INTENSIVE THERAPY

A NOVEL

JEFFREY DEITZ

GREENLEAF
BOOK GROUP PRESS

To JoAnn

Published by Greenleaf Book Group Press
Austin, Texas
www.gbgpress.com

Distributed by Greenleaf Book Group

For ordering information or special discounts for bulk purchases, please contact Greenleaf Book Group at PO Box 91869, Austin, TX 78709, 512.891.6100.

Design and composition by Greenleaf Book Group
Cover design by Greenleaf Book Group
Cover images: ©iStockphoto.com/totallyPic.com, ©iStockphoto.com/Materio, ©iStockphoto.com/OSTILL Library of Congress, Prints & Photographs Division, HABS/HAER/HALS, Reproduction number HAER PA,51-PHILA,729—2
Back cover images: ©iStockphoto.com/Tongshan

Stopping by Woods on a Snowy Evening" from the book *The Poetry of Robert Frost* edited by Edward Connery Lathem. Copyright © 1923, 1969 by Henry Holt and Company, copyright © 1951 by Robert Frost. Reprinted by permission of Henry Holt and Company, LLC. All rights reserved.

Publisher's Cataloging-In-Publication Data is available.

ISBN: 978-1-62634-186-9

Part of the Tree Neutral® program, which offsets the number of trees consumed in the production and printing of this book by taking proactive steps, such as planting trees in direct proportion to the number of trees used: www.treeneutral.com

TreeNeutral

Printed in the United States of America on acid-free paper

15 16 17 18 19 20   10 9 8 7 6 5 4 3 2 1

First Edition

Other Edition(s):
eBook ISBN: 978-1-62634-187-6

1

Friday, November 19, 2004

As Victoria Braun surveyed her closet deciding which suit to wear, she caught sight of the black negligee she had hung on the far side of the rack weeks earlier. She had been hoping to surprise her husband with a steamy night, only that night kept getting pushed back. *It's because of all the late afternoon appointments and last-minute conference calls*, she tried to persuade herself. But the lawyer in her knew the argument was far from convincing. Her schedule was no more hectic than it had been for years.

Facing her reflection in the makeup mirror moments later, she heard a commotion break out down the hall. Gregory, her ten-year-old son, couldn't budge his older sister, Melinda, from her room, which meant keeping the carpool driver waiting for the third time in five days. Friends Select School, on Benjamin Franklin Parkway, was ten minutes away from the Brauns' townhouse by car, but it was a good half hour on foot, weather cooperating, which it wasn't. An enormous front descending from the Great Lakes through the eastern seaboard had shrouded the Mid-Atlantic sky in battleship gray, with a cold drizzle veiling Philadelphia's glass towers behind a glaucous scrim.

"Come on, Melinda," Gregory urged, pounding on her bedroom door. "Mrs. Caruso will be here any minute. This time, I'm going whether you're ready or not. Please. I don't want you to be late again!"

"Go away," Melinda grumbled. "Stop bothering me."

"I'm not trying to bother you," Gregory said. "You're in enough trouble already. I hear Mother talk about it all the time; those calls from the guidance office are getting to her. Next thing we know, the school will send a truant officer."

Melinda cracked open the door. "I hate that you and Mother talk about me behind my back. She's such a hypocrite. She's always late herself."

"So? You're in ninth grade; she's finished law school. You know, Melinda, being in the gifted program doesn't mean you don't have to go to school."

"So, now that you're in sixth grade, it's okay for you and Mother to gang up on me?" Melinda said.

"Don't be so paranoid, Melinda. I'm trying to help."

"Fuck all of you," Melinda yelled loudly enough for everyone to hear. "I'm tired of your shit."

"Do you hear this, Martin?" Victoria said to her husband, standing next to her adjusting his collar and tie. Something's wrong with that girl. Dammit," she exclaimed when her eyebrow pencil broke. "Now what! Take me away, Martin. Anywhere. I'd be happy with a long weekend."

"Oh Vic," Martin responded kindheartedly. "Hopefully, Melinda's just going through a phase. I know how your mind works. Even if we went away—assuming we could get away—you'd find something to worry about."

"You're probably right. There's just so much to do. It's so dark out. I wish we could get some sun."

"Maybe after Christmas," Martin said.

"Jury selection for Barlow v. Duke's starts Monday," Victoria fretted. "I have to meet with Mrs. Arrestia in fifteen minutes. Then I have to be at Broad Street by ten o'clock to defend Dr. Ramey at the performing arts center deposition. All this rushing . . . I hate it."

Martin said, "You know the Colazzo hearing begins at ten o'clock, too. I need an hour to prepare him."

"What's with your outfit?" Victoria teased affectionately, noting Martin's spanking white shirt and red tie dotted with American flags. "You're not running for office, are you?"

Martin Braun, six years older than Victoria—not that anyone could tell because he was so fit—looked especially handsome that day.

"No," he smiled at his wife's comment. "The presiding judge is a World War Two veteran, so I'm leveraging the patriotic look. You like?"

"Very nice," Victoria replied, trying to stay in the moment. Soon she was preoccupied with Melinda and the rush to get to the downstairs office. "If Melinda needs a ride to school, my schedule will be shot. I'll never get to that summary judgment motion that has to be filed before Tuesday."

"If only you'd learn that voice recognition software I got us, you could bang it out in ten minutes."

"Martin, please. Don't get me started," Victoria said. "I'm technologically challenged enough. Thank God Gregory showed me how to do word-processing and e-mail. I can't possibly manage another thing."

"Okay, okay. Take it easy," Martin said. "Let's send Snyder to the Ramey deposition."

"Snyder? Are you crazy? He's worthless. Chris Buddinger is representing the plaintiffs. One look at Snyder and Buddinger will smell blood. He'll tear Ramey to pieces if I'm not there. I should have listened when you said not to hire Snyder. I can't deal with Melinda this morning. Can you take her to school? It's not fair for Gregory to be late."

"Speaking of fair," Martin said. "Since it's my parents' year for Thanksgiving, they asked us to bring dessert. How about fresh cannoli from the Italian Market?"

"That's another thing to worry about," Victoria said. "No matter what I bring your sisters will give me grief. Sophia and Lydia treat me like a gold digger. I can't help it if your family got here a century before mine. My grandfather waited until Kristallnacht and spent every last penny to get out. At least he got us here. The way your sisters treat me, I wonder if they're sorry he made it out at all."

Approaching from the side, Martin drew his arms around Victoria's waist affectionately, as he always did when she was having a fit. "Calm down, Vic. Calm down," he cooed, peering over her shoulder as she repaired the smudged eyebrow. He stood back to admire his wife's profile. "Look at you," he beamed. "You're radiant. As for Melinda, let it go. Just let it go."

A floor below, the smell of freshly brewed coffee suffused the Braun's Center City townhouse with the aroma of morning. Another level below, a glass partition delicately etched with the names Schone and Braun separated their law practice from the privacy of their home. Gail Heath, their paralegal-cum-office manager, was already at work preparing for the day.

Outside, the usual morning cacophony had begun: the groan of a bus on its way up Walnut Street; honking geese gathered by the gazebo on Rittenhouse Square; the whistle of the doorman hailing a taxi for a tenant of The Dorchester. Pots upon pots of yellow and orange mums lined the eight curvilinear steps leading from the pavement to 1912 Rittenhouse Square South's front door.

"I don't believe you, Melinda. I'm leaving," Gregory said as he slung his backpack onto his shoulders. "What a narcissist," he muttered on his way to the stairs.

Victoria stepped to her bedroom door. "What happened?" she asked as Gregory passed.

"Melinda. I don't know what's with her," Gregory said. "I feel sorry for you. I tried to get her up and out."

What a dear boy. So considerate, Victoria thought. Gregory Braun was Victoria's nimble skateboarder, merrily grinding his way towards puberty. It was far more than his book smarts—he was already in double-accelerated math and science—that Victoria adored. Gregory was so creative. His way with words made Victoria feel that he got her. Gregory was proof she had made the world a better place.

"That's not your job," she said about Melinda. "Is that new?" she asked, pointing at his backpack.

"Martin got it for me on South Street. Look," Gregory said, showing his mother several zippered pockets. "There's room for my laptop, my calculator, and my Palm Pilot."

"Martin? Since when do call your father, 'Martin?'"

"Since today. I'm trying it out to see how it feels. 'Martin,'" Gregory said, mimicking his mother's inflection. "'Martin' sounds more mature than 'Daddy' or 'Dad.' 'Father' is much too stiff. What do you think?"

"I think you're special," Victoria said with a delight she felt only in Gregory's presence. How she wished she could feel that way about Melinda, too.

"I'll pronounce it like you do," Gregory said. "You always say 'Martin.' Not 'sweetheart,' not 'dear,' like Mrs. Lester calls Brad's father. Just 'Martin.' Very professional—like your business suits."

"Is that a compliment?"

"I like your business suits. They make you look put-together. Not like my friends' mothers in their sweatpants. I've got to go. Sorry about leaving you with Melinda." Gregory hugged his mother.

"You can still kiss me," she said, offering a cheek.

"I know, but I don't want to mess up your makeup," he said, disappearing down the stairs.

After she finished dressing, Victoria marched down the hall. "Melinda!" she demanded. No response. "Melinda!" she shouted loudly enough to rattle the door. "Get up and get dressed. I have to be downstairs in five minutes, and your father has a hearing at ten o'clock. It's out of his way, but he'll drive you. Do you hear me?"

"Stop trying to run my life," Melinda shouted back. "I'll get dressed when I want to. I don't care what you and Daddy do."

Martin came up behind Victoria.

"Something's wrong, Martin. Something's very wrong," she said over her shoulder.

"Leave it to me, Vic. I'll deal with her. Go downstairs and have your tea."

As she headed down the steps, a horrible feeling overcame her; something Victoria had not felt in more than twenty years.

2

Friday, September 18, 1981

Descending the creaky stairs of The University of Pennsylvania's College Hall after her last class, Victoria Schone was terrified about what was happening to her. Every time she passed an emergency exit door, she went into a panic, plagued by thoughts of jumping off one of the tall buildings on campus. These impulses, which had started weeks earlier during her family vacation in Italy, were becoming stronger and more tempting. *What is wrong with me?* She kept asking herself. The more she focused on the bad thoughts, the more intense they became—racing through her mind day and night, to the point that she could barely sleep.

Although the clock atop the architecture school read 2:30, Victoria's 3:00 PM appointment seemed hours away. She had been counting down the hours for ten excruciating days. Stopping for tea at the student union, she collapsed into an armchair and tried reading her English literature book to calm her mind. It didn't help.

Victoria crossed Spruce Street and entered the Hospital of the University of Pennsylvania's Gates Pavilion. She felt nauseated every time the elevator lurched to a stop on its way up to the ninth floor psychiatry clinic. At precisely 3:00 she arrived in the vestibule, where the secretary directed her to room 921, the office of the chief resident, Dr. Jonas Speller. Walking down the narrow corridor, Victoria imagined her doctor-to-be as a bearded, bespectacled nerd-type. Neutral and non-threatening. *What will he do?* she wondered. *Call my parents? Send me to the hospital? Tell me to stop school? Say I'm beyond help?*

The last thing Victoria wanted was for her parents to know how badly she felt, which could give them even more ammunition with which to snipe at her for moving into the dormitory. Her relationship with her mother, Lorraine, was already tenuous. Grandma Jeanine, Lorraine's mother, paid for Victoria's room and board, enabling her to leave home against her parents' wishes and to make the appointment at the psychiatry clinic without having to ask her parents for money.

The door to room 921 was open; Victoria peeked inside cautiously.

She was startled. Dr. Speller looked nothing like she had imagined. He was a moustached and vigorous-looking man in his late twenties, dressed in a fashionable checked shirt with a contrasting bow tie. Caught off guard, Victoria felt self-conscious.

"Good afternoon," the man said, as he rose from his desk. "I'm Dr. Jonas Speller. You are . . . ?"

"Victoria Schone," she said tersely, her fear transmuted into resentment that her name had become Dr. Speller's business.

"It's good to meet you," the doctor said, gesturing for her to take a seat. "Make yourself comforta—"

"Is this the only time you can see me?" said Victoria, still standing. "I'm missing class."

Dr. Speller seemed unsettled. He remained upright while Victoria looked about the sparsely furnished office. He sat down first, withdrawing into his chair-on-rollers, with an expression like the one that usually presaged her father's alcohol-lubricated assaults on her character. The longer Dr. Speller stayed silent, the angrier Victoria became.

"Don't you have anything to say?" she asked.

Dr. Speller asked her to sit. Victoria plopped down onto a chair close enough to his desk that she could rest her right elbow and arm on it. She waited, drifting into a far-off stare, her fingers tracing circles.

"So," the doctor said gently after a few moments, "Tell me about yourself and your situation."

"I don't know where to start." Telling her story felt unfair; revealing the suicidal thoughts was unimaginable. "I wake up every day with a knot in my stomach. I'm always afraid."

"Afraid of . . . ?"

"I don't know. I used to know. But now it's everything. Everything!"

"Everything? Can you put that feeling into words?"

"It's like dread. Whenever the phone rings, I think it's horrible news. Horrible."

"Horrible as in . . . ?"

"Horrible as in horrible. I just said that," Victoria barked.

Dr. Speller waited. Sounding more detached and clinical, he said, "This horrible feeling, does it resonate with anything? Does it bring anything to mind?"

Victoria felt she had driven Dr. Speller away. *I do this all the time*, she thought. "I do this all the time," she whispered aloud.

"I beg your pardon," Dr. Speller said.

She was surprised when he spoke. "What?" she said.

"I thought I heard you say, 'All the time.'"

"It doesn't matter."

"It doesn't matter?"

"Why would it matter?" she said.

"Why would it matter?" he echoed incredulously.

"Yes. Why would it matter?"

"Because I'm interested in what you think and feel," he said.

"What I think and feel? Like you care about what I think and feel. How much does this cost?"

"We'll talk about that in a minute. Can we get back to—?"

"How much?" Victoria insisted.

"We usually discuss that at the end of the visit."

"I don't give a shit what you usually do," Victoria erupted. "You're telling me you care what I feel, but I have to pay for it."

Dr. Speller rolled his chair back and was silent for a long time. He turned to face Victoria head on. "Yes, I'm interested in what you think and feel," he said passionately. "That's what I do. That's what we do here."

Victoria knew he was telling the truth. She could tell when her mother lied; this was different. "But I have to pay for it, don't I? Don't I?" she said, bitterly.

"You sound very bitter," Dr. Speller observed.

"What did you just say?"

"I said you sound very bitter."

Victoria wondered if the doctor had read her mind. The thought made her head spin. She replayed his words like a mantra. *I'm interested in what you think and feel. I'm interested in what you think and feel.* She pictured receding waves at the Jersey shore where she summered as a child. "What did you just say?" He didn't answer. "I asked a question." Again no response. "This is fucking ridiculous," she huffed and stood up as though to leave.

"This?" Dr. Speller responded.

"Yes, *this.* What *is* this? You don't talk for minutes at a time, and you can't remember what I said two seconds ago."

"I was thinking. I'm trying to get a sense of where all this anger is coming from."

He certainly wanted to understand her, Victoria had to concede. But she had no intention of letting him off that easy. "Really," she scoffed.

"Yes, really," he mocked, mirroring her tone with just enough bite to smart. He sounded pissed. "*This* is called psychotherapy; that's what *this* is. *This* is where someone talks about their thoughts and their feelings. *This* is about two people working together, and *yes,* you pay to get a handle on your issues."

Victoria knew she deserved the reprimand. He spoke with just enough "I don't need to take this shit from anybody" to make her think he might send her away. She slumped into her seat, her anger giving way to profound sadness and the image of an eddying swirl of water spiraling down a toilet.

"Whatever," Victoria uttered dismissively, after which she responded sullenly to the standard questions: where she grew up—a big house in Abington Township; her age—she was twenty; where she lived—Hill Hall; her major—English literature; her family—her parents hated her. Eventually Dr. Speller asked about friends and if she had a significant relationship.

Victoria wanted a boyfriend, because that's what other girls had. But despite all the admiring glances from boys on campus, no one made it past the third date because she lost interest. "What kind of question is that?" she asked. "How long have you done this?"

Dr. Speller sighed and looked elsewhere. Victoria thought he glanced at his watch. *Why do I do this?* she berated herself. *Push people away and then feel bad.*

"Has anyone ever said you push people away?" Dr. Speller ventured.

That was twice in half an hour. "How did you know what I was thinking?"

Dr. Speller smiled, setting his glasses on his side of the desk.

In truth, Victoria had picked a psychiatrist-in-training not just because it was all she could afford, but also because she figured the therapy would hurt less. Somehow, though, Dr. Speller had already poked her sore spots. She had been nasty to him, but he kept coming back, unlike her drunken nebbish of a father who took his wife's abuse without standing up for himself.

Victoria looked across the room. Atop the bookcase rested a sculpture of an orchestra conductor next to a thick blue paperback and an aged hardcover entitled *Guide for the Perplexed*. What did she have to lose?

"I'm angry all the time. All the time. And," she said, holding her breath, "ever since I went with my family to Florence, I'm terrified of high places. I think about walking off tall buildings all the time." She braced for the worst.

Dr. Speller pincered his glasses by their earpieces, twirled them around, and said, "Both ideas are intertwined, you know."

The notion bowled Victoria over. She looked out the window for the first time. "It never occurred to me they were related. You really think so?"

"I know so," Dr. Speller said. "As for your anger, how long have you felt this way?"

"I don't know. It seems like forever."

"Can you remember when you didn't feel this way?"

"You don't give up, do you?" she said. "I wish my father was like that, but there he sits night after night downing double martinis in front of Walter Cronkite, while my mother bitches at him or me. I had to get out of there."

The room started to spin and Victoria's stomach heaved. Too proud for anyone to see her on hands and knees over a trash can, she bolted down the hall seeking relief; the men's room, the women's room, it didn't matter. She made it to the commode just in time.

* * *

When Victoria returned, it was five minutes to four. Room 921's door remained open. Dr. Speller was quietly reading the newspaper. He seemed pleased to see her. "Are you okay?" he asked.

"Yes, thank you. I feel much better." Victoria searched Dr. Speller's face, trying to get a read. "It was nice of you to wait for me. I'm sorry I was so nasty. I get that way when I'm overwhelmed. That's not really me."

"I get it," he said with a smile.

Relieved that Dr. Speller had accepted her apology, Victoria said, "We've run late. I'm keeping you."

"There's still time."

"When can we meet again?"

Dr. Speller seemed surprised. "How soon would you like to come?"

"The next time you can."

He surveyed his appointment book. "That'll be this Monday afternoon. When does your class end?"

11

"At four forty-five."

"I have someone then. How about five twenty?"

"How long do sessions last?"

"Around forty-five minutes, although some take longer to wrap up than others. I try to stay flexible, but I don't like making people wait."

"Five twenty, Monday, it is. See you then," Victoria said, feeling as though a cannonball had been lifted off her chest.

"Good-bye," Dr. Speller said grinning. "See you Monday."

3

Monday, September 21, 1981

"To her surprise, Victoria had not thought about tall buildings all weekend. Upon entering room 921 for her second session, she studied Dr. Speller more carefully. "Before we get into anything," she said, "how old are you?"

"That matters, doesn't it?" Dr. Speller replied.

"What kind of answer is that? You know about me; I need to know about you."

"What does knowing my age mean to you?"

"Mean to me? It means I want a straight answer. Jesus Christ, it's a simple question."

Dr. Speller hesitated. "I'm twenty-seven years old. I'll be twenty-eight next month," he said.

"That's good." His age reassured her; it made him seem worldly. "So, what happens next?"

"First, let's decide on a schedule. You should come often enough that we can follow the themes in your thoughts from session to session. What feels right to you?"

"How about Mondays and Thursdays, after class?" Victoria said.

"Sounds good. If it's too much or too little we can always change," Dr. Speller responded.

Victoria nodded.

"So let's get going," he said. "The basic idea is to say what's on your mind, uncensored, just as it goes through consciousness."

"My mind is like a carousel spinning out of control. There are so many thoughts racing through it, I don't know where to start."

"Pick one. Any one."

"How will I know if I'm on the right track?"

"It doesn't matter. You'll see. Thoughts are associated. Your mind connects them unconsciously. Among other things, my job is to see the connections."

"What other things?"

"I try to put your thoughts and feelings in perspective. To see the world through your eyes."

Victoria looked around the room, settling on a photograph of Philadelphia's Academy of Music. "Okay, here goes," she said. "I called my mother Saturday night. Lorraine drives me crazy. You never know what mood she'll be in. This time, she was complaining about Daddy's drinking. Morris Schone hasn't said a civil word to me in two years, except to complain about how much money I cost.

"See this?" Victoria touched her Italian leather coat. "Lorraine took me shopping in Florence. When we got back to the hotel, he had a shit fit about how much it cost; but she was the one who wanted to buy it, telling me how good it looked on me. Which is another thing. Lorraine has this thing about my body. She hates certain skirts, because she thinks my hips and legs are too narrow. It's all about appearances with her. Even though she was furious about my moving away to college, Lorraine would never send some Cinderella to Hill Hall wearing rags, not with the rest of the girls gallivanting around campus in Burberry skirts and cashmere sweaters. So, she bought this jacket just as much for herself as she did for me. I liked it, but I didn't have to have it. But when Daddy blasted me, she turned on me like I was a greedy pig. That's what I mean. You never know what kind of mood she'll be in."

For the next half hour, Victoria surprised herself with how eagerly she shared her thoughts and feelings about life in Abington Township.

"I see," Dr. Speller said when Victoria stopped to catch her breath. "You mentioned that there were other thoughts on your mind. Feel free to include your memories, your daydreams, and your night dreams."

"I never talk about what goes on in my mind," Victoria said. "Do you have any idea how weird this is for me? Sitting with a perfect stranger, saying things out loud I haven't even said to myself?"

"It's hard, I know, especially if you've never done it before, but that's your job in therapy. Sometimes it's best for me to remain quiet, so I don't disturb your train of thought. Then we try to figure out what your thoughts mean. And one other thing," Dr. Speller added. "Keep a pad and pencil by your bedside and write down your night dreams. Dreams are a peephole into the unconscious mind—more for us to work on."

Victoria liked his "we" and "us." There was no "we" at Abington. Abington was Lorraine and Morris telling her what to think and feel.

"Dr. Speller," Victoria said as the session drew to a close, "you have no clue about the shit that goes through my mind, hour after hour, day after day."

"You're right. I don't," he said. "But this is a safe place to share it."

Outside the tiny window, the afternoon sky had turned dark orange and pink. "There is one more thought on my mind today," Victoria said. "It's about the girl in the book I'm reading. Her name is Esther. Esther catches smallpox and barely survives, but while she's recuperating, she meets her mother—who she's been searching for her whole life—for the first and only time. Her mother has always known Esther's true identity but was ashamed, because she bore Esther out of wedlock. Now, she was frantic, worrying whether her daughter would survive her illness.

"I was thinking about Esther's pock-marked face, about how scarred I feel, that there must be something grotesque about me that repulses my family." Victoria burst into tears. "They don't like me. I've been alone for so long. I have friends so to speak; I have a brother, but except for Grandma, no one knows the real me. They wouldn't like it. Can you understand that?"

"I want to. Very much," Dr. Speller said empathetically.

It had taken only two sessions for Victoria to open up. This she did not expect.

Victoria and Dr. Speller shared a brief silence that felt like a memorial service. At that moment, she felt the loneliness of childhood begin to die. Not with the explosion she expected, more like the bitter sweetness of her favorite poem by Robert Frost.

4

Friday, November 19, 2004

"I can't believe you get nervous before these things," Jennie Speller said to her husband. "You must have given this talk a hundred times."

"More like thirty, Jen," said Jonas, checking himself in the hotel room mirror. "I prefer panels. It's nerve-racking when everyone's looking at you."

"You're not fooling anyone, Jo. We know you love the attention."

"Well, maybe," he laughed.

"What's so funny?"

"Remember that German psychoanalyst I trained with when we lived in Philadelphia? Hannah Schmidt. The one who looked like a Berlin disco bouncer?"

"Sort of. What made you think of her?"

"You reminded me of my first presentation after residency. What a hoot! Hannah—a die hard devotee of psychoanalyst Melanie Klein—was on the panel that day. She showed wartime pictures made by English children, claiming the aerial bombs and antiaircraft weapons represented turds and shriveled penises. It was all I could to do to keep from breaking up. But she got me thinking how literal children are. Tell a child he has chicken pox and he's liable to start looking for a rooster! Ironic, isn't it? That I learned from her."

"And me? Have I taught you a thing or two? Or would you rather fantasize about Fraulein Schmidt?"

"You should see pictures of Melanie Klein, Jen. Hannah cut and dyed her hair to look exactly like her heroine. Her head looked like Brillo." Jonas ogled Jennie. "You look good enough to eat," he said. "How come I can't get enough?"

"Must be all those adoring lady patients and residents you spend your days with. But there're still a few lessons I could teach you, Herr Professor."

Dressed in olive pants, a yellow blouse, and brown loafers, Jennie looked more beautiful than the day they met, the twenty-third anniversary of which was approaching on Thanksgiving. Jennie's dark brown hair had kept its lustrous sheen, and her green eyes looked out from a flawless face that defied time. Jonas couldn't help admiring the subtle way Jennie's waist contoured into her hips. A jolt shot up and down his spine, centering deep in his core. "When does class start?"

"After the girls and I finish our spa day courtesy of the Foxwoods Resort and Casino. They must think you're some kind of high roller. What did you tell them?"

"Eddie's partner made the arrangements for the Connecticut Bar Association's fall meeting. When you bring in four hundred lawyers for a long weekend, you get perks. Everyone connected with Speller and Bodenheim is comped for whatever they want."

"'Whatever they want?'" Jennie said, perusing the room service menu. "Suppose what you want isn't on the menu?"

"Huh?"

"Remember that article I showed you in *Cosmopolitan* about ten ways to drive your man wild in bed? Maybe I should order a blonde wig and four-inch stilettos?"

Jonas looked at Jennie from the bottom up, stopping at her chest. "That won't be necessary. I like you just the way you are."

Jennie made one of her sounds that drove Jonas wild, but just as he went to embrace her, three loud knocks on the door announced that Eddie, Jonas's brother, had come to fetch him for the conference. "To be continued," Jonas murmured into her ear.

"Hi Jen. You look nice," Eddie said when she opened the door. Then to his brother, "Jonas, did you know that more than two hundred people registered for your presentation? If I had known how renowned you were gonna become, I would have syndicated your speaking rights, like thoroughbred stud fees."

Jennie and Jonas smiled at each other. He said, "Bye, Jen. We'll look into that stud business later and see if there's anything to it."

Jonas was to give one of the keynote presentations after his first order of business, an appearance on a panel with several distinguished litigators about the psychodynamics of cross-examination.

Since the conference center was on the far side of the sprawling complex, Jonas decided to go by car. All the way down in the elevator, Eddie gabbed about how people were praising the conference and how proud he felt of his brother.

By the time they reached the lobby, Jonas's BMW had arrived from valet parking. Another encounter from his training days popped into mind. About a woman far more important to him than Hannah Schmidt. "Get in," Jonas told his brother. "I'll drive."

5

Friday, September 18, 1981

As Jonas Speller drove hurriedly from the clinic to his 4:30 psychoanalysis session, he laughed, thinking about what had just occurred: the Penn undergraduate girl teetering into his office at five minutes to four. What a sight. A fractious filly dressed like an aristocrat. She spent the first forty minutes with her nostrils flared but left wearing a smile that lit up the hallway.

By the time he lay down on Dr. Fowler's couch, Jonas was five minutes late. His father's sudden death just before Jonas's medical school graduation had driven him into psychoanalysis three years earlier. At first Jonas was so flattened he would have laid down his life for Dr. Philip Fowler, the hot new training analyst at the Philadelphia Psychoanalytic Institute. Within months, Jonas entered formal psychoanalytic training, and since all trainees had to be in analysis, it was natural to continue with Dr. Fowler. But as Jonas felt better and better, he began challenging Dr. Fowler's rigidity about classical psychoanalysis. That's when Fowler unsheathed his switchblade of a tongue, and the analysis deteriorated into a battle of wits and wills. Because he was training to be a psychoanalyst, Jonas felt trapped, convinced he would be dismissed from the Institute if he broke with Dr. Fowler.

The couch felt scratchy that afternoon, like lying on burlap. "I did something today you're going to hate," Jonas opened the session warily.

"You should know by now," Dr. Fowler scolded, pouncing on a theme of that week's sessions, "that you're projecting onto me the unconscious hatred you harbored toward your father."

"There you go again." "Hammering about hatred."

"Hammering?" Dr. Fowler interjected smartly. "What does hammering bring to mind?"

Jonas's first thought was of helping his father with home repairs, but he kept quiet, his mind returning to staying late for the Penn girl, a no-no in analytic practice.

"Hammering reminds me of jackhammerers who need headphones for ear protection," Jonas said, hoping Dr. Fowler would get the dig. "You know, Dr. Fowler, it feels like you're more interested in your theories than in my psyche. This business about me reliving a love-hate relationship with my father is your idea, not mine. This analysis feels like lying naked on a butcher block with my hands tied behind my back."

"Naked on a butcher block? No doubt with me wielding the meat cleaver?"

"Good God," Jonas said. "Not castration anxiety again."

Dr. Fowler's pen scratched, the sounds reminding Jonas of clawing mice at the lab where he had worked summers to help pay for Johns Hopkins medical school.

"I broke the rules today," Jonas said. "I had a new patient. She left my office five minutes before her session ended. Instead of shutting the door, I waited until I was sure she was okay. I was reading the review of yesterday's Philadelphia Orchestra concert. The program starts with *Invitation to the Dance*, a piece I adore. The strings are so lush. I'm living in the wrong century. It should be 1881, not 1981."

Dr. Fowler remained silent.

"The girl came back fifteen minutes later. It made a difference that I had waited."

"Clearly, you want me to admire your bedside manner," Dr. Fowler said, "while in fact you indulged her dependency and allowed her to manipulate you."

"It was a first session, for God's sake. The girl really needed help. She was thinking about killing herself. You call that indulgence; I call it being humane. I'm a doctor. And a damn good therapist for someone three years into training."

"Three whole years," Dr. Fowler snickered. "Quite the prodigy!"

"I don't care what you think. I did what was right."

"I see," Dr. Fowler said. "Now I'm supposed to admire your defiance. Haven't you read *Oedipus Rex*?"

"Yes, I have. The whole trilogy," Jonas said. "Ever since I told you my dream about moving into the office next door to you, you've been making the relationships with my father and with you sound perverted. What I want is for you to show me the psychoanalytic ropes and encourage me to become my own man. This isn't quantum mechanics. Why complicate things with all this song and dance about sex and aggression? Last night, I dreamt about airplanes dodging bridges on takeoff and landing. What do you think that means?"

"This constant need to out-analyze me—it's about wanting a bigger analytic penis."

"Penis, schmeenis. What's wrong with wanting to be better than you? You make it sound like a disease. Every time we disagree on an interpretation, I catch a ration of shit about Oedipus killing his father. Oedipus didn't set out to kill Laius, Dr. Fowler. Laius's chariots drove young Oedipus off the road. Like you; you knock me off track. I have serious issues we never deal with. I keep dating women who don't challenge me, and the relationships go nowhere. If anything, my grief is worse, not better. Meanwhile, analysis feels like a battle for self-preservation."

Jonas drifted through the rest of the session, ending with a story about the Philadelphia Academy of Music box office. "I know a blue-haired woman named Mrs. Paquette. As long as I show up early and make eye contact, she finds me a ticket, even when the concert is sold out. Sometimes, there's a student discount. I've never been shut out."

Jonas decided to take one last shot at being frank. "You know," he said, "the concert thing is very painful, Dr. Fowler. Sure as shit, you and your entourage will be there, which means that awkward moment seeing you at intermission and feeling ignored because I want you to say, 'Hey everybody, this is Jonas Speller. He's going to be a terrific analyst,' after which everyone asks my opinion about the orchestra, because you've told them I'm conservatory-trained and read more scores than contemporary fiction. Well, I'm going tomorrow night. I'll get in again somehow."

"I see," Dr. Fowler said. "Paulette—"

"Her name is Paquette, not Paulette. Mrs. Paquette."

"Mrs. Paquette gets you in. Just like you want me to make it easy for you, give you a reduced fee and be your admission ticket to the analytic 'entourage.'" Dr. Fowler, a devotee of puns and word-play, sounded especially tickled with his admission ticket double entendre.

"I resent that," Jonas said. "I've always paid my own way here. Full fee and don't you forget it." The clock read 5:14. Jonas left without waiting for Dr. Fowler to end the session. He felt relieved. "Today is an ending," he said to himself on his way out. "Of what, I'm not sure."

6

Half an hour after leaving Fowler's office, Jonas was back at his apartment, half-hoping his date—another sultry graduate student looking for her MRS degree—had called to cancel. No such luck.

Energized, he pulled on his running gear and bounded out into the late afternoon sun, completing the four-mile loop to the Schuylkill and back in less than thirty minutes, record time for him. He headed straight into the shower where, of all people, he thought of the Penn girl, whose last name he couldn't remember. The Serengeti Plain came to mind; next, the emerald castle from *The Wizard of Oz*. "It's her animalism," he said aloud. "Dressed like a duchess. Family outings to Europe. Fancy suburb. I hereby christen you Miss Abington." Jonas turned contemplative. *Some night I'll stroll into the Academy of Music to hear* Invitation to the Dance *with my own Miss Abington. Not tomorrow night . . . but some night*, he told himself as he climbed out of the shower.

Toweling himself off vigorously, he reached for the telephone.

"Hello," answered Jonas's older brother, Eddie, a lawyer in New York City.

"Good, you're home."

"Greetings, Professor Freud," Eddie said. "Any new shrunken heads today?"

"You should have seen me today. I thought this gal was going to chuck a spear at my *cojones*."

"The warrior type, eh? You've always had a thing for that archetype."

"Archetype? I didn't know you studied Jung."

"Throw me a bone. Tell me about your Amazon."

"She's a ball of fire. I've christened her Miss Abington. She's from a prosperous suburb north of here, not exactly where we grew up."

"You'll get there," Eddie said.

"Probably not. I'd prefer New York. Lincoln Center. Carnegie Hall. Besides, Miss Abington might aim too high and nail me in the heart."

"Sounds like she's gotten there already."

"You know me; I can look out for myself."

"Are you sure? Maybe I should send you some chest armor and a codpiece. They're made of titanium now."

"You're just jealous," Jonas said. "Besides, my date tonight is a dark-haired Kim Basinger. Eat your heart out."

"You sound good. How's Philadelphia?"

"It's great. How's everyone? Margo and the kids?"

"We're great," Eddie said. "Think of this: While you're making omelets with Ms. Basinger tomorrow morning, we'll be schlepping the double-stroller to Central Park."

"We'll see. Besides, who says I'll be with anyone in the morning?"

"What are you going to do? Call a limo and send her home?"

Jonas's voice trailed into a whisper, as a pang of grief erupted. "I wish we were together," he said.

"Jesus, Jonas. What just happened? You sound so different."

"Dammit," Jonas said. "Does this ever fucking end? 'Limo' made me think about the car we rode in on the way to the cemetery, and shoveling dirt on our father's casket."

"You keep talking like it happened yesterday, Jonas. Not three years ago. I thought that's what therapy was for. What does your analyst say?"

"Oh, him? Dr. Fowler thinks I'm angry at Dad."

"He's not helping?"

"I don't know. I think he gets his interpretations from a cookbook. Everyone knows I should have had Dad go to Hopkins Hospital. The only reason I chose GBMC was because I sub-interned there, and I figured he'd be treated better since the nurses knew me. At least if he was at Hopkins, they could have tried to pull the clot out of his lungs."

"You can't keep talking this way," Eddie said. "Nobody blames you. It kills me that you still think that. He died because he waited too long to have the operation, because he wouldn't get out of bed. You didn't answer my question. Is Fowler helping?"

Jonas looked out his window at the scraggly yard, where the descending sun cast shadows resembling tombstones. "Everyone tells me Fowler's the best," he said. "That I'm so fortunate to have him. Meanwhile, I think he's more interested in my conflicts than he's interested in me."

"That doesn't sound right," Eddie said. "You know, if you take the early train tomorrow, we can all go to the park together."

"Thanks, but I'm staying here this weekend. There's a concert I want to hear tomorrow night."

"Fine. Just don't let Miss Abington mess with your head."

"Jesus Christ, Eddie, she's a patient. I'm taught to handle all kinds of characters."

"Then again, maybe that's why you avoid certain women," Eddie quipped.

"'Certain women?' What's that supposed to mean?"

"Whoa. Time out. I was just kidding."

"What kind of women?"

"Don't be so thin-skinned, Jonas."

"Since when did you become the expert on my love life? Besides, you never asked what I felt about your getting married."

"What?" Eddie reacted sharply. "What are you saying?"

Jonas bit his lip hard. "That I had feelings about whether you were ready to get married; but I was your kid brother whose opinion wasn't worth two cents. Admit it, you still think of me that way."

"What? That's not true. Where is this coming from?" Eddie said. "I'm sorry, Jo. I didn't mean to upset you."

"Have a good weekend," Jonas sulked.

"You, too. I worry about you sometimes, Jonas. This is one of them. Margo and I love you."

"I know, I know," Jonas said, but Eddie's gibe felt like one of Dr. Fowler's tongue-lashings. "We'll talk later," he said, knowing that later wouldn't be for a while. He glanced at the portrait of his father atop the table on which he replaced the telephone. Willy Speller's eyes looked pained.

Spending more time at his closet than usual, Jonas fussed over what to wear that evening. Something about Miss Abington's dress stuck with him. He finished dressing hurriedly, wondering what she was doing that very moment.

7

Tuesday, September 22, 1981

The day after Miss Abington's second session dawned clear and crisp. Jonas awakened from a series of dreams overlaid and intertwined like a Bach fugue. In the most vivid, he was playing first violin in a Philadelphia Orchestra performance of *Invitation to the Dance*, Dr. Fowler conducting. Jonas's father appeared and snatched away the baton, berating Dr. Fowler for being musically obtuse, whereupon Jonas's gut-wrenching grief transformed into sublime joy, the pianissimo of the cello's concluding notes enfolding him like the farewell embrace he longed to have shared with his father before he died. Jonas awoke feeling incredibly sad, and incredibly peaceful.

Enveloped in the afterglow of the dream, Jonas drove to analysis hearing the melody.

The Institute of the Pennsylvania Hospital in West Philadelphia, where Dr. Fowler practiced, had seen better days. The fenced-in property was ringed by graying, cracked pavement that looked like aged scrimshaw. The first-floor offices had identical, room-wide windows reaching from radiator to ceiling. To protect patient identity, the exterior was guarded by a row of boxwood hedges, silent witnesses to the hourly drone of murderous dreams and incestuous fantasies confessed on the couches within by Philadelphia's finest and brightest.

Jonas lay down at 9:10 AM.

"Wasn't the Tchaikovsky inspiring?" he began, hoping for the umpteenth time to extract a dram of affirmation from his analyst. "I loved it, but . . . " He fell silent, replaying his morning dream.

"What's happening?" Dr. Fowler inquired.

Jonas had attended the concert alone. Mrs. Paquette found a seat in the parterre. At intermission, he and Dr. Fowler had made eye contact briefly. As Jonas lay on the couch that morning, he saw his future flash before his eyes: a Dr. Fowler clone. It felt awful. Next, Jonas imagined looking through the telescopic sight of a high-powered rifle, panning the faces of the concertgoers until he pinpointed Dr. Fowler in the crosshair.

Ready. Aim. Fire.

"This isn't what I want anymore," Jonas said. "Lying here day after day, acting out a part scripted by a self-aggrandizing prick who doesn't get who I am or what I'm about. You know I hate it when you ignore me at concerts, but you do it anyway. Outside this room, I don't exist to you, do I?"

"I didn't ignore you. I didn't acknowledge you the way you wanted," Dr. Fowler said. "What does that mean to you?"

"I'll tell you what it means. It means you put your bullshit ideology ahead of basic human kindness. What a wonderful role model! Thank God I have Stan Amernick to talk with," Jonas said, thinking of his favorite supervisor, a man who encouraged Jonas to follow his instincts, instead of spouting old-school psychoanalytic dogma.

Jonas heard papers rustling, the scratching of pen on paper. "What are you doing? Writing your shopping list?"

"What does it mean to you to hear me writing?"

"I'm done with that."

"Done with what?" Dr. Fowler said.

"Done with your 'What-does-that-mean-to-yous.' You say that so much, it's meaningless. I need analysis to get over my father so I can become a better man. I need analysis to understand my mind so I can become a better doctor. What happens here? I wind up with neither.

"So what if I have a sentimental streak. It's what makes me, *me*. So what if I had a dream about occupying the office next to you and having a door that connects us. It was a beautiful dream, and you spoiled it with all those interpretations about repressed homosexuality you ram down my throat. You know why I dream about airplane crashes? It's because their pilots don't know how to steer. Just like you. You have no clue where my analysis—or my life—is headed. If I keep going like I am, I'll be shredded through your analytic mill like tractor tires. I'll wind up recycled into another you. Enough of this; that's not going to happen. I won't let it."

"I'm honored by your oration," Dr. Fowler said. "As long as you're at it, is there anything else you'd like to say? I'm all ears."

"You fucking bastard."

"Don't stop there. By all means, keep going."

"I don't care whether you believe this or not, but you apply your ideology to me the way internists pigeonhole patients into catchall diagnoses. It's time to update your thinking. That's what competent analysts do."

"I see."

"What exactly is it you see?"

Dr. Fowler said nothing. Thinking of when Victoria asked him his age, Jonas said, "I asked you a simple question."

"If it's so simple, Dr. Speller, enlighten me with the answer."

"This analysis has become a joke."

"I don't follow you."

"Of course you don't. That's the point. This whole thing is ludicrous."

Dr. Fowler's chair creaked. Jonas began to feel more sorry than angry. Sorry he hadn't taken better care of himself. Sorry he'd assumed Dr. Fowler would understand him better than Jonas could himself.

Neither man spoke for minutes.

Jonas said, "You must know by now that I don't tell you what's on my mind when I'm here. Or are you too arrogant to know that?"

"Oh," Dr. Fowler said, followed by a long silence during which Jonas heard *Invitation to the Dance* in his head.

He hummed the melody out loud: "Bawm bibawm bum bah, dah diddle dada, dah diddle dada; bawm bibawm bum bah, dah diddle dah daaah." Double stops in the violins on each attack. Then, the sweet violin melody: "Bawm 2, 3, 1 diddle dum. Bawm 2, 3, 1 diddle dum. Dum diddle dum, dum diddle dum, dum diddle dah-dah dum." The fingers of his left hand danced up and down the neck of an imaginary violin, his right wrist and arm bowing in synchrony.

"Can you put what's going on in your mind into words?" Dr. Fowler said.

"Sure, I can, but why should I?"

"Because you're supposed to say what's on your mind."

"You don't deserve it." Jonas sat up on the couch and faced Dr. Fowler, the first time in three years he looked the man in the eye. "I like my new patient. She's full of fire, like I used to be. If I let you, you'll puree my soul into mousse for your next before-the-concert dinner party. Do you know the name of the piece I was just humming?" Jonas persisted. More silence. "I asked for the name of that piece. I'm not going to stop until you answer." Dr. Fowler's chair creaked again, like the rusty door hinge of the Institute Library—old and musty, like a mausoleum. "Don't be scared. I won't tell on you."

"It's *Invitation to the Dance*," Dr. Fowler said in an unfamiliar, wavering voice. But by that point, it didn't matter.

"I dreamt about it last night. I felt the music in a place you've never earned the right to enter, someplace sacred."

"I'd like to hear about it."

"It's too late for that."

"Too late?"

"Too late for us. We're done. You'll have four open hours once I'm gone. It's time you took a refresher course. That's the only way you'll be invited to my dance."

Jonas rose to leave. "I was wrong to say I got nothing from you. You saw me through my darkest hours and taught me to trust my unconscious mind. For that, I'll always be grateful. You tried. I know that."

He paused at the door. "I'll miss Friday afternoons here; they reminded me of how much I looked forward to Saturdays when I was a kid, singing in the children's chorus. We sang beautiful Christmas carols in four-part harmony. Maybe it was too much to hope you'd understand me. That's over now, like my childhood. I'm no kid anymore. It's time to take care of myself. That's what my father would have wanted. Not you. Not this. Thank God it's over."

8

Victoria's thirty-second commute to work had advantages, but the biggest disadvantage was the lack of transition time. Like the stuffed prize in an arcade game, she felt plucked from her kitchen each morning and dropped into the legal mill downstairs.

Throughout the morning, Melinda was on Victoria's mind. Melinda, so angry with the world, was far prettier than Victoria had been when she was fourteen. So active that she needed her tennis racket restrung monthly, Melinda had not been to the pro shop since June. And despite growing two inches over the summer, she hadn't asked for new sneakers either. She was so much younger than Victoria was when she began to need therapy. Melinda couldn't be as distraught as Victoria had been back then. Could she?

For her first appointment of the day, Victoria met with Flora Arrestia. Schone and Braun had taken on Barlow v. Duke's as a favor to the Arrestias' accountant, who golfed with Martin Braun's father in Upper Merion. Although no one would be funding their retirement based on the outcome, the case reminded Victoria of a novel she read in college—a book that changed her life.

Flora Márquez Arrestia was the heiress to Duke's, a family-owned restaurant chain founded by her father, Luis José Márquez, a Cuban refugee who made omelets and sandwiches for years in West Chester. By 2004, his business had expanded to seven locations in the Philadelphia suburbs.

Donato Arrestia, an Italian tenor whose opera career went nowhere, settled down with Flora after years of affairs with his students. Donato assumed control of the restaurants when Luis retired. The Arrestias had one daughter.

Duke's was predominantly a cash business. When an audit revealed a three-hundred-and-fifty-thousand-dollar discrepancy, Donato installed security cameras, which caught the operations manager, Horace Barlow, raiding cash registers at all seven branches. A private detective tailed Barlow to the Atlantic City casinos where he lost much more than he won. However, Barlow was never charged, because the security films were inconclusive and Duke's bank deposits didn't fully correspond with the missing loot.

Someone besides Horace—most likely Donato—was skimming, too, Victoria realized.

Barlow sued his former employers for lost wages, defamation of character, and age discrimination, retaining flamboyant lawyer Denise Mather. Martin and Victoria quickly realized that publicity-hound Mather—already a talking head on CNN—would relish having a bully pulpit from which to broadcast her indignation over ageism, her cause de jour. So the real agenda behind Schone-Braun's involvement was to muzzle Barlow and Mather and prevent a scandal that might expose Duke's dirty dealings and implicate the accountant.

"How can they think we're going to pay him?" Flora Arrestia asked Victoria. "We have it all on tape."

"The tapes are going to be a problem," Victoria counseled. "Barlow's attorney is very shrewd. She'll turn them against you—that's what I would do—alleging you harassed Barlow into quitting so you wouldn't have to pay his benefits and pension. We cannot have you acting outraged in front of the jury. That'll make you look worse in their eyes. Remember, we want the jury to believe how pained you were by Barlow's behavior, how hard it was to accept that someone you trusted would steal from you. It had to hurt, didn't it?"

Victoria saw something in Mrs. Arrestia's eyes. Had she and Horace been lovers? Did Horace blackmail Flora, taking the money as a payoff to keep him from telling Donato? Or was Barlow, whose arrest was splashed all over the newspapers, out for revenge against Donato, a tacit partner-in-crime who had ratted him out? No matter what, the case smelled.

Victoria prompted Flora, "Horace Barlow wasn't an employee; he was family. The pain of being robbed by someone you trusted—this is what the jury has to see on your face." Victoria imagined supplying Flora with a bottle of fake tears. "We want the jury to feel your pain—the tapes, the detective; you did that because you didn't want to believe it."

Looking at Flora's face, Victoria wondered, *Are you acting your part, too?*

For the rest of the meeting, Victoria made notes about jury selection, the key as she saw it to settling the case before it deteriorated into a media circus.

She was still preoccupied with Melinda. What would her daughter do next?

The ten o'clock deposition at Attorney Buddinger's office was even worse. Geologist Jonathan Ramey presented diagram after diagram about the underpinnings of a newly constructed Bucks County outdoor amphitheater whose foundation was crumbling. To rebuild would cost a fortune. Everyone involved in the design and construction blamed each other. Schone and Braun represented the architects.

Victoria, who usually relished thinking on her feet, spent three grueling hours defusing Buddinger's attacks on her witness's qualifications, disrupting the flow of his intimidating questions by objecting every time Buddinger raised his voice. By the end she felt like a tenth grader expected to compare and contrast Elizabethan poets. Her mind wandered from Flora Arrestia to Martin's inconvenience taking Melinda to school. Did Donato and Flora have an understanding, an arrangement? Could the same be said of Martin and her?

Back at her desk after the deposition, flowers from Martin awaited, along with an invitation for a late lunch at Bookbinder's in Old City. "Meet me at 2:00 PM," the message said in Martin's handwriting, his signature above a Cupid's arrow. *That's nice*, Victoria thought, wondering if Martin had noticed the negligee and got his hopes up for a romantic evening. Although she really wanted to, her heart just wasn't in it.

* * *

Victoria tried to stay in the mood, but she couldn't. Soon she and Martin were squabbling over the Duke's case, from which Victoria was sure Schone and Braun would never receive a dime, seeing as the brouhaha in the papers had reduced Duke's business to a trickle, and the detectives, video surveillance experts, and forensic accountants had all but bankrupted the company.

"Why are we doing this stupid case?" Victoria asked over her tea.

"Because Dad's been very good to us, Vic," Martin said. "He could have cut me off years ago when I left Braun Brothers to become a lawyer. Instead, Dad gave us the money to start Schone and Braun."

"You're right. And I do want to help your father," Victoria said.

"If Barlow doesn't go quietly, everyone who had anything to do with Duke's will wind up under a microscope. The fallout could tarnish the reputation of Dad's most loyal friend. You know how touchy it is."

"That could happen anyway," Victoria said.

"True, Vic, very true, but Dad wouldn't have asked us to get involved unless he trusted us. I owe him a lot, Vic. This is the first time he's ever asked for our help." Martin took hold of Victoria's hands. "I love my father. I love him very much. He loves you, too. When I brought you home for the first time, Dad saw your sparkle—how you made me come alive. If it hadn't been for you, I might still be languishing in the family business; I would have never have gone to law school, never made a life of my own. He saw how good we were for each other. Dad wanted us to be together—to have a family."

Some family, Victoria reflected silently, Melinda weighing heavily on her mind. For the moment, hers and Martin's courtship seemed like it belonged to someone else. She squeezed Martin's hand with as much affection as she could muster. "Even so," she said. "All this work for nothing."

"Is that what's really bothering you?"

"No, you're right, Martin. Melinda has me incredibly upset. If anything ever happened to Gregory . . ." she paused to consider what she was saying, "or to Melinda. I don't know what I'd do. I have to speak with her when we get home."

"Are you sure you should to do that?"

"I'm not sure about anything Martin!" Victoria flared. "But I can't just sit by and let her destroy everything I've worked for."

"Destroy? Isn't that going too far? And what about me? I'm part of this family, too."

"I didn't mean it like that, Martin," Victoria said. "But you have no idea what's going through my mind. I went through a terrible time in college. A total nightmare. I thought it was over. The Arrestia case reminds me of *Bleak House*, the Dickens novel. A property dispute destroyed a family and drained the estate. One of the heirs couldn't cope. He killed himself. I grew up in a bleak house. I can't live in one again."

"I remember that book."

"That book changed my life."

"The girl's guardian was a real *mensch*. His name is on the tip of my tongue."

"John Jarndyce. The case was Jarndyce versus Jarndyce. I remember it like yesterday."

9

Victoria's class before therapy on Mondays was nineteenth-century British literature. They were reading Charles Dickens's *Bleak House*, a story that gripped Victoria as if the novel had been written about her.

Her preoccupation with tall buildings had not recurred since the first session, but she had descended into a pervasive sadness. She found solace in talking about it to Dr. Speller, but her mood remained black.

"Why am I so sad?" she began that day's session.

"You're mourning," the doctor replied.

"For whom? For what?"

"I'm not sure. Why not do what we always do? Let your thoughts come freely and say whatever comes to mind. We'll figure it out."

"I never told you how *Bleak House* ended," Victoria said. "Esther's guardian considered marrying her but stepped aside to let her marry a dashing physician who had loved her for years. Because of her smallpox scars, Esther believed no man would ever want her. But in the end, her guardian encouraged the relationship between the younger people and outfitted a cozy cottage for them."

Dr. Speller opened his file cabinet's bottom drawer to prop his feet on.

She continued, "The night I finished it, I dreamed about the book. I didn't want it to end. In my dream, I was at a wedding on a spring day at a park. I assume it was Esther's. A string quartet was playing. People were dancing. I looked all over, but I couldn't find the bride. I wanted to see her face, to see how she felt about the groom.

"My parents were there. A bartender served drinks to my father, who was conversing animatedly with someone. Lorraine was in another group. I felt shunned, like they were ashamed to introduce me. Grandma was there, too, carrying a gold necklace for the bride. I followed her, hoping she would leave it where I could pick it up.

"When I tried to dance, my head spun, and I felt nauseous. A man talked with me. He made me feel better.

"In the dream, I thought, 'This can't be my family's wedding, because we don't have that many relatives.' It felt like the hosts had invited me as an afterthought, not because they really wanted me. I woke up sad, very sad." Victoria eyes welled with tears. "How long will I feel like this? It seems like it's gone on forever."

"Perhaps your dream can explain your feelings," Dr. Speller said. "Let's start with the park. Are there any thoughts, memories, daydreams, or associations with it?"

"It reminds me of Fairmont Park in the spring. I hate being cooped up all winter, so I go walking in the park the first weekend I can. I visit Grandma Jeanine. She lives on Ben Franklin Parkway near Boathouse Row. I usually go by myself, but I always wish I had company. Talking about it makes me sad and lonely."

"It's a memory about loneliness."

Victoria reached for a tissue. "Usually it's chilly, and after a bad winter, there are grayish mounds of snow that won't melt completely until the spring thaw, until the crocuses bloom. I love flowers. When I have my own home, I want lots of flowers. It looks like the grass won't ever start growing. The ground is muddy, and my feet sink in."

"Was the park in your dream sad?"

"No, it was warmer, brighter. The grass had turned green. There was a warm breeze. That's right! I must have been wearing the clothes I got in Florence—Lorraine hated everything I chose. Shopping with her was torture.

"I just thought of something. Remember that leather jacket? Lorraine bought it for me the morning we climbed the Duomo—at a fancy leather-goods store across from the Medici Palace. Florence was warm that day; I remember beads of sweat on my forehead, like in my dream.

"The more clothes we tried on, the more excited Lorraine became. She didn't care how much things cost, which I knew would make my father mad. We picked two things for me: a short leather jacket, and a mid-calf leather skirt. In the wedding dream, I must have been wearing them. Lorraine and I finished shopping early that afternoon."

"Like in the dream?"

Victoria nodded. "On the way to the checkout—and this really happened—I saw a coat I thought Grandma would like, but when I mentioned getting her a present, my mother's face contorted with rage."

"Do you know why?" Dr. Speller asked.

"When Jeanine was younger, she ran the fine jewelry department at John Wanamaker's. Her father was a goldsmith. Lorraine always maintained that Jeanine took the job to get away from her, but she just wanted her own life."

"As for your mother's anger about getting your grandmother a gift?"

"It ruined the moment. When we tried on clothes, Lorraine sparkled like a diamond, but then her whole persona changed. When the bill came, she looked at me like I was a pig. When we rejoined my father, she blamed the high cost on me, saying I had demanded she buy the clothes. Both my parents barely spoke to me that afternoon. It makes my blood boil to think about it."

"You felt angry at them."

"Angry? I was furious. But also confused, very confused. I kept asking myself what I did wrong. I must have done something wrong. All I wanted to do was disappear." She went silent. A moment later, she blinked.

"Did something just happen, Victoria?" Dr. Speller asked.

"That explains it," she said. "I can't believe it took me this long to see."

"To see what?"

"How I felt at the top of the Duomo—that's when my fears about tall buildings began. Thinking about it makes me nauseous, like I'm really sick."

"That's what happens when you come in touch with powerful feelings. Trust me. You'll feel better when you say it out loud."

"I felt how easy it would be to climb over the stone wall of the observation deck and disappear. That began all those bad thoughts."

"They enraged you," Dr. Speller said. "They pushed you over the edge, metaphorically speaking."

Stunned by his interpretation, Victoria couldn't speak. "How come I never looked at it that way?" she said several moments later.

"Because you needed to understand yourself better. That's what we're doing here. You're searching for yourself—like the bride you can't find—at someone else's party, not yours."

"Who would want to come to mine? I don't know anybody I feel that close to."

"That needs to change."

"I liked what you just said about the dream. It makes me look at things differently. I felt that way the first time I told you about Esther's scarred face. Right then, I felt my childhood ending. Will I ever stop being so sad?"

"Does anything in your dream resonate with the sad feeling?"

"The yearning to find the bride. It feels like heartbreak."

"I think your heartbreak comes from looking for love in the wrong place." Dr. Speller paused, then added, "One thing's for sure."

"What's that?"

"You won't find it in Abington."

"You're right about that. Everything feels so up in the air. I don't know where I belong anymore."

"I know where you belong," Dr. Speller said. "You belong here, in therapy."

10

Monday, November 2, 1981

On the first Monday in November, Victoria awoke in a good mood from a dream she could not remember. One thing was certain; her sadness had lifted.

Working on dreams in therapy had become enjoyable with Dr. Speller as a trusted ally. *I have to remember that dream. I want to tell him*, Victoria said to herself. But the harder she tried, the more it eluded her, like grasping for the vapor she exhaled on crisp mornings.

Carol Hancock, her dormitory suitemate, noticed the change immediately. "Well, well, you're all smiles this morning," she said. "Most mornings, you drag yourself around like the boy in *Peanuts* with a cloud over his head."

"It's that bad?"

"'Fraid so," Carol said. "Are you mad at me? You've been avoiding me."

Victoria felt it was time to say what was on her mind, even though it might upset Carol. That, Victoria had learned in therapy. "The truth is that I think I'm disappointing you because I don't come along when you invite me to mixers and fraternity parties. I know you're trying to include me, but the boys are so infantile—bragging about Daddy's Pep Boys franchises and what they're going to do after graduation. They really turn me off. And they ply me with alcohol and marijuana—which makes me nauseous—and try to get me in the sack. Not that I don't want to sleep with a man. I'm no prude. I think about sex as much anyone, probably more. But I want someone older, someone who knows what he's doing. I like that you care about me and want me to have friends, but I don't want to be part of that scene."

"I was just trying to be a big sister," Carol said.

"I know, but it can't depend on me doing what you want. I've had a lifetime of that. My mother is forever telling me what to think and how to act. I can't do that anymore, Carol. I hope you still want to be my friend," Victoria said as if she were facing an executioner.

"Are you out of your mind? Of course I want to be friends! My sister went here, and she showed me how to have a good time at Penn. I wanted to do that for you. I'm glad you told me. You're such a good person, Victoria. We'll always be friends. Besides," Carol confessed, "you're not the first person who ever said I'm too pushy."

They laughed and hugged. It was the first time Victoria had embraced a friend so affectionately, which brought the previous night's dream so close to mind she could almost taste it.

* * *

Bursting with pride, Victoria skipped down the hall toward room 921 that afternoon. "You're going to be happy to hear what I did today," she told Dr. Speller. "Something I've never done before."

He returned her smile. "Terrific. Let's hear it."

"I had an honest talk with my roommate. It was about something stupid. I knew she was coming from a good place, but I didn't want to keep up an act. So, I told her how I felt."

"Good for you! What was the 'something stupid'?"

"She wanted me to go to parties with her, and I felt obligated, because I was afraid she wouldn't like me if I said no thanks. It sounds ridiculous when I say it out loud."

"Ridiculous?"

"My mother is always saying how ridiculous I am."

"Always?"

"Well, maybe not always, but often enough that I don't know what to expect from her. You can't believe how hot and cold she blows. Sometimes, she's in a fabulous mood with me; other times she dismisses me with a 'You're being ridiculous' that makes me feel like two cents."

"Intermittent reward and punishment," Dr. Speller said. "It's the worst."

"Huh?"

"Basic psychology. Learning theory: conditioning, reward, reinforcement, punishment. Unpredictability is the worst. Intermittent reinforcement, it's called. Someday you'll take the course."

"You know I hate to say it, but predictable is boring," Victoria admitted.

"That *is* a problem. What's that about?"

"It must have to do with how my mother and I interact. That's a whole issue in itself. We should get to it sometime, just not now. There's a dream I wanted to tell you. It has to be important, because I woke up smiling, and my mood's better. I've been close to remembering it all day."

"You didn't write it down?"

"No. I woke up in such a good mood all I wanted to do was savor the feeling."

"Did the dream have to do with eating?"

"That's amazing. I just remembered it. How do you do that? It's like you can read my mind."

"All I'm doing is connecting the dots. You used the word, 'savor,' which goes along with tasty food."

"In the dream, I was with my mother at the supermarket where we always shopped when I was little. There were these sugar cookies I loved, but the only way she bought them was if I snuck a package into the shopping cart when she wasn't looking. I told you she's always had a thing about how I look. Back then—it must have been before puberty because I didn't thin out until after I got my period—I must have looked chubby to her. I suppose she didn't want me getting any fatter. At the checkout line, she always gave me a dirty look when she found the cookies, but she never said 'No.' I'm sure she didn't want the cashier thinking, 'What kind of mother wouldn't buy her daughter what she wants?'

"So, in the dream, Lorraine and I became separated, and then it switched to me being my real age, shopping for my own food; that meant I could get exactly what I want, which felt so liberating." Victoria tossed her head back and started to blush. "Here's the funny part. I went to a bakery, and you were there."

Dr. Speller's eyes widened. "Me?"

"Yes, it was definitely you. It was one of those bakeries where you see past the end of the counter into the kitchen. I had come to buy sugar cookies. The person behind the counter said, 'Wait a moment, they're just coming out of the oven.' You were the baker. Only, I could see just your face, which cracked me up because you looked like a bobblehead. When I asked why you were there, you said in your clinical mode, 'We need to look into your feelings about this.'"

"Clinical mode?"

"Of course."

"What are you talking about?"

"You must be kidding. You don't know?" He shook his head. "How can you not know?" Victoria laughed. "You have two ways of operating, which you bounce back and forth between. In clinical mode, you sound detached. I like it much better when you're relaxed and conversational. Your voice is sweeter. I can't be the only person who's told you this."

Dr. Speller's face went from pink to red. "Well . . . You know . . . Someone once said—"

"I didn't mean to upset you."

"I'm not upset," he countered, like the character in Hamlet who protested too much. After a moment, he smiled. "I get it. You just did with me what you did with your friend—saying directly how you feel. Good for you. I can stand the feedback."

"Then you still like me?" Victoria half-joked.

"Yes, I like you."

"This is good," Victoria said as she left, feeling playful and happy for the first time since she had begun therapy.

11

Friday, November 19, 2004

Jonas Speller had long accepted he would never be a professional violinist—lectures and courtroom appearances had become his recitals. He'd rehearsed and performed the day's opus, "The Psychiatric Expert in Mental Damage Cases," many times.

After his morning panel, Jonas lunched with Eddie and his partner, Pete Bodenheim. Pete had been Jonas's fraternity brother in college, and Jonas had introduced him to Eddie. Pete, an all-Ivy backcourt standout, and Eddie, a huge college basketball fan, hit it off immediately. When Pete finished law school, Eddie recommended him for associateship at his firm. Later, they founded the law firm bearing their name. Nowadays, Pete and his wife, Beth, and Eddie and Margo Speller spent nearly every holiday together with Jonas and Jennie, the three sets of children like brothers and sisters.

Jonas lounged comfortably with many of the lawyers for whom he often testified, until Eddie retrieved him shortly before his main performance. "Time to make sure the audiovisuals are locked and loaded," Eddie said on the way to the Esquire ballroom. "It's show time."

* * *

"It's just not that complicated," Jonas began his presentation. "Mental damage cases are like those with any other type of injury."

Jonas took his audience through what to expect when collaborating with mental health professionals. "When it comes to your expert," he said, "pick someone who doesn't patronize the jury or use jargon. Otherwise, no one will believe their testimony."

Jonas kept the technical parts of the talk entertaining, presenting a series of color-enhanced brain scans to demonstrate the difference in brain functioning between a normal person and a psychologically traumatized September 11th victim. "Technology is revolutionizing psychiatry. For decades defendants have argued that mental damage doesn't really exist because no one could see it. Those days are gone," he said, stressing each syllable as he pointed a laser at the X-rays projected on the screen. "Now we can see and measure brain activity like never before.

"And be sure to get medical records from every doctor your client has seen, not only his psychiatrist or psychologist. Get job evaluations and employment physicals, too, anything that documents baseline levels of functioning.

"I leave you with the case that taught me the most. I had a great mentor, Paul Fremont. Some of you may have been fortunate enough to know him. Paul coached me to make eye contact and read the jury's body language, but the best thing he impressed upon me was the importance of having your expert read every document in the medical record word for word. It is *so* tempting to scrimp on record reviews. Don't do it.

"I testified for Paul in a multi-million-dollar case in which a borderline mentally retarded twenty-six-year-old woman nearly died in a car accident. At issue was whether the accident rendered the woman— we'll call her Carmen—who had been able to make do on her own prior to the accident, totally disabled. Everyone assumed she had been so traumatized by her near death experience.

"The defense engaged a highly regarded institution's department of psychology—note, not psychiatry—for expert testimony; the important distinction being that psychiatrists have medical training. Their report asserted that Carmen's pre-accident IQ was so low that the experience could not have made her functioning level any worse.

"I dissected the report word by word. Same with the medical records—five loose-leaf notebooks so thick they looked like the operating manual for the space shuttle!

"When I examined Carmen at the nursing home, she was totally bewildered. She remembered nothing of the accident or the hospital, not even what she ate for breakfast that morning. Her capacity to make new memories had been entirely wiped out. She could dress and feed herself only if her clothes and food were prepared for her. I contended that psychological trauma was not the critical issue. The plaintiff's team had missed Carmen's short-term memory deficits, something psychiatrists routinely screen for.

"I'll never forget that courtroom scene," Jonas went on. "The reflection off the defense attorney's bald head looked like it could pierce titanium. 'Doctor,' he turned on me scornfully. 'How can you tell us that the accident caused the plaintiff's deficits? Look how poorly she functioned for her entire life.'

"I measured my words carefully before I spoke. 'The medical record indicates that prior to the accident this woman could function on her own. When I examined her after the accident I found that she had no short-term memory. No mentally retarded individual, even borderline retarded, with short-term memory loss can subsist without round-the-clock care. Six weeks in a coma with a fractured skull damaged this woman's brain. I'm certain of it.'

"'And where does it say that the plaintiff suffered a fractured skull, Dr. Speller?' the attorney pressed.

"'It's in the medical record,' I responded.

"'Exactly where in the medical record?' he sneered. 'We found no such mention.'

"'*She did have a fractured skull, didn't she?*' I wondered to myself. If I was mistaken, it would have undermined the credibility I'd worked so hard to establish.

"So, there we were: me rustling through binder number five trying to find a skull X-ray report. I looked everywhere, with no luck. But then, like a lighthouse beacon on a foggy night, the answer appeared before me.

"'It's right here,' I said, and I showed him the CT scan.

"The attorney said, 'I see nothing about a skull fracture.'

"I read aloud. 'Twenty-six-year-old comatose female with CSF leakage from the nose. That's it.'

"'What do you mean, "That's it?"' What does CSF have to with anything?'

"I turned to the jury. 'CSF stands for cerebrospinal fluid, the liquid that bathes the brain and spinal cord. CSF leakage through the nose after head trauma is always the result of a fracture of the bones in the base of the skull.'

"The attorney's face turned beet red. He'd broken the first commandment: Never ask a question you don't know the answer to. 'No more questions.' he mumbled quickly.

"The records were key. The cerebrospinal fluid leakage registered in my mind subconsciously. I'm sure of it. And even if the plaintiff's team had reviewed the records as diligently, they missed the short-term memory defect and the subtlety about the skull fracture, not having studied neuroanatomy and radiology, something every medical student—including students of psychiatry—learns. If you need a medical record review, get a medical doctor. P.S.: We won. Big time. Thanks for listening. I'll be around if anyone has questions."

Through the applause, Eddie and Pete smiled broadly. "Jesus, what a performance," Eddie said when the three shared a private moment. "It's like *Mark Twain Tonight*. I've heard this speech more times than I can count, and yet every version sounds fresh. How do you do it?"

"Nothing complicated. I stay current. And I try to make each person feel I'm talking to him," Jonas grinned deviously. "That's what Samuel Clemens did when he lectured. Now, there's a man with a phenomenal grasp on human nature."

"Damn, you're good," Pete said. "Even though she keeps kosher, you could sell my mother pork-belly futures. Have you considered a sales career with Amway?"

"I don't know about that," Jonas laughed. "What I do know is I can't wait until the meetings are over. Tomorrow, I'm strictly a tourist. Then, I'm heading to the craps tables to set my inner child free. I hope you both come, too."

"Sounds great. Let's see what the girls are up to," Eddie said.

"I know exactly what they're doing," Jonas said. "They're getting the full spa treatment, probably just finishing up. Let's go out to dinner tonight to celebrate."

Eddie borrowed Pete's Blackberry. "I hear you three are at the spa," he said when Margo answered. "Jonas hit another grand slam today. I swear, every time he lectures, we get three more cases. The guy's a walking ATM. Tell Jennie her husband was terrific. He had everyone mesmerized, including me."

"I heard that," Jennie chimed in. "Put me on speaker."

"After reflexology, they treated us to avocado, eggplant, and oysters for lunch; they claim it rejuvenates a woman's sex drive. I hope they're right, but even if they're not, we'll be ravenous by dinnertime. We'll be here until five. What time is it now?"

"Four-thirty," Eddie said.

"Let me talk to Jonas in private."

Jennie asked her husband, "So, how was it?"

"Great. Everyone liked it," Jonas said, his mind and body consumed by a very different appetite. "How's this? I'll meet you back in the room as soon as I can and finish your treatment the proper way. After a nap, the six of us will go out to eat. What do you say? Eddie and Pete agreed to amuse themselves until dinner."

"How soon can you be here?" Jennie asked.

"If I get going now, I'll be waiting when you get back to the room."

"Mmm. Can't wait to see you, love. I'll be ready. I'm so proud of you, Jonas. So proud. And even though he's not here, so is Dad. Especially Dad."

12

Jonas stared ahead as he passed Dr. Fowler's open door on the way to Dr. Amernick's office. Dr. Stan Amernick, Jonas's supervisor, had been in Switzerland for six weeks teaching psychotherapy. Jonas could hardly wait to tell him about Dr. Fowler and about Victoria.

"I have something to tell you," Jonas said as soon as he sat down in Amernick's office. "I had a blowout with Dr. Fowler. I'm done with him." Dr. Amernick, his pearly hair combed front to back over a ruddy pate, smiled faintly. "To tell you the truth, I'm relieved. I stopped telling him my free associations a long time ago." Amernick broke into a wide grin.

"Why are you smiling?" Jonas said.

"Thank God you got it! You and Fowler were a terrible match."

"Why didn't you say anything?"

"Why? Because criticizing someone's analyst is like bad-mouthing their girlfriend. And Philadelphia's a small town. Everybody knows everybody's business. It's a big deal when a candidate dumps his training analyst."

"And everyone assumes the candidate is unanalyzable."

"Don't assume, Jonas. Don't assume. It was Henry Plummer, director of your clinic, who backed Fowler's promotion to training analyst. It was political. Plummer steers residents like you to Fowler in return for favors."

Dr. Amernick removed his feet from the ottoman and inched forward in his Eames chair. "Just between you and me," he confided, "after college, Fowler's daughter Morgan went wild. She even had a romp with one of her father's patients, an older female college professor. When Fowler heard about it in the woman's analysis, he sent Morgan to Plummer for therapy, hoping Plummer would keep a lid on it. I found out because Morgan was friends with the daughter of someone we knew. That's what I mean about Philadelphia being a small world."

"You know, when you cross him, Fowler's tongue turns into a chain saw."

"I'm not surprised," Dr. Amernick said. "Whenever I challenged his ideas at Institute functions, he twisted my words so much, I wasn't sure what I believed. Anyway, the good news is that you're free of him. Good for you."

"Won't Plummer hold it against me?" Jonas asked.

"Maybe, but let's look at the big picture. Do you mind if I smoke? I analyze better with a Macanudo." Dr. Amernick cranked opened the window for ventilation, guillotined the end of an impressive cigar, then lit up. "Where do you want to be in five, ten years?" he asked after a few minutes.

"In New York City, near my brother. Married, family; I can see our kids growing up near each other."

"Career-wise?"

"I get along great with all the residents. Psychology interns, too. We've evolved into what amounts to peer supervision. Sometimes, so many people show up in my office, it feels like an overcrowded Volkswagen. They're a riot, those sessions. You should hear the things they say about their patients and how they gripe about the faculty."

"That's great and all, but how are you going to pay the bills?"

"Teaching, supervising, private practice of psychoanalysis."

"Sorry, Jonas, but the days of psychoanalysis are numbered. The federal government dropped insurance allowances for it from unlimited sessions to fifty a year. It'll go even lower. You'll see. No one can show that analysis is cost-effective. Don't get me wrong; I still think it's the best way to learn how the mind works, but twenty sessions of cognitive therapy treats depression and anxiety better and faster. Analysts will be swimming against the tide, so don't pin your hopes on having full-fee patients, especially when you're just starting out. And New York has tons of competition. Mark my words. In twenty-five years, the only people coming for therapy four or five days a week will be psychoanalysts-in-training, and the training-and-supervising analysts will be in a feeding frenzy to get their jaws into those cases. You really want to get mixed up in that?

"Look what's happening in biological psychiatry. Not to mention combining medication and psychotherapy. It's very exciting. Who knows where we'll be in twenty years? You could be leading the way if you keep an open mind."

"Most every analyst maintains that medication interferes with analysis by covering over the underlying causes," Jonas asserted.

"Hogwash! Rationalization: pure and simple. If anything it's the other way around. When symptoms are under control, therapy works better. Analysts are scared because combining medication with psychotherapy gets people better quicker. Less business for them."

"Well, I still want to finish analytic training first," Jonas said. "And I can't do control cases without having a training analyst."

"Of course, you should finish training. It'll make you a better therapist and a better person. You're so musical; I can't believe no one told you about Scott Frantz, head of the Institute's education committee."

"When I started analysis I didn't feel I had a choice."

"Well you do now! Scott's the man I would have recommended for your training analyst. His wife, Johanna, plays cello for the Philadelphia Orchestra, and he's a decent pianist. They play duets, which says a lot about how the man relates. He'd be perfect for you. I'll call him and tell him about you, okay?"

"What a relief. And here I was worrying the Institute would throw me out."

"I see potential in you, Jonas. Strength, courage, and imagination. But I know how the psychoanalytic gristmill works. If you're not careful, it can grind away your creativity and churn your interpretations into aphorisms. Look at Fowler, a brilliant mind trying to cram his point of view into other people's mindsets. His daughter's a mess, while he plays word games. Plummer, Fowler, they're hanging on by a thread. Once word gets around about you leaving Fowler, you'll be more of a threat to them than they are to you."

"Really? I never looked at it that way."

"Define life for yourself, Jonas. Don't live someone else's. When I was your age, I lived in Switzerland for a time. What an eye-opener. My patients stopped being obsessives or hysterics; they became people. I stopped analyzing solely in terms of 'intrapsychic conflict' and began helping them find their way. There were two men there who changed my life. Maybe I'll tell you about it someday. It's quite a story."

"I'll think about it, Dr. Amernick."

"It's time you started calling me Stan."

"I'd like that, although it'll take some time to get used to. Meanwhile, there's this new patient I have to tell you about. She's a huge part of what's been happening to me."

"Tell me about her," Stan said.

Jonas grinned. "Victoria is her name. If you took her at face value, you'd say she's a spoiled Jewish princess, but beneath the surface, she's full of fire. If it hadn't been for her, I wouldn't have had the balls to confront Fowler. There's an amazing connection between us. It's uncanny. I'll be thinking something, and two seconds later, she's saying the same thing. She soaks up my interpretations like a sponge. She came in overwhelmed with thoughts of walking off tall buildings, which stopped the moment I connected the impulses to her rage at her parents."

"She's what I call a sports car."

"Huh?"

"Very responsive to what you say. With all that oomph, she sounds like a Ferrari." Stan chuckled. "The Institute drones would call her a 'phallic woman,' jargon for any woman who intimidates them. Does she have a boyfriend?"

"Nobody's made it past the third date. Says she's a virgin, although she's plenty interested. Dresses royally, too. Always in designer outfits, never without makeup."

"My God. All detailed and still in the showroom!"

"The first dream she brought into therapy was about a wedding."

"Aha," Stan said. "There it is. She wants a serious relationship. She wants to be the bride. She must feel alone."

Jonas nodded.

"How old?"

"Just turned twenty."

"Are you considering her for one of your control cases?"

"She would do it if I pushed, but I don't want to share her with a supervising analyst I don't know. It would be like throwing her to the wolves."

"How's her therapy going?"

"Just fine. We meet twice a week, face-to-face. She emerged from a big funk after I appeared undisguised in a dream."

"The first dream about the therapist is a hallmark event. So, how did she portray you?"

"At first, Victoria-the-child wanted her favorite sugar cookies, but her mother wouldn't let her. Later, the grown-up Victoria was in a bakery, looking for her own cookies. Guess who the baker was?"

"Sweetness—that's what she wants from you. I bet her mother can be very bitter. And what were her associations to you in the dream?"

"That sometimes I sound too detached, in what she calls 'clinical mode.' She likes it better when I'm 'relaxed and conversational.' I think I get clinical when I'm unsure of myself."

"I bet 'clinical mode' is connected with your ex."

"My ex?"

"Your ex-analyst. You've probably been mimicking Fowler's style without realizing it. He's a know-it-all. Don't be afraid to be unsure of yourself with Victoria, with all your patients. It'll make you more human in their eyes. And don't worry. Victoria's not going anywhere as long as you keep doing what you're doing."

"You don't think I should focus on the orality in the dream?"

"Leave that to Phil Fowler and his cronies. They've made their living off those interpretations for the past fifty years. This girl hungers for sweetness and consistency. There'll be sparks between you and her," Stan said, his eyebrows dancing. "But that's how it is in our line of work.

"By the way, Jonas," Stan said as time was running out. "My wife, Marta—she's a psychiatrist, too—and I are having a few couples for Thanksgiving. You'd like them. I hope you can join us."

"Whoa, that's some invitation!" Jonas said.

"Please try and make it. There's someone I want you to meet."

13

Thursday, November 26, 1981

J onas was excited about Thanksgiving for the first time since his
father died. This would be his first without family.

Stan had invited him for 3:00 PM. They would have dinner
later, after several other couples arrived. In the morning, Jonas took off
for his run in the blustery wind. As he crossed Broad Street, napkins
and hot-dog wrappers from the Thanksgiving parade swirled around
the gutters like pigeons scavenging for their holiday meal.

The Amernicks lived on Delancey Street in a landmarked colonial
townhouse. Jonas often jogged through the neighborhood, but he had
never been inside any of the historic houses.

Barely able to contain himself, he arrived punctually, toting two
bottles of Dezaley.

"Make yourself comfortable," Stan said, collecting the wine and
Jonas's overcoat.

The Amernick foyer opened into a great room, the kitchen at the
rear, a working fireplace on the brick wall to the right. Crackling flames
reflected the colors of the holiday table's china, polished silver, and

glimmering crystal, making the entire space glow as if it had been lit by a giant candelabra.

Marta rushed to the door. Stan said, "Jonas, this is my wife, Marta."

Marta smiled. "Hello, Jonas. Stan's said so much about you."

"It's nice to meet you. Your home is fabulous," Jonas said. "I've seen these houses for years, but only from the outside."

Stan said, "We bought it for a song in the sixties. It looked abandoned." He turned to Marta, his face full of admiration. "We renovated it over time, room by room. It's been a labor of love."

Professional women usually intimidated him, but not Marta, whom Jonas took to instantly. He said, "Stan's told me about that journal club you're in, and about your training abroad."

"Dezaley!" Marta exclaimed as Stan showed her the wine. "The Swiss hardly ever export local wines. Where did you get these?"

"My brother, Eddie, lives in New York. You can find anything there."

"How thoughtful," she said.

"Remember our first Dezaley?" Stan asked her.

"Who could forget? The night you proposed," Marta said as she caressed the labels. "They're even chilled, too. Is it too early to make a toast?" She moved toward the staircase. "I'll see if Jennie wants some."

Stan took her arm. "She's getting dressed, dear. There's no rush."

"Jennie?" Jonas quizzed Stan.

"It must have slipped my mind," Stan chortled as if he were struggling to keep a straight face. "Jennie's our daughter. She's been staying here. She's on leave from Sotheby's in New York. She's a docent and tour guide for prospective buyers in Europe, mostly France."

Jonas's heart skipped a beat. *Jennie; so this was the someone Stan wanted me to meet*, he realized. He had never been abroad; the furthest he'd ever traveled was across the country with the Mask and Wig Club during his college years at Penn.

Marta said, "I thought the four of us could have a moment before everyone arrived."

Stan whispered something to her, and she said, "Okay, later."

"Anything to drink now?" Stan said.

"Something soft," Jonas replied, as they headed for the kitchen.

"There's club soda," Marta offered. "We keep it for Cuthbert Boening; Cutty, we call him. He'll be here later. He's on a first-name basis with every neuron in the brain of the sea snail *Aplysia*."

"What a character," Stan chuckled. "Cutty's in at the same time each day. His rats practically stand and salute when he enters the lab. At twelve-thirty sharp he lunches with the same colleagues before retiring to his favorite chair in the library to review the latest publications."

"Sounds like the man likes order. And predictability," Jonas said.

"Don't we all?" Marta added. "We wrestle with that all the time in the neuroscience group—where we discuss patients and journal articles. It's like a monthly infusion of new ideas. You'd like it, Jonas. Come sometime. Lately we've been wondering, what if people we've been calling 'moody' are *not*, in fact, dealing with unconscious conflict. Suppose their brains are merely more vulnerable to stressors, like body temperature?"

"I like that analogy," Jonas said. "When I was interning, we admitted a prostitute with a burning fever from pelvic inflammatory disease—"

"That reminds me," Stan interrupted. "You heard about those unexplained sarcomas in gay men? It wouldn't surprise me if the cause was sexually transmitted. Sorry for interrupting. You were saying . . . "

"The woman's self-esteem was in the toilet. Not one person visited her. But I was nice to her, and she felt better long before the antibiotics could have worked. My resident called it a placebo effect, but I knew my interaction with her made the difference. That's one of the reasons I chose psychiatry."

Marta said, "Wait until you meet Rebecca Kahn. She's coming, too. She's a child psychiatrist who gave up the analytic ghost after eight tortuous years on the couch. She felt well for the first time in her life once she took Lithium."

"Is that where you got the idea to analyze a patient on Lithium?" Jonas asked Stan. "I read that paper after we talked about combining medication and psychotherapy."

"I get a lot of ideas from Marta." Stan turned to her and asked, "Remember the night you came home from group all charged up about a European study of a new drug for depression? Zima . . . Zima . . . something."

"Zimeledine," she said. "The first drug to specifically increase serotonin. I better seat you and Rebecca at opposite ends of the table," she said to Jonas while basting the turkey, "or you'll monopolize each other all night."

Jonas heard someone approaching.

"There she is," Marta beamed. "We've been waiting for you. Jonas Speller, this is our daughter, Jennie."

Jennie Amernick, around Jonas's age, looked like a tulip curled up against a biting wind. She had dark brown hair and was more slender than her mother, her hips and thighs tapering softly beneath a tailored skirt. She had huge green eyes. Such sparkling eyes—they looked like polished jade. A large emerald pendant dangled from her neck.

"Hello," she said to Jonas. "From what he's said, Dad really likes you."

"Well, your father is the best teacher I ever had. Your necklace is mesmerizing. Where did it come from?"

All three Amernicks began speaking at once. Stan broke in, "You tell the story, Jennie. It belongs to you."

Jennie hesitated.

"C'mon, sweetie," Marta cajoled, eyes admiring Jonas. "We're friends."

"You'd have to really know my parents to understand," Jennie said. "My father's the son of a rabbi from Long Island. My mother is German Catholic, one of nine children, raised on a farm in southern Indiana. At Christmas time in 1954, Mom flew home from Switzerland where she was studying medicine. Dad was headed to Kentucky, where he was best man at a friend's wedding. They were both waiting for the same plane from New York to Louisville when a freak snowstorm buried the airport in two feet of snow, stranding everyone. Mom was carrying a duffel bag stuffed with Toblerones. All Dad had was his coat and a psychoanalytic journal.

"When Mom saw him reading *Psychoanalytic Quarterly*, they started talking. She shared her duffel bag for him to sleep on. That was it. Their paths crossed once, and from then on, they were inseparable. Dad moved to Switzerland. Otherwise, I wouldn't have been born. It's enough to make you believe in fate. They named me Genevieve after Lake Geneva."

Across the room, a burning log tumbled in the fireplace, unleashing a brilliant burst of colors. Jennie's pendant gleamed. So did Jonas's eyes.

"My grandfather, Rabbi Amernick, never pestered Mom or Dad about religion. When they saw how happy Dad was, my grandparents loved Mom like their other daughter." Jennie cradled her necklace gently. "As a symbol of acceptance, my grandmother gave her this pendant, specifying it be passed on to the first granddaughter. If I have a daughter, the pendant will be hers."

Jonas said, "What a story. I love the part about paths crossing once."

Stan said to Marta, "How about that toast you talked about?" He ushered Jennie and Jonas to the sitting area, and he and Marta conveniently disappeared to the kitchen to open the wine.

Jonas and Jennie sat quietly by the fire. He liked her smile and her soothing tone, although there was a crackle to her voice that told him there was far more to Jennie Amernick than met the eye. In no time, they were talking about all the great opera houses Jennie had seen throughout Europe.

Stan returned with a tray bearing four glasses of Dezaley. "We have so much to be thankful for," he said, clinking glasses with Jennie. "Welcome home, sweetie. We're so glad you're here. And," he said, turning toward Jonas while Jennie and Marta smiled, "welcome to our home, Jonas. To the first of many visits."

14

Victoria went to the ladies' room while Martin waited for the bill. Her face in the mirror was haggard; her mood was worse. As soon as she got back to the table, her cell phone rang. It was Gregory.

"Hello, Gregory. Are you all right? How's Melinda?"

"I'm fine, Mother. It's quiet. Melinda's in her room. When will you be home?"

"Soon. We're leaving the restaurant. Why?"

"Brad invited me for the weekend. His family's going to Mount Snow. It's been cold enough to make snow in Vermont. Brad snowboards, and he says I'll pick it up right away. If we leave now, we'll beat the traffic and be settled in early tonight, so we can be there when the lifts open in the morning. The lifts close at four on Sunday, so I'll be home by ten. I'll do my homework in the car. Can I go? Please?"

"I'll ask your father. How can you read in a moving car? The thought makes me nauseous."

"I researched your condition online, Mother. It's a neurological disorder called benign positional vertigo. There are exercises you can do to make it better. We'll work on it together if you like. I'll e-mail you the link."

Such an amazing child, Victoria thought. She and Martin agreed that Gregory could go on the trip.

"They can get me in fifteen minutes. So I might not see you. Is that okay?"

"All right," Victoria replied. "Make sure you wear your helmet."

"You worry too much, Mother. Google 'progressive muscle relaxation.' It'll help you control your mind."

"Wear your helmet. Promise or I won't let you go."

"Okay. I'll take my skate helmet with me."

"Promise you'll wear it. Swear."

"I swear. Progressive muscle relaxation, Mother. Promise me you'll do it."

"We'll see."

"Swear."

Victoria laughed. "I swear I don't know what I'd do without you."

"Stop being a lawyer, Mother, and swear."

"Okay, I swear."

"I'll do my homework, but you have to do yours. Fair?"

"Fair is fair. Have a wonderful time, Gregory."

"Love you. Tell Martin I love him, too. Bye."

* * *

When Victoria and Martin returned home, Gregory was gone. He had made his bed, straightened his desk, laid out his clothes, and arranged the pillows and throws precisely the way she preferred.

Victoria tapped gently on Melinda's door. No answer. She knocked harder; still nothing. It took four more tries, each progressively louder. Finally, she hollered, "Melinda, open this door now."

"What is it?" Melinda responded lethargically.

"Melinda, honey, there's something we need to discuss."

The knob twitched, setting the door ajar. Looking at Melinda's room made Victoria's stomach turn. Dozens of books lay strewn about. Melinda hadn't touched dinner, which she'd deposited on the floor next to two half-empty yogurt containers and a banana skin. Melinda's shoulders slumped, and her skin looked pasty.

"Cut the 'honey' crap, Mother," sneered Melinda, sitting cross-legged by her bed. "You say 'honey' whenever you're going to complain about me."

"Melinda, you have to get to sleep early enough to get up on time for school. You're up all hours with the iPod piped into your headphones. And that disgusting sound your phone makes croaks all night long like a bullfrog."

"No way. You shut off the Internet at eleven."

"We're not morons, Melinda. We know about text messages. There were hundreds a few months ago."

"Admit it," Melinda snarled. "You hate me."

"Hate you? This isn't about me liking you or not. It's about life in our house."

"Our house? Since when do I have any say here?"

"We've always let you pick your furniture, your clothes, your food, your friends."

"Friends. What friends? Everybody hates me."

"We don't."

"'We'? Which we? You? You and Daddy? You and Gregory? You love Gregory a hundred times more than me. Why did you even have me?"

"Why? Because we wanted you. I wanted a daughter more than anything. Don't you know that?"

"Whatever. It doesn't matter."

"Melinda, I don't want to fight," Victoria said, trying to be patient. "I just want our family to work. Your job is to get educated, and you can't do that if you're sleeping until noon. And I hate being your human alarm clock."

Melinda walked to the opposite corner and turned her back. "School is a fucking joke. All my teachers want is for me to sit like a doofus while they preach."

"We've been over that, honey . . . "

"Stop the 'honey' shit. I told you I don't want to hear it."

"I'm sorry," Victoria said. "Daddy and I have talked with your teachers. They understand you have a lot to say, but they don't want you interrupting class. They want you to wait until discussion time."

"You never take my side. It's always my fault."

"That's not so. We'll send you to another school if you want. You could get into Andover or Exeter. You're brilliant. And witty."

"Sure; ship me off to New Hampshire, so you don't have to deal with me."

"That's not true. We want you to feel challenged. Wouldn't you love being around students whose minds work like yours? Why won't you consider it?"

"You can't wait until I'm eighteen, can you? I can just see you signing me up for the Army. 'Please take my daughter. She's got a lot of talent, but she needs discipline.'"

"What's so wrong with discipline? Raw talent's not enough, Melinda. Look at your father and me. We didn't turn out so bad."

"Spare me the litotes, Mother. You think you're such hot shit, don't you."

What a nightmare—Abington in a reverse mirror, Victoria thought. "I know I'm no 'hot shit' of a mother to you, Melinda. You've made that perfectly clear. But what I am or am not has nothing to do with when you go to sleep. You make noise at night. It keeps us up, and it's not good for you. Surely you can apprec—"

"Appreciate what? I love this speech. The 'after all we've done for you . . . ' It's such total fucking bullshit. You don't give two shits about me. You never did."

"This can't go on. We have to do something. Maybe counseling."

"Great. Pack me off to some shrink, because you don't like me. You're fucked up, and I get blamed."

"Look, Melinda, there are rules. If you can't follow them, we'll make other arrangements. There are other people in this house besides you. And yes, we are going to counseling, whether you like it or not."

"Fuck you." Melinda grabbed a porcelain figurine of an ice dancer she had won at a skating competition and hurled it to the floor, smashing it to pieces at Victoria's feet. "Are you happy, now? See what you made me do?" Melinda screamed, breaking into tears. "I wish you were dead."

*   *   *

"She's so awful," Victoria told Martin moments later. "There's no reasoning with her. It wasn't a discussion, it was a diatribe. My head feels like a punching bag. I'll be awake all night for sure."

"Do you want some tea?" said Martin, leading Victoria into the kitchen.

"I heard it in Gregory's voice; he was relieved to get out of the house. I can't believe this nightmare. I couldn't wait to get away from my parents' house. Now my son can't wait to get away from his."

"What happened in there?"

Victoria reported the details like a war correspondent.

"This changes things. I agree, we have to do something," Martin said. "What are you doing next week?"

"Jury selection in the Barlow trial starts Monday at ten. Tomorrow, I have to prep the rest of my witnesses. They're in from out-of-state; I can't stand them up."

"We've got to help."

"There's someone I'd like to talk to," Victoria said, wondering how receptive her old therapist from college, assuming she could find him, would be to hear from her. "Whatever we're dealing with, I'm afraid."

"Afraid of what?"

"That something horrible will happen. I'm failing as a mother, Martin. I'm failing. And I don't know what to do."

15

On the last week of the term, Victoria arrived for therapy in a panic about failing biology. The impending catastrophe would blemish her otherwise perfect transcript.

She promptly spilled her herbal tea on her skirt and on her lab notes, which scattered on the floor. She shot out of her seat in a fury. "Goddammit! Now what?"

"Here, let me help you," Dr. Speller said, barely containing his smile. The more flustered Victoria became, the harder he choked to keep from laughing. "My, my, what a mess," he said, helping to wipe everything up. "We should write a paper together about this: 'Advances in Psychoanalytic Technique.'"

Victoria laughed with him, then said, "I don't know what I'm going to do about biology. The only reason I took it was because my suitemate said educated women need to understand medical terminology. But everyone in my class is pre-med or a science major who's already taken biology and chemistry in high school. It's not like English, where I remember every character from every novel I've ever read. I don't think scientifically, and there's just too much to memorize. My GPA will be ruined for sure."

"What are you working on now?"

"DNA transcription. The professor uses an overhead projector. This morning, a fly landed on a transparency of a DNA helix. It lolled across the screen like it was laughing at me. I have no idea what's going on."

"There must be someone who can help you."

"There's my TA, Leslie Kilway. She teaches lab and recitation. She's preparing us for finals."

"Can't she help you?"

"I'm not sure how I feel about her."

"Are you saying there's a connection between how you feel about Leslie and whether or not she can help you?"

"Like I said, I'm not sure how I feel about her."

"Well, do you like her?"

"'Like?' I don't even know what that means. 'Interested' is better. I'm interested in her, and I think she feels the same way about me. But there's something about her that turns me off."

"How so?"

"I know Leslie wants to help—even though I'm standoffish she's offered to go over the material; she must know how much trouble I'm in grade-wise—but the way she acts makes me think she's dull."

"Dull. Do you know anything else about her?"

"She's finished medical school and is doing brain research."

"You say she's trying to help. Let's talk about what that feels like for you."

"Jesus Christ, do we have to do this today?" Victoria said irritably. "All I said was that someone is trying to help me. Why do you have to make such a big deal of it?" When Dr. Speller kept silent, she glared at him; when he didn't respond right away, she asked, "Don't you have anything to say?"

"Not yet," he responded firmly.

Victoria glared at him. He didn't flinch; it was clear he was going to outwait her. She resumed, "Leslie asked if I wanted a one-on-one review of photosynthesis and the Krebs cycle. She said that and a question about the genetic code would be on the exam."

"Can you tell me more about Leslie?"

"Look. I don't have time."

"Make time. It's important."

"Are you sure?"

"I'm sure your feelings about Leslie are important." Dr. Speller leaned forward and removed his glasses. "Look, Victoria. It's crunch time with your bio course, and this person has been trying to help you. But something's gotten in the way of your accepting it. Finals are in two weeks. Our last session before winter break is next Thursday. We don't have time to fuck around!"

"Don't yell at me."

"If I raised my voice, it was only for emphasis."

"I don't like it when you do that. It makes me think of *her*."

"I had to get your attention."

"Well you did, all right. What do you want me to do?"

"What we always do. Like when we work on dreams. Your job is to say your thoughts about Leslie without censoring them, just as they go through your mind."

"Suppose there isn't enough time today?"

"Then we'll find time later."

"I thought sessions were only Mondays and Thursdays."

"Therapy is supposed to fit your needs, not just my schedule. Let's get going and see how far we get today. Tell me about this person."

"She's older than me, around your age. She dresses in faded jeans and sweaters that look like they come from J. C. Penney. I picture Leslie changing her own motor oil. She looks like she spends time outdoors. I think she's tougher than me, that she could beat me up if she wanted to."

"Why would she want to do that?"

"I don't know. You asked me to say what's on my mind. That's what I was thinking."

"That's fair. She's intimidating?"

"She turns me off."

"Is it that she's stronger than you? Or does she remind you in some way of Lorraine?"

"We're going down the wrong path," Victoria said. "This isn't about being scared of Leslie. I could figure out how to change my oil if I had to. It's something else." Victoria mulled over her thoughts. "I've got it. It's not about her; it's about being with her."

"Good. What comes to mind when you think of being with her?"

"Annoyed."

"Annoyed?"

"I know she's smart. How else could she be a doctor and a researcher? Here's the thing. She talks *so* slowly and *so* methodically, I just want to scream, 'Hurry up and get to the point!' So, my mind wanders, and I tune in and out. I only hear bits and pieces of what she's saying."

"Like when a record skips?"

"It's more than that. Sometimes, I wake up in the middle of conversations and can't remember what was happening. People like Leslie bore me, and I get snippy with them."

"Well, whether or not she likes you, she's definitely interested in you."

"How do you know that?"

"I hear it in the way you describe her. She wouldn't have asked to help if she was indifferent."

"Maybe she feels sorry for me."

"That's your default position," Dr. Speller said. They'd been over that before, how Victoria fell back on automatic assumptions when she wasn't sure what something meant. "It sounds like she takes pride in her teaching and wants her students to do well. But the fact is you don't know why she's interested in you."

"That's true. I don't like the feeling of not knowing."

"Here's what I think," Dr. Speller said. "Your mind works very fast, Victoria. Lorraine and you go back and forth lickety-split. Not every time, though, because she's not always in the mood. You, however, usually are in the mood, so you look for that kind of interaction. Are you with me so far?"

"I'm trying. Keep going."

"Those rapid-fire back-and-forths have become the standard against which you judge whether a conversation is interesting."

"That's true. The content doesn't matter that much; it's *how* we're talking."

"Exactly. It's about engaging each other's minds, but not everyone's mind works like yours. Having a quick mind is good when you're problem solving, but it gets in the way when you rush to judgment about people. People like Leslie have something to offer, too. You know, someone could be smart and interesting even if they speak more slowly than you. They might even say something worthwhile," Dr. Speller said, titrating his sarcasm carefully.

"You know, that's how my mother gets with me. She's impatient. I guess I treat people that way, too."

"You guess?"

"You're right. I do treat people like that," Victoria admitted.

"That wasn't so bad, was it—working it out together?"

Victoria flushed, her body warm, almost glowing. "I'm feeling weird, now. Something I never felt before." She described the heat on her face and skin.

"It's called warmth. You *liked* what I had to say."

Victoria felt warm down to her toes. "Well, whatever it is, I want more!"

"You know you could get used to it," he teased.

"What's happening to me?"

"Well, not wanting to get into clinical mode . . . " They laughed. "I'd say you're getting desensitized to intimacy."

Her eyes moistened.

He said, "It's waiting for you, even with Leslie. I hear it in how you describe her. You're not some charity case; she genuinely likes you. 'Warm' and 'like,' they're all around you. Give it a try, okay?"

"Okay," Victoria said through tears for which there were no words.

16

As soon as she returned from the session, Victoria called Leslie Kilway, who agreed to meet the next morning. Leslie had already staked out a table in the student union by the time Victoria arrived.

Notes and textbook in hand, Victoria said, "Thanks so much. How much time do we have?"

"No hurry," Leslie said. "I'm free until my three o'clock meeting with the chairman of the research committee. What would you like to cover?"

"I can't wrap my head around photosynthesis and the Krebs cycle."

"Photosynthesis is how plants capture and store the sun's energy," Leslie offered, diving right in.

"And the Krebs cycle?"

"That's inside the part of cells called mitochondria. Think of the Krebs cycle as a refinery that converts potential energy into a usable form.

"And DNA?"

"DNA codes for the proteins that make cells work."

"Proteins?"

Leslie flinched. "I think you need more than just definitions. Let's start at the beginning."

"It's that bad?" Victoria said.

"Well . . . " Leslie sighed, rolling up her sleeves as if she were about to tackle a lab experiment. Except for a ten-minute break at 11:00 AM, they worked together for the next five hours. Leslie wouldn't give up until Victoria understood that photosynthesis captured the sun's energy to build hydrocarbon molecules, without which life would be impossible. Leslie didn't stop until Victoria could conceptualize, not just memorize.

The following Wednesday, Leslie concocted a mock final for the class. Victoria came away confident she could eke out a B. "I can't thank you enough," she told Leslie on her way out. "The way you stuck with me until I got it. I never had a teacher who was so patient."

"I knew you could do it. I enjoyed the challenge of figuring out how to help you understand. Besides, you hung in there the whole time. Most people would have given up. Talk about determination; that was impressive. Hey," Leslie added, "would you like to have pizza with me and some friends tonight?"

"Really? Aren't they all older researchers? What could I say that's interesting?"

"Don't sell yourself short. You know literature and philosophy. We're so into science we lose sight of the rest of the world. We're meeting at seven at Sam's Pizzeria on Pine Street. I'll pick you up, okay?"

"You know, I'd like to walk around Society Hill first, since it's close to Sam's. I'd enjoy some company."

"Sure. Should be fun," Leslie smiled. "I'll get you at six."

* * *

That evening, as they walked past a contemporary house on Seventh and Spruce, Victoria said, "This place looks like a giant refrigerator.

Some discount appliance store must have dragged this monstrosity here and plugged it in."

"That's so funny; I love how you put things," Leslie laughed. "Like when you said your English professor's muttonchops and tweed suits make him look like a dehydrated cell membrane. You crack me up."

Victoria felt a ripple of warmth rise through her spine. "You have to admit this building is atrocious. The city should demand demolition or face charges of abetting cultural depravity."

Soon the girls were chatting amiably about Philadelphia history. Victoria loved having someone to share ideas with. Time flew as they ambled through the neighborhood.

Just when Leslie and Victoria arrived at Sam's, a couple leaving the restaurant barged into them. There, arm-in-arm with a dark-haired woman about Leslie's age, was Dr. Speller.

"Excuse me, miss. I'm so sorry," he said before recognizing Victoria. The woman with him was taller and curvier than Victoria. Her eyes glistened like gemstones as she looked down on Victoria with disdain.

As if she had been punched in the solar plexus, Victoria couldn't breathe for a moment. She had imagined running into Dr. Speller many times, but never with someone like this. Dazed and dissociated, Victoria was overcome by déjà vu. Even though it made no sense, she *had* felt this way before—less of a woman. Victoria fled to the ladies' room where she splashed herself into the present with cold water. "How could he! How could he!" she fumed out loud, subliminally aware that she was more disturbed by the woman than she was by Dr. Speller.

Although the conversation was convivial and she felt welcomed into a new social circle, Victoria struggled throughout the rest of dinner to keep from thinking about the sinister look in the dark-haired woman's eyes.

17

After they had eaten, the crew gathered for drinks at Leslie's apartment, which was different from anything Victoria knew: garage-sale area rugs, Marimekko wall hangings, mismatched couch and armchair, and science journal reprints strewn on every surface. Someone passed around a jug of Mateus, and everyone clinked different-sized plastic tumblers, toasting neurotransmitters and new friends. Two sips went straight to Victoria's head.

The group included an attractive man who had not been at dinner. Although he had tangles and tangles of blond hair, his friends called him Mr. Clean. His real name was Bucky Bleyer. He, too, was a researcher on the neuroscience track. It took Victoria the rest of the evening to realize Leslie was playing matchmaker for her and Bucky.

Later, Bucky offered to drive Victoria home. As they walked to his car, she grazed his jacket gesturing toward the houses along the way. "This block looks just like Society Hill," she said.

"That's my apartment over there," Bucky pointed across the street. "If it hadn't been for Leslie, I'd have stayed in L.A."

"You know her from California?"

"Didn't meet her 'til I moved here. She read one of my journal articles and sent me a note asking me to consider Penn's neuroscience program. She even found me an apartment on her block."

"Leslie helped me with biology," Victoria said. "If it weren't for her, I'd be slaving away right now memorizing the Krebs cycle."

"That's so Leslie. She's the earth mother who looks out for everyone. Want to see my place?"

"Sure," said Victoria, still quite tipsy. She liked the way Bucky paid attention to her.

Inside, Bucky pointed at a wall-mounted electrified bookshelf as he showed her around the apartment. "See this? I built it myself," he said with laugh. "What a fucking disaster. I crossed the wires, so when I plugged it in, sparks shot down my arm like lightning. I jumped as high as a kid in a haunted house."

Victoria laughed, too. She felt even warmer than before.

"The next thing, the whole building went dark. People congregated in the hall. When we went into the basement to look for the circuit breaker, it was so cobwebbed and creepy we expected to trip over a corpse. I was so embarrassed."

"It's not like you murdered anyone," Victoria said.

"You're right. Everything turned out fine. We reset the circuit breaker and then I reversed the wires. Voilà!" Bucky said, as he turned on the bookshelf light.

Victoria liked what she saw. "Umm. It makes the room feel very cozy," she said. She caught sight of a clock. "Isn't it late for you? What time do you have to be up?"

"I was having such a good time, I forgot. Psych residents meet once a week at nine AM on Thursday mornings with the chief resident. Everyone loves him. He wears really colorful bow ties."

"Which clinic?"

"Penn has a terrific outpatient clinic on the ninth floor of the hospital. Are you interested in neuroscience?"

"You could say that," she replied, imagining Bucky and Dr. Speller comparing notes.

Bucky drove Victoria back to her dorm. "Can I call you?" he asked, reaching for her hand.

"Of course," she said, pulling him closer for a good-night kiss.

*   *   *

Once she was settled in her suite, Victoria took a leisurely shower, relishing the pulsating stream of hot water. The thought of Bucky touching her made her skin tingle all over.

Slipping under her covers, she imagined cuddling next to Bucky after having sex for the first time. About that, she had no reservations. But her thoughts shifted to the next day and her last therapy session before the semester break. She knew she couldn't avoid talking about Bucky and her feelings about Dr. Speller and the dark-haired woman, which felt like too much to deal with. So before going to sleep, Victoria left a message on Dr. Speller's answering machine canceling her appointment, saying she would see him the Monday after they returned from vacation.

As soon as her head hit the pillow again, her imagination lit up with impressions of the evening: the dark-haired woman's face, Leslie's apartment, the warm feeling from the wine and Bucky's attention. Didn't he mention a haunted house? And a creepy basement?

Creepy haunted house. Those words jogged a memory of a place Victoria hadn't thought about in years. When she was a little girl, Victoria's family spent several Augusts at a posh resort north of Saratoga Springs, New York. Her father's client Bill Brendel, who owned racehorses, had invited the Schones to visit during racing season. She could vividly remember being dressed up and trotted out on race days. One morning, eight-year-old Victoria visited the barns where hundreds of high-priced yearling racehorses were on display for auction. She saw sadness in their eyes and wondered if her parents might auction her off, too.

One August, the family visited Lake George Village, a tourist town south of the resort featuring an amusement park with a gaudy arcade, an ice cream parlor whose skeleton-like proprietress chain-smoked Lucky Strikes, and a dingy haunted house. Everything was so creepy it made Victoria's skin crawl.

As Victoria lay still in the darkness of her dorm room the smell of stale tobacco smoke began drifting through Hill Hall. She felt as if she were floating through time. Suddenly she was eight years old, wandering through mazes in a dimly lit house. When she looked in a mirror, she saw no reflection. It had vanished. People laughed at her. Then she heard a barker shout through his megaphone, "Ladies and gentlemen, step right up and see the amazing girl without a shadow. You won't see this anywhere else." When Victoria looked toward the barker, his megaphone had metamorphosed into a grotesque black rose.

Half awake, Victoria saw the outline of her dresser. It looked so much like the barker's lectern she couldn't tell where she was.

The scene transformed into a dry goods store selling cheap pajamas and dresses that looked like the wall hangings at Leslie's apartment. Victoria tried on a polka-dotted skirt. When she returned from the fitting room, a dark-haired clerk resembling Dr. Speller's date laughed, because Victoria's left breast was twice the size of her right one.

Then Victoria was in an ice cream parlor, where a dark-haired woman called her "little miss piggy" because she ordered two scoops of her favorite flavor.

For the rest of the night she drifted among vivid dreams and periods of hazy lucidity—the same dark-haired woman weaving in and out of scenario after scenario of humiliation and freakishness.

The next morning, Victoria awoke hungover and panicky. When she couldn't get through to the clinic, she tore across campus through cold rain to reclaim her appointment, but the secretary said that when Dr. Speller heard about the cancellation, he left early for vacation. Victoria's first thought: *He couldn't wait to get away from me.*

Cold-soaked and miserable, Victoria wandered through that

interminable day until 5:20, when alone in her dorm room, she imagined herself in Dr. Speller's office. *I can do this*, she told herself. *It was a dream, only a dream. I can get hold of my thoughts.*

For the next forty-five minutes, Victoria let her thoughts go just as she would in therapy. She started with the haunted house barker, wandered through the amusement park past the dark-haired woman, and ended up outside Bucky's apartment, by the rustling trees that reminded her of the copper beech in her Abington backyard. Its brilliantly colored fallen leaves had always made her sad. Then she remembered what she had learned in biology: The leaves die, but their hydrocarbons form the soil from which new life springs. Death followed by rebirth. The idea brought her peace. She ended her "session" promptly at six.

At 6:15, Bucky called.

18

Jonas arrived at his hotel room in a fever. Jennie, who had set the hotel room thermostat to boiling, was already in the bathroom getting ready. When she revealed herself in a black satin bustier and thigh-high stockings, there was no stopping her.

"Look at us," Jonas said, as they avoided the wet spot to cuddle. "We're like a couple of twenty-year-olds."

"Ouch," Jennie exclaimed involuntarily. "Damn. It's sore under there," she said, referring to her reconstructed left breast.

"I hope I wasn't too rough. I get carried away."

"No, it's not that. It happened this morning on the massage table. The masseuse used a lot of pressure. She must have mashed my chest."

"You didn't tell her to stop? If some guy was squeezing my balls, I sure would let him know it."

"You're right. I should have told her to stop."

"So, why didn't you?"

Jennie rolled onto her back. "Not now, Jonas. Not now."

"What?"

"You know what; I tell you all the time. So do Gil and Gracie. We hate it when you analyze us. I'm the daughter of a psychoanalyst; I'm used to it, but it bothers them."

"Bothers them?"

"Yes, Jonas, it bothers them. Very much. You're always saying, 'Why didn't you do this?' or 'How come you didn't do that?' They take it as criticism. Meanwhile, they hear how proud you are that *this* resident got a fellowship to Karolinska Institute, or *that* resident is on the fast track to tenure. They need that from you, too. Desperately."

"They never say anything about it to me."

"What do you expect? They're kids. And they're adopted. You're the expert on adolescents. Gil may look like a model, but he's shy. You know that teenagers who don't get a handle on social anxiety before college can end up seriously depressed. Or binge drinking. Is that what you want to happen to your son?"

"And Gracie?"

"I worry about her, a lot. She's just started her period. All of a sudden she stopped talking to me—not that it's so surprising—but I don't like the crowd she's hanging out with. They act like they're thirteen going on thirty. Next stop, sex. Then drugs. Things could go downhill really fast. I wish she would talk with you more. How would you feel if you came home and saw her with a nose ring or God-knows-what-other body piercing? Or with tattoos? Then what will we do?"

"Oh, Jesus," Jonas said. It was so much simpler when it was just the two of us. I love you so much, Jen, but I feel like I'm drifting when it comes to the children."

"I love you, too, Jonas, but there's two other passengers on our boat now, and like it or not, we're in for rough seas. We have to work together. My parents did a lot of things right, but not this. They weren't together when it came to raising me. I wasn't sure enough of myself to resist temptation, and it cost me big time emotionally. I was fortunate I didn't get pregnant or something even worse. But now there are drugs we hadn't even heard of when we were growing up, and girls give blow jobs the way we used to make out. I don't want that for Gracie, and neither do you."

"You're right, Jen. You're right—I'm sorry. I just wish I had a better sense of how to relate to them."

"Well, like it or not, Jonas, the storm's brewing, and there'll be times you need to take the helm."

"Jesus, Jen. You sound like a sailing instructor."

"No sassing your way out of this, Captain Courageous!"

"You're right, Jen. You're right. I just wish I we could chart a different course."

19

Thursday, December 17, 1981

Swissair flight 101 began the transoceanic portion of its journey to Geneva, Switzerland. Glowing with anticipation, Jonas settled beside Jennie Amernick. She had booked them a week-long ski trip in Zermatt. Ever since Thanksgiving, Jennie had become more than a friend, although they hadn't slept together. And she hadn't talked about her divorce yet.

Jonas looked out upon a silver-yellow canopy of moonlit clouds stretching to the horizon. Claude Debussy's *Clair de Lune* came to mind. He felt a new world opening. "It's so beautiful out there," he said. "It was great how you arranged for us to get away a day earlier."

"All I did was call Swissair. Their Thursday flights are never sold out. They'll remember it, too. We just opened up two seats on the Friday flight, which they'll sell for five times what we paid. If we get some sleep tonight on the plane, we'll have a whole extra day. I know a place named Villars that's right on the way from Geneva to Zermatt. Miles of cruising trails. When the sun shines, it's heavenly. I have friends we can crash with."

Jonas went after an itch between his shoulders.

"Here, let me," said Jennie.

"God, that feels good." Her touch felt tender. "If you like, I'll return the favor."

"When we get there," she replied with a mischievous smile.

Jonas raised his wine glass. "Here's to—"

"Your first time," Jennie finished his sentence. "Excited?"

"Thrilled! Like getting ready to go to a great concert. Do you play any instruments?"

"I took flute in grade school, but I was so bad, it felt like noise pollution. So, I drew and painted."

"That's amazing. I hear melody everywhere, but I can't draw a circle, let alone a face."

"You're always talking about music. Why didn't you become a musician?"

"Honestly? I loved piano and violin but I wasn't good enough to make it professionally. Besides, unless you compose or play improvisational jazz—which I never studied—you're playing other people's music, not making your own. That's why I chose psychiatry; I wanted to be creative."

"Do you still play?"

"Not since my father died three years ago."

Jennie frowned. "That's a long time to be away from your instrument."

"Where do you paint?"

"I had a studio."

"Had?"

"In my apartment in New York. I took it apart when I moved out. I stored everything in my parents' basement."

"You haven't said what happened."

"No one knows the whole story. My parents, my friends—they know bits and pieces." Jennie gazed out the window and then turned to Jonas with tears in her eyes.

She was going to tell him. With the overhead reading lamp slightly askance, the amber light turned Jennie's luminous eyes dark aquamarine. Jonas imagined adjacent ponds, the color of Monet's water lilies. He brushed away Jennie's tears with his cocktail napkin and waited.

"I met Peter and his father on a tour of a French castle. His father's a Hollywood psychiatrist, and the names of the rich and famous rolled off Peter's tongue like they were his best friends. He dogged me across Europe and then back to the States, where his father bought him an apartment on Central Park West. It was so intoxicating to be pursued; I didn't see things as they were."

"What do you mean?"

"That I was a trophy. He didn't love me; he loved the idea of me, and he thought people would take him more seriously with a chic wife— which is how he saw me—at his side. Peter was twenty-seven, and aside from jobs his father's patients got him as favors, he hadn't become anything on his own. He drifted around the Mediterranean coast with a crowd of producers and directors, pretending he belonged. He told himself he was an up-and-coming movie producer but he was really just a hanger-on.

"Peter's family wanted a huge wedding, but my parents didn't have the hundred thousand dollars. So Peter's family humiliated my parents by limiting their guest list. I'm sure they were afraid Mom's relatives would show up looking like the Beverly Hillbillies.

"When my father pointed out that Peter hadn't accomplished anything on his own, it infuriated me. He had no respect for Peter's father, who crossed the country with a medicine chest of Valium and Dexedrine for impresarios and entertainers who wanted pills. I thought Dad envied Peter's father because he charged ten times more than Dad did. I was so mixed up. I didn't know who to believe.

"The wedding was a disaster. I felt so alone. None of my aunts and uncles, not even my closest cousins, were there.

"Then, one day I showed up at our apartment unexpectedly when one of my tours ended early. The place looked deserted, but I heard noise coming from the bedroom.

"I walked in on Peter, grunting like a pig on top of a long-legged blonde who was squealing like a porn star. She couldn't have been more than twenty.

"I couldn't believe it. I yelled at them so loudly it's a wonder the neighbors didn't call the police. The girl—some ingénue model—leaped off the bed and bolted into the bathroom, leaving me staring at her purple thong on the bed. She claimed that Peter never told her he was married.

"Please, Jonas, please don't tell my father. Promise me," Jennie pleaded.

Jonas said, "It's over. It's done." He put his arm around Jennie's shoulder.

"You're the only one who knows."

"Why me?" he said.

"Because I believe you won't judge me, and that you'll see the whole me, not what you need me to be."

Jonas held her while she cried. "You must have gone for therapy," he said.

"Where? I couldn't go in Philadelphia. Mom and Dad know everybody."

"How about Marta? She seems so nurturing. Couldn't you confide in her?"

"Nurturing? You don't know her, Jonas," Jennie said stridently.

Jonas was taken aback by the fervor in her voice. He hadn't realized that she felt this way about her mother.

She continued, "The last thing I needed was to be preached at by someone who spent my entire childhood telling me what a spoiled brat I was. If it had been up to her, she would have packed me off to the farm every summer to pick strawberries like she did when she was young. Thankfully, Dad saw it differently. He knew I wanted to spend summers at art camp and on writing retreats. When I have children I want them to be themselves. Growing up is complicated enough without your parents sending you mixed messages."

"What about New York? There's a therapist on every corner."

"I felt like such a fool. Retelling the story would have just made me relive the nightmare."

"You've been sitting on this all by yourself?"

"Yes," Jennie said.

"How long?"

"Too long. For months, I dragged myself to work. The girl's voice was burned into my brain. As time passed, I felt angrier at myself for being such a victim than at Peter for being such a schmuck. We settled quickly. The divorce was quick. I could have blackmailed him for alimony, but I knew that would keep me tied to him.

"My folks eased up on me. Mom wants to make things better between us—I know she feels guilty. Dad promised not to say, 'I told you so.' I told the people at work I needed time off. They said I could come back whenever I want."

"Does that mean you're moving back to New York?"

"Not necessarily. Sotheby's has an office in Haverford. I could rent a place in Center City and reverse commute. The bulk of my job is on the road." Jennie drew Jonas close to her. "I can't believe I told you. You must think I'm such a—"

"Don't assume. If I told you half of what I did during my *jeunesse* . . . "

"That's a wonderful French word! Have you been studying?" Jennie sounded eager to move on from her story. She pulled out ski maps of Villars and Zermatt, which she shared with Jonas.

After dinner, they staked out two empty rows of seats and lay down facing each other where they could brush hands and talk.

A veil had lifted. Jonas knew he was traveling with someone very special. By the time the subject returned to skiing, Jonas knew it was a metaphor for their future. "Are you sure I won't fall off a cliff in Zermatt?" he asked drowsily.

"You'll be fine. I know every trail like the back of my hand. I promise not to take you anywhere you don't feel safe."

20

Saturday, November 20, 2004

Martin and Victoria spent Saturday trying to conduct business as usual even though Melinda had barricaded herself in her room. Martin got the names of several psychiatrists, but Victoria convinced him to hold off until Monday, saying there was someone she wanted to speak with first.

When she wasn't upstairs hovering about Melinda's door, Victoria was in the office conferring with several former Duke's staffers. The disgruntled employees delighted in the chance to see their ex-boss get his comeuppance. Everyone agreed that Horace Barlow had an arrogant, nasty streak. If the case wasn't handled delicately, he would readily make a big stink.

The Arrestias' daughter was on the calendar, as well. She confirmed how convoluted the relationship was between Barlow—who used to be a frequent guest at her home—and her parents.

Victoria and Martin took turns checking on Melinda, tacitly agreeing that she couldn't be left alone. Not a sound issued from her bedroom, although the quiet felt like the silence before a cannon barrage.

When she heard Melinda's door open Victoria rushed upstairs, trying to sneak a peek at her elusive daughter, but by the time she got to the third floor, Melinda had already locked herself in the bathroom.

Victoria waited on the landing, unsure whether or not to say something. Before she could open her mouth Melinda said through the closed door, "I know you're out there. Stop following me."

Sometime during the late afternoon, Martin and Victoria ventured into the living room for some R-and-R. When the conversation turned to holiday plans, Victoria said, "You know we can't go anywhere until Melinda is settled. I don't know about Thanksgiving."

Martin said, "Well, the Cruickshanks will have their usual New Year's Eve bash. We can always show up at the last minute."

"Ah yes, Martin, New Year's Eve," Victoria said dreamily.

"What about it?"

Victoria forgot her troubles for the moment; the tension in her face dissolved into a warm glow. "I was remembering my first New Year's Eve away from home," she reminisced. "It almost feels like it was another me."

21

Winter vacation in Abington wasn't nearly the nightmare Victoria had anticipated. Mornings, she sneaked out early and caught a train to be with her friends. In the evenings, Bucky drove her home.

The morning of New Year's Eve, Victoria bounced downstairs toting an overnight bag, which she deposited by the front door. Lorraine spotted the suitcase immediately.

"Victoria, I didn't know you had plans."

Victoria thought, *Yes, Mother. I'm sleeping with my boyfriend for the first time tonight.* She said, "You know the new friends I've made, Mother? Leslie—she helped me with biology—she's throwing a party tonight. Bucky usually drives me home, but because it's New Year's Eve, Leslie said I could stay with her."

"I like this Leslie. She sounds like a girl with a good head on her shoulders. It's reassuring that you're in good hands tonight."

Victoria grinned, having carefully studied erotic massage in *The Joy of Sex* the night before.

"How old is Bucky?"

"Twenty-five."

"What does he do?"

"He's a neuroscientist and a psychiatrist. He was a gymnast at UCLA." Victoria said, certain her mother would notice the allusion.

"A gymnast? Like you see on TV? At the Olympics? They're so . . . They're so . . . I thought they were all gay."

"I really don't think Bucky's gay, Mother."

"Are you sure?"

"Yes mother. *Very* sure."

"Oh." A moment later, Lorraine's face turned pink. "Oh, I see."

"I'll call you about the rest of the weekend. I might be staying more than one night," Victoria said, departing gracefully before Lorraine could recover.

Although the thermometer outside read 22 degrees, Victoria felt pleasantly warm.

"Victoria?" Morris Schone called after her. "Would you like a ride to the station? I'm headed into the city, too."

Victoria hadn't realized her father was still home. "Thanks, Daddy," she said, recalling long ago when Morris used to twirl her in the air to their mutual delight. *What happened to that man?* she wondered. *Where did he go?* Victoria couldn't recall the last time they had spent any time together, let alone side by side on the train for an hour.

Morris dropped Victoria at the station and parked. By the time he caught up with her, she had already purchased her one-way ticket.

"You didn't have to do that," he said.

"Oh yes, I did," she said, remembering the last time her father bought her something. "I'm never going to be on the receiving end of a rant like you pulled on me about the coat in Florence. Maybe you don't remember, but I do."

Morris hung his head. "I felt bad about that."

"You could have fooled me. I can't take that shit anymore. I don't deserve it. Besides, it was Mother's idea to take me shopping that day, not mine."

Morris shifted his weight from one foot to the other. "It's not easy living with your mother. She expects. She demands."

He father looked older, even frail. Victoria said, "That's her. Not me. I never nagged you for things. All I wanted was for you to feel happy with me. You were the handsomest daddy around, and I was so proud to be your daughter. Look what's become of you. You let her walk all over you. You drink yourself into oblivion, then you vilify me for getting the hell out so I can live a normal life around normal people."

"I didn't know you felt that way. Why are you telling me this now?"

"Because I love you. Otherwise, I wouldn't care. It hurts that you don't have the balls to stand up to her."

An icy wind lashed their faces on the train platform. Morris positioned himself aweather, to shelter Victoria from the cold. When the train arrived, he found adjacent seats and hoisted Victoria's bag into the overhead compartment. She felt protected for a moment. Then, she laughed out loud.

"What's so amusing?"

"I was thinking about my new friends and the party. They really like me, Daddy. Except for Leslie's friend Charlese—she's a nurse Leslie likes a lot; Leslie's pushing her to go to medical school—they're all graduate students. It's amazing how well they manage on very little money. We have so much fun."

"I'm happy for you, Victoria. I had a fraternity brother in college named Izzy Stein. Before we got married, your mother and I did things with Izzy and his fiancée, Lizzy. Everyone joked about their names. Izzy was a good friend. After they got married, they had a boy—Isaac. We had a birthday party for you at their house when you turned two. You probably don't remember, do you?"

"No. I wish I did."

"You and Isaac always played together. You were so happy. I can still hear you giggling."

"What happened to them?"

"I lost touch. Your mother didn't like something Lizzy said or did, and we didn't see them again. I ought to look him up."

"Yes, you should. It would be good to have your own friends. And your own life."

Morris looked at Victoria seriously. "I want you to know I heard what you said before."

"Good. I meant it."

"About this young man you're seeing?"

"His name is Bucky."

"You've become an attractive young woman, Victoria. No matter what you think of me, I'm still your father. What does he do?"

"He's a psychiatrist-in-training, and a researcher. I respect him a lot."

"Does he treat you well?"

"Yes, he's a gentleman. I feel safe with him."

Morris winced. "Maybe I could take you two out for dinner after work some evening."

Victoria looked past her father. "We'll see," she said.

"Is this about my drinking?" he asked.

"I've made it clear how I feel about that," she replied.

They got off the train at Suburban Station and walked several blocks in silence. Approaching City Hall, Morris brightened. He produced his credit card. "Here, Victoria. Please take this. I'm really sorry about what happened in Italy. Stop at Wanamaker's," he said gesturing across the street, "and get something special for tonight. Okay?"

"That's sweet, Daddy. I know just what I want," she smiled, thinking about some racy lingerie she had seen in *Cosmopolitan*.

When they reached the compass in the City Hall courtyard, the heart of Old Philadelphia, she kissed her father good-bye, and they headed their separate ways.

22

Sunday, November 21, 2004

M elinda remained in seclusion throughout the rest of the weekend. Frightened her daughter might have done something to
hurt herself, but afraid to set off another explosion, Victoria
didn't know what to do. Martin agreed to check on Melinda but all he
got through her closed door was, "I know you and Mother are trying
to get rid of me."

"At least we know she's alive," Victoria said.

Martin pressed Victoria about getting Melinda help.

"I'm going to call Dr. Speller—my psychiatrist during college—
tomorrow," she said. "I trust him. He'll know what to do . . . I hope. I'm
falling apart, Martin. How can you just sit here reading your *Sunday
Times* while I'm going out of my mind? I can barely keep my thoughts
straight."

Victoria had never told Martin the details about her therapy and
how ill she was during college. All she told him was that the relationship with her parents had been awful and that therapy helped with the
transition from Abington to living on her own. Beyond that, Victoria
never spoke of her feelings for the man she felt had saved her life.

"I'm not just sitting here," Martin said, moving closer to Victoria, who stiffened involuntarily.

"Try and relax," Martin said. "This Dr. Speller. Where is he?"

Victoria moved to her favorite chair, a recliner from Grandma Jeanine's apartment. Her fondest memories of childhood were sitting on her grandmother's lap, listening to stories. She drifted into dissociation, her fingers tracing circles on the armrest. "He practices in New York City. I hope he remembers me," she said, her voice trailing into a whisper.

"He helped you?"

"Yes. He helped me." Martin's cellphone buzzed once. Victoria asked, "Did we hear anything from Gregory?"

"He just texted," Martin said. "They're done for the day. He had a great time. He wanted to know how your breathing exercises were progressing. He also said to tell you his skull is intact."

"Oh," Victoria smiled. "Guess he wore his helmet."

"Breathing exercises?"

"He said it would help me stop worrying so much."

"That's a good suggestion. They're just getting on the road now. Gregory won't be home until late. How about take-out for dinner?"

"I'll go to Whole Foods and get something we can nuke," Victoria said. "It'll be good to get some fresh air. We should ask Melinda what she wants to eat, don't you think?"

Martin concurred.

"I don't want her feeling we don't care. Then again, I don't want to set her off, either. You go up and ask. The last time I got near her she thought I was following her around."

"'Following her around.' The last thing she told me was that she thought we wanted to get rid of her. Back in law school clinic, I had a case where a family argued that their son was incompetent to manage his trust fund, which he wanted to spend on electronic surveillance. I represented the son, who thought his brain was being controlled by a neighbor's television remote. He said he heard voices commanding him to file a class-action suit unless the manufacturer recalled their devices.

He was up night after night trying to get the telephone number and address of RCA's CEO. He turned out to be schizophrenic."

"You don't think . . . " Victoria shuddered.

"God, I hope not," Martin said. "Gregory's right. Take some deep breaths. And get some air. You know how to read text messages, don't you?"

"Yes. Gregory showed me."

"Good. Why don't you go to the store now? While you're out I'll speak to Melinda. Keep your phone in sight and I'll text you whatever she wants."

"How am I ever going to get through this?" Victoria lamented.

"Let's just get through today. Hopefully your doctor will set us in the right direction tomorrow."

"Call me if anything changes with Melinda," Victoria said on her way out the door.

Whom should Victoria encounter in the prepared foods section but Denise Mather, her opposing attorney in the Duke's case? Not that Victoria couldn't hold her own, but Mather was a street-tough bulldog inside the body of a Sophia Loren. Typically, nothing bothered Victoria about work, but today was far from typical. Denise looked good in her open beaver coat, her dark hair shining and a handsome man on her arm. Enough to remind Victoria of another dark-haired woman from long ago.

23

Monday, April 5, 1982

In therapy, Victoria and Dr. Speller worked hard to understand the dark-haired woman, who, in Victoria's mind, epitomized power, grace, and womanliness—a sexual dynamo without compunction about satisfying her carnal appetite. Ten times tougher than her dainty nail polish, the dark-haired woman was just as formidable in tights and track shoes at the Penn relays as she was in an evening gown at the opera, or the naughty négligée she slipped into and out of if and when she wanted a nightcap.

"There's something we need to talk about," Victoria began her Monday session. She blushed. "I realized it after Bucky and I had sex two nights ago. Understand, Bucky is cute, and I like him. But I want someone bigger. More manly. And I finally understand something about the dark-haired woman. No matter what I do, I'll never be like her."

"Never?"

"There's more. It goes back to the summer before I turned twelve. You know I was such a tomboy. I acted cocky around girls; I liked showing them up. One day on the playground, everyone was admiring a new girl who was tumbling like a cheerleader. She landed perfectly after a cartwheel, ending in a twisting backflip. She goaded me into trying, but I got all dizzy and fell on my face. I get dizzy when my head moves too fast. It's something I was born with.

"The girl was a grade older, and she had dark hair and a contemptuous sneer like, 'Who do you think you are?' Her chest bulged, and she wore pink ribbons. I had always thought that pink looked silly on girls.

"I wanted to outdo her, so even though my head was still spinning, I climbed up the swing set. The crossbar was really high. When I looked down, I remember thinking how easily I could fall. Sound familiar? The people on the ground yelled for me to come down.

"I felt a tingling between my legs, but I ignored it because I had to concentrate on scootching across to the other side. Well, that night I felt the tingling again. I remember worrying that I had hurt myself, so I went to the bathroom and locked the door."

Victoria caught Dr. Speller's eyes. "Please don't laugh at me," she said. "This part is so humiliating. I decided to look at my vagina in the mirror to see if anything was wrong—not that I knew what to look for. I brought a chair into the bathroom to stand on to see between my legs in the mirror.

"Somehow, I touched myself in a way that made the tingling stronger. Then, I felt an ache inside. It got so intense, I almost screamed, but I didn't want my mother to know because she'd make me go to the doctor. And he'd have to examine me down there, because that's what doctors did when something was broken. And I didn't want that."

Dr. Speller barely stirred.

"Then, I went numb between my legs, and I figured I had really damaged myself, because it didn't seem right that I should be tingling one moment and then feeling nothing the next. So I touched myself again, and the tingling and the ache came back stronger than ever. I didn't know if I wanted to make it stop or keep going. My vagina felt dry, so I put some Vaseline on one of my fingers and found the spot that ached. I rocked back and forth, and when the ache finally went away—which felt so good—some liquid squirted out, which made me even more convinced I had done something to hurt myself.

"After it ended, all I wanted was to go to sleep and hope I would be all right in the morning, so I wouldn't have to tell my mother."

Dr. Speller started to talk, but Victoria hadn't finished.

"I had no idea what had happened. I walked around in a fog for days, hoping the tingling wouldn't come back, but I couldn't forget how good the release felt. I don't know how any man can understand. You're the first person I've ever told."

"It was masturbation and orgasm," Dr. Speller said matter-of-factly.

"Lorraine was useless. I had no girl cousins. My friends were all boys. What was I supposed to say?"

Dr. Speller looked on sympathetically.

"Don't you understand? By the time girls in gym class were budding breasts and giggling about second base, I was fantasizing about someone touching my vagina. I didn't connect sexual intercourse with that feeling until later. But by the time I was thirteen, I dreamt about sex night after night. I told myself it was because of what I did to my vagina—that no normal girl would feel this way. The feeling went on and on, even in my dreams, the release always accompanied by the fluid. I still don't know what it means."

Dr. Speller said, "This explains why you feel so different from other young women, Victoria. No one told you that sexual longings can develop early, especially in tomboys. There's a name for the spot inside the vagina where the ache comes from. It's in all the women's magazines—the G-spot, it's called. Men have one, too, at the base of the prostate gland. This isn't about good or bad; it's about health. You have a very healthy sex drive. In fact, you have a lot of drive, period."

"And the fluid?"

"It's quite common and very normal."

"Really? How can you be sure?"

"I'm a doctor. I read about it," Dr. Speller said in his clinical mode. The next moment, he turned bright red.

"What is it?" Victoria said.

"Nothing."

"I know you better than that. Out with it."

"Let's just say I've experienced it first-hand." The mood changed instantly.

"Oh, probably with that dark-haired woman of yours," Victoria said with a smirk. "You can't tell me it's normal for a thirteen-year-old girl to be dreaming about having sex."

"It's not as weird as you think, Victoria."

She liked the way he said her name. It reassured her that he wasn't disgusted.

He said, "However, you need to get a handle on your balance. It sounds like you don't think it can be developed."

"Can it?"

"You won't know unless you try. Your natural gift is mental agility; lots of people would kill for your mind. But balance-wise, you have a handicap. That doesn't mean you can't work at it. You may never become as graceful as you want, but you'll never improve unless you try."

"How would I do that?"

"I treated someone who wanted to learn golf so he could play with his father and older brother. The trouble was that the man had horrible balance, which ruined his swing and his pleasure in being with the family. Instead of bemoaning his fate or giving up, he took ballet and strengthened his core. Yoga, too. It centered him. Now he enjoys the game."

"I'll never be as graceful as I want."

"Probably not, but you can get better. So, stop complaining about being klutzy and work on becoming more graceful. It's not that complicated."

"Are you sure I can really change?"

"If I weren't, I'd be doing something else with my life."

Victoria liked that Dr. Speller shared some of himself during the session. It meant he liked her.

24

Saturday, November 20, 2004

"The conference couldn't have gone any better," Eddie told Jonas and Pete. "Everyone's thrilled. People are still talking about yesterday, Jonas. They can't wait to have you back. You sure know your medicine and psychiatry. What a dynamite combination."

"That's right," Pete said. "You told us a long time ago not to underestimate you."

"Time to celebrate," Jonas said, hoping to shake off the malaise from his previous day's pillow talk. "The girls gave us the night off. What do you say to some juicy steaks and a stint at the craps table?"

"Feels like old times," Pete said. "You know what I mean?"

"Oh, I remember everything about that weekend." Eddie said. "We wouldn't be here if it weren't for that, would we?"

Saturday, October 8, 1983

The minute the Philadelphia Phillies clinched the National League championship, Jonas's telephone rang.

It was Eddie. "Hey, Jo. What are you doing next weekend? Since I made partner, I get a few perks, including tickets for the Series. How about a birthday bash? That is, if you've got next weekend off."

"No problem. Between teaching and practice, I don't have to moonlight anymore. Only I'm not third-generation Philadelphia, so I'm a psychiatric trash receptacle; I get the cases no one else wants. Not exactly what I had in mind."

"Dad won't let that happen," said Jennie, nestled comfortably next to him.

"Listen," Jonas said for both to hear. "I love Stan, but I have to be my own person. So, understand this, Edward Speller, Esquire. It's only a matter of time before we contact a realtor who knows your neighborhood." Jennie purred at *we*. "Are you serious about the tickets?"

"Absolutely," Eddie said. "Four on the third base line. Everyone here's a Yankees fan, so they could care less. Who else should we invite?"

"Bodenheim for sure."

"I already put him on yellow alert. What about Stan?"

Jennie intervened, "That's very considerate, Eddie, but Dad's not really into baseball. Ask Steve Rothman? He's a die-hard Phillies fan. I'll make a dinner reservation at Victor's for Saturday night. You know the place where the waiters and waitresses break out into arias. It's time my parents met Eddie and Pete."

"Sounds great." Eddie lowered his voice. "And leave time for you and me, Jonas. There's something I want to discuss."

"What is it?"

"Nothing that won't keep until Friday."

Annoyed, Jonas said, "Whatever you say. I'll call Steve tomorrow. Call me later in the week. Thanks for thinking of me." He hung up abruptly.

"What was that about?" Jennie said.

"Eddie says he wants to talk about something, but he wouldn't say what. I love him to death, Jen, but he has this way of upsetting me."

"Well, whatever it is, it worries me how your mood changes around him."

"He thinks it's perfectly fine to stick his head into my business. If you had a sister who treated you like that, you wouldn't like it, either."

Jennie curled her lip. "You're wrong! You can't imagine how much I've wanted a sister or a brother. Once, when I was at the Geneva airport, I saw two little children playing peekaboo; the way they giggled at each other made me want to cry. When the brother put his arm around his sister, I felt like part of me was missing. That day, I swore I would never have an only child."

"Of all places on Earth, Jen, how did your mother wind up in Switzerland?"

"She did well in French and biology. She put the two together and applied to medical schools in Belgium and Lausanne. I asked her why they never had more children, but I never got a straight answer. She said there was a problem with her uterus, and that I should have mine checked out, which I did. Everything turned out to be fine. The best I can do now is to raise the family she never had. You're lucky to have a brother who cares about you," she said enviously. "Next weekend should be a celebration; don't spoil it."

"You're so good for me," Jonas said. "No matter how far I stray, you always put me back on track."

Friday, October 14, 1983

Eddie and his law firm associate, Pete Bodenheim, arrived early Friday afternoon. When Jonas caught up with them for lunch, they were talking shop.

"We were discussing mental damages," Eddie said. "I told Pete what you said about the field changing."

Jonas said, "You'll see. Chemical assays and brain scans will show how stress damages the brain. If I were a trader, I'd go long on psychiatry. Fortune smiles on the well-prepared."

Eddie squeezed a puddle of mustard onto his sandwich. "I'd take him seriously, Pete, if I were you."

"You realize the defense will try and pound any expert into scaloppini," Pete said.

"Don't sell my brother short. A lot of people have tried and a lot of people lost."

"What is this?" Pete said. "Two on one?"

"You stepped in it, pal," Eddie said. "This isn't some early-season game where Duke beats up on the Little Brothers of the Poor Community College."

"Knock it off, you two. You sound like braying jackasses," Jonas gibed.

Pete said, "That surprises you? We're litigators. We fight all day."

"What a wonderful life," Jonas joked. "Makes me want to pawn my stethoscope and take the LSAT. But listen up, Pete Bodenheim! Just because I never had to sink a foul shot in front of eleven thousand screaming maniacs at the Palestra, doesn't mean you can sell me short on nerve. I can hang in there with the best. Remember Tau Delta Phi on Sansom Street? I took down the biggest poker pot ever played there, because I wouldn't let those thugs push me around."

Eddie beamed. "Close to a thousand dollars. They shoulda put up a plaque. This isn't college hoops anymore, Pete. We're talking professionals."

"Listen," Pete bristled. "Basketball taught me offense and defense. I prepare for trials like I did for games. I'll be as ready for the big leagues as anyone. Don't either of you doubt it."

"Congratulations, Pete," Jonas cheered. "You've been drafted by the NBA."

"Huh?" Eddie and Pete said.

"New York Bar Association," Jonas said. "You're our number-one pick."

Jonas and Eddie saluted Pete with another round of black cherry soda.

Eddie said, "You know, if we set up shop carefully, we can take on all comers. Jonas needs experience in court. Pete can take the depositions and try the cases. I'm in the backcourt, calling the plays. I know we can do it."

Several sodas later the threesome bounded off to the Broad Street subway, looking more like a pack of horny teenagers than the future of American jurisprudence. Led by Steve, who joined the group at Veteran's Stadium, the men raised their beers in an impromptu bachelor party.

"Here's to your birthday, Jonas," they said as one. "And the end of an era: Your days as a single man are over."

"Welcome to the rest of your life," Eddie teased.

"What?" Jonas protested half-heartedly. "Who said anything about getting married?"

"Married?" Steve feigned disbelief. "You already are. Didn't anyone tell you?"

Just before game time, an older man and a young couple descended the aisle on the way to their seats. The women wore a Phillies hat and Mike Schmidt jersey. Between innings she ascended the aisle and tried to hail a peanut vendor. Jonas did a double take. Victoria Schone smiled at him and his companions. Eddie, Pete, and Steve looked curiously at the attractive young woman who did not budge.

Nodding at his companions, Jonas said, "Guys, this is Victoria Schone. Victoria, I'd like you to meet my brother, Eddie Speller, and my friends, Pete Bodenheim and Steve Rothman."

"Nice to meet you," Victoria said.

"So, how do you know each other?" Eddie said.

"Dr. Speller's my doctor."

Pete said, "Is he as good as he claims?"

"He sure turned my life around."

"Thanks," Jonas said. "It's been a pleasure."

"Nice to meet you," Pete and Steve said. Eddie remained silent.

"Go Phillies!" she said. "See you Monday," she whispered to Jonas before leaving.

Eddie said to Jonas, "That was Miss—"

"Not now, Eddie."

Several uncomfortable innings later, Eddie broke the silence. "They're talking like you and Jennie are a done deal."

"I'd rather you put it another way."

"That's what I wanted to talk with you about."

"I figured as much when you wouldn't say anything on the phone with Jennie next to me. Let me enjoy the rest of the game in peace, Eddie. Then we'll talk."

25

Friday, October 14, 1983

The game remained tight until the Orioles, Jonas's home team, went ahead for good in the top of the seventh inning. Afterward, everyone headed to Jonas's neighborhood tavern for a beer. Later, Eddie went along to Jonas's apartment.

"Thanks for the terrific evening, Eddie," Jonas said.

"I have this picture, too," Eddie said, looking their father's portrait. "I have to hand it to you, brother," he added, noting several pastel landscapes hanging over the couch and loveseat. "Compared to when you moved in, this place definitely has a woman's touch."

"These are Jennie's paintings. Aren't they fabulous?" Jonas crowed. "Look at the colors. And the intensity. Just so you know, she's moving in next month."

"Did I miss something? There's no rush, is there?"

"I didn't get her pregnant, if that's what you're thinking. Look, Eddie. It's late. If you have something to say about Jennie, please say it."

Eddie turned to the picture of their father and paused thoughtfully. "C'mon, Jonas," he said. "Be honest. What are you doing with her?"

"Doing with her? What kind of question is that?"

"I'm trying to tell you I'm concerned. Are you sure you're ready? Jennie's a terrific girl; I know how fond you are of her and her family. But fond isn't enough to get you through the tough times. It doesn't take Sigmund Freud to know that a big reason you're with her is because of her family."

"You're wrong. I'm with her because of her. Take one look at these walls and you'll see exactly what I mean."

"There's something missing. I saw it in your eyes tonight when you introduced your patient to us. That was her, wasn't it? Miss Abington?"

"Yes, it was her."

"Your faces lit up when you saw each other. I've never seen you look that way. Look me in the eye and tell me you don't care about her."

"Care about her? I spend my life caring about people. Miss Abington is a fantasy."

"What I saw on your face tonight was very real."

"She has transference to me. I have countertransference to her transference."

"What a load of horseshit. You never use words like that and you know it. There's something about her, isn't there?"

"Yes, there is. She's full of life. She inspired me. She still does."

"And Jennie?"

"It's different with her. We love each other for real. You've spent a total of twelve hours with Jennie in three years. You don't know what she's like behind closed doors. Jennie's got a helluva lot more oomph than you give her credit for."

"But what about Miss Abington?"

"What about her? All my patients are special in their own way. I'm just a toll booth on their journeys."

"I'm not talking about all your patients. I'm talking about her. How can you be so sure?"

"Sure? There's no 'sure' in what I do. You want 'sure,' teach math. The Egyptians believed Pythagoras had discovered the laws of the universe."

"So, if you believe you're just a rest stop, that's what you'll be."

"Look, Eddie, it gets complicated when a shrink has feelings for his patient."

"Don't you talk with your analyst about her?"

"Dr. Frantz is terrific. We talk about her all the time. He knows exactly how I feel."

"Which is . . . ?"

"Jesus, Eddie, if you're this ferocious in your legal life, Pete and I will make a mint."

"Confess your sins, my son, and all shall be forgiven."

"Look, Eddie, Victoria's a diamond in the rough. Because of the therapy we've done, she believes in herself. Because of the therapy we've done, I believe in myself. I'm a psychoanalyst. My patients and I *talk* things out. We don't *live* them out. You have no idea what crossing that boundary means, how it could destroy her trust and taint my career."

"You can do it if it means enough to you. This is the most important decision you'll make in your whole life."

Adrenalin shot through Jonas. "You're going somewhere you don't belong, Eddie. I love Jennie; I do. We were both three-quarters dead when we met. She means the world to me."

"Does she make you feel like that girl from Abington does? Because that's what you need."

"Who the hell are you to tell me what I need? Since when do you know what it's like to be part of people's lives the way psychoanalysts are? So don't come around here like Elmer Gantry preaching I need psychological enlightenment."

"That's not fair, Jonas."

"Life's not fair. Our father was supposed to be at my graduation. It killed me that he wasn't."

"I was there for you. I always will be."

"I know. I know," Jonas relented. "You mean the world to me, Eddie, but you can't show up like Father Earth bearing World Series tickets and expect me to say, 'C'mon in, Dad, let's have a heart to heart.' Jennie wants a family with me. She knows how much you and Margo mean to me; she wants to be a part of that."

"But you care about someone else. What do you do about that?"

"*Do*? There's nothing to do. Victoria's therapy ends in eight months. I'll never see her again. I can't have you and Margo second-guessing me about Jennie."

"Are you sure about this?"

"What about when you—?"

"What?"

Jonas took two deep breaths and bit his lip hard. "You and Margo were a lot younger than me when you got together. Were you sure about her?"

"Yeah, as sure as anyone my age could've been. Listen, I'll stand by you, brother, no matter what you decide. I just want to make sure you have your eyes wide open."

After Eddie left, Jonas unwound with the late news. That night, he dreamt about Jennie. In the dream, she wore a Phillies cap.

*　*　*

Since the Sunday game didn't start until 4:00 PM, the foursome gathered for a late brunch.

"That was fun last night," Pete said over his omelet.

"Victor's is always fun," Jonas said. "How'd you like it when the waitress broke out with *Un bel di*? I love that aria."

"You and your opera," Pete said. "Give me Simon and Garfunkel, a fireplace, and a good Burgundy."

"I'd just as soon go to a Stones concert," Steve said.

"I was twenty-two during Woodstock," Eddie said. "You three were riding three-speeds while we were scared shitless about Vietnam."

Jonas said, "My generation's nightmares are about AIDS. There's no test for it yet."

"You're the last bachelor. Doesn't it scare you?" Steve asked.

"You bet," Jonas said.

"What do you tell your patients?"

"Wear a condom and know who you're sleeping with. Better yet, take a sexual history. How's that for foreplay!"

"In college they ran us around so much in basketball practice," Pete piped in, "that by the time we finished studying, we couldn't get it up enough to beat off, let alone get laid. Thank God I met Beth before AIDS came along."

"What a fun conversation," Eddie said. "I'd rather talk about the death tax."

* * *

Late that afternoon the Orioles won the World Series, as Jonas's youth slipped beneath the horizon along with the October sun.

When Jonas hugged his brother good-bye at the Thirtieth Street Station, he knew his grief for Willy Speller was finally over.

26

Monday, November 22, 2004

For Victoria, the rest of Sunday felt like a vigil. On Monday morning, Melinda refused to leave her room, but Victoria had to work. The voir dire for the Duke's case turned out to be even more contentious than Victoria had imagined, with Denise Mather challenging potential juror after another. When the judge adjourned court at 3:00 PM, Victoria returned home immediately and sequestered herself in her office, wondering what was ahead. It was more—far more—than just fear about how he would react to her after all these years. Did she really want to open up about her mother and about her own mothering? Not to mention her feelings about Martin and what was and wasn't happening inside their bedroom. Old wounds, newer wounds, already inflamed and oozing.

One look at the most treasured document in Victoria's life aside from Gregory's birth certificate, even more precious than her marriage license, convinced her to reach for the telephone. The last thing Victoria looked at before dialing was her college diploma.

27

Sunday, May 20, 1984

Victoria's commencement day was gloriously sunny. She was graduating summa cum laude, with a GPA of 3.98. She had one B+—in Biology.

She scanned her cheering section of friends and family, including Lorraine and Morris—his last drink two years ago—and Victoria's surviving grandparents, Grandma Jeanine Cohen and Grandfather Samuel Schone, who had battled prostate cancer to the bitter end to see his granddaughter graduate from an Ivy League school. When she saw Dr. Speller smiling through the crowd, she approached him, sheepskin in hand.

"I felt your presence," she said.

"Congratulations, Victoria," he said, eyeing her cap and gown. "Look at you. You look like a nun."

"Fat chance. You know me better."

"You worked incredibly hard."

"So did you," Victoria said. "I couldn't have survived those awful days without you. At graduation from therapy tomorrow, I'll have something special for you."

A handsome couple edged toward them through the crowd. Dr. Speller said, "Your parents, right? Weren't you with your father that time at the baseball game?"

"I can't believe you remember that. Look at him; I'm so proud. He has his life back. Isn't that remarkable?"

"It's why I do what I do," he said. "You've gotten a handle on yourself, and the effects rippled through your entire world. The Talmud says, 'Save a life, save the world.'"

"Who was that?" Lorraine said after Victoria rejoined her family.

"Oh, that's Dr. Speller," Victoria said. "He's my . . . my advisor."

"He's obviously fond of you. Judging from the look on your face, I'd say you feel the same about him."

"What look?"

"I know that look. I looked at your father that way when we first met. He was so handsome."

"Was? Look again, Mother. Besides, Dr. Speller is much more than a handsome face. Without him I'd never have become the person you see today."

"Ah, young love," Lorraine sighed. "To project onto your beloved the power to make all things possible. He becomes the blank canvas onto which you paint your hopes and dreams."

"My beloved? You know nothing about him, Mother. Or me."

"Touchy, touchy," Lorraine said with a duplicitous lilt. "All this, because I said something about your handsome professor. You don't think you'd be the first girl who had an affair with one of her teachers?"

"An affair? That's ridiculous. Besides, he has someone."

"Silly goose; since when did that keep a professor from plucking a blossom from his garden? You could at least introduce us."

"Why? So you can bat your eyelashes and hurl your innuendos at him? It would be humiliating."

"Come on, Victoria. We're grown-ups now. Why don't we let bygones be bygones and be friends? I've missed you since you moved out."

"Missed me? What did you miss?"

"Our talks."

"Our talks? They upset me for days. I'm different now. Same with Daddy, or haven't you noticed?"

"There you two are," Morris interrupted. "It's so nice to see you two talking, just like the old days." Victoria turned to her father without flinching. "Time to celebrate, everyone," he added. "There's a table waiting for us at Bookbinder's. Off we go."

28

Victoria walked into her final therapy session toting a brown-paper-wrapped rectangle the size of a small picture.

"This is for you," she said, placing the package on the couch. "So you don't forget me."

"How could I forget you, Victoria, after all that we've been through?" he said.

After he had finished residency training, Dr. Speller moved across the hall into a larger office with a huge picture window that faced south. The décor was the same except for the addition of a couch and a larger desk. On it rested a portrait of a smiling woman with dark hair, her arms draped around Dr. Speller's neck from behind; the same woman from that night at the pizzeria.

Victoria looked out at an airplane disappearing behind the sea of oil tanks dotting the confluence of the Delaware and Schuylkill Rivers. At twilight, she could make out the Walt Whitman Bridge.

"What are you looking at?" he said.

"Airplanes. Bridges. The future, I guess."

"Journeys and connections," he said in a distant voice.

"Is something bothering you?" she asked.

Dr. Speller looked out the window.

"You didn't answer me."

"Sorry," he said. "I was thinking about how much I'm going to miss you. You have such a way with words and ideas. Your mind works so fast. And you have a terrific sense of humor."

"God knows where it comes from," Victoria said. "Abington felt like growing up in a funeral home."

Dr. Speller's head drooped, and his eyes, usually so lively, gravitated toward the window.

"Hello, anyone home?" Victoria said, rapping her fist against an imaginary head. "What's going on in there?"

Dr. Speller remained silent.

"What is it you aren't saying?" she said. "You're not dying, are you?"

Dr. Speller grinned, then shook his head.

Victoria said, "Look, you've always told me to be honest. And I've upheld my end of the bargain. No one knows better than you how hard, sometimes humiliating, it's been to tell you the truth. This doesn't have to do with me, does it?"

Dr. Speller nodded enough for Victoria to see.

"Look at me, then," she said. "You can't leave me hanging. I never knew where I stood with Lorraine. You have to be honest with me. After all we've been through, you owe me that much. C'mon, out with it."

Dr. Speller's lips moved silently as if he were struggling for words. "Here it is," he said after a moment. "I like you."

"I know. I knew it the day I told you about the dark-haired girl."

"It's more than that. I wonder what would have happened if we knew each other outside this room."

"That never would have happened," Victoria said.

"Probably not, but I think about it sometimes."

"So do I. But here we are, and that's that," Victoria sighed. "Besides, you made all the decisions about us. You set the rules. How close, how distant. Intimacy without being intimate. You know everything about me, but what do I know about you? This was never fair."

"It's not supposed to be."

"Who says? Whose rules are you playing by?"

"I've been trying to figure that out as we've gone along," Dr. Speller said. "You picked up on it long ago when you clued me in about 'clinical mode.' My teachers spouted propaganda about therapists being blank screens on which patients play out their conflicts. I knew they were wrong. It misses what therapy is all about."

"Which is?"

"The relationship between the participants. I don't have rules for this. I made them up as we went along."

"And 'this' means?"

"You and me."

"You and me?"

"Yes, you and me."

"How can you talk about you and me? I don't even know what to call you. You've always been Dr. Speller to me."

"That's only part of who I am."

"I see," she said. "We're not just talking about 'Dr. Speller' anymore, are we?"

"No, we're not. You're not just a patient to me."

"Well, you're not just a doctor to me. You told me a long time ago that your job was to put things in perspective. So, do it. Do your job. Tell me who you are, what you believe, what you feel about me. Don't you see? I can't leave here without knowing that."

"I agree," Dr. Speller said. He hesitated for one last moment and then sat on his desk, legs dangling as he faced Victoria. "My name is Jonas Speller. I'll be thirty years old on October fifteenth. I was always interested in the mind and the brain, but I didn't figure out what to do with it until I started working in this clinic. I've learned more from you about therapy than in all the courses and supervision I've ever had. As I saw you change, I had the courage to change, too.

"I have an older brother, Eddie, who lives in New York. He has two young children and a wife named Margo. My father died of complications from surgery in my last year of medical school, and it tore me up—which is how I wound up in therapy myself. After we began your therapy, I switched analysts, because I realized I couldn't be as straight with mine, a man I'd seen for three years, as you were with me the first two times we met.

"I come from much humbler surroundings than yours. The closest I ever got to Florence was my art history course. See this blue book?" He pointed to the bookshelf. "It's the score from my favorite opera, *Die Meistersinger*."

"What's it about?" Victoria said.

"In order to win his beloved's hand, an out-of-towner named Walther has to win a song contest judged by a guild whose rules are rigid and antiquated. Someone helps him transform a dream into a breathtaking song that pushes the rules to the limits but gains the admiration of the townspeople. That's me trying to come up with my own rules for therapy, not just parroting the party line. Making my own music, not singing someone else's. That's us. We've created our own song. Have you heard enough?"

"No, you've got two and a half years' worth of catching up to do! You know everything about my relationships; what about yours?" Victoria pointed to the photograph on the desk. "Who is she?"

"Her name's Jennie. I met her soon after your therapy started."

"Do you love her?"

"Yes."

"Why didn't you say something before?"

"I was a young psychiatrist. You were in terrible shape, and you were just starting to get better. I'm your doctor. I would never put your well-being at risk."

"Who would have known?"

"I would have."

"This is fucked up. I pay you. Outside of two minutes at a baseball game, I've never even talked with you outside this room."

"I know. I'm always in my therapist mode. I wouldn't be telling you all this if I didn't think it would help you."

"Well, whatever you do, I wouldn't have made all the changes without you. Besides, honestly, would you have done it if I didn't pay? Tell me you would have taken the time to understand that crazed bitch who walked into your life back then."

"I saw something in you from the beginning. You never were indifferent."

"Neither were you. And you have to appreciate what that meant to me, coming from a family where nobody gave two shits about the real me. I felt so lonely as a child. So terribly lonely. What about you?"

"This is *your* therapy, Victoria. Not mine."

"I understand that. I'm asking you to share yourself, like I've done with you. You just said that was what therapy was about. You have to know how much better it makes me feel about myself to know you have issues, that you're not some god."

"Outside of playing music," Jonas said, "making friends didn't come naturally. I was shy, so I had to work at it. Of this I'm sure: The connection between us is special, something far beyond your being my patient. Look for it with whoever you get involved with."

"Thank you for sharing yourself. I needed that," Victoria said. "You're a brave man, Jonas Speller." She looked out at the bridge in the distance. "I can't ever go back to that awful place I was in before you."

Jonas searched his bookshelf.

"What are you looking for?" Victoria said.

"My Maimonides book, *Guide for the Perplexed*."

"Oh, I wondered what happened to it."

"I didn't know you noticed it."

"Trust me. I notice *everything*."

"I took it with me on vacation, the one when you cancelled your session at the last moment."

"I can't believe you remember that."

"Believe me. I *remember* everything," Jonas said.

They both smiled.

"Are you going to marry *her*?" Victoria asked.

"Yes."

"I hope you're happy together."

"Thank you."

"Where are you headed?" she said.

"New York City."

"Soon?"

"When I finish training to be a psychoanalyst."

"Is it supposed to feel this sad?" Victoria asked, reaching for a tissue. "We're saying good-bye to this whole part of our lives, aren't we?"

Jonas nodded.

Victoria looked toward the descending sun. "It makes me think about a ferry ride to Martha's Vineyard I took when I was little. I looked way off into the distance and thought I saw our destination, but when we got there, it was a mirage and I realized we had more to go."

"We're headed into the unknown," Jonas said.

"Can I call you if I need you?"

"Of course."

Victoria retrieved her gift, which she presented to Jonas, saying, "This is very special to me; it's my favorite poem. Think of it as your diploma."

"Thank you," he said, unpacking a wooden frame that held sixteen lines of hand-inscribed verse on vanilla parchment:

Stopping by Woods on a Snowy Evening
By Robert Frost

Whose woods these are I think I know.
His house is in the village though;
He will not see me stopping here
To watch his woods fill up with snow.

My little horse must think it queer
To stop without a farmhouse near
Between the woods and frozen lake
The darkest evening of the year.

He gives his harness bells a shake
To ask if there is some mistake.
The only other sound's the sweep
Of easy wind and downy flake.

The woods are lovely, dark, and deep,
But I have promises to keep,
And miles to go before I sleep,
And miles to go before I sleep.

Thank you for being there for me.
Victoria Schone May 21, 1984

Victoria approached Jonas, cautiously. Then, she buried her head against his shoulder and embraced him as though she was afraid to let go. "It's time for me to leave. Good-bye, Jonas," she said. "I like using your first name. It's how I want to remember you," whereupon she departed, head held high, without turning back.

29

Monday, November 22, 2004

Jonas tried to save the hour between 3:00 and 4:00 PM on Mondays to catch up on patient call-backs and prescription refill requests that had come in over the weekend. Since the conference at Foxwoods started the previous Friday, Jonas's to-do list was longer than usual because of the extra day away.

He wasn't especially pleased when his colleague Christopher Cantley, assistant director of residency training, stopped in for a curbside consult. Cantley wanted an opinion about which medication to use for a traumatized patient whose wife had died in a gruesome car accident. A recent study had touted Paxil for combat-related posttraumatic stress disorder, but the patient wouldn't take it because of sexual side effects. Cantley wanted to know what Jonas would prescribe.

"Are you sure the man needs medication?" Jonas inquired.

"He says he's having panic attacks," Cantley replied.

"Hmm. Sexual side effects . . . Is the man dating?"

"Yes. For the first time in three years."

Jonas said, "Maybe that's what has him upset. You know, how old stuff gets stirred up."

"I didn't think about that."

"How often do you see him?"

"Once a month, for medication management."

"You might want to try meeting more often and for longer sessions," Jonas said tactfully. "I treated a widow whose husband died on September 11th. She had a guilty depression once she started dating again. It turned out the new man was much more sexually satisfying than the dead husband. For her it felt like cheating! We met regularly for a while; she got well quickly once we talked it through."

"How often did you meet?"

"Twice the first week. Then once a week for the next couple of months; about ten sessions, that's all it took. It always felt like she was flirting with me, but I just let it be. She kept saying how I was the only man she ever talked with so frankly. How special I was. I was like her summer romance. I remember her last session because she came in dressed to kill. Unconsciously she had acted out the affair with me, got it out of her system and went on with her life. No medication could have done that. Talk about the power of psychotherapy."

"You know," Cantley said on his way to the door, "I think you're onto something. My patient's probably a wreck worrying about sexual performance. Before I prescribe anything I'll tell him to come in and talk about it. Thanks, Jonas."

"Sure thing," Jonas said. "You can always find a medication that doesn't cause sexual dysfunction, but therapy can be just as powerful; besides, I like the side-effect profile a lot better."

Glad to be alone, Jonas rushed through his checklist without much enthusiasm. The talk with Jennie about Gil and Gracie was still on his mind. Jonas surveyed the three haphazard stacks of journals on his couch, which hadn't been used for classical psychoanalysis in twelve years. The view across Madison Avenue was dismal, Mount Sinai's Guggenheim Pavilion looking like the Titanic on end just before it sank.

At 4:30 PM, the telephone began droning: *meep-meep*, pause, *meep-meep*; *meep-meep*, pause, *meep-meep*. Had his family or a colleague needed him, they would have called on his cell phone. Maybe it's a new patient, he thought; although, that seemed unlikely.

The sounds reminded Jonas of the heart monitor in the intensive care unit the night his father died, the trauma of which propelled him into psychoanalysis with Fowler.

"This is Dr. Speller," he said dispassionately into the handset.

"Oh," said a surprised woman's voice. "I didn't expect anyone to answer. I thought I'd get a message. My name is Victoria. I doubt you remember me . . . "

Jonas's heart flipped over backward. "You don't know if I remember? How could you think such a thing? What is it, Victoria? What's happened?"

"I . . . I . . . it's . . . it's . . . my Melinda. I have a daughter. I have a son, too. Gregory. This is so strange. You can't imagine, or maybe you can. Or even if you can't it doesn't matter. Well, here I am. Or is it here we are? I told Martin I was going to call someone. I can't believe I . . . Martin, that's my husband. I looked online. I thought I might not find you, or that maybe you had died. I knew that was silly. But I thought it anyway. Thank God you're alive. It's been so awful. You won't believe it." Victoria stopped abruptly, as if she needed to catch her breath. "Where are you?"

"In my office on Madison Avenue at Ninety-eighth Street, on the seventh floor. Guess I haven't moved up in the world much. And you?"

"I'm a lawyer in Center City. So's my husband, Martin. We live on Rittenhouse Square in the townhouse we practice in. I'm looking out of my office now. It's drizzling. Everyone's wearing raincoats and carrying briefcases and umbrellas with wooden handles. The only things missing are the derbies and apples. I'm becoming one of them."

"I love Magritte," Jonas said. "This is amazing. I was just thinking about Philadelphia before you called. What's the matter? You sound worried."

"It's about my daughter, Melinda. Something's very wrong with her. She's been just horrible."

"Are you sure it's not about you?"

"That, too. I told my husband I was losing my mind. But you're two steps ahead of me—let me catch up. Either your mind is faster or mine has slowed down, although it never stops racing."

"Someone's coming for a session in a few minutes. Let's set a time for us to talk."

"I need to see you. Soon," Victoria said.

"Fine. I can probably shake loose sometime tomorrow."

"Now that I hear you, I don't want to wait. What about this evening?"

"Seriously?"

"I'm fifteen minutes from the Thirtieth Street Station. Trains leave every hour. There's a five-fifteen Acela train that gets in around six thirty. What's the fastest way from the station?"

"A cab'll take forever. Come by subway. Follow the signs and look at a transit map. Take the blue line . . . "

"I'll figure it out."

"When you get to Ninety-sixth Street, turn right on Madison and go two blocks. The building looks like a hairbrush; it's so ugly you can't miss it. I'm in 716. You'll have to sign in. What name shall I say?"

"My license says Victoria Schone-Braun. I should be there by seven. Are you sure that's not too late?"

"Not at all. I have a dinner meeting I can miss. Call my cell phone if you have any problem." He gave her the number. "I'll call Jennie and tell her an emergency came up."

"I'm on my way."

Victoria. Jonas was so glad to hear her voice. A slide show of memories played through his mind: waiting for her after she tore out of his office that first day; running into each other at the pizzeria and the baseball game; the bakery and the Lake George dreams; even her identification with Esther in *Bleak House*; and their emotional farewell. Her poem had hung in every office he ever occupied.

So much had happened in the last twenty years: marrying Jennie; moving to New York and starting a practice; Jennie's breast cancer;

adopting Gil and Grace; Speller and Bodenheim's ascendancy in New York's legal world; the accolades Jonas received for his papers and workshops integrating psychodynamic theory, behaviorism, and neurobiology as the Prozac era evolved. Yet Victoria's call reminded him that something was missing.

Jonas's next session was at 5:00 PM. Prominent Manhattan socialite Jill McCutcheon had been arrested for shoplifting a four-carat diamond from Tiffany's while in a cocaine-enhanced hypomania. The scandal made the front page of both of New York's tabloids: *The Daily News*, "Gotham's Diamond Jill"; and *The New York Post*, "The Party's Over."

"So, Jill," began Jonas, imagining Victoria on her way to Penn Station. "How've you been this week?"

"The medication is finally working," Jill said. "You were right about my needing huge dosages."

"That's because your metabolism is still revved up from all the cocaine. Your body burns medicine like a furnace. Is the Lithium blunting your thinking or making you gain weight?"

"No. So far so good," Jill responded. "Although I wish people at Narcotics Anonymous didn't recognize me. It seems like everyone knows what happened to me. Something touching happened at Saint Vincent's last Thursday. After I told my story, a purple-haired girl who sounded higher than the Empire State Building said, 'That's so fucked up.'

"A Hassidic man hooked on Oxycontin said, 'I've felt like stealing diamonds for years. It would be easy to palm one. The one I wanted most was flawless; it must have weighed five carats. And it had nothing to do with money. I felt it was looted by the Nazis, and I imagined being God's messenger returning it to its owner's descendants.'

"'Yeah, yeah,' the girl said. 'You kleptos are all the same. You've got an excuse for everything.' That whacked me in the gut, because somehow in my mind, I felt I had a right to the diamond I stole."

Even with half his brain on task, Jonas picked up on Jill's sense of entitlement. He said, "Did anything come up in connection with the last session?"

"You mean about my parents?"

Jonas nodded.

"You remember me saying that when my father was a state senator, he trotted me and my mother out for his election campaigns. He treated us like the family jewels, which has to be why I stole one. Then, it hit me. I coveted the diamond pendant my mother used to wear. Get this. The diamond I stole was bigger than hers."

"Diamond envy?" Jonas chuckled aloud.

"I know. It's so trite, wanting a bigger diamond than my mother's."

"You wouldn't have acted out the fantasy if the urge hadn't been fanned by your cocaine-laced soirees."

"It's all connected. My parents hosted a notorious salon for New York's glitterati. The city's most famous writers, composers, and actors sipped and sniffed away their evenings right in my living room. Sometimes, I'd wake up in the middle of the night hearing the piano and the laughter. I felt left out. I promised myself that when I grew up, my parties would be the envy of all New York."

"Some psychiatrists might call that a delusion of grandeur," Jonas said later, as Jill's session drew to a close. "But I disagree. I think you've been intoxicated with the belief that in order to be worth something, you have to be the hostess of hostesses in the world's most glamorous city. Dreams like that die hard. Believe me, I know. Diamonds are pretty, but time is more precious. You're thirty years old, Jill. Do something with your life. The clock's ticking."

And so were the minutes until Victoria appeared.

30

Thirty seconds before seven o'clock, Victoria arrived, pulling a Tumi Rollaboard. One glance and Jonas felt as if her last appointment had been only a week ago. Victoria had become a stunning woman. The way her eyes darted around his office was so familiar it reminded him of their first appointment.

"Well," she said, still breathless from rushing. "Here I am."

"So you are. It's so good to see you," Jonas said.

"I need a moment to settle." Victoria meandered around the office. There was the old—the Academy poster, her Robert Frost poem, and the new—a three-generation family picture of Jonas and his family in front of the Matterhorn, a letter from the dean confirming Dr. Speller's promotion to full professor of psychiatry. When she saw the couch, she smiled. "Is this an antique or do you actually use it?"

"Nope. The real thing. I see you haven't lost your sense of humor."

"I always wondered what couches were for," Victoria said.

"We used them to encourage people to say their thoughts and feelings out loud. We called it free-associating."

"Did it work?"

"You and I did fine face-to-face instead, which is the natural way people communicate. It's how infants connect with their caregivers. The couch fosters regression—going down the ladder of time—which helps recover buried memories, but it doesn't always help therapy. It can just as easily lock someone into his past."

"That's what must have happened with my mother and her analyst," Victoria said. "She never got past being upset with me."

"Is Lorraine a factor in what's happening now?"

"You remember her name?"

"I told you a long time ago, I remember everything. What's happening now?"

"My daughter is driving me absolutely insane. I can't figure out why she's so hateful. Do you have children?"

"A son and a daughter. They're adopted."

"How old?"

"Gil is sixteen. Gracie is twelve."

"So, you know what adolescents are like to live with."

"Oh, God, yes. Without them, I wouldn't have realized how stupid I am."

"And your son?" Victoria said.

"Is there a reason you want to know more about him?"

"I'll get to that in a minute."

"Gil, short for Guillaume. William in French."

"How are you and Jennie?"

"We're good. For a while, I was afraid I was going to lose her to breast cancer. I think the fertility drugs did it."

"That must've been awful."

"We were scared for a long time. But she's fine now. And your family?"

"My son's name is Gregory," Victoria said. "I wanted to name him Jonathan, but it didn't work out. You have no idea how important he is in my life. Gregory's the only one who really gets me. Do you have that with your son?"

"I wish I could say yes, but I can't."

"Maybe that has to do with being adopted. I love Gregory so much, it frightens me. If anything happened to him, I would dissolve completely. Melinda's envious."

"What about Melinda?"

"I'll get to her. Gregory makes me feel like I'm a good person, not just a good mother—that I'm leaving my mark on this earth. Remember that last session, when you said how special the connection was between you and me? Well, that's what it feels like with Gregory. We finish each other's sentences. He knows what I'm thinking even before I do."

"And your husband?"

"Martin is . . . Martin is Martin. He's very handsome. Like my father, but in a different way. He's good to me, and we work together beautifully. He's my exact opposite. He rarely gets riled up. I know he's mad at Melinda now, but that's because she has me upset. I can't remember the last time he was mad at me."

That didn't sit right with Jonas. It sounded as if she took her husband for granted. "And as a lover?"

"We'll get to that if and when we need to, "Victoria responded sharply.

"You don't think it's important?" Jonas asked.

"I said, 'we'll get to it.' That's not why I'm here." Victoria shifted in her chair. "But as long as you're asking about sex, you should know I had an affair before we got married. 'Affair' might not be the right word; it happened only once. Martin doesn't know. Martin must never know.

"Remember how I took ballet classes to work on my balance? After therapy, I kept it up during law school. All the instructors were women, except for one man who had such a beautiful body, it drove me crazy."

"Crazy?"

"I don't know what happened. It was like someone turned on a switch. I was in a frenzy for days—all I thought about was sex. Anyway, I figured nothing would happen, because everyone knew male ballet dancers were gay. Apparently not this one. He spent extra time with me one-on-one.

When he touched me to accentuate a pose, the feeling was delicious. He asked me for coffee one evening after class; I knew what he wanted. Martin was busy with exams. By the time we got back to his apartment, I was so hot, I almost orgasmed in his hallway. I didn't feel guilty. I figured, why not give into it?"

"Jesus, that was reckless," Jonas said.

"Not completely. I knew enough to ask if he was safe. He said he was bisexual, which got me worrying about AIDS. So, he wore a condom, which felt like throwing cold water on my crotch. He wanted more, but the condom thing killed it, and that was that. Martin's been the only man inside me without a condom."

Jonas said, "Are you going to tell me about Melinda?"

"I'll get to her in one more minute. But since we're talking about marriage, I want to ask you about your wife."

"I'll tell you, but what's behind your question? We're here about Melinda. And about you."

"Are you happy with her?" Victoria said.

"Jennie? Yes, Very happy."

"Does the sex mean as much now as it did when you were younger?"

"This has to do with you and your husband?"

"Yes, it does. But you didn't answer my question."

"What do you want to know?"

"I don't think about sex like I used to. So with Jennie, it's not like when you and she were younger, right?"

"No, sex is better. We're in a different place than years ago."

"I wish I had that," Victoria said. "Does she work outside the home?"

"My, you certainly are curious."

"You want to kid around, that's fine," Victoria snapped. "I can use some levity in my life. But no patronizing bullshit. Agreed?"

"I was trying to be lighthearted. I didn't mean to offend you."

"You hit a nerve," she said. "Let's leave it at that."

"Fine. Just don't expect me to read your mind. Suppose you take a moment to reflect out loud on how you're different from twenty years ago. It'll save us time."

"I have a whole work persona now," Victoria said. "I'm good at what I do. I go to court, and I fight. I claw like a tigress. I don't give up. Plaintiff or defense, makes no difference; I'm with you for the duration. I just started a trial today that could explode at any minute."

"That's good, Victoria. I always hoped you'd end up someplace where you could use your natural instincts."

"It's the wifing and mothering I'm insecure about. Except for Gregory. That's why I asked about your wife. I need to know how other people do it."

"Jennie used to work for Sotheby's, shepherding high rollers around Europe and preparing them for the auctions. You want to see raw instinct, watch an auction. It's war. After we adopted our children, Jenny developed an antique home-furnishing business. It keeps her hand in the art world but lets her set her own schedule. Everyone loves her, especially her customers."

Victoria said, "She mixes her work life and her home life. I wish I could. You remember how much my parents hated me? Now, I have this creature in my house who despises me. Three nights ago, I tried reasoning with her about going to bed earlier. She got totally out of control and threw a glass figurine at me. She could have killed someone."

"How old is she?"

"Almost fifteen. Her birthday is one month after Thanksgiving."

"How long has she been this way?"

"It's been really bad the past four months, but it's been coming on since she turned twelve."

"When did she start menstruating?"

"Around the same time."

"And before that?"

"Melinda was always high-strung, hard to settle down. Always begging for one more story, or one more song at bedtime. And if Martin or I said no, she'd be upset for hours, thrashing around like a maniac. When we tried letting her cry herself to sleep, she wailed so loudly, you'd think she'd been dismembered. It would go on for hours."

"Did anything calm her down?"

"Not really. Sometimes I'd find her curled up in bed with all the covers and pillows piled around her like a womb."

"Did Melinda like cuddling?"

"More with Martin than with me. After Gregory was born, Melinda used to rock him. At first, it looked cute, but then she kept doing it even when he didn't want it, and she'd get angry at him for being upset."

"She was trying to comfort herself."

"Ever since, I'm afraid to leave her alone with him. Meanwhile, she's brilliant. She took the SATs in seventh grade to get into the Johns Hopkins program for the gifted and talented. You wouldn't believe her scores."

"Did you ever consider that Melinda could be bipolar?"

"You can't open any newspaper or magazine without reading about Bipolar Disorder in children. Do you think that's it?"

"You know it runs in families?"

"I knew you were going to say that. Lorraine has it. Me, too, I suppose."

"That's exactly what I think. You probably had it way back when. Bipolar Disorder went unrecognized and undiagnosed for years. It wouldn't surprise me if you had it all along."

"As for it running in families, nothing could compare to Lorraine's ups, but when she got down on me, she was merciless. Melinda tears me to shreds, too. Only now, I can't get away from it. I'm reliving the same nightmare all over. I rarely have ups; mostly I'm agitated."

"I should have asked: Did you get depressed after your children were born?"

"You mean postpartum depression. I didn't call it that; I called it 'worried.' After Melinda was born, I worried for months, thinking I'd done something wrong during the pregnancy. I barely slept during her infancy. Lorraine did better with her than I did."

"How so?"

"It didn't bother her if Melinda had trouble going to sleep. She'd stay up half the night rocking her, but of course, Lorraine didn't have to go to work like I did."

"Did you get any treatment?" Jonas said.

"Not really. My ob-gyn gave me samples of Zoloft. The first pill drove me through the ceiling. My head felt like it was exploding. The doctor said I'd get used to the medicine, so I tried for a few more days. But I couldn't take it."

"Why didn't you call?"

"Because I felt like a failure. You had never prescribed medication. I assumed you'd be upset with me."

"We've learned so much since then. Sensitive people like you often react violently to medication. Besides, medications like Zoloft can make bipolar patients worse. Much worse. We'll take care of you, but Melinda has to be seen right away."

"How about after Thanksgiving?"

"That's too long. Whatever we're dealing with, I want it addressed right away."

"You're scaring me," Victoria said.

"You're not leaving here until there's a plan for Melinda. I have someone in mind. Rob Milroy. We worked with teenagers years ago in Philadelphia, and we stay in touch. I don't know if I can reach him tonight. How do I get you tomorrow? If I can get him to see Melinda on short notice, I'll need to get you the information right away. Do you know how to text message?"

"Between Martin and Gregory, I can manage."

"Good. I don't want us playing telephone tag tomorrow."

Jonas didn't finish with Victoria until close to nine o'clock. He prescribed tiny doses of medication to calm her, nothing that would dull her or make her more agitated. They agreed to meet in a week and have a phone session after Dr. Milroy evaluated Melinda.

"How much do I owe you?" Victoria asked.

"How's this? Pay me the same rate you get per hour. I'll keep track of the times and phone calls and bill you every month. Agreed?"

"Very fair. That was easy. Do sessions still last forty-five minutes?"

"Sessions last as long as they *need*," Jonas said for emphasis. "The forty-five minute hour was more about the doctor than the patient. For me, combining medication and therapy is as much art as it is science. I generally schedule patients an hour apart, unless it's someone new or a more complicated family session, then I block off more time. It all depends."

"What about those doctors who see six patients an hour for medication and send them to social workers for therapy?"

"I don't know how they do it," Jonas said. "It's impossible to evaluate someone's mood and response to treatment based on a howdy-do and a self-report questionnaire. I tried it for a few months and I hated it. I can't do my job with a meter running. It would be like telling someone having a heart attack he has forty-five minutes to get better because the doctor has another patient."

"I'm glad you operate that way."

"What can I tell you, Victoria? I'm an analyst. It's what I do. It's who I am."

The next train to Philadelphia left at ten o'clock. Jonas walked Victoria to the hospital entrance where she could get a cab. On the way, she said, "It was very kind of you to see me on such short notice. I'm still worried about Melinda, but at least there's a plan. I feel less alone."

"Bring Martin along next time," Jonas said as they approached a line of taxis. "It would be good if he's in the loop."

"That's not necessary. I'll fill him in myself," Victoria said, which made Jonas wonder what she was and wasn't telling Martin and what, if anything, it had to do with him.

31

D r. Milroy had juggled his schedule to arrange the consultation the next afternoon, but Melinda wouldn't leave her room. He told Martin and Victoria to come anyway, to provide her history and decide what to do. Leaving Gail Heath, her paralegal, to keep an eye on Melinda's door, Victoria brought Gregory with them to the doctor's office, where he sat quietly doing math puzzles.

Like Jonas, Dr. Milroy also had a couch that looked more like a decoration. *What is it with these guys?* Victoria wondered. *They show off their couches like Purple Hearts.*

Dr. Milroy had a jovial, round face, a full beard, and a carefully trimmed mustache. His eyebrows rose and fell rhythmically with his "ah-hahs," "um-hmms," and "I sees." After hearing about Melinda's behavior, his expression turned serious.

Victoria said, "She's stopped changing her clothes. Her room is filthy, littered with dirty dishes and half-drunk glasses of chocolate milk and cans of Red Bull. No one can get her out of her room, not for school, not for dinner, not even to shower. When I spoke to her about her bedtime and going for counseling, she had a shit fit and threw one of her skating trophies at me. Then, she blamed me for upsetting her. She thinks I'm following her; that we're trying to get rid of her."

Dr. Milroy's eyebrows furrowed. "Melinda's not going to make it easy for us," he said somberly. "I've met lots of adolescents like her. Unfortunately, they become so consumed by their distorted views, that they misinterpret the intentions of people who really care for them."

Victoria said, "She's constantly feeling misunderstood and unappreciated, criticized for expressing her thoughts, some of which, frankly, are rather out there. She's incredibly bright—you should hear her vocabulary, and her SATs were off the charts—but she can't see how her behavior affects other people."

"Don't be misled by her fancy language," Dr. Milroy said. "I've seen many youngsters flaunt their grandiosity with big words, but underneath it all, they're insecure about themselves and seek affirmation in self-defeating ways that leave them even more isolated."

"I've told . . . no, we've told her she can go to boarding school wherever she wants—Andover, Choate, Exeter—where she can be with people like herself. It's such a paradox. How can someone so bright not get it that you can't treat people like garbage and still expect them to tell you how smart you are?" Victoria winced, remembering how she used to devalue people, especially girls, the way Melinda did.

"She'll never agree to boarding school," Dr. Milroy said. "Not now. That's because of her dread that she'll be found ordinary and untalented."

"It sounds like you've met her already."

"Believe me, I've known more than my share, so bright and full of rich ideas, yet locked in their own world. Their minds race a mile a minute. That's why they barricade themselves in their rooms, to regulate sensory inputs on their already overstimulated brains. Music can block out intrusive images. Every moment is a struggle to control their bad thoughts.

"Try not to be upset by what I'm about to propose," Dr. Milroy said. "Pennsylvania Hospital has an excellent inpatient adolescent psychiatry unit. I wish there was another way, but I'm afraid she won't go for help unless she's dragged in kicking and screaming. But, because she's under sixteen, you can admit her. She should be admitted as soon as possible—waiting will only prolong everyone's misery and protract Melinda's brain dysregulation, which will only get worse."

"Are you sure hospitalization is necessary?" Martin asked.

Dr. Milroy looked at Martin and Victoria without wavering. "Yes."

Victoria pictured Melinda shot full of tranquilizers, writhing and howling, carted off by linebacker-sized orderlies in white coats. "What's going to happen there?"

"She'll get medicine that will slow her mind and quiet her irritability."

"How do you know she'll go along with the program?"

"Although we can never be totally sure, there's something comforting about being with one's peers. She'll meet teenagers with similar issues. They'll confirm that medication and therapy help. The mood-stabilizing medications we use promote sleep and clear thinking, and we teach mindfulness and breathing exercises, and other techniques that help regulate thoughts and feelings. Think how empowered Melinda will feel, knowing she can control what's rattling around inside her head."

"What about the stigma of being psychiatrically hospitalized?" Victoria said. "Won't she hold that against us?"

"Not in the long run. You'll see; she'll come around. I genuinely like teenagers, especially bright ones like Melinda. I can usually find a way to speak their language and hop aboard their metaphors. I like figuring them out. After that, it's about getting them to see what's special about themselves while accepting their limitations. I share stories about myself, my family, and my friends when we were young. Kids eat them up. I also run outpatient groups for mood-disordered teenagers. I try to introduce prospective members while they're still in the hospital. It gives them hope they'll get better. I'm sure the other kids will welcome her. She'll feel at home in no time."

Dr. Milroy continued, "There are several groups, one for the more withdrawn schizoid types—that's not Melinda. There's one for depressed teenagers without mood swings, and one for the grandiose genius-wannabes. I mix and match the kids carefully, depending on their needs. No bullying. We're there for support, not to knock anyone down. I also see every patient individually, so I can regulate his or her medication and discuss where they're at. I'll have to convince Melinda that mania is no way to influence people.

"You know who pioneered this approach, don't you? Dr. Jonas Speller, the man who referred you to me. I finished training two years behind him. By then, he had developed many innovative strategies, all in the era before today's mood stabilizers."

Victoria liked Dr. Milroy's association to Jonas. Reluctantly, she and Martin agreed that waiting would only delay the inevitable.

Dr. Milroy said, "Because psychiatric hospitals employ skeleton crews for holiday weekends, and only minimal therapy is available, I think it makes the most sense to intervene after Thanksgiving. If we admitted Melinda tomorrow, it wouldn't be until Monday that she'd get the full attention that will ease her into the milieu. I wouldn't want her isolated in her room for five days. That could make her even harder to reach. We can always admit Melinda between now and Monday if she threatens to hurt herself or someone else, but that's unlikely unless she's provoked."

"Should we take her with us for Thanksgiving dinner?"

"That's a very good question." Dr. Milroy paused thoughtfully. "I wouldn't want her to feel excluded. Give her the option and see what she makes of it. Follow her lead. If she decides against going, someone should stay home with her." After discussing the logistics of getting Melinda to the hospital, he produced his card and cell phone number. "I'm reachable any time. Don't hesitate to call. As it stands now, I'll see you on Monday morning."

* * *

Victoria had a phone session with Jonas the day before Thanksgiving. Although it had been less than two days since they last spoke, it felt like a month.

"Your vocal cords sound tighter than my violin's E string," Jonas said after hearing her first words.

Victoria tried to re-create the feeling of being in Jonas's presence. She said, "You have no idea what's been going through my mind. I have awful thoughts about Melinda, of tussling with her to the point that someone gets bloody, and I can see her stabbing herself or someone else. There are times I get so angry at her, I imagine garroting her, like in the Godfather movies. Imagine having thoughts like that about your own child! They're so sickening they make me nauseous—that same feeling I had in your office way back on the first day we met."

"Well, the good news is that you're aware of your anger. Back then you were totally dissociated."

"I'm not sure this is any better."

"Well, we better up your medication. We'll find the right level. It's going to be a day-by-day, sometimes minute-to-minute battle to keep your mind calm. Keep doing the deep breathing and yoga. Think of those techniques as medicines without side effects. Try to get to the gym, too, where you can burn off some steam. Can you focus on work?"

"It's a struggle. I'm always feeling guilty, like there's something more I should be doing for Melinda. Meanwhile, this trial has me amped up like I'm on speed."

"Tell me about Dr. Milroy."

"He says great things about you. We couldn't get Melinda out of her room, so Martin and I met with him alone. Dr. Milroy said we should hospitalize Melinda, but suggested we wait until after Thanksgiving."

"I understand," Jonas said, "but I don't like waiting."

"Is there anything we can do?"

"It's very hard, because no one knows what's going on inside Melinda's mind. Is there any way you can get a look at her, at least for the holiday?"

"We're supposed to go to my in-laws' tomorrow afternoon for dinner. Dr. Milroy said to give her a choice about coming. He doesn't want her feeling excluded. God knows it'll take an act of Congress to get her out of her room, but we'll try. What are you doing for your holiday?"

"Jennie and I and our children will be with Eddie's and Pete's families. You have my cell phone; call if anything comes up."

"I'll try not to bother you."

"Bother me?"

"Yes, bother you. Sometimes I feel like I'm making this all up, that I have no reason to feel as bad as I do. Look at my life from the outside: handsome husband; fascinating career; gorgeous house; two beautiful children; heading to my in-laws on the Main Line for a holiday feast. Can't you just hear someone saying, 'What's her problem? She has it all.' Meanwhile, inside I feel as if my whole world could crumble any second. You're the only person who understands what's going on, Jonas. The only person."

"Believe me, Victoria. I get it. The outside of a person is like the exterior of a building. It's all a façade until you're invited in to see what really happens inside. I know that if I hear from you before Monday, it won't be because you want to talk about how much fun you had with your sisters-in-law. Let's meet in person as soon as Melinda's situated. Milroy's a good man. Try and have a good holiday, and call me after Melinda's been admitted."

32

Thursday, November 25, 2004

Gregory wanted to see the Thanksgiving Day parade, a Philadelphia tradition, where Mummers bands strutted and colorful floats brightened the morning. Victoria had barely slept the night before; she asked Martin to take Gregory to the parade. Dinner would begin at three that afternoon. The weather forecast called for a mixture of sleet and freezing rain from a storm moving up the coast, followed by a frigid air mass moving in from Canada.

Unexpectedly, Melinda agreed when her parents asked if she wanted to go to her grandparents'. She appeared in jeans with holes over both knees, a faded T-shirt, and a red kerchief knotted around her tangled hair. She said little on the ride out of town, having plugged herself into her iPod as soon as she settled in the car.

Melinda's grandparents, Charles and Danielle Braun, lived west of the city on the Main Line, in an historic brick colonial mansion. As Charles welcomed everyone and took their coats, he said, "I can't thank you enough for taking on the Barlow case. Whatever happens, I know you'll do your best, which is all anyone can hope for."

The dining room, with working chimneys at both ends, was furnished opulently. The faces and profiles of former lords and ladies of the manor watched over the meal from ornate picture frames, while the musty odor of fireplace residue permeated the rafters and plaster walls.

Martin's relatives were already there. Everyone except Melinda wore either dresses or jackets and ties, leaving her looking like a mutt brought in from the street.

At dinner, Melinda gobbled her turkey ravenously. Martin's sisters eyed her and Victoria more critically than ever.

Silver-haired Charles Braun had the same oblong face as Martin. Victoria had liked Charles from their first meeting. Impeccably dressed, he was the incarnation of a vigorous man aging well. Morris Schone and his second wife, Carolyn, got on with the senior Brauns splendidly.

With a diplomat's sensitivity to the malaise in the room caused by Melinda, Charles steered the dinner-table discussion to an uncontroversial subject, Pennsylvania's colonization by William Penn.

"Did you know," Charles said after the plates were cleared, "that Penn received huge tracts of land in 1681, from England's King Charles II, in repayment of a large debt owed to Penn's father by the throne? But unlike the Commonwealths of Massachusetts and Virginia, Penn paid the Indians for the land."

Preoccupied, Victoria said, "I never realized that."

Charles turned to his granddaughter. "Melinda, you go to Friends Select, a Quaker school. What do they say about how William Penn treated the Native Americans?"

Gregory and his cousins, all younger than Melinda, looked at her wide-eyed.

Melinda rolled up her napkin and flicked it from side to side. "My school is full of hypocrites. The teachers say how important acceptance is, but I see them whispering behind our backs. Those polemicists make William Penn into an icon of religious tolerance, but it's all for show. He fucked over the Indians, the indentured servants, the women, and the slaves, with impunity, just like every other colony. William Penn treated the Native Americans the same as Hitler treated the Jews. Those he couldn't buy off, he had no use for." Melinda stood up abruptly and began swaying back and forth. Victoria cringed.

"Genocide," Melinda continued. "We're still doing the same fucking thing. Look at what we did in Korea, then Vietnam and Cambodia. Now Afghanistan and Iraq. The government wraps up the package with a red, white, and blue bow, but I know different." Melinda picked up one of the serving plates bearing an image of the Pennsylvania state flag. "Look at this," she said.

Victoria, who knew the true value of the antique plate, was terrified. "Melinda, I—"

"Just look at this place," she interrupted Charles, pointing around the room with the plate. "William Penn got the merchant class to build manors like this, but slaves did all the heavy lifting. He didn't give two shits about how many of them died from yellow fever. You don't think someone constructed this house for union wages?"

Victoria reached for the plate. "Please, honey, let's calm down. Your grandfather didn't mean anything."

Melinda jerked the plate away. "I know exactly what he meant. That we have so much to be thankful for, just like you're always saying I'm such an ungrateful bitch."

Victoria said to everyone. "I'm so sorry, so sorry."

"That's right," Melinda said. "Apologize, because you're ashamed of me. I can't say what I really feel without you thinking I'm wrong."

"Please give me the plate, Melinda. Just put it down," Victoria said. She counted to ten and remembered the plan she and Martin had discussed with Dr. Milroy. "Can we go home now, Melinda? It's been a long day for everyone."

"It's quite all right," Charles said to Melinda, like an ambassador dealing with squabbling dignitaries. "I had very strong opinions myself when I was young. They didn't endear me to everyone, but I earned a lot of respect." He nodded to his children. "It turned out okay, didn't it? Let me tell you something about that plate, Melinda, my dear. It has been in our family for many generations, and as the oldest grandchild, it will be yours some day. Your great-grandmother received it from Benjamin Franklin's family. Let me show you something interesting about the inscription on the back. You'll appreciate the calligraphy."

As Charles diffused the situation, Victoria wondered about her father-in-law's calming influence. *How did he do that?* she asked herself. He had appealed to Melinda's intelligence and curiosity. He made her feel special, something Victoria wished she could do.

With Melinda quieted down, Charles and Danielle led the six grandchildren on a tour of the house. As darkness overtook the landscape, thick wet snow began falling rapidly, forming a layer of mushy slush on the roads and sidewalks.

When the adults adjourned to the library, Victoria implored Martin to leave before Melinda could make another scene. She just wanted to get home.

Martin's sisters, Lydia and Sophia, began to talk about their holiday vacation. "I hope it won't be too much of a rush to get to Pier 26 the day we leave for the BVIs."

Victoria could tell how relieved they were that they wouldn't have to deal with Melinda. Sophia whispered to Martin, infuriating Victoria so much she wanted to slap him. Unable to stand her sisters-in-law another minute, Victoria said, "I'm going to check on the children," and left the room abruptly.

She headed for the center-hall spiral staircase, at the base of which stood a nineteenth-century grandfather clock enclosed in an ornately carved, sharply pedimented cabinet. She could hear Gregory and her nephews talking, out of sight on the second-floor landing. The others must have stepped away.

Lydia's son Mark said, "She's so weird. There's a kid in my class like that. He needs a teacher's aide with him to keep him from going off. I think they called him autotic."

"Did you see the way she's dressed?" his cousin Richard said. "She looks like one of those orphan kids in old movies, and she uses the F word every other sentence, like rappers. What's the matter with her?"

Gregory said, "I don't know what's wrong, but she's not well. My parents are worried about her. They went to see a doctor about it. Don't be so hard on her—she's your cousin, you know. Families are supposed to help each other when someone's sick."

Victoria broke into tears. *He's so compassionate*, she thought. She took her shoes off, so she could creep closer undetected.

"I didn't mean it that way," Richard said.

"What way?" Gregory said.

"That she was psycho or something."

Gregory said, "Suppose someone called you weird?"

"He *is* weird," Mark said. The boys giggled.

"Watch this!" Mark said. The next thing Victoria knew, Mark, legs astride the mahogany banister, flew around its curved railing. Coming out of the curve, Mark yelled, "Wheee!" just before nearly decapitating Victoria, who was midway around the turn. Soon the other boys came barreling after him. Gregory, the last, lost his balance when he plowed into them, but he recovered in time to avoid plunging over the side and impaling himself on the clock case. Everyone had a good laugh except for Victoria.

"What were you boys thinking?" she said harshly. "Someone could have fallen over the side!"

Gregory said, "You worry too much, Mother. Remember? We talked about this." He told his cousins, "That was fun. Let's do it again."

Victoria said, "No way, boys. It's too dangerous. Besides," she fibbed, "tomorrow is a work day. We have to get home soon."

When at last it was time to go home, Victoria stormed to the car, dreading the call to Dr. Milroy she would have to make in the morning. *Just get me home in one piece before anything else happens*, she prayed, fixating on the sickening image of Gregory impaled on the clock.

33

By the time the family left, several gelid inches had accumulated, and the temperature had plummeted into the low teens. Since Lancaster Pike hadn't been salted and plowed, the road was a patchwork of shards and ruts of ice mixed with puddles. The cars ahead of Martin's Mercedes churned up opaque slushy liquid that coated his windshield. When he tried the windshield washer, a warning light blinked, indicating that the washer fluid had run low. The wipers left smeared arcs nearly impossible to see through. With the glare from oncoming vehicles nearly blinding, Martin squinted as he drove.

"Dammit," he said. "I should have filled up on washer fluid. I can barely see." Martin pulled into an abandoned gas station and tried to clear the windshield with a wad of slush. The freezing liquid penetrated Martin's gloves and loafers. Back in the car, he winced in agony.

"What's wrong?" Victoria said.

"My toes feel like they're encased in ice."

"This should help," she said, turning the heat on full blast and directing it downward.

By the time they got under way again, the windshield was smearing up. Martin turned left at City Line Avenue. "I'm going to take the Schuylkill Expressway. It has to be better than this."

A high-pitched noise sounding like a beehive emerged from Melinda's half of the backseat. Her iPod was overflowing its headphones.

Trying to avoid another rampage, Victoria told Gregory, "Tell your sister to lower the volume. Your father needs to focus on the road."

Gregory shouted, "Melinda," but she remained oblivious. "Muh-linn-dah," he yelled louder.

As Martin approached Center City, the light from the Art Museum intensified the glare. "I can't have all this noise," Martin said. "The driving is treacherous. I have to concentrate. Gregory, please. Make her stop."

Gregory poked Melinda's thigh. It took three tries to get her attention.

"What do you want?" she snarled.

Gregory pulled the plugs from her ears. "Melinda," he shouted. "Martin needs you to lower the volume, so he can concentrate on the road."

"Go fuck yourself," she said, repositioning her earpieces.

Gregory snatched them and disconnected the iPod with a jerk. "Listen, Melinda. Cut it out! You want to get us all killed?"

As the sparring escalated, Victoria hollered, "Stop it, you two. Don't miss the exit, Martin. We're almost there."

Melinda said, "Keep your fucking hands off my headphones." She grabbed for them.

Something hit the hood and windshield with a heavy thud, sending Victoria and Martin into a panic. A huge wad of slush had dislodged from an overpass and pelted the car like a missile.

"Jesus, Melinda," Gregory yelled. "How can you behave this way? After I just stuck up for you with Mark and Richard."

"Give them to me!"

"How much longer?" Victoria asked Martin.

"Only a couple more blocks. Shit! The light at Market Street is red." Martin looked both ways, then ran the stoplight in desperation.

Melinda tried to slap Gregory's face. He parried most of the blows, but not the last, which reddened his right cheek. Victoria turned around and tried but couldn't grab Melinda's flailing arms.

Gregory screamed at his sister, "You asshole, crazy asshole! Nothing matters to you except what you want."

Martin turned left onto Rittenhouse Square South and pulled up in front of their house. A blast of frigid air hit Victoria's face when she opened her door. In a rush to open the rear door and separate the combatants, she slipped and twisted her ankle on the slippery street. Gregory got out, key in hand, and ran up the eight ice-caked steps to the house, trying to get away from his rabid sister.

Melinda tore after him. Victoria tried to regain her footing but went down on her other knee. When her hand reached the pavement, she heard the snap of her wrist bones breaking. Searing pain radiated up her arm. Looking up from the curb, Victoria saw Gregory frantically trying to unlock the door.

Melinda charged up the ice-coated steps after Gregory. Martin, whose thin-soled shoes had little traction on the icy pavement, tried to catch up with her.

Gregory lurched to the left to avoid Melinda, as she tried to wrench the key out of his hand, but his right foot slid on the ice and he fell over backwards, smacking his head on the top step. Stunned, he careened down the steps feet-first, but at the bottom step his body cartwheeled around, cracking the left side of his head violently against the point of the granite threshold.

Unable to get up from her fall, Victoria saw it all unfold as if in slow motion. Cradling her broken wrist in her left arm, she scrambled to her feet and minced her way to where Gregory lay lifeless, blood oozing from his ear and his nose.

"Oh my God!" Victoria cried. "Oh my God! No, please, no. Not my

Gregory. Oh my God. Oh my God." Victoria cradled Gregory in her good arm and rocked him, wailing, "Gregory, Gregory."

Victoria looked up the steps at Melinda, who was staring back down at the carnage. "You!" Victoria hissed. "What did you do to my Gregory?"

It took all of Martin's strength to restrain Victoria from going after Melinda, who fled into the frigid night.

"Call the police! Call an ambulance! Call an ambulance!" Victoria pleaded. "Call an ambulance, call an ambulance," she continued, until the sounds came out as throaty whispers.

34

Jonas looked expectantly at Jennie, while Pete and Beth Bodenheim, hosting Thanksgiving at their Old Greenwich, Connecticut, home, sat contentedly at the head and foot of the table. A pair of college-aged girls served coffee and soufflés. Beth Bodenheim had just delivered a light-hearted tribute to life in the locker room with Pete and their two sons, and it was Jennie's turn to reflect on what she was thankful for.

Jennie paused thoughtfully. She put her hands on her children's shoulders. "I give thanks every day for my husband and children. Without them, I would not be the woman you see today. Gracie, your kindness has always delighted me. Gil, I marvel at your solidity and self-discipline. Before you two, I never appreciated how much of a privilege it is to be a mother. Raising you has been a chance to grow up all over again. Seeing the world through your eyes as you've developed has been an amazing journey. The little things: the way Gracie changes the pictures on her wall to mirror the coming and going of the seasons; the sensitivity Gil shows by lowering the volume of his bass when Dad comes home, even when he's working on a new song;

how he always calls home when he knows we might worry about him. While other children are sullen and self-consumed, Gracie and Gil never take their families and friends for granted. You've made me into a kinder, more forgiving person. I never think about what I don't have or what I didn't get when I was growing up. You're such a joy. I want you to know how much I wanted you both. I give thanks for you every day."

I try so hard to feel like she does, Jonas thought, wondering if it had to do with his children being adopted. *Why don't I?*

Jonas's cell phone began vibrating. He excused himself to answer it. The call originated from area code 215. Jonas had given his number to only one person in that area code, Victoria Schone-Braun, but it was not her calling.

He meandered into a corner of the Bodenheim's family room, and said, "This is Dr. Speller. Can I help you?"

A frantic man's voice exclaimed, "Dr. Speller, I'm so glad it's you. My wife said to call you. I know it's a holiday, but it may be a matter of life and death."

Jonas's throat tightened. "You're Martin, aren't you? Victoria's husband? What's happened?"

"It's unbelievable. Victoria's in the ambulance with our son Gregory. They're taking him to Children's Hospital. I think he's dea . . . "

"Oh my God, no," Jonas cried loudly enough to hush everyone. He retreated into Pete's den and closed the door. "What happened? What's Gregory's condition?" Someone knocked tentatively on the door. Jonas said, "Don't go away, Martin. I'm at dinner."

It was Jennie at the door. She said, "My God, Jonas. Your face is the same color as your shirt. What's happened?"

"My patient's family just suffered a catastrophe. The child of someone I saw on Monday is in critical condition. I have to figure out what to do. Tell everyone I'll be back in as soon as I can."

Jennie squeezed his hand. "It'll be all right."

He tried to believe her.

Martin said, "I'm so sorry to disturb your holiday."

Jonas ran his hands through his hair, preparing himself for a very long night. "It's okay. Tell me what happened to Gregory."

"It's his head. We both saw the fall. He slipped down our cement steps and cracked his skull against the pavement. I'm no doctor, but I think he's hurt very badly. He's out cold. When the EMTs got him into the ambulance, they said that his breathing was irregular and his heart rate was slowing down. They also said his left pupil was much larger than the right."

Oh no, thought Jonas, who knew that bleeding inside the skull causes downward pressure on the base of the brain—the part called the brain stem—which regulates breathing, blood pressure, and heart rate. Brain stem compression traps the nerve that controls dilation and contraction of the pupils, which would account for what the EMTs said about Gregory's eyes.

Martin continued, "I don't know what it's like where you are, but we've just had a slush storm, and everything turned to ice when the temperature turned bitter."

Jonas looked around. Everywhere, he saw pictures of Pete, Beth, and their children. He said, "Did this have to do with Melinda?"

"Yes. On the way home from Thanksgiving at my parents', she got out of control with Gregory and attacked him like a maniac. We barely got home in one piece. Our front steps were solid ice. When Melinda charged after Gregory, he fell down and slammed his head. Then Melinda ran away. The police are looking for her now. God knows what she'll do if she thinks her brother's dea—" Jonas shuddered. "Melinda knows how close Victoria is to Gregory. If he dies . . . she knows her mother will never forgive her. Melinda could do something desperate."

Jonas had to breathe deeply to keep from vomiting. "Goddammit," he said. "I was afraid something like this would happen. How's Victoria?"

"I think she broke her wrist falling on the ice. She moaned on and on about Gregory, and then she started talking mechanically until the ambulance headed off for Children's Hospital."

"She's overwhelmed."

"What are they going to do at the hospital?" Martin said.

"First they'll secure Gregory's airway by inserting a breathing tube—the EMTs may have done that already—but even if they did, the hospital will want to make sure it's positioned properly. Then they'll try and stabilize his heart rate and blood pressure, and rate the depth of the coma. They'll want a CT scan of his head right away to check for bleeding and assess the swelling. Swelling is the real enemy in head injuries." Jonas felt confident that practice with head trauma in Philadelphia had kept pace with the latest techniques used in New York.

Martin said, "Excuse me, the police just pulled up. A policewoman is asking about Melinda."

"She'll get frostbite and hypothermia if we don't find her," Jonas said.

Martin said, "Please call Victoria. She begged me to put you in touch with her. Do you have her cell phone number?"

"Yes, I do."

"She may have some life-and-death decisions to make in the next hour. I know it's a holiday, but please do what you can. She trusts you with her life."

Jonas was glad he hadn't had much wine, knowing he needed a clear head. He called Victoria.

"Hello, Martin?" her voice resounded after the first ring.

Jonas shot up from the chair. "No, it's Jonas. Martin just called. Have you gotten to the hospital yet?"

"No. The roads are caked with ice. It's taking forever."

"Did they put in a breathing tube yet?"

"Yes. He may have stopped breathing. I can't tell. They also put a brace around his head." Jonas heard Victoria talking to an EMT. She sounded detached, just as Martin had described.

Jonas said, "The brace is just a precaution in case he hurt his neck—that's unlikely, given what Martin described. Gregory's probably hooked up to a heart monitor. It looks like a mini-TV with green blips. Can you see if the blips have a regular rhythm? Do they all look the same?"

"I can't tell."

"Give the EMT your phone."

"What?"

"Just do it, Victoria."

Jonas heard the phone hit something. An angry voice said, "Who's this? We're busy trying to save this boy's life here."

"This is Dr. Jonas Speller. I'm the boy's mother's doctor. Has he stopped breathing?"

"We're not sure. He's intubated and we're bagging him."

"Is his heartbeat steady?"

"It's slowing."

"What about his blood pressure?"

"It's going up and down. We're not sure we're getting an accurate read."

"And his pupils?"

"The left is barely responding."

"Okay. Do you have mannitol?"

"We're just starting to administer it."

"Good. He probably has a bleed that needs to be evacuated. We may have only one chance to save this boy's life, so listen carefully. Children's Hospital has a pediatric neurosurgeon on call. Radio ahead and get him and his team ready. Every second counts. Have him call me on my cell phone the instant you get in touch with him." Jonas gave his number. "When you radio in, do you talk with triage, or do you speak with the ER doctors directly?"

"We've already notified the trauma team."

It's a teaching hospital, Jonas thought. *It's a holiday. What if there are only residents and interns on duty tonight? God help us if we get some arrogant know-it-all who doesn't respect his elders.*

Jonas asked the EMTs to have the neurosurgeon call. Then he asked him to hand the phone back to Victoria. He told her, "I'm trying to get the neurosurgeon on the line."

"Neurosurgeon. What do we need a surgeon for?" she asked, terror returning to her voice.

"You're going to have to trust us, Victoria. That's all I can say for now. I have to speak with the doctor, and I'll get back to you the minute I do."

35

For the next ten minutes, Jonas paced around Pete Bodenheim's den, feeling as though his own son was en route to the hospital. The Connecticut weather had turned frigid, but the ice storm had not advanced that far north. He hoped the turnpike remained passable to Philadelphia. In good weather with no traffic, he could be there in two and a half hours. With icy roads, who knew how long it would take? Using Pete's computer, Jonas checked the National Weather Service. No updates had been posted.

His phone rang. "This is Dr. Speller," he said.

"This is Dr. Anna Breckenridge, pediatric neurosurgery fellow at Children's Hospital. I was told to call this number." She sounded neither irritated nor arrogant.

Jonas said, "Who's your attending?"

"Dr. Liddle, Larsen Liddle. Please, who am I speaking with?"

Larsen Liddle. Just like Stan Amernick had mentioned to Jonas years ago. What a small world Philadelphia was.

"I'm sorry, Dr. Breckenridge. I should have introduced myself. My name is Dr. Jonas Speller, and I'm Professor of Clinical Psychiatry and Neurology at Mount Sinai Medical School in New York. One of my patient's children—her ten-year-old son—is coming your way any minute. He's had a horrible closed-head injury; his left pupil is blown and his vitals are deteriorating."

"How do you know that?"

"I just got off the phone with the EMTs in the ambulance."

"Are there any other injuries?"

"Not that we know of. The boy's mother is with him. She's been a patient of mine for years. Gregory, that's the boy's name, is intubated. I hope you don't mind my asking, but what's your protocol for severe head trauma?"

"We use the standard trauma life support protocol. The trauma team will be ready the moment he arrives. They'll examine him for internal injuries and make sure he didn't break any bones. While they're stabilizing his vital signs, I'll examine his cranial nerves and use the Glasgow Coma Scale to assess his neurological status."

"Excellent."

"Did the EMTs say anything about the boy's blood pressure?"

"They were having trouble measuring it. Why?"

"Low blood pressure in the field is a bad sign."

"I'll make sure they stay on top of it," Jonas said. "Is there anything else I should tell them?"

"See if they can administer mannitol."

"They already started."

"That's good," Dr. Breckenridge said. "Once the boy gets here, the trauma team will X-ray his cervical spine. Then we'll go straight to CT, where we'll look for a bleed, determine the extent of the swelling, and see if there's any midline shift or hydrocephalus."

Jonas held his breath. His palms felt clammy. "Do you do craniectomies? Hemi craniectomies, I mean?"

"Yes, if we have to."

"Good. What do you do with the skull?"

"We used to implant it in the patient's abdomen. Now we put it in a freezer, so there's no need for another incision."

"Good. That's what we do here, too. Mount Sinai gets all the bicycle, skateboard, and rollerblade accidents from Riverside and Central Parks. Plus the motorcyclists who're too macho to wear helmets. I hoped you weren't still relying solely on mannitol, or hyperventilation, or cold perfusion."

"We do give mannitol or hypertonic saline acutely, which is why I want the EMTs to start now. But the definitive treatment is to remove the blood, if the swelling is severe enough, we leave the bone flap off. We try and avoid hyperventilation. We gave up on cooling a while ago."

"Do you do a CT scan on every patient, even when their vitals are deteriorating?"

"It only takes a few minutes. From what you're saying, most likely there's blood on the same side as the blown pupil. But since we're not sure, we should know how much and where. If there's no bleed, we can put in an ICP to monitor the pressure. But from what you said, it sounds like we'll have to open the skull."

"That makes sense. You're going to have a tough time getting the mother to consent to the procedure. That's where I come in. Let me handle Gregory's mother. You've done this operation before, Dr. Breckenridge? I mean you, personally."

"I've assisted at several in the last year. Children's Hospital is the regional trauma center, so we get head injuries from all over the Tri-State Area. As soon as I get off the line, I'll call Dr. Liddle and tell him what's happening. From what I hear, the roads are bad. I don't know how soon he'll be able to get here, but I don't want to wait. This would be my first unsupervised as the chief surgeon, but I've opened the skull innumerable times for brain tumors, aneurisms, and vascular malformations."

Jonas had no time to quibble about her qualifications. Gregory would be in her hands. Dr. Liddle would get there as soon as he could, but no one could say when.

"I know you'll do just fine, Dr. Breckenridge," Jonas said. "Gregory's fortunate to be in such good hands. I know you'll take good care of him."

"I will, I promise. Thanks for the heads up and the vote of confidence."

36

Just as the ambulance was pulling up to the emergency room, Victoria's phone rang. She put it to her ear but she was too overwhelmed to speak.

"Victoria?" Jonas said. "It's me. Are you still in the ambulance?"

"No, we just arrived at the hospital. They must have known we were coming because everyone dashed out the minute we pulled in. There's a lady in blue pants and a white coat sprinting toward us. What's going on?"

"Listen to me, Victoria. That's probably Dr. Anna Breckenridge. She's an experienced neurosurgeon. We don't have time to wait for the attending. It could take hours for him to get to the hospital in the storm, and that's too long."

A passel of aides and nurses whisked Gregory through three sets of automatic doors into the trauma bay, where the team was ready to take over. A woman in civilian clothes carrying a clipboard intercepted Victoria as the trauma bay doors closed.

"They closed the doors," Victoria said, shocked at how fast the doctors had taken control of Gregory.

Jonas said, "They have to get a CT scan of Gregory's head. We suspect there's been a leakage of blood that's increasing the pressure inside Gregory's head. Pressure, that's the enemy. The skull is like a rigid box. It's not like your skin that can expand when there's bleeding or a bad bruise. Imagine a water balloon inside Gregory's skull: If you press on the top the bottom bulges. That's what's happening inside his head—the pressure has nowhere to go except downward to the base of the skull, at the brain stem. That's the area that regulates blood pressure, breathing, and heart rate. Unless we relieve the brain-stem pressure, Gregory's heart will stop. Or, just as bad, the increased pressure will choke off the arteries and keep blood and oxygen from nourishing his brain, which will cause a massive stroke."

"Oh my God! You mean he could wind up . . . ?"

"That's what they're trying to prevent."

A bright light from inside the trauma bay drew Victoria's attention to the door's window. "Wait a second. They just turned on a giant overhead light. My God. There must be eight or ten people in there. Jesus! They're poring all over him."

"That's right," Jonas said. "They have to make sure he's getting enough oxygen and that his circulation is okay."

"The doctor in the blue pants is rubbing his chest and shining her penlight into Gregory's eyes."

"That's right," Jonas said. "She's rating the depth of the coma and she's checking his brain-stem reflexes, trying to assess how bad the brain is injured. That's exactly what she should be doing."

"She's coming out of the room. She wants to talk with me."

"Fine. Talk with the doctor, Victoria. Make sure she knows I'm listening. Tell her to speak up so I can hear."

A minute later, the doctor spoke. "I'm Dr. Anna Breckenridge. I'm covering pediatric neurosurgery this weekend. I've been in touch with Dr. Speller. We don't have a lot of time to discuss options now, Mrs. . . . . Mrs. . . . . ?"

"Braun. Victoria Schone-Braun. Dr. Speller is listening." Victoria pointed at her cell phone. "I want him to hear what you say. He's already explained the pressure issue. What can you do about it?"

"Based on the history and my examination, I think the fall ruptured a blood vessel on the left side of your son's brain," she said, pointing to a spot midway between her temple and the crown of her head. "If it's what I think it is, he'll need an operation."

"An operation! Did you hear that, Jonas?"

"Yes, I did, Victoria," he said.

"What kind of operation?" Victoria asked Dr. Breckenridge.

Dr. Breckenridge said, "It's too early to tell. We'll know more after the CT scan. That's the best test to look for bleeding and skull fractures. I'm leaving for the radiology scan suite now; it's on the third floor." She pointed to the woman with the clipboard, who had been at Victoria's side all along. "This is Mrs. Siskind, our social worker. She will take you to the radiology waiting room. I'll meet you there in about fifteen minutes." She departed hurriedly, joining several people who were rushing Gregory's gurney past Victoria into an open elevator. One of the people was squeezing an inflatable bag connected to the breathing tube inserted into Gregory's throat.

Chilled by the sight of Gregory attended by so many people, Victoria, still on the phone, said, "I don't believe this, Jonas. She's talking about an operation. Are they serious?"

Jonas said, "I'm sure they won't do anything unnecessary. You better hang up now and get to radiology. Call me after Dr. Breckenridge gives you the results of the CT scan."

Mrs. Siskind led Victoria into a different elevator, which took them to a small waiting room on the third floor. "I know how upsetting this must be, Mrs. Braun," the woman said in a consoling voice. "But we do this all the time. There's no better hands your son could be in than the neurosurgery team at Children's Hospital."

Not long after, Dr. Breckenridge entered the waiting room. "Good. You're here," she said to Victoria. "Mrs. Braun, the scan confirmed my diagnosis. There is a considerable amount of blood inside Gregory's skull under what we call the dura mater, the tough membrane between the brain and the skull. The medical term is subdural hematoma. I can't be one hundred percent certain if the bleeding has stopped completely, but either way we must operate immediately to relieve the pressure.

"There is a good chance we will have to do what is called a hemicraniectomy. It's a relatively new procedure, Mrs. Braun. But it works dramatically well. It's the best chance your son has to escape devastating consequences from traumatic brain injury. Gregory has unmistakable signs and symptoms of brain-stem compression because of increased intracranial pressure."

"Procedure? What's involved here?"

"First, we shave Gregory's head. Then we make a large, question-mark-shaped incision and elevate your son's scalp and muscle off of his skull. Then we remove a large piece of the skull, and we evacuate the blood clot and make sure the bleeding is stopped. We keep the piece of bone sterile and place it in a freezer. With the bone off, the brain can swell against the soft and pliable scalp tissue, which we sew over to protect the brain from infection. When the brain swelling goes down we reattach the skull, but that can take weeks, even months."

"You must be out of your mind!" Victoria said. "You want to remove my son's skull?"

"I wish I had more time to explain, but we can't wait. Increased pressure keeps blood from flowing into your son's brain, and that means anoxia—not getting enough oxygen—which causes brain-cell death."

"I know. Dr. Speller explained it to me. This isn't some kind of experimental procedure, is it? Gregory's not going to be a guinea pig, is he?"

"Oh no, Mrs. Braun, I can assure you this procedure is the state-of-the-art treatment for life-threatening closed-head injuries."

"Life-threatening?"

"Here, let me show you. Follow me." Dr. Breckenridge conducted Victoria through a doorway into a crowded, windowless space that looked like a war room. The walls ahead and to the left contained light-boxes, computer screens, and X-ray equipment. Through the glass wall on the right, Victoria saw several people transferring Gregory from the CT machine back onto his gurney.

"Quiet, everybody," Dr. Breckenridge spoke up, stilling the crush of doctors and technicians scurrying about. "This is Gregory's mother. Make room so I can show her the scan."

Dr. Breckenridge led Victoria to the main screen and pointed to a large glob of white inside the outline of a skull. "See this, Mrs. Braun? That's the blood clot inside Gregory's brain." Dr. Breckenridge enlarged the image and pointed to what looked like an inward-jutting jagged rock surrounded by a thin line. Everyone huddled closer so they could see and hear.

"This is where the skull is indented," Dr. Breckenridge said. "See how the white from inside traverses the line? That tells me that the blood is under pressure, probably from a ruptured artery on the surface of the brain. We have to get in there now, not only to evacuate the clot but to identify and cauterize the artery. Otherwise, it will start spurting once the pressure is reduced."

Dr. Breckenridge ushered Victoria back into the waiting area and said, "Wait here with Mrs. Siskind. I have to go back inside for a moment. Would you like to call your husband now?"

"I'll call my doctor first."

"Fine," she said, as she left waiting room.

Victoria called Jonas, who picked up immediately. "Victoria?" he said.

"I don't believe this, Jonas. They want to operate. Gregory was just riding the banister with his cousins. He just stuck up for his sister. It was only an hour ago, and now they're talking about taking out part of Gregory's skull. Can this really be happening?"

"The operation is the best option for acute traumatic brain injury," Jonas said. "We've been doing the same procedure at Mount Sinai. It's particularly effective in children. There's been a flurry of case studies from all over the world, and every patient got better. Every patient. Dr. Breckinridge assures me it's done routinely at Children's Hospital. She doesn't strike me as scalpel-happy. Listen to her."

"Are you sure?"

"As sure as anyone can be. The older, more conservative therapies don't work well, especially when there's a lot of swelling. It's the pressure, Victoria. Remember that. The operation reduces the pressure immediately. The earlier that happens, the better the results."

"Jesus, Jonas. You want me to put Gregory's life in the hands of this doctor? She looks like a kid."

"Victoria, opening up the skull is something neurosurgeons do all the time. She's had plenty of experience, and it's the only chance for Gregory to come out unscathed. You've got to give your consent to the operation, Victoria."

"You mean he could wind up . . . ?"

"Permanently brain-damaged. That's right."

"Like those children who spend their lives in wheelchairs with horrible impairments?"

"That's right," Jonas said.

"My God, you're telling me this could happen to my Gregory?"

"Yes, Victoria. It's what we're fighting against."

"No. Not my Gregory. Not my Gregory," she cried.

"Trust this doctor, Victoria. We don't have much time. Now, I have to get back to Martin about Melinda. I have to get hold of Milroy, too. We'll need him to deal with her."

Victoria's hair stood on end. "Melinda. What about her?"

"She's missing. The last I heard, the police were mobilizing a search. As soon as Melinda is located, if exposure hasn't lowered her body temperature, I want her brought to wherever Milroy can get her a bed. I'm leaving for Philadelphia now."

"You're coming here? Why?"

"I'm not sure why, but something tells me you might need me."

"What should I do until then?"

"Trust the doctor. Give her permission to operate. It's the right thing. I'm going to hang up now and get going. I'll try and call from the road. I'll see you as soon as I can. Okay?"

The line went quiet.

"Okay?" Jonas repeated

Victoria could hardly speak.

"Victoria? Are you still there?" Jonas asked.

"Yes," she managed weakly before saying good-bye.

Dr. Breckenridge returned to the waiting room with a white-jacketed young man who handed Victoria a manila folder.

She said, "I know this is hard for you, Mrs. Braun, but I need you to sign this consent form so we can operate. I also need to know when Gregory last ate and if he has any medical problems or bleeding problems. We also need to know if he takes any medications. It makes a difference in the anesthesia."

Victoria looked at her watch. "He had dessert at my in-laws' two hours ago. Are you sure about this . . . ?"

Dr. Breckenridge looked Victoria in the eyes and said, "If we don't operate now, your son's heart will surely stop within the next half hour."

"Do you have any children?"

"No. But I hope to someday."

"Do you have family?"

"I have two younger brothers. I always looked out for them when I was younger. I still do."

"Can you save my son's life?" Victoria asked, tears streaming from her eyes.

"I'll try. I promise you, I'll do everything in my power to keep Gregory alive."

"Where do I sign?" Victoria said. Dr. Breckenridge indicated where to sign and initial.

Dr. Breckenridge said, "I wish we had more time, Mrs. Braun, but I have to get to the OR and scrub up." Pointing to the young man at her side, she said, "This is Dr. Jonathan Bell. He's a first-year resident; he'll explain everything."

"Please. Please save my son."

Dr. Breckenridge touched Victoria's good arm lightly. "Someone will talk with you as soon as we know anything," she said.

Dr. Breckenridge left hastily, then reappeared with the trauma team, who whisked Gregory's gurney past Victoria on the way to the elevator.

Victoria barely had time to squeeze Gregory's hand and kiss his pale cheek.

"Is anesthesia ready?" Dr. Breckenridge asked someone.

"They'll be waiting when the elevator opens on the fourth floor," an intern replied.

"I want four pints typed and cross-matched, in case there's rebleeding once I remove the clot."

"Already done."

"Good. Let's go, let's go," the doctor commanded, as they wheeled Gregory into the elevator.

Once inside, Dr. Breckenridge turned to Dr. Bell, "As soon as you're done with the consent form, get to the OR and scrub in. I'm going to need you."

As the elevator doors closed, the bottom fell out of her stomach. Victoria wondered if she would ever see her Gregory again.

37

Jonas apologized to the Bodenheims for departing abruptly. He hugged his wife and children tightly after Eddie reassured him that he and Margo would transport everyone home safely.

At the door, Eddie said quietly, "It's *her* again, isn't it? Miss Abington. I knew you two weren't done with each other."

"Not now," said Jonas, slipping on his coat and gloves. "I don't have time to argue with you. Think what you like. I have to go."

Jonas set out for Philadelphia, glad he had driven the four-wheel-drive SUV to the Bodenheims. On the way, he phoned Rob Milroy's answering service and left his number. Then he called Martin.

"Hold on one second, Dr. Speller," Martin said. "I'm talking with Inspector Ruby Pale. She's in charge of the investigation. This whole nightmare is turning surreal; Melinda might be charged with assault and battery. God knows what kind of trouble she'll be in if Gregory doesn't make it." He, too, sounded dissociated.

The stress these people are under with their children, Jonas thought as he drove across the George Washington Bridge. From the middle of the span, he saw New York's skyline to his left; it looked so incongruously peaceful compared to the mayhem occurring only ninety miles to the south.

"I'm back," Martin said. "Inspector Pale has some more questions."

"I'm on my way to Philadelphia," Jonas said. "Hopefully Dr. Milroy will call back soon. Would you mind putting your phone on speaker, so I can hear what you and the inspector are saying?"

Straining to hear every syllable, Jonas heard Martin say, "Inspector Pale, there's a doctor named Jonas Speller on the other end of the line. I want him to listen in. Is that okay?"

"That's fine," the inspector said curtly. "Is your daughter athletic? Is she in good physical condition?"

"She used to ice skate competitively. Up until this past summer, she played tennis and ran regularly."

"A runner, eh? Were there any favorite routes she'd take?"

"That's very clever, Inspector Pale," Martin said. "Melinda liked to run past the museum onto Kelly Drive. She was wearing sneakers tonight. Do you think that's where she might have gone? She hasn't been there for months."

"People under stress tend to revert to old patterns. The cold won't bother her until her adrenaline wears off."

"That's exactly right," Jonas broke in as he negotiated the maze of ramps connecting the bridge with the Jersey Turnpike.

Inspector Pale continued, "Then she'll feel spent, like a marathoner hitting the wall. She's already desperate. I just don't like her being so close to the water. As her body temperature goes down, she'll become uncoordinated, then lethargic. Especially in these slippery conditions, she could fall in. Does she have any favorite places in the park?"

"She likes the view of the bridges from the river. She knows all their names."

"Good. That's a start. Let's concentrate on Kelly Drive. I'll radio in a description. We'll post squad cars on the bridges."

"On the bridges?" Martin exclaimed.

"They're right to do that," Jonas said. "She could become suicidal."

"How long ago did she take off?" Inspector Pale said.

Martin said, "About an hour, give or take a few minutes."

Jonas's cell phone buzzed. He said, "Martin and Inspector Pale, I have to stop to talk to the doctor who'll be taking care of Melinda. I'll jump back in when he and I are done."

He toggled to Dr. Milroy's call. "Rob, is that you?"

"Yes, Jonas," Milroy said. "I hope this isn't about the Braun girl."

"It is, and unfortunately it couldn't be much worse." Jonas accelerated to seventy-five miles per hour. "Melinda had a meltdown at Thanksgiving dinner. On the way home, she and her brother got into a fight, and the boy wound up cracking his head on the pavement in front of their house. He's in critical condition at CHOP, undergoing surgery to relieve intracranial pressure. There's brain-stem involvement, and his vital signs were deteriorating quickly. I've already spoken to the neurosurgeon who's operating. They're probably going to do a hemi-craniectomy. We won't know much for several hours."

"And Melinda?"

"Melinda ran off into the frigid night. The police are searching for her, but the inspector in charge of finding Melinda sounds very sharp. Melinda's in all kinds of trouble, legal and emotional, and I fear the worst unless someone can talk her down before she does something impulsive. Mania and hypothermia are a deadly combination. I know you've only met her through her parents' eyes, but I think you should hook up with her father and the police trying to track her down. You could be instrumental."

"Goddammit!" Rob exclaimed. "Goddammit. What was I thinking? What made me think we could wait until Monday?"

"This isn't the time for hindsight, Rob. You did what you thought was right. Most likely, I would have done the same thing. It doesn't matter now. The girl's missing, and we have to act fast."

"I'll do everything I can. What's the boy's prognosis? When we find Melinda, she's going to want to know how her brother is."

"It's too early to tell, Rob. I'll know more after I talk with the neurosurgeon. I'm in touch with Gregory's mother. He won't be out of surgery for several hours. Right now, I'm on the road to Philadelphia."

"Just so you know, the roads are caked with frozen slush."

"I know. I've got Martin on the other line. He's with the police inspector looking for Melinda. They're concentrating around the Art Museum, along the river where she used to run."

"I don't know how anyone could run given what's on the ground tonight. It's bitter cold outside, and the wind is howling."

"That's why we have to get to her soon. Her thinking will only deteriorate as she gets hypothermic. Right now, I've got to get back to Martin. I'll probably see you in a couple of hours. I wish the circumstances were different."

"Me, too. Look out for black ice as you get closer, okay?"

"I promise," Jonas said. He switched back to Martin and Inspector Pale.

He heard Martin telling her, "My father, Charles, calmed her down during dinner. She feels he likes her."

The inspector said, "Good. Please call him and see if he'll join us. It'll be good to have someone along who Melinda trusts."

"Of course."

"Have you heard about your son?" Inspector Pale said.

Martin said, "Nothing yet, but Dr. Speller said the doctors at CHOP are operating now. He's in very critical condition."

The word "critical" made Jonas's stomach heave; he pictured Dr. Breckenridge opening Gregory's skull with a rotary power saw.

"Children's Hospital's is as good as it gets. I'm sure they're doing everything they can," the inspector said. "Let's get on with finding Melinda."

"Hold on just a minute, Dr. Speller." Martin said. "I'm going inside to put on warmer clothes."

Jonas heard Martin's footsteps on a wooden floor. After a few seconds, Martin said, "I'm back. Are you still there?"

"I'm here. You just reminded me of something," Jonas said to Martin. "Can you find me some warm things for Victoria? She might need them. Maybe something for my feet? I left right from dinner and didn't have time to get warm clothes."

"I'll put them inside our vestibule, and I'll leave a key under the vase on the top step." Martin gave him the address.

Jonas said, "Dr. Milroy's coming to join the search. I gave him your number. I'll get into warm clothes at your place and then drive to CHOP to see Victoria before joining the search for Melinda."

* * *

An hour later, Jonas's phone rang. The caller ID read Edward Speller. Jonas said, "Eddie, are Jennie and the children okay?"

"Yes, I dropped them off back home. It was crowded, but we all made it. What the hell are you doing, Jonas?"

"You wouldn't understand," Jonas said, sipping sludgy cold coffee from a travel mug. "So don't pull your stern father routine on me. I have no choice. She could lose both her children on the same night. One's at death's door in the operating room; the other ran off into the night and is probably suicidal."

"You don't get this involved with any other patient or their family. I hear the roads are treacherous. Jesus, Jonas! Think of your wife. Think of your family."

Jonas gripped the steering wheel, scanning the roadway for black ice.

"Don't tell me what I should or shouldn't feel for Jennie and our children, Eddie. I could list fifteen reasons why I'm on the road right now, but I don't need to justify myself to you or anyone. It's about what I feel. And where I belong right now. It's about who I am."

"What is that supposed to mean?"

"I'm her doctor, for Christ's sake."

"We both know you're more than that."

"So what? I'm doing what I have to do. Let's leave it at that. Okay?"

"You're not being objective."

"You're wrong, Eddie. I am. She needs me. They both do. Her *and* her husband; I haven't lost sight of him. Besides, you don't know the half of it. There's a young neurosurgeon in the operating room right this minute battling to save their ten-year-old boy's life. Their daughter's gone AWOL into this frigid night, and we're all scared to death she'll become hypothermic and frostbitten, that is unless she kills herself first. So, let's postpone the lecture about right and wrong until next semester."

"Why do you feel so responsible?"

Jonas decelerated as the three lanes of the turnpike merged into two, past the exit for the Pennsylvania Turnpike. "I'm not responsible for what happened. But I might have a say in what's *going* to happen. My instinct says they need me, and I learned a long time ago to trust my instinct. It's the same instinct that serves you well when I'm on the stand under pressure. Stop and think about that."

"You said she came back into your life on Monday. Are you having an aff—?"

"What the fuck is that supposed to mean?" Jonas said. "Since when is that your business? And the answer is *No* with a capital N."

"All right, all right. Just drive safely. You're driving into an ice rink. The black ice could sneak up on you any second."

"The psychiatrist working with the family said the same thing."

"Don't break Jennie's heart. You hear me? She'd never get over it. And neither would I."

"Why do you always have to get in the last word. Eddie? Can't you just leave it alone? Why not say you're proud of me for doing the right thing?"

"Okay, I'm sorry, but please be careful tonight. Call me when you know anything. I don't care what time it is. Do you want me to call Jennie?"

"I'll call her when I can."

Jonas drove on. The northbound lanes of the turnpike were eerily empty. Thirty miles from Camden, ice crystals began sprinkling the windshield, lighting up in the headlights like swarms of moths. He slowed down instinctively. Wanting the solace of familiar music, he inserted the remastered Arthur Rubenstein edition of Chopin's Mazurkas and Polonaises into the CD player. He felt himself sinking back in time and place, beckoned by some ill-defined sense of unfinished business.

38

Victoria had been pacing the waiting room for two hours; its characterless décor reminded her of a motel lobby. The nauseating pungency of hospital disinfectant permeated the entire floor. Just after 11:00 PM, an older gentleman in a white coat over hospital scrubs glided gracefully toward her. He had long, perfectly manicured fingers. He reached for Victoria's hand, then winced when he saw her contorted wrist.

"Look at your wrist," he said with alarm. "You should have this taken care of right away. Your fingers are turning blue."

Victoria looked at her discolored hand as if it belonged to someone else. "I'll get to it when I can."

"Please don't wait much longer." He motioned her to sit down.

"You must be the boy's, I mean Gregory's, mother." He sat down a comfortable distance away. "Mrs . . . ?"

"Mrs. Braun. Victoria Schone-Braun. You are—?"

"Dr. Liddle. Larsen Liddle, chairman of the Children's Hospital of Philadelphia's Division of Pediatric Neurosurgery. Anna Breckenridge is my fellow. She called me when Gregory arrived at the hospital. I agreed with her decision to operate without delay. I'd have gotten here sooner, but the roads were impassable. I had to wait for the highway department to send a salt truck. I've been in the OR with Dr. Breckenridge for an hour."

"What's going on in there? Is he still alive?" Victoria was terrified that the doctor was going to ask permission to donate her son's organs.

"Given the seriousness of Gregory's injury, it's gone as well as it could. Dr. Breckenridge explained the procedure, didn't she?"

"Yes, she did."

"Gregory's brain is massively swollen, Mrs. Braun. He developed a subdural hematoma—a leakage of blood, which we've evacuated—caused by a depressed skull fracture that ruptured a small artery. Removing the skull gives the swollen tissue room to expand, like opening an eggshell whose contents are about to explode. The good news is that Dr. Breckenridge reduced the pressure and stopped the bleeding as soon as possible. There's no way we could have treated Gregory without surgery. Thankfully, Gregory's vital signs have improved, but there is a long, long way to go before we'll know the outcome."

"How long are you talking about?"

"Weeks. It could even be months. "

"What's happening now?"

"The technically challenging part of the operation is over. No one could have done better than Dr. Breckenridge, and it's a good thing she didn't wait. She reduced the pressure before I got there. There is one thing, however." Dr. Liddle's lips moved silently as if he was rehearsing his next line.

"What's that?"

"We had to remove more skull than we usually do, because the swelling was so extensive. We're sewing the scalp over Gregory's brain to protect against infection. When the swelling goes down, we'll replace the skull and reattach the scalp; somewhere around three weeks from now depending on how things go. The skull was dented and cracked, but not fragmented. The rest of the operation is quite straightforward."

The elevator doors opened, and a maintenance man sporting a tool holster headed down the hall. Hospital business was proceeding as usual. Victoria went from terror to dissociation and back again. "What will happen to Gregory now?" she asked.

"We wait; once he's settled in the pediatric ICU we'll attach an EEG machine to monitor the electrical activity of his brain. We'll know more when we get an MRI, which is better for assessing damage to fine brain tissue; the CT scan we used when he arrived is better when looking for blood or skull fractures. We'll repeat it after the surgery's done. The good news is that Gregory is only ten years old. Young brains are much more resilient than adult brains; youngsters Gregory's age heal better and faster. We've seen children who were in coma for months make remarkable recoveries.

"When Gregory gets out of the OR he'll be taken directly to the intensive care unit on the seventh floor. Now that the clot is out and the bone is off, the pressure is lower. It'll take vigilance, but my team will work diligently with the ICU doctors to manage the pressure. Be prepared, Mrs. Braun. The swelling hasn't peaked yet; that won't be for another two to four days. His face may swell so much that you don't recognize him, but that's to be expected and it will resolve quickly. Over the coming days and weeks we need to watch for infection, hydrocephalus, seizures, and stroke.

"Keep this in mind though, Mrs. Schone. Even though Gregory did great with surgery, he's still critical. He'll be attached to a breathing machine and he will have a drain coming out of his scalp. He's receiving anti-seizure medication as well as concentrated intravenous fluids to keep his minerals in balance and decrease brain swelling. He'll be sedated to keep him from thrashing, but," Dr. Liddle added solemnly, "it remains to be seen when, and even if, he wakes up. Until then, I can assure you he won't be in pain. Once we get the MRI, we'll know more."

"When and if?" Victoria said. "You make it sound like a death sentence."

"I'm sorry. I didn't mean to do that. Anna Breckenridge is the most talented and humane fellow I've had in the last twenty years. She sees three-dimensionally and she has great hands. She really needed them tonight. If Gregory were my child, I'd have wanted her on the case."

On the waiting room wall, a painting of flowers reminded Victoria of her rooftop garden where Gregory sat on her lap while she read him Dr. Seuss. The idea that Gregory might never see her flowers bloom in the coming spring was so overwhelming, she could barely speak.

"Dr. Breckenridge looks so young," Victoria said. "She reminds me of a friend who studied here twenty years ago; she worked on brain imaging. Leslie teaches at the medical school now."

"You don't mean Leslie Kilway, do you?"

"Yes. She's one of my dearest friends."

"Everyone knows Leslie Kilway. Without her research, we wouldn't have the procedure we use to evaluate brain tumors."

"I've known her since college."

"Talk about small world. Image that . . . two degrees of separation," Dr. Liddle smiled. "I'm going back to check on how Anna and the rest of the team are doing. We'll get back to you when we know more." He walked toward the operating room, but after two strides, he turned back abruptly and stared at Victoria.

"What is it?" she said.

"You're part of the Schone and Braun I read about in *Philadelphia Magazine*, aren't you?"

Her mind flashed back to the article, which mentioned how much fear her law firm struck into the hearts of adversaries. "That's just media hype, Dr. Liddle. I'm here as a mother. Don't think for a minute I would ever—" Victoria knew the damage had been done. "Please. Please, Dr. Liddle, just save my little boy. He's so special. He's so smart and compassionate. My doctor already explained how pressure damages the brain. Please do what you can to give him back to me. I won't blame you if—"

"Let's hope it turns out well. The body is resilient, especially in young boys and girls."

"I know. My doctor told me."

"Your doctor? Your neurologist? Or your GP?"

"No. My psychiatrist."

"Your psychiatrist knows about brain swelling and closed head trauma?"

"Of course he knows. He's teaches at Mount Sinai in New York," Victoria said proudly. "He also lectures on how brain circuitry interfaces with psychiatric disorders. He's been an expert witness in head trauma cases."

"That's impressive. What's his name?"

"Dr. Jonas Speller. He trained at HUP back in the early eighties. I was an undergraduate and he was chief resident in the outpatient department."

Dr. Liddle rolled his sleeves up and sat down closer to Victoria than before. "What a coincidence," he said.

"What is?"

"In 1986, Dr. Speller saved my own son's life. Jock nearly died from a heroin overdose at Cornell. We brought him back to Philadelphia, and Dr. Speller treated both his substance abuse and psychiatric disorders. It's so ironic, isn't it? I felt the same then as you do now. I remember looking at Dr. Speller and saying to myself, 'Look at this fellow; he's just out of residency. How can I put my boy's life in his hands?'"

Dr. Liddle stretched his shoulders. "It's as it should be, Mrs. Braun. Each new generation supplants its elders. Anna's got more natural ability than I ever did. She's a sculptress, you know. For her, neurosurgery is more than a profession; it's a calling. Twenty years from now, Anna will be sitting here with a parent who loves her child as much as we do. I hope I live to see it.

"I'll never forget what Dr. Speller did for my family," Dr. Liddle added. "Even though Jock was over twenty-one, Dr. Speller insisted our whole family be involved in the treatment, which forced me to look at my life and my relationships. I owe Dr. Speller a lot. He was a very special person."

"He still is. He's on his way here right now."

"Maybe I'll get to see him, then. You're very fortunate to have him on your team. I don't know many psychiatrists who would drive all the way from New York on a night like this to be at their patient's side. He must care for you a great deal."

"His support means the world to me," Victoria said.

"We'll do everything possible for Gregory, Mrs. Braun. I'm going back to the OR. One of us will come out to see you once we're done."

39

Alone for the next hour, Victoria kept picturing Gregory hooked to a respirator in a permanent vegetative state. She seesawed between helplessness and dissociation until her cell phone rang at midnight.

"Who is it?"

"It's me," Jonas said.

"I'm falling apart. I can't stop these awful thoughts. Where are you?"

"I'm in your house, changing into some boots Martin left for me."

"How was the drive?" Victoria asked.

"The last thirty miles took forever. I got stuck behind every salt truck between Exit 4 and the Ben Franklin Bridge."

"Where's Martin?"

"Martin's with the police searching for Melinda. They're meeting up with his father and Dr. Milroy."

"Charles? What does he have to do with this?"

"Inspector Pale—she's directing the search for Melinda—told us to find someone Melinda trusts. It could be useful when the time comes."

"When what time comes?"

"We're afraid Melinda might act impulsively. It's extremely cold. As her body temperature goes down, her thinking will deteriorate. She'll get clumsy, maybe even stutter. The more people she trusts, the better. I'm coming to the hospital now."

"Dr. Liddle gave me a progress report an hour ago," Victoria said. "He's the senior neurosurgeon. He remembers you, Jonas. He said you saved his son's life. He wants to save Gregory's, too. I could lose him, my Gregory; he might never wake up. Dr. Liddle said as much." The line went silent. "Are you still there?"

"Yes." Jonas sounded shaken. "I'm leaving for CHOP in two minutes. I'll be there as soon as I can."

* * *

As Jonas sat on the foyer steps putting on the boots Martin had left for him, he noticed the hall closet was open. A multi-colored skateboard stood on end, its bottom indented with black streaks, probably from sliding down outdoor handrails; the edges were scratched, no doubt by half-pipes like the ones Jonas had seen on television. A helmet and knee- and elbow pads rested on the top shelf. Gregory's, he surmised.

Next to the skateboard were two pairs of well-worn ice skates: figure and speed skates. A tennis racket and two sealed containers of tennis balls sat on the shelf beside the helmet. Melinda's, no doubt. A vivid image of Victoria's children playing sprang to mind. *How vulnerable these children are*, Jonas thought, followed by an idea he never expected: *Could they have been my children? Victoria's and mine?* Locking the front door behind him, the frozen night jarred him back into the present.

* * *

Slowly, Victoria became aware of the pain in her wrist, and her head-spinning sensation recurred. At 12:15, Jonas stepped off the elevator.

They looked at each other, whereupon she flung her arms around him and buried her head on his shoulder and sobbed. Jonas patted her back tentatively, as if he were comforting someone else's child.

"Someone should have prevented this," Victoria exclaimed. "You weren't there to see my beautiful Gregory lying on the pavement with his skull bashed in. I'll never be able to forget that. Ever."

"We'll deal with it." Jonas looked at Victoria's disheveled hair and terror-stricken eyes, then her broken wrist and cyanotic fingers. "Oh my God, Victoria. What happened to your hand?"

"I think I broke my wrist when I fell. I heard something snap."

"Well, we've got to get this taken care of. Now."

"I can't leave him. I can't."

"You're not leaving him. You said he's in good hands. Dr. Liddle must have said something about getting your wrist taken care of."

"Yes. So what?"

"So what? You have to listen to him. Swelling is preventing the blood from getting to your fingers. Do you want to lose them?"

"It doesn't matter."

"Don't talk that way."

"What way?"

"Like you're giving up. Like you don't care. Not now. They need you."

"Need me?" Victoria said. "My son needs brain surgery. God knows what my daughter needs."

"Well, before anything, your wrist has to be set. That's what *you* need."

"I'm not leaving here."

"Then, we'll go to the emergency room. If you're lucky, it'll turn out to be a simple Colle's fracture. It happens to kids all the time. The ER doctors probably see hundreds a year. If it's not complicated, they can fix it in no time."

"How poetic, a Colle's fracture. I've become a dog. Lassie, come here, girl. Come home."

"That's the Victoria I know. As for Melinda, she needs you. The night's far from over. We're going to the emergency room now. Don't argue."

"You have to make them understand they cannot put me under."

"Suppose you need an operation to save your hand? Be reasonable, Victoria. Please."

"Don't yell at me."

Jonas drew a deep breath. "How about this, then? Let them examine you and tell you what they think. We'll deal with the rest later."

Victoria acquiesced reluctantly. Unsteady on her feet, Jonas supported her on his arm as they walked down the hallway.

The Childrens Hospital emergency department waiting room—a cross between *Sesame Street* and *MASH*—overflowed with a horde of West Philadelphia's and Center City's children who had fallen on the jagged ice. On one side of the room, a chorus of overtired toddlers with broken bones, lacerations, and abrasions screamed continuously. Once one howl ceased, two others took its place. The other side looked as if the Sharks and Jets had called a truce. Bloody bandages, splints, and ice packs appeared everywhere.

Victoria was too dazed and shaken to speak for herself. Jonas explained her situation to an understanding triage nurse, who prevailed on the overworked staff to treat her promptly. After studying the X-ray, the on-call orthopedist diagnosed displaced fractures of Victoria's ulna and radius bones.

"That's what's restricting blood flow to her fingers," the orthopedist explained. "I can try to reset the bones with a closed reduction. The circulation should improve immediately."

"There's no way she will allow you to put her under," Jonas told him.

"That's fine. I'll give you a nerve block, Mrs. Braun, then put you in a cast," the doctor said. "You won't feel anything for an hour or so. Just make sure to see an orthopedist for a follow-up."

While a technician applied Victoria's cast, Jonas returned to the waiting room, where a steady stream of adults were shepherding their young from the treatment area—every child on crutches or in a sling, most wearing fresh casts.

Parents and their children, Jonas mused—a thought that disappeared abruptly when his cell phone rang.

40

"We need to leave now," Jonas said when Victoria rejoined him in the waiting room. "Let's get going."

"Where are we going?"

"I'll explain on the way."

"On the way? On the way to where? I told you I'm not leaving Gregory."

"This is more important. Here, take my arm." Jonas draped the parka he had brought from the Braun house over Victoria's shoulders, and led her firmly through the ER door.

"What is it?" Victoria said. "Where are you taking me?"

A plump secretary ran into the frigid night after Victoria. Sliding to a halt on the icy pavement, she handed Victoria a CD case and said, "You'll need this, Mrs. Braun. It's your X-rays. Your orthopedist will want to see them."

"Thank you," Jonas said to the woman, who retreated backwards into the biting wind. "I'll make sure Martin gets it," he told Victoria. By then, they had reached Jonas's car. "Get in, please."

Jonas revved the engine and put the car in reverse. He said, "Martin called while they were setting your wrist. The inspector was right; Melinda did head for the park. Police dogs found fresh blood where she must have fallen on some ice past Boathouse Row. Fifteen minutes ago, a squad car spotted her on the Strawberry Mansion Bridge. She's perched on top of an observation post overlooking the river. She's convinced Gregory is dead, and she's terrified of what you and the police will do to her. Martin said that when he and Charles approached, Melinda threatened to jump. She believes you'll never forgive her for murdering Gregory. No one can reason with her except you. You have to go to her, Victoria. You're the one person who might get her to change her mind."

"Me? I want to tear her apart! Look what she did to her brother, her own flesh and blood. I could choke her to death with my own bare hands. We should have sent her away to boarding school when we had the chance. Goddamn Martin; he talked me out of it."

Jonas felt like a battlefield surgeon operating on a patient hemorrhaging to death. He put the car in park and said quietly, "Look at me, Victoria. Look at me and focus. How long have we known each other?"

"What are you talking about?"

"How far back do we go?"

"What does that have to do with anything?"

"We knew each other back when we were kids; before we had children. I remember how much you wanted a daughter to love and cherish. Remember that?"

Victoria grimaced. "That was then. I gave birth to a monster." Victoria's eyes darted from Jonas's face to her broken wrist and back. "I should have known better. I hated my mother; now my daughter hates me."

"This is about more than your daughter. This is about your whole family."

"It's falling apart, like me."

"What about Gregory? You love mothering him. Gregory is easy."

"So?"

"Melinda is hard. She's very hard to mother. You know that's true."

"What about it?"

"It's not like you to quit."

"Is that what you think?"

"That's exactly what I think. The you I know doesn't give up. You hated that in your father; then he fought for his life. He battled for his sobriety, like you battled for your sanity in college. We faced it together."

"That was then."

"Think about Melinda, Victoria. Is she that different from you at her age? Angry with the world. Self-absorbed. You needed help."

"It's not the same. I *wanted* help, but I had to do it on my own. My parents never understood how sick I was. Like they cared."

"You're not that kind of parent. You do care. When you came to me for help, you were ill; you weren't bad. You weren't a freak, even though you felt like one in some of your dreams."

"You remember that?"

"I told you I remember everything. Remember when you climbed the swing set? You were fortunate you didn't fall off."

"What if I had?"

"You might have bashed *your* head in. Think about a world without Gregory."

That got Victoria's attention. "So what's your point?" she said.

"This isn't about you, Victoria; it's about Melinda. And even though he's fighting for his life, it's not about Gregory, either. It's come down to this—your daughter's fate rests in your hands."

"I don't want the responsibility."

"It's yours whether you want it or not. It goes with being a parent. She didn't ask to be born, and she didn't ask to be ill."

"Neither did I."

"Well, you were, and you got help. Right now, Melinda is ill, and she's terrified, and she doesn't know what she's doing. She's holding on for dear life, just like you were when you came to me. There had to have been moments when you held her and loved her."

"You don't understand, Jonas. She was so hard to love. I gave her the best I had, and she still wound up hating me."

Jonas looked at his watch, the second hand pulsating like a heartbeat. He took two deep breaths. "Victoria," Jonas said, straining to keep his voice under control. "Believe me, I understand. I remember a mother and daughter I saw for therapy. The woman was one of the most conscientious mothers I ever met, but both she and her daughter had mood disorders. One day right in front of me, the daughter emotionally eviscerated the mother mercilessly, told her she was a selfish bitch; told her that everyone in the family made fun of her behind her back. Every time the daughter stuck the knife in, I saw the mother bleed more. But the mother stayed strong, and a year later, they were friends again. They got help and turned their relationship around. The same can happen with Melinda and you, but she has to survive the night."

"What do you want me to do?"

"You're asking the wrong question."

"Goddammit, Jonas. Just tell me what to do."

"You have to find your love for her, even though right now you're ready to kill her. That's what parents do for their children. Just like a long time ago, you needed me to tell you who I was and what I felt about you."

"The last day."

"You said, 'Do your job.' Remember?"

"I remember."

"And I did it. I did it, because that's what you needed."

"I remember."

Jonas said, "Do it, Victoria. She didn't ask to be born this way. Do your job. Find your love and compassion for her. It's her only chance."

"Do you mean that?"

"Yes, I do. It *is* her only chance. Please, Victoria, it's up to you."

Exhausted, Jonas recalled seeing his son Gil for the first time at the adoption agency. He had longed for a son ever since his father died. When Jennie couldn't conceive, Jonas was devastated. He'd always dreamed of being in the delivery room when his wife gave birth, cutting the umbilical cord as fathers had done for generations.

Victoria was Melinda's lifeline. He was Victoria's. "You can do it. I know you can," Jonas said.

"How much time do we have?"

"I don't know. Every second counts. I brought you some boots. Can you put them on with your good hand?"

"I'll figure it out. Let's go. We'll talk on the way."

41

As Jonas drove to Fairmont Park, Victoria rehearsed what she wanted to say to Melinda. Jonas's presence felt inhibiting, so she muttered to herself, trying to commit the words to memory like she did during trial preparation.

"You're talking to yourself," Jonas said.

"I'm trying to stay focused. I want to believe this whole business with Melinda is only a nightmare. I'm trying to remember the good things."

"Maybe this will help," Jonas said. "How did you feel when you were pregnant? Did you know you were having a girl?"

"We found out at the first ultrasound."

"What was it like when you first saw her heartbeat?"

"I felt detached, like I was in hygiene class."

"And when she was born? When you saw her? What did you think?"

"Honestly? I thought, 'God that hurt. I'm glad it's over with.'"

"You didn't bond with her?"

"You have no idea what the delivery was like. The pain was unbearable. It felt like she clawed my insides into shreds with her fingernails on the way out. I felt so violated."

"You never bonded with her?"

"I tried so hard. The more ferociously I mothered, the more disconnected I felt from her."

"Okay, then. Think of this as your second chance to bond with her."

"A second chance? Really? I never thought of that."

"People don't get many second chances in life," Jonas said. "This is yours and Melinda's."

As Jonas turned onto Lancaster Avenue, one of his rear wheels skidded, and the car fishtailed.

Victoria started. "What was that?"

"It's the ice. I'm going as fast as I can," Jonas said. "That postpartum reaction you had after Melinda was born—it screws up the brain-bonding chemical system."

"I want to do it all over. I know my feelings about Lorraine must be mixed up in this, too. After I learned I was having a girl, I let my mother back into my life. She told me not to take any painkillers during the delivery, that all I needed was natural childbirth classes. After Melinda was born, she bombarded me with advice. 'The baby needs this, the baby needs that.' I didn't know what the hell Melinda needed, but I was sure she wasn't getting it from me. I started doubting myself again."

"Of course. You doubted you could mother a daughter. If I'd been in your life, I would have shaken you by the neck until you realized what was happening."

Victoria swallowed hard. "I was afraid you'd be mad at me for screwing up the hard work we did by letting Lorraine back into my head. That's the real reason I didn't call. It wasn't just the medicine thing."

"I figured there was something else. Upset or not, we would have dealt with it. Either way, we're in it together now." Jonas glanced out the window, craning his neck to see the cross-street signs, which were caked over with ice. "Stay on the lookout," he said. "The directions were to take Lancaster Avenue until Forty-fourth Street, and turn right."

"Okay."

"What was it about mothering that you doubted?"

"I didn't want the pregnancy to end. I knew I wasn't ready to give birth. I just wanted to keep Melinda inside me until I figured things out. By the time I was writhing in pain on the delivery table, it was too late for an epidural. I blamed Martin for not keeping Lorraine out of my head. Everything was screwed up. Melinda and I never recovered."

"That had to affect your relationship with Martin, too."

"That's a whole other story—for another time," Victoria deflected Jonas's observation. "How long until we're there?"

"It depends. We're supposed to make a right on Monument Avenue."

"All I want now is to hold her." Victoria began crying. "That's all I ever wanted to do, but Lorraine said too much holding would spoil her, that she'd never learn to comfort herself."

The streetlights disappeared once Jonas and Victoria entered Fairmont Park, the view turning into one contiguous blur of ice and snow. Drooping tree branches turned the road into a maze of crypt-like passageways, sword-like icicles attacking Jonas's windshield as if he were plowing through a medieval armory. With the headlights no longer reflecting off objects as usual, the contours of the road all but vanished. Jonas slowed to a crawl.

"We must be getting near the bridge," he said. "I see blue and red flashing lights in the distance."

He eased to a stop where two police cruisers had blocked the roadway leading to the Strawberry Mansion Bridge. As he lowered his window, a blast of frigid air pummeled him and Victoria while an officer blinded them with a flashlight.

"This road is closed," the officer announced.

Victoria said, "It's my daughter out there. Her name is Melinda. Please let us through."

The officer said something into his walkie-talkie; the reply sounded unintelligible. He said, "The doctor thinks it would be better if you approached on foot."

"Which doctor?" Jonas asked.

"There's a Dr. Milroy in the car with the girl's father and grandfather."

Victoria said, "Officer, pass me the radio. I need to speak to Dr. Milroy."

"Sorry, ma'am. I can't do that. I need to keep in touch with Inspector Pale and headquarters. You'll have to call on your cell phone."

"How far away is she?" Victoria asked the officer.

"She's in the middle of the bridge, about two hundred feet from here. She's sitting on top of an observation post, facing the water."

Victoria told Jonas, "Call Dr. Milroy on your phone and put it on speaker."

Milroy answered on the first ring.

"Rob. It's Jonas. Victoria and I are at the bridge on western side of the river. Where are you?"

"Exactly opposite you." Dr. Milroy's voice sounded strained.

"Martin?" Victoria said. "Martin, are you there?"

"Yes, I'm here."

"Did you talk with her?"

"When Charles and I got within twenty feet, she told us not to come any closer. I begged her to come to talk things out. She's convinced the police are after her for killing Gregory and that you'll hate her for the rest of her life. She said she'd rather be dead."

Martin continued, "I told her we love her, that Gregory is still alive and that the doctors were operating on him. But Melinda wouldn't hear it. She insisted he was dead; that she saw him lying on the sidewalk. She believes you want her to be tried for murder and that it'll be all over the Internet that Melinda Braun killed her brother."

"Give me the phone, Mr. Braun." Victoria recognized Dr. Milroy's voice.

"That's her grandiosity speaking," Dr. Milroy said. "She thinks the whole world is as caught up in this as she is. When you talk to her, avoid saying 'we' and 'all of us,' which she could misinterpret. Say 'I' or 'your father and me.' And tell the truth about Gregory; she'll know if you're lying."

"Okay," Victoria said. "I'm getting out of the car now."

Jonas said, "Be careful on the ice. Take short steps with your feet apart. Here," he handed her a stocking cap. "Cover the fingers of your right hand with this. It should fit over the end of your cast."

Victoria proceeded slowly. Once she reached the bridge proper, sepia-toned floodlights styled to look like gas lamps illuminated the roadway every thirty feet. Bitter winds swirled off the rampaging Schuylkill River below. She gripped the handrail tightly with her good hand and fought to keep her balance.

Advancing, Victoria discerned the hazy outline of a dark figure swaying back and forth, feet dangling over the ledge of the bridge's central observation post.

"Don't come any closer," Melinda said, her voice weak and raspy.

Victoria crept forward.

"I said, 'Don't come any closer.' I mean it."

Victoria shouted something, but the wind swallowed her words. She kept moving. "Melinda, please, please listen to me," she tried again.

"Who is it? What do you want?"

"It's me, Melinda. Your mother."

"Mother? What are you doing here?"

"Don't do anything until you listen to me. You *have* to listen to me. Gregory's still alive."

"I don't believe you."

"I just came from the hospital. The doctors are operating on him now."

"How bad is it?"

"It's critical, but they've seen children in Gregory's condition recover."

"I know how you feel about him. You love him sooo much more than me. Why couldn't you love me like him?"

"I want that more than anything in the world. Please believe me."

Victoria's tears froze on her cheeks. "Give me another chance. I'll make it better. I understand what's been happening to you. We can help make it better if you let us help you."

"What if Gregowy dies?" Melinda lisped.

Melinda never lisped. It had to be the cold. "The three of us will deal with it together. Please let us help you."

"I'm sawey," Melinda wailed. "I didn't mean to hurt him. No matter what happens, you have to *bewieve* that."

As Victoria progressed to within ten feet, her eyes leveled with Melinda's back. Melinda sat facing away on a slightly elevated cement slab that overlooked the river, her feet dangling over the ledge. A blast of wind sent her sliding toward the precipice; her body lurched forward within inches of perpendicular. Victoria gasped. "I know you're sorry."

"Something's wong with me, I . . . I . . . I . . . "

"Your father and I love you. You must be so cold, honey. So cold." Closing in, Victoria saw streaks of clotted blood on Melinda's cheek.

"I'm afwaid, Mutha. Pwease help me, Pwease. Gwegowy, Gwegowy. Pwease fuhgive me."

When the next blast of air knocked Melinda off balance, she pitched forward toward the river.

Ignoring her cast and sling, Victoria reached up from behind and hooked both hands and arms under Melinda's armpits just as Melinda slid past the point of no return. Victoria alone had hold of Melinda. Victoria held on for their lives. She was pulled forward, her feet lodging against a crossbeam at the foot of the observation post. Victoria pulled Melinda back, the pain reminding her of expelling her daughter from the womb. Melinda was still pivoting over the edge when Victoria pulled one last time with all her might. Melinda tumbled backward into her arms. They hit the ground together, in a heap.

"I'm here, honey," Victoria said. "You need someone to hold you. I'm here to take care of my girl."

After thrashing about violently, Melinda stopped moving. They were still too far from the end of the bridge for the police to see or hear them. Knowing she couldn't leave and run for help, Victoria reached for her phone. "Shit," she said, realizing she had left it in the car.

Victoria removed her hat and pulled it over Melinda's head and neck, then double-plied the hat from her cast over it, too. She tugged on one of Melinda's feet until her body began sliding along the ice-caked walkway. Victoria pulled her to safety, foot by foot.

Along the way, Victoria felt faint and almost collapsed. After what seemed like miles of dragging, a policewoman jumped out of a cruiser and ran to them. Within seconds, a crew of police and EMTs lifted Melinda's half-frozen body onto a gurney, then into the ambulance standing by.

The ambulance door closed, and for the second time in less than twenty-four hours, Victoria accompanied an unconscious child to the Children's Hospital of Philadelphia.

42

The treacherous drive from the Strawberry Mansion Bridge into town afforded Jonas little release in tension. His energy drained by hours behind the wheel and the drama leading to Melinda's rescue, he thought about Jennie and his children. The car bore the faint scent of Victoria's perfume, which felt like it didn't belong, like a violation of his and Jennie's privacy. Jonas felt guilty about how compelling Gregory and Melinda's fates had become to him. That he'd been sitting contentedly at the Bodenheims' dinner table earlier that evening seemed utterly incomprehensible.

Victoria's description of her pregnancy and her difficulty bonding with Melinda preoccupied him, as did the memory of the packed emergency room full of parents and children traveling in pairs like they were on their way to Noah's Ark.

He said to himself, "It doesn't matter whether Willy Speller is dead or alive; I will always be his son. Is Gil really my son? Do I even know what that means?"

Victoria called to say that she and Melinda had made it safely to the hospital. Jonas drove by the Brauns' town house. Yellow tape cordoned off the area, which the authorities must have designated a crime scene. The nauseating vision of Gil tumbling down the steps headfirst went through his mind.

Jonas parked in view of the Rittenhouse Square gazebo, which the ice storm had turned into a giant snow cone. He tried to quiet his mind. Instead, he recalled a warm July day after he and Jennie moved to New York. By then, Jonas had joined the faculty at Mount Sinai Medical School and was starting his private practice.

Jennie had called, leaving a terse message: "Come home now." The intensity in her voice made his blood ran cold. He rushed home with his heart pounding.

"There's a lump in my breast," Jennie told him the minute he walked in. "I can feel it. I had a mammogram and the radiologist sent me immediately to a breast surgeon who said the lesion looked malignant but most likely curable by mastectomy. He wants to operate right away, followed by radiation and chemotherapy. Do you understand what this means?" Jennie had begun to cry. "No one will ever prescribe fertility drugs for me again. The surgeon said flat out not to get pregnant because estrogen and progesterone could make the cancer come back." She stared out their picture window overlooking Roosevelt Island. "What are we going to do?" she said.

Jonas held her close. He said, "It's all right. You're all that matters. If we want children, we'll adopt. Or we can go the surrogate mother route."

"Suppose she decided to keep the baby or wanted visitation, and we wound up in some terrible legal mess? I can't bear the thought of someone raising my child. I'm so sorry, Jonas. I know how much you wanted a son to name after your father," she wept.

The prospect of losing Jennie was unbearable. "Don't think about that now. I'll call the chairman of surgery in the morning and find out whom he trusts at Sloan-Kettering. We'll get you scheduled as soon as we can." Jonas poured himself a scotch. "I can't believe I made you take that goddamn Clomid. I saw what it did to you."

"Nobody made me do anything," Jennie said. "I wanted it as much as you."

"It's like pouring gasoline on a smoldering fire. That's what I tell my patients about fertility drugs. Why didn't I take my own advice?"

"It's nobody's fault." Jennie clutched him tightly. "I'm scared. I don't want to die young. There's so much I want to do, so many places I want us to go."

"Without you, nothing matters," Jonas said, and he meant it. "No more about children for now. That settles that."

But did it?

Still thinking of that day and all that had followed it, Jonas called home. It was 2:47 AM.

Jennie picked up on the first ring. She sounded wide awake. "Where are you and what happened? I've been worried."

Jonas choked up. "Yeah, I'm okay," he managed. "Well, not really. It's been a very hard day. I hope you understand."

"What is it?"

"I just want you to know how much I love you and our children."

"Of course you do. We know that." Jennie cleared her throat, as she did when she was troubled. "Are you all right?"

The question gave him pause. The sequence of events that brought Jennie and Jonas together shined on Jonas like Venus on a moonless night. Had Victoria not inspired him, Jonas wouldn't have left Dr. Fowler, and his relationship with Jennie's father wouldn't have blossomed, which meant they would have never been introduced.

"This is the twenty-third anniversary of the day we met. Remember? You wore your grandmother's emerald. I couldn't take my eyes off you."

"Jonas, what is going on down there?"

He interlaced his hands on his lap the way he did when he was in psychoanalysis. "It involves a woman I knew years ago, a clinic patient. We became close. Don't take that wrong, Jennie. You know I would never do anything to hurt . . . "

"You don't have to say that."

Jonas felt his heart breaking, but he had no idea why. "She has two children—a girl, and a boy a few years younger than ours. She showed up in pieces the other day, because her daughter had fallen apart. Tonight, the children got into a fight. Both of them wound up in intensive care at Children's Hospital. I'm heading there after we talk. It made me realize how fragile this whole thing is, our wonderful life. It could all fall apart in a minute."

"That's why we have to cherish every moment," Jennie said. "Every single one. That's why you drove to Philadelphia tonight. It made a difference, didn't it?"

"We saved her daughter's life."

"I'm so proud of you. No one could have done that but you, could they? Dad always knew you had a big heart. So did I."

"Once the situation is stable, I'm going to crash at your parents'. I have a key and the alarm code. I'm so tired I wish I could go there now, but there's more to do. Once things are okay tomorrow, I'll head back to New York. Everything's canceled tomorrow anyway, so there's no big rush."

"Please drive carefully, Jonas. You know, I can always take an early train to Philadelphia, and we can drive home together."

"I don't know what I'd do without you." Jonas began to feel better. "Plan something for the weekend that the four of us would enjoy."

"I could try to land tickets for *The Nutcracker*. Everyone likes that. There are usually three performances on holiday weekends, so we might be able to wiggle our way into one of them. How's that sound?"

"I don't care if we go window-shopping on Fifth Avenue, as long as it's something everyone enjoys. I just want us to be together. I'll be back in time for dinner. I'll call from the road. I love you, Jennie."

"Come home safe, you hear. I love you, too."

43

When Jonas returned to CHOP, the families of patients in critical condition were waiting in designated rooms outside intensive care. Comfortable chairs and recliners allowed family members to sit quietly or even to snooze. Jonas understood the layout all too well; the curtained Plexiglas walls were soundproofed, so that a doctor could deliver bad news privately. Martin and Victoria were pacing one of the rooms when Jonas entered and met Martin for the first time.

Before long, a white-coated man with an olive complexion, older than the typical intern or resident, emerged from the intensive care unit. Jonas bolted to intercept him.

"I'm Dr. Jonas Speller, Mrs. Braun's doctor."

"I'm Dr. Carlos Meninas, senior pediatric ICU fellow. I'd like to speak with Mr. and Mrs. Braun."

"Is there anything I should know before you speak with them?"

"You understand, Dr. Speller, that I'll need their permission before I talk with you," Dr. Meninas said.

"Dr. Goodman, the chairman of psychiatry, granted me temporary privileges."

"Oh. Good, then. Glad you're here. As you probably know, both children are in critical condition."

"Melinda, too?"

"Her body temperature was so low in the ER that we needed an esophageal probe."

"How low?"

"Seventy-eight degrees."

"Wow, that low? Is she stable?"

"For now, yes. We're watching her very closely."

"And Gregory?"

"He's stable, too."

Jonas breathed a sigh of relief. "At least they're both alive. Have you been in touch with your attending?"

"We inform Dr. Renehan of every admission. He goes over every protocol."

They went over to the Brauns, and Dr. Meninas introduced himself to Martin and Victoria.

Martin said, "I'm glad we're all here. Dr. Speller can clarify anything we don't understand."

Dr. Meninas closed the door. "Gregory remains comatose after surgery, but his vital signs are normalizing, which is what we were hoping for. The ventilator is working well. His oxygen saturation is ninety-eight percent. So far there's no seizure activity on his electroencephalogram. Neurosurgery is happy with the post-op CT scan; thankfully there's no more bleeding. Once he's more stable, we'll get an MRI, which is much more sensitive in assessing tissue damage. He has a mild leukocytosis that is normal post-operatively."

"That means Gregory's white blood cell count is slightly elevated— that's normal after an operation—" Jonas said, "and that his brain is getting enough oxygen."

"He's sedated for now, but in another day or two we'll ease off some and try to get a good neurological exam."

"How long before the skull is reattached?" Martin asked.

"The neurosurgeons are estimating three weeks at the earliest, but I've seen them wait as long as three months. It all depends on how quickly the swelling goes down. Gregory's in very good health, which will help. But there was massive swelling, which will take longer to resolve. For now, we'll give him medicine to keep him from moving, which means we have to breathe for him—not only to give him oxygen, but to expand his lungs fully. When the lungs don't fully inflate the lower lobes often collapse, and that can cause pneumonia."

"My God," Victoria said. "So many complications to deal with."

"We try to be proactive," Dr. Meninas continued. "Dr. Breckenridge did a terrific job. She isolated the artery with one hand and cauterized it with the other, entirely by feel. Imagine the skill and sensitivity it takes to do that with blood gushing and totally obscuring her view. The biggest risk right now is seizure, which we're treating aggressively with anticonvulsants. Even after the swelling goes down Gregory may not awaken fully for weeks, and even then, he'll regain consciousness slowly. I want you to understand, people with Gregory's degree of trauma don't awaken suddenly, like in the movies. They come out of coma a bit at a time.

"But be prepared, though. When Gregory awakens, he'll likely be weak on the contralateral side, and he'll have contracoup symptoms until the brain heals completely."

Victoria sat up erect. "You're saying he *will* wake up? Dr. Liddle didn't sound that certain."

"I don't want to give you false hope, Mr. and Mrs. Braun, but as long as we get through the next forty-eight hours and nothing unexpected turns up on the MRI, I really think he'll wake up. What's not knowable is what he'll be like. Only time will tell. But because Gregory's young and was healthy to begin with his nerve cells are resilient. A lot of rewiring will need to happen inside his brain, but therapy will help with that. All of Gregory's senses should be stimulated. Some families read to their children, even when they are in a coma. Others play music. Also, try to provide familiar smells. That's important, too.

"For now, we can get away with intravenous fluids, but until he wakes up we'll have to tube-feed Gregory or else his GI tract will go into starvation mode."

Jonas said, "That's right. The intestinal lining is intricately ridged to absorb nutrients. The ridges flatten if there's nothing to digest. I like what I'm hearing. These doctors have everything covered."

"What's does 'countercoup' mean?" Martin said.

"The word is 'contracoup,'" Jonas said. "Since the brain sits in an enclosed space, the mini-shock-waves from a blow to the head reverberate back and forth like ripples in a pond. The major damage is to Gregory's left hemisphere, which controls the right side of the body, so that's where he'll be the weakest. But because of the shock-wave effect, he'll have symptoms on the left side, too."

Martin reached for Victoria's arm.

"What about Melinda?" Victoria said.

Dr. Meninas said, "Melinda arrived with a core temperature of seventy-eight degrees, borderline severe hypothermia. Hypothermia slows the heart, but for the time being, she's in a normal sinus rhythm. That could deteriorate into a ventricular arrhythmia at any time until her body warms up."

Jonas jumped in, "That could stop the heart from beating."

"We're up to eighty-seven. Her heart rhythm is being monitored very carefully," Dr. Meninas said. "And we can do prolonged resuscitation if necessary."

"ECMO?" Jonas asked.

"That's right," Dr. Meninas said.

"What's that?" Martin asked.

Dr. Meninas replied, "'Extracorporeal membrane oxygenation.' We have machines that can take over for the heart if necessary. Meanwhile, we'll raise her body temperature slowly by infusing warm fluids."

"How warm?" Jonas said.

"One-hundred seven degrees Fahrenheit. It's as fast as we can go. Melinda's fingers and ears are another matter; we're warming them from the outside. I don't expect any problems as long as her heart behaves well. When Melinda's temperature hits around ninety, she may seem as if she has DTs."

"What's that?" Martin said.

"Delirium tremens," both doctors said simultaneously.

Dr. Meninas went on, "Melinda might look like she's in alcoholic withdrawal; if that happened she might shake uncontrollably and become disoriented. I'm worried that she could become agitated, which is why I want a psychiatric nurse with her. I don't want to sedate her, because tranquilizers might destabilize her brain's temperature regulation center. If we need something, we'll pick the safest medication possible."

"Melinda told her mother she'd agree to getting help," Jonas said, "but who knows what she'll be like when she comes to."

Victoria asked, "When can we see them? I need to see my children."

"I'll make sure it's okay to visit. Family only."

Jonas looked at Dr. Meninas intently.

"Right, you have privileges, Dr. Speller. Let's leave the visiting to your discretion."

Dr. Meninas's pager went off and the overhead alarm sounded. He raced out of the room.

"Wait here," Jonas told Martin and Victoria brusquely. He tore off after Dr. Meninas.

44

A hoarde of doctors and nurses converged on the pediatric ICU like firemen rushing to a five-alarm blaze. Jonas knew some life-threatening catastrophe had occurred. He hoped to God it wasn't Melinda's heart or Gregory having a seizure. Jonas chased a ponytailed intern through the swinging doors. The doctors and nurses crowded into a corner room while a single clerk manned the telephones at the central nurse's station.

"What's going on?" the intern said to an intensive care fellow.

"It's the girl with bacterial meningitis we admitted this morning," he said. "The bottom just dropped out of her blood pressure. Septic shock. The only thing to do now is push fluids, corticosteroids, and vasopressors. And hope."

Reassured the crisis didn't involve Gregory or Melinda, Jonas introduced himself to the unit clerk at the nurse's station and then went to Melinda's room. She was hooked to a maze of wires, and a black and green monitor displayed her heart rate, blood pressure, and body temperature, which had climbed to eighty-nine degrees. She had begun to shiver. The psychiatric nurse noted that Melinda was floating in and out of consciousness but hadn't awakened fully.

Looking at Melinda's face was like going back in time. She looked so much like Victoria had when she was angry or frightened. Jonas briefed the nurse about Melinda then moved on to her brother's room.

Gregory's head was bandaged and connected to a drain by a plastic tube. Purple and amber stains on his temples indicated the spots where the scalp had been scrubbed before the operation. Ribbed, plastic tubes connected his endotracheal tube to a breathing machine, while his expression—angelic yet resolute—looked as though he was determined to recover.

Gregory looked exactly like Victoria had described him, right down to the peach fuzz. He had Martin's forehead and chin, but everything in between was his mother's.

While Jonas was studying Gregory's face, a fair-skinned woman in a white lab coat entered. A penlight and a reflex hammer protruded from her pockets. Even before he could read the red embroidery above her vest pocket, Jonas knew she was Dr. Anna Breckenridge come to check on Gregory one last time before going to bed.

Jonas felt an immediate sense of connectedness, as if he knew her from a previous life. After introducing himself, he said, "You're very much like I imagined. You remind me of a woman psychiatrist who trained with us at Mount Sinai. On September 11, 2001, she was visiting her husband, who worked for Cantor Fitzgerald at the World Trade Center. No one above the 85th floor survived. I'd like to think some of her lives on."

"I was a PG-five on September 11th," Dr. Breckenridge said. "They were ready to send us to New York to help with the head trauma cases. But there weren't any survivors, so we stayed here."

Jonas recognized the Maryland accent. "Is that Baltimore I hear?"

"Hopkins undergraduate and medical school; 1991 and 1996."

"Penn undergraduate, 1974. Hopkins med school, 1978," Jonas said. "For all we know we sat in the same seats at grand rounds on Saturdays."

"Could well be," Dr. Breckenridge said as she checked Gregory's pulse, then lifted his eyelids in succession and shined her light at them. She smiled. "It's better now. The left pupil was practically fixed when I saw him in the ER. Here," she handed Jonas the penlight. "Take a look."

"He has his mother's eyes," Jonas said as he examined Gregory. "Word has it that you did a great job tonight."

"I hear you were pretty busy, yourself," she said.

"How did you know?"

"Philadelphia's really a small town. Everyone knows everybody's business."

Jonas laughed. "So I've heard."

"Dr. Liddle and I are rounding at 6:30 AM. In case he doesn't see you, he said to tell you Jock's youngest is thinking about medical school. He wants to be a psychiatrist."

"That's wonderful. If I miss him, please tell Dr. Liddle that I'm happy it all turned out well." Jonas looked at Dr. Breckenridge with admiration, then turned back to Gregory. "Amazing organ, isn't it; the brain?" Jonas said. "We both touch it. You with your hands and instruments. Me with words. I thought about going into neurosurgery, but I knew I couldn't survive the training. Put a scalpel in my hands when I'm tired and I'm a danger to society."

"Do you remember the first time you saved someone's life?" Dr. Breckenridge asked.

Jonas nodded. "Of course."

"What happened?"

"I had just gone into practice. A woman with postpartum depression called to say good-bye. I was treating her with medication and psychotherapy and it looked like she was perking up. I usually let calls ring through to my answering service, but I was between sessions so I picked up. She sounded strange, so I asked what was happening. She said she wanted to thank me for trying.

"'Trying?' That sounded strange so I asked what was happening that moment. She said she had just lost her temper and slapped one of her toddlers. She hadn't slept for two nights because her ten-week-old had developed colic. She said her children would be better off without her. She was holding the phone with one hand; in the other she had her pill bottle—before Prozac was widely prescribed we used tricyclics. She had already taken ten and was about to swallow the rest. Fortunately her husband was home. I had him take her to the hospital immediately. By the time they got to the ER she was in a coma. A few minutes later she went into cardiac arrest. They started chest compressions, gave her IV bicarbonate and sympathomimetics; then they shocked her back into sinus rhythm. She survived. After three weeks on the psychiatry ward she went home. We got her a doula and counseled the couple. Today she's fine. Three children under three—can you imagine what her death would have done to that family?"

"Torn them apart, no doubt," Dr. Breckenridge said.

"Do you think Gregory will make it?"

"I think so," she said. "It was good that we got to him early. Your heads-up saved us precious time. The first forty-eight hours will tell. As long as he doesn't develop intractable seizures he should live. What he'll be like is another story.

"I won't forget this night, will I?" she said.

"How did it feel?" Jonas asked.

"I was surprisingly calm. Even though I'd been in ORs for years, when they shut the doors tonight, I felt I had entered another world. I knew exactly what to do."

Jonas smiled. "I played violin. I used to feel that way when I had a big solo. I couldn't wait for my turn."

Dr. Breckenridge said, "I learned to sculpt in elementary school. I made my first model of the brain out of Play-Doh when I was in second grade."

Jonas smiled at her. "It's late, Dr. Breckenridge. I'll let you get some rest. Thank you for giving Gregory a chance."

She hesitated. "Just so you know—it was a bloody mess in there. The bone fragment nicked an artery. The clot and the swelling were as bad as anything I've seen. If he had been anywhere else, he wouldn't have had a chance. Still, it could be a very long vigil. And even then, who knows what there'll be on the other end."

"Good luck with your future, Dr. Breckenridge. You know, cracked skulls aren't going away anytime soon in the Big Apple. We could always use a hand."

"Call me Anna. Say, did anyone ever tell you you're easy to talk to?"

Jonas grinned and produced his card. "Pleased to meet you, Anna." He took a step back and smiled at her. "Jonas Speller. Call anytime."

Anna's eyes welled up. "Thanks," she said. "I see some awful stuff. It would be good to have someone to talk about it with."

Jonas looked into the woman's eyes, shook her hand gratefully, and then departed.

45

Jonas was returning to Martin and Victoria when Dr. Meninas caught up with him. "Do you have a moment?" he asked.

"Sure," Jonas managed feebly, his vision blurring from fatigue.

"Word has it that you saved Melinda's life by helping her mother keep her from jumping off the Strawberry Mansion Bridge."

"Where did you hear that?"

"The neurosurgical attending pieced the story together from the police. How does it feel to be a hero?"

"I don't feel much of anything except the overwhelming need to sleep."

"I won't keep you long, then." Dr. Meninas said. "Lately, I've been thinking about psychiatry, but my peers say child psychiatry is a waste of a medical education; that I'll spend my life writing Ritalin prescriptions and battling school boards to get kids into therapeutic schools. They say I should go into pediatric oncology if I want to save people's lives."

"That's absurd!" Jonas said. "Look at tonight. One child with uncontrolled mania winds up on death's doorstep after nearly killing another. Tell me psychiatry's not about life and death."

"Just so you know, a police inspector named Ruby Pale is here some-place."

"If it wasn't for her, we wouldn't have found Melinda."

"Also, a Dr. Milroy called. He is . . . ?"

"Melinda's psychiatrist. He's on his way in. We want him to meet Melinda as soon as he can. He's terrific with teenagers. Her transfer to the Pennsylvania Hospital psych unit will be a lot smoother if she feels good about her doctor."

"I can see you've done time in the ICU," Dr. Meninas said.

"My first job in New York City was running the consultation-liaison service at Mount Sinai. That was before Prozac, when patients died all the time from antidepressant overdoses. What a horrible period!"

"I know about those days," Dr. Meninas said. "My Uncle Umberto was a revered pediatrician in Brazil. Whenever he lost a patient, he took to bed for days. His psychoanalyst got the family doctor to prescribe an antidepressant. My uncle hoarded the pills and then took an overdose after his best friend's child died of leukemia. Umberto barely survived."

"How's he doing now?"

"Fine. Turns out he was manic-depressive. He's on Lamictal and Seroquel and is doing well. I have a lot of respect for your profession, Dr. Speller. Imagine what would have happened to our family had my uncle died."

"'Save a life, save the world,' I tell my residents. Look us up. Mount Sinai has excellent psychiatry programs. I'd be happy to put in a good word for you. Lots of pediatricians pursue child psychiatry. Knowing child development puts you miles ahead. Our chairman was a pediatrician, and he's a wonderful teacher."

"I'll think about it. Thank you, Dr. Speller."

"Just give me a minute with Mr. and Mrs. Braun, Dr. Meninas, and I'll be out of your hair."

Jonas turned to Martin and Victoria. "Dr. Meninas and the staff have the situation well in hand," he said. "It's been a long night for all of us. I'm going to crash at my in-laws', but I'll stop by in the morning. I'd like to catch up with Dr. Liddle."

"I can't tell you how grateful we are," Martin said, extending his hand.

Victoria squeezed Jonas's arm firmly as he turned to leave. "Thank God you were here. I don't know what I'd have done without you."

As they walked down the corridor toward the elevator, Martin extended an arm around Victoria's waist as if he wanted to comfort her. She responded with indifference, which made Jonas wonder even more about what was happening between them, and inside her.

46

Ten minutes later, Dr. Milroy, still in his parka and galoshes, knocked gingerly on Martin and Victoria's door. Martin seemed grateful. For the moment, Victoria wasn't. Despite her venomous stare, Dr. Milroy did not avoid Victoria's eyes.

He said, "I'm so sorry, Mr. and Mrs. Braun. I thought we could wait to admit Melinda. I was wrong. I'd like to see her now, but I'll understand if you want someone else to treat Melinda."

Satisfied with the sincerity of Dr. Milroy's apology, Victoria's anger dissipated. "No," she said, looking toward Martin, whose body language was conciliatory, as well. "None of us wanted Melinda locked up against her will over Thanksgiving. Fortunately, both the children are alive. We'll visit them soon. If Melinda's awake, I'll tell her you want to see her." She noticed Dr. Milroy's tousled hair and salt-stained boots. "Thanks for being there tonight. Your advice about how to talk to Melinda made a difference."

"I'm glad. Where's Dr. Speller?"

"He just left. He was exhausted. Martin and I are going in to see

Melinda and Gregory. The nurse said they'd let us in for fifteen minutes each hour."

* * *

The sight of Gregory attached to a respirator with a plastic tube coming out of the side of his head overwhelmed Victoria with helplessness and rage, alternating with periods of such absolute dissociation she felt as if her emotions had been deactivated. Even though it made no sense, Victoria's first thought was that Martin could have prevented the disaster.

While Martin hovered about Gregory, Victoria went to Melinda's room.

Melinda regained her faculties gradually as her body temperature climbed, her wild eyes searching for clues to what was happening.

As soon as she saw her mother, she spoke. "It really happened? Please tell me it was a bad dream."

"I wish it was," Victoria said.

"Where's Gregory?"

"He's two doors away."

"He's still alive?"

"Yes."

"You promise he's still alive," Melinda said.

"I promise. I wouldn't lie to you."

"You said he needed an operation. They operated on his brain?"

"It's all over now."

"On his brain? I can't believe I did that to my brother. It makes me sick. Give me that thing," she said, pointing to a lavender basin on the window sill. "I feel like throwing up."

"It's all right, honey," Victoria said. "It's all right."

"What did the doctor say? Will he be okay?"

"The doctor said we were fortunate we got him here as soon as we did. They won't know for a long time how well he'll recover."

Melinda tried to sit up in bed. She seemed confused by all the wires connecting her earlobes, fingers, and chest to a computer monitor across the room. "What are these for?"

"For a while it was touch and go with you. The doctors have to watch your heart and temperature carefully."

Victoria helped Melinda maneuver her legs over the bedside, whereupon she dissolved into her mother's arms, crying, "I'm sorry. I'm so sorry."

"I know. I know," Victoria said tenderly, holding Melinda with more affection than she ever had before.

After she cried herself out, Melinda said, "Before you came, there was a strange woman over there. Who is she? Where did she go?"

"The doctor wanted a nurse here in case you got upset. I asked her to step outside to give us some privacy."

"I don't like her. She looks like she's angry with me." Melinda pointed to her hospital gown and made a face. "I hate this thing," she said. "I feel so naked with nothing on underneath."

"I would, too. But it's hospital policy," Victoria sympathized.

"Did you mean what you said at the bridge?"

"Every word. I promise."

"What happened to your arm?"

"I broke my wrist when I slipped in front of the house," she said, looking down at her swollen purple fingers. "I must have reinjured it when I pulled you off the ledge. I should go back to the emergency room."

"You're coming back, aren't you?" Melinda said.

"Of course."

"What did you mean when you said you understood what was wrong with me?"

"That I know what it's like to have thoughts and feelings so jumbled that you can't think straight—that make you want the world to go away."

"That's exactly how I feel. That's why I don't want that woman in here. It's one more thing to deal with. Can't you make her go away?"

"I'll try. She's here because one of the doctors taking care of you was afraid you might hurt yourself. Your body temperature got so low the doctors worried that your heart might stop, but I don't think we have to worry about that anymore. There's another doctor, too. Dr. Milroy."

"Who's he?"

Victoria took a slow breath. She wanted the words to come out right. "He's the doctor who's going to help with your moods and thoughts."

"He's a psychiatrist, right? You think I'm crazy, don't you?"

"Not at all. Dr. Milroy works with lots of teenagers. You're probably just like me. My doctor says I have bipolar disorder and that I've had it for years and didn't know it. My mind got so jumbled from all the thoughts racing through it I thought it was normal."

Melinda looked relieved. She got out of bed and pulled her IV pole to the vinyl chair where the nurse had been sitting.

"Here," Victoria reached over to her, covering Melinda with a hospital blanket. "Before long, you'll be in your own warm bed at home."

"Ugh. My room is such a mess; I don't want anyone to see it. It'll take forever to clean it up."

"I'll help you," said Victoria, putting her good arm around Melinda.

"It's been so awful," Melinda said, tears streaming. "Everyone at school hates me. Whenever I speak in class, they laugh behind my back. I'm afraid to say anything. I went to my English teacher, because I couldn't do the reading—no matter how hard I tried nothing stuck in my mind—and she accused me of being lazy. It wasn't always that way." Melinda sighed. "I used to like reading." She pointed at her forehead. "Something bad happened. I did it to myself."

"What do you mean?"

"It's too . . . too . . . I'm so ashamed. I'd rather tell the doctor."

A nurse entered the room. "It's time, Mrs. Braun," said Melinda's charge nurse, a comely woman whose name tag said 'Robin.' She was sympathetic but businesslike. Robin turned to Melinda. "It's so nice to see you up and out of bed. How are you feeling?"

"Are you talking to her or me?" Melinda said.

Robin smiled. "I guess I meant both of you. You both look like you could use a cup of hot tea and a piece of honey cake." Victoria started to knead Melinda's neck with her good hand.

The pain in the other one was becoming unbearable.

"God, that feels good," Melinda said.

"Rough night?" Robin said wryly.

Melinda and Victoria laughed.

"Dr. Milroy wants to introduce himself to you, Melinda," Robin said. "He may talk with you later, Mrs. Braun. We'll let him decide." Robin's jaw dropped when she saw Victoria's hand. "Mrs. Braun, your fingers look like they're about to explode. Let's get you down to the ER. We'll get you back up here as soon as we can."

Victoria gave her daughter's neck one last squeeze and left, passing Dr. Milroy on his way into the room. Martin walked her into the elevator and accompanied her to the emergency room.

"You know what, Martin?" Victoria said as they entered the last of a set of swinging doors. "I'd rather you went back upstairs in case something happens."

"I'd like to be with you," Martin said.

"I know," Victoria said, disconcerted that she found such little consolation in Martin's presence—which brought to mind talking to Jonas about feeling dissociated from Melinda.

Martin looked hurt. "Are you okay?"

"I'll be all right. You know where I am if you need me."

47

Victoria returned to the emergency room in time to vomit; the pain had become that intense. A technician ushered her directly into the treatment area, where an aide removed the cast seconds before a lead-aproned woman re-X-rayed Victoria's wrist.

The orthopedist walked in holding two enlarged radiographs, which he affixed to a light box. "This is before," he said indicating the one on the left. "This is now," he pointed to an area circled in red. "You didn't break anything new, Mrs. Braun, but you pulled the bones out of alignment. I can give you the same local anesthetic as before and reposition the bones. You'll need something for the pain after the nerve block wears off though."

Although the injection into her armpit felt like being impaled by a fireplace poker, the nearly instantaneous relief from the pain was divine.

"What did you do to your hand?" the doctor asked while waiting for complete numbness.

Victoria replayed the scene at the bridge in her mind, shuddering at how close Melinda had come to falling. "Will it change what you do?" she said.

"Not really." By then, the doctor was starting to manipulate her hand and arm, pulling down, away and then up. The crunching sounded like someone stepping off a gravel road onto bubble wrap.

"I did what any mother would do to save her child," Victoria said quietly.

"I'm sure you did," the doctor said. He and Victoria were silent until he finished the procedure. "What do you say, Mrs. Braun, no more heavy lifting tonight? Seriously though, I hope everything turns out well."

"Thank you," Victoria said as he left to attend to a screaming child.

*   *   *

Victoria returned to the ICU waiting area in time to catch Dr. Milroy on his way out. He and Martin were at the doorway talking. Victoria accompanied Dr. Milroy down the hallway toward the elevators.

"I was just telling your husband that Melinda and I had a good talk," Dr. Milroy said to Victoria. "She promised she wouldn't hurt herself, so I sent the psychiatric nurse on her way. There's a lot Melinda wants to talk about, which is a good thing. She also agreed to come to Pennsylvania Hospital. It's late," Dr. Milroy said, stifling a yawn. "Let's all get some sleep and reconnoiter when we can think straight. The doctors here want to monitor her over the weekend to make sure her heart remains stable. See her as much as you want this weekend. After she's moved on Monday, visiting will be restricted for the first week. We'll start family sessions when the time is right. I'll stop by on Saturday to talk with Melinda, and I'll keep you in the loop about what's happening. Any questions?"

"Not for now. I'm glad you came," said Victoria.

When she returned to her waiting room, Martin was dozing lightly, reminding her of Morris drowsing in front of the television the nights he'd had an extra martini. She wandered down the hall to the pediatric ICU intercom and asked to visit. Once inside, she passed an empty corner room with two orderlies in hazmat sealed suits, complete with helmets and faceplates, scouring the floor and walls.

When Victoria returned to Melinda's room something didn't feel right. It was the absence of noise. The 'drip, drip, drip' from the IV had stopped, and the cardiac monitor displayed a continuous flat line. Alarmed, Victoria approached the bed only to see that Melinda's bed covers were scrunched together; there was no movement or sounds. Victoria shouted, just as Robin came into the room.

"She's not breathing," Victoria screamed. "She's not breathing."

Robin quickly pulled the covers back. No Melinda; just an empty bed.

"Where is she? Where is she?" Victoria yelled. "Not again!"

"Let's not panic," Robin said. "She has to be somewhere. Follow me." She led Victoria to Gregory's room.

"I knew it," Robin said, patting Victoria's shoulder. There Melinda lay, asleep in a big chair she'd dragged over to Gregory's bedside, clasping his hand.

48

Within ten days of his operation, Gregory was stable enough to be moved farther away from the nursing station. Victoria noticed a gradual decline in the nurses' attention, but the neurosurgical team rounded on Gregory every morning and evening. Although the doctors were pleased that the brain swelling had gone way down, they still wanted to wait before replacing the skull. Concerned that Gregory hadn't awakened, they were forever running the butts of their reflex hammers across the soles of his feet and mentioning the Glasgow Coma Scale.

Dr. Meninas finished his pediatric ICU rotation the last day in November. The new fellow, Dr. Narissa Hyung, circled the bedsides of the most seriously ill patients like a hawk.

Several children had head injuries, but none as bad as Gregory's. One had epilepsy the doctors couldn't control. Another was in liver failure after drinking a bottle of liquid Tylenol. But the worst cases were the bald preteens and adolescents with cancer. One sixteen-year-old boy had his leg amputated because of a bone tumor. His father looked like he'd had his own leg ripped off.

When Drs. Hyung and Bell disconnected Gregory's respirator for brief periods to see if he would breathe on his own, he did.

"This is good," Dr. Breckenridge said to Victoria. "It means the brain stem is working properly, but we won't remove the breathing tube until we're certain Gregory can maintain his oxygen level. Brain cells are exquisitely sensitive to oxygen deficiency, especially the part of the brain called the hippocampus, which is the seat of working memory. It's like RAM in your computer. Without it you can't function."

"Gregory's the one who speaks computer. I don't," Victoria said. "I can e-mail and type documents, but that's it. As far as I'm concerned, rams belong on a farm."

* * *

The first week Melinda was in the psychiatric ward, Dr. Milroy called to say she was adjusting well and that the medicine was taking hold.

"She doesn't mind taking it?" Victoria said.

"On the contrary, she says it makes her feel better. We'll start family sessions sometime around the two-week mark; the medicine will help her become stable enough that the sessions won't disrupt her progress. Here's some good news: Melinda has bonded nicely with a girl who's a couple of weeks ahead of her recovery-wise. They're looking forward to seeing each other in group."

Visiting hours at Children's Hospital began at 10:00 AM. Victoria was always the first person to sign in at the visitor's desk. Her presence on Gregory's floor was so regular it looked like she had become a permanent addition to the house staff. Someone even suggested getting her a security badge.

Gregory's bedside became a monotonous, malaise-filled blur. Something about the colors: everyone in uniforms, like the army. Victoria learned to tell people's jobs from their outfits. LPNs wore blue bouffant scrub caps and speckled tunics. RN's wore white jackets and green blouses.

The doctors had distinguishing outfits as well. Pediatric interns and residents had their names embroidered in blue script on their white coats. Surgical residents always wore hospital scrubs beneath their lab coats but, instead of mingling, they hung together, and the alpha males played up to their female counterparts like GIs parading through Paris.

The neurosurgeons were at the top of the food chain. Victoria saw it in the way they moved: They didn't just walk, they didn't swagger—they strode. The respect they commanded upon entering a patient's room was palpable. Hundreds upon hundreds of students and surgical fellows applied for neurosurgery training at Penn, but the program accepted only two per year. Their lives were their work, and everyone knew it.

It surprised Victoria to learn that Dr. Breckenridge was thirty-five years old, and had already completed seven years of neurosurgical residency before entering pediatric neurosurgery. She looked much younger. It comforted Victoria immensely to see Drs. Liddle, Bell, and Breckenridge hovering over Gregory as if he was their prize pupil. Convinced Gregory was stable for the time being and that Melinda was safe, Victoria traveled to New York to see Jonas.

He said, "You look better than the last time I saw you."

"So do you," she said.

"How's it going?"

"I'm reading *Harry Potter* to Gregory. I want him to hear my voice; I get the feeling he knows it's me. We're in the middle of *The Goblet of Fire*."

"And how's it going in there?" He pointed to Victoria's head. "Your mind-racing? And your sleep?"

"The medicine helps, but the nights are hard. Thank God I can sleep. Otherwise they'd need to admit me. I'm not sure why, but I'm dreading family therapy. Dr. Milroy thinks Melinda'll be ready next week."

"Can you focus? Concentrate on reading?"

"When I'm with Gregory, I can stay on track. I try to get some work done. Thank God the judge recessed our big case indefinitely. My colleagues have been great. I was worried I'd be blackballed by the legal community."

"You worry so much," Jonas said. "How is it when we talk by phone?"

"Not the same, but better than nothing. Being in your presence has such a calming effect. I remember our conversation in therapy when we first talked about Leslie Kilway. Do you remember her?"

"Sure. She was your biology tutor."

"Leslie teaches at the medical school. She looks in on Gregory every day. I hadn't thought about that conversation in years. You think memories are gone when bang, they're there, like yesterday. It amazes me."

"Speaking about yesterday," Jonas said, "did the doctors say anything new?"

"Didn't I tell you? They're using a new kind of bed that turns Gregory to keep him from getting bed sores."

"That's good."

"Other than that, everything's the same. The doctors come early each morning and before they leave for the day. They say the brain swelling is gone, but I think they're concerned that Gregory hasn't woken up. They say to be patient, but I get the feeling they're talking to themselves as much as to me."

"Anything else?"

"They're still concerned that the pressure inside Gregory's head might increase. They mentioned it on rounds. They were talking about hydrocephalus and something that sounded like 'NIH.' They're not thinking of medevac-ing Gregory to D.C., are they?"

"No. The term is NPH, not NIH: Normal Pressure Hydrocephalus; that's more common in adults."

"Whatever it is, they need to be sure about it before reattaching the skull."

"Did they say when they're going to do that?"

"Somewhere around the three-week mark; which should be pretty soon. They may need to use plates and screws, but if they do, Dr. Liddle says they're made of titanium, so Gregory can still get MRIs and won't set off metal detectors."

"Amazing," Jonas said. "They think of everything."

"What's this NPH thing?"

"The brain has four fluid-filled cavities called ventricles," Jonas explained. "If the filter becomes plugged, like it can after a head injury, the pressure can rise. I'm sure they've been monitoring the pressure in Gregory's head very carefully since they operated. Speaking of which, I bet if you look at Gregory's heart rate and blood pressure, the numbers go down when you read to him."

"I hope so. But if they put the sensors on me, the machine would go haywire when Lorraine visits."

"How are you and Lorraine doing with each other?"

"We coexist; that's all. She blames me. I can tell."

"And how do you feel about her?"

"I go back and forth between hating her and feeling sorry for her. Most of her friends deserted her after the divorce. I guess they didn't want her flirting with their husbands. It's awkward when Morris visits while she's there."

"What happened to Morris?"

"He's been in AA for years. He sponsors newcomers, and he married a woman he met there. Her name's Carolyn; I like her. It's wonderful to see the way they touch each other. I can tell she cares about Gregory, too, but she won't visit when Lorraine is there."

"We still haven't talked about Martin."

"I know, I know," Victoria said testily.

"I know this isn't a good time, Victoria. But something's going on with you and Martin. Something's not right."

"It's not him. It's me. My feelings about him are so complicated, I don't know if I'll ever be ready to deal with them."

"We have to get to it sometime, Victoria," Jonas said. "You can't keep putting it off."

"Don't push me, Jonas," Victoria flared. "I'm doing the best I can! I'll deal with it when I'm ready."

Jonas sighed. "The way you say that worries me, Victoria. Something's going to blow; I see it coming. And when it does, it could be ugly. Very ugly."

49

As Gregory's coma dragged on and on, so did Victoria's anomie. Between shuttling back and forth from Gregory's bedside to Melinda's family therapy at Pennsylvania Hospital, Victoria had not seen Jonas in person for two weeks. Phone sessions were the best they could manage.

"I haven't told you what's happening with Melinda," she told him in mid-December. "Dr. Milroy wants to keep her in the psych unit until after New Year's. I think he's afraid of another debacle like Thanksgiving. Melinda likes talking with him. I get the sense she's confiding in him. Has he said anything to you?"

"No, there's nothing to tell," Jonas said. "From the beginning, I told Rob not to tell me anything about Melinda that I couldn't tell you."

"Do you have any idea what's she talking about with him?"

"Anything I say is pure conjecture, nothing more. Understand, Victoria?"

"I understand."

"Melinda might have experimented with drugs, or with sex. Either one might have pushed her over the edge."

"You know, I didn't make much of it at the time, but during the summer, Melinda hung around with a friend-of-a-friend of someone at school. The text messages cost us a fortune. She was obsessed with him for two weeks; then he vanished. When I asked her about it, Melinda made out like it was no big deal, but she hasn't been the same since."

"It wouldn't be the first time a guy sweet-talked a girl, then ditched her after he got what he wanted. She's so young."

"You don't think he got her pregnant? Or gave her a disease?"

"I hope not."

"Martin and I visit her every evening. A social worker named Pamela Blount is assigned to us for family therapy."

"Blount? I know that name. If it's who I think it is, her husband was an analyst in town. He was a big mahaf back when I was training."

"'Mahaf!' Nobody who isn't from Philadelphia knows that word."

"I spent my psychological adolescence in West Philadelphia and Center City, Victoria," Jonas said. "It's in my blood. So tell me about this Blount woman."

"Well, whoever she is, this lady has wrung out every drop of contentiousness that ever existed between Melinda and me. As far as she's concerned, my emotional life is her property. She must know there's no way we'll follow up with her after Melinda's discharge, so for now, she's like a jackal gnawing on a carcass. She makes a big deal that she studied family therapy with someone whose name sounds like Munchkin. She drops his name all the time, like he's some kind of guru."

"The name is Salvador Minuchin. He's a family therapist from South America. According to him, children's psychological issues come from dysfunctional families."

"Do you agree?"

"Not completely. The mind is much more complicated. Biological predisposition to mood disorders plays too huge a role to be discounted. Minuchin's followers want the therapist to become part of the family; then the therapist riles things up, telling people to leave the room, or to sit in a corner, or not to talk. I understand the rationale, but that invites the therapist to become a dictator. Like most therapies, there's good and bad. Minuchin's work gave me the idea of using a one-way mirror in therapy with adolescents. In my practice, instead of forcing families to look at themselves, which makes people defensive, I get permission to record other families' sessions; having parents look at the behavior of people they don't know makes it easier to identify maladaptive patterns in their own families.

"In my experience, a Family Systems approach can help once you get past the totalitarianism, but the therapists have to watch themselves, or else they can become tyrannical and rationalize it as good for the therapy."

Victoria's wrist, still in its cast, began to itch. "Oh, this is just wonderful. Mrs. Blount must think she's doing a good job when she makes me feel horrible. You should see her in action."

"What does she look like?"

"She's painfully thin; I can see her bones. Her skin sags like it's melting off her face and arms, and she wears shapeless dresses that hang off her shoulders. Her voice is so caustic it could penetrate a missile silo. She has no chest or rear end." Victoria laughed. "She looks like she's wearing a Halloween costume."

Jonas laughed, too. "Good Lord, she sounds like a character from *The Night of the Living Dead*."

"She harps on what she calls Melinda's assigned role in our family. That Gregory is the golden child who can do no wrong, while I over-identify with Melinda's faults and devalue all her strengths."

"There is some truth to that, wouldn't you agree?"

"I accept the concept, I do. But Mrs. Blount's formulation is too black and white. I've always acknowledged Melinda's accomplishments. People play more than one role, don't you think?"

"Of course they do. Did you tell her that?"

"Yes. But when I did, she accused me of being confrontational, which she assumes is how I treat Melinda. She does nothing but criticize my parenting. One night, she made Melinda role-play Gregory with me, which Martin and I understood and found helpful, but then Mrs. Blount attacked me like a pit bull. Even Melinda told her it wasn't fair. If the goal of family therapy is getting us to bond, Mrs. Blount's doing a fine job of turning Melinda and me into trench buddies, united against a common enemy. I remember you once saying something about changing therapists, didn't you?"

"I was just thinking about that. Your family therapy reminds me of how I felt trapped with my former analyst. It took guts, but I extricated myself. It was one of the best things I ever did."

"I just realized something. Mrs. Blount makes me feel like I did growing up with Lorraine."

"You stood up to Lorraine on graduation day. You were so proud of that. Remember that Mrs. Blount works for you, not the other way around."

"But what will Dr. Milroy say if I tell him we want someone else?"

"Rob's a pro. Things like this happen all the time. He's interested in results. How's Melinda doing?"

"Better. She's not so infuriated with me. But I have to watch myself; when Melinda gets irritated it's hard not to take it personally. I'm glad we talked about Mrs. Blount. It gives me something to work on."

"About Martin . . . ?"

"I'm trying."

"'Trying'? What does that mean?"

"It means what it means," Victoria reacted more intensely than the last time Jonas brought up the subject.

"Victoria, I can't emphasize enough how important it is to get a hold of your feelings about him."

"I'll talk about it when I'm ready."

"What if you never feel ready?"

"Goddammit, Jonas!" Victoria erupted. "How many times do I have to tell you to stop pushing me on this? There's enough on my mind already."

Jonas fell silent. Victoria remembered the feeling from years ago, when she felt she had driven him away. She wanted to keep the conversation going. "How are your children? I'd like to know more about them."

"They're fine," Jonas said tersely.

"You said they're adopted?"

Jonas responded hesitantly. "Gil never talks about being adopted, but our twelve-year-old daughter Grace has been asking about it a lot recently."

"A lot?" Victoria said in the same inflection Jonas always used to draw her out.

"You're still plenty sharp, Victoria."

"Must come from years of depositions and cross-examinations. Right now you sound like a reluctant witness."

"Do you know people with adopted children?"

"Leslie and Charlese adopted a girl from Croatia. So did a friend from the neighborhood, who adopted domestically."

"I'm assuming this woman adopted when the baby was an infant," Jonas said. "Did she talk about bonding with her newborn?"

"Why?"

"Just curious."

"This doesn't sound like you, Jonas," Victoria said. "Something tells me we've been here before. Like twenty years ago."

"It's not for me to burden your therapy with my issues."

"Burden me? Before every session, I worry how much of a pest I've become. It's still liberating to hear that you have issues, too. It makes you more real and makes me feel less like a freak. Without that, I couldn't talk like we do."

As their time drew to a close, Victoria resolved to see Jonas in person more often, and to steel herself for the discussion about Martin, for whom her mixed emotions were festering like an abscess.

50

Three hours later, Mrs. Blount ripped into Victoria about neglecting Melinda's needs. Victoria had had enough; she left the room abruptly, but Mrs. Blount followed her to the elevator and continued the harangue.

"What's the matter with you?" Victoria cried. "I thought therapists were supposed to be understanding and compassionate. My son's in a coma, and I'm trying to reconcile with my daughter. We're finished with you. My husband and I want another family therapist."

"Well, I never!" Mrs. Blount huffed.

"Well, you just did! I give opposing counsels' experts more respect in a two-hour deposition than you've shown me in the whole time we've known you." Victoria motioned toward the room. "This is about my daughter. And," she said, pointing at her chest, "this is about me."

"I'm going to . . . I'm going to . . . "

"You're going to what? Report me to the principal? Go ahead."

Mrs. Blount's face contorted like a gargoyle's. "No wonder your relationship with Melinda is so terrible."

"Leave my daughter out of this. What do you know about relationships?" Victoria had done her homework. "Everyone in Philadelphia knows your husband is always fucking one of his patients and that neither of your children speaks to you."

Victoria marched back into the therapy office and slammed the door. "We're done here," she told Martin and Melinda. "I'm sure Dr. Milroy will get us someone we can work with."

Mrs. Blount barged into the room.

Victoria yelled, "Get out and stay out!"

"Good for you, Mother." Melinda applauded.

Martin glowered at Mrs. Blount. "I don't care for how you've treated my wife." Turing to Victoria, he said, "I'm sorry, Vic. I should have said something sooner."

"We'll talk about it later," Victoria said abruptly. She hadn't intended to be so short, which brought to mind Jonas's warning about getting a grip on her feelings about Martin.

Dr. Milroy entered the room. "I heard a commotion. What's going on?"

Mrs. Blount opened her mouth, but Melinda interceded. "This woman is an asshole. All she does is upset my mother."

Mrs. Blount said to Melinda, "Your mother *is* the problem. She's nasty, confrontational, and obstinate. No wonder you're so ill, you poor thing."

"I'm not poor, you stupid bitch!" Melinda yelled. "And it's not all her fault. I played a role in it, too, not that you have the brains to understand. As for nasty, confrontational, and obstinate, look in the mirror, lady. That's you, not her."

"Let me talk with the Brauns alone," Dr. Milroy said to Mrs. Blount, who slithered out, fangs still bared.

"Can't you help us?" Melinda said to Dr. Milroy. "You work with groups. You must know how to work with families."

Dr. Milroy looked at his watch. "Stay here, everybody, while I call home and tell them I'll be late."

51

During Dr. Milroy's absence, Melinda withdrew several tissues from a Kleenex cube.

"What is it, Melinda?" Victoria asked.

"I've made such a mess. I love Gregory, too. I understand how much he means to you. I know I'm not as easy as him. It doesn't matter anymore. I know you tried to love me the best you could."

"I did. I tried so hard," Victoria said. "But I can do better, now. You'll see."

When Dr. Milroy returned, Victoria and Melinda were embracing. He waited while Melinda composed herself and sat facing her parents.

"This is hard," she began. "But here's what really happened. Do you remember the boy I hung around with this summer? I met him through someone at school, Nancy Grogan. I was so lonely; it made me happy she wanted me to hang out with her. The boy's name was Todd Kramer; he was a friend of Nancy's brother.

"Todd went to Choate. He was visiting Philadelphia because he had an interview at Penn; he said he wanted to be a doctor. I told him you were smart and that both of you went there.

"Todd had long hair, and his stubble made me think of Jack Sparrow in *Pirates of the Caribbean*. I said something about the movie, and it turned out he liked it, too. So, we got into this thing where he'd say a line from the movie, and I'd say the next line; or he'd imitate one of the characters, and I'd say who it was. It was fun. I felt like someone finally *got me*. He'd talk with me and stuff, and he intrigued me, because he was so much older and wiser. Todd started texting me and, like, I couldn't believe it. I really got the feeling he liked me.

"Once, he and I texted back and forth all night, and I wouldn't go to sleep because I was afraid I'd miss something. So, I stayed up even though I was exhausted. He said everyone was going to Atlantic City in the morning, and he asked me to go. Remember that day? I asked permission to go to Atlantic City, and you said yes."

"I remember that," Victoria said, recalling how pleased she felt that Melinda had friends at school.

"Todd said there would be a lot of supervision, but when I got to the Grogan's house, Todd was the only one there. He said the Grogans had left when he overslept. This was the first time I was alone with him, and I liked it. Actually, I liked it a lot, a whole lot, and I got . . . I got . . . I felt . . . " Melinda's face turned pink.

Martin started to speak but Victoria shushed him and told Melinda to continue.

"Todd asked if I wanted to eat. He said he had something that would make food taste really good; then he produced something that looked like half a squashed cigarette and he asked if I knew what it was and I guessed it was marijuana. Everyone in school had tried it, and I felt stupid, because nobody asked me to smoke with them, so I pretended I knew about it, so he wouldn't think I was, like, some clueless moron."

Melinda searched Dr. Milroy's face. He rolled his neck around as if he had a crick. If anything, he seemed pleased.

"Todd took me into the bathroom and turned on the fan. He told me to inhale as deeply as I could. At first, it felt like sucking in gravel; I coughed so hard, it hurt my sides. The second and the third times were easier.

"Then I started feeling weird. My legs felt heavy, and I wanted to lie down. I stumbled over to the nearest couch, and I remember looking at Todd's shirt and becoming obsessed by the buttons, which I thought were amazing. I started thinking about who invented buttons and how it changed the world, and what people did before buttons. I started counting Todd's buttons from the top down, and the bottom up.

"Anyway, I was really tired from being up all night, so I fell asleep, but Todd must have thought I was dead, because he woke me up. I told him to let me be, which he did, but then he woke me up again and said he was afraid that if I went to sleep, I might stop breathing. That got me really scared."

Melinda said to her mother, "I didn't want to call you or Daddy, because I knew you would yell at me."

The corners of Dr. Milroy's mouth tightened.

Victoria said, "That's going to change, Melinda. I mean it."

Dr. Milroy smiled at Victoria and nodded for Melinda to continue.

"Todd disappeared and came back with some blue pills. He told me to take one; he said it would keep me awake. I figured that someone who was going to be a doctor would know what he was doing, so I did what he said. I took a pill but nothing happened. Then I took another one, and that's when everything went crazy. My heart beat out of my chest, my skin felt like it was on fire, and it felt like someone was pulling my hair. I pictured running in front of a bus or slashing my throat. I couldn't make the thoughts stop."

Victoria recoiled, realizing how alike she and Melinda were.

"I was hoping and hoping it would all go away, but it just kept getting worse. I asked Todd what the pills were. He said it was his ADD medicine, and I asked how to get it out of me. He went online and found out that too much ADD medicine could cause schizophrenia, and I thought how awful it would be to turn into some schizo. It went on and on. I remember telling myself, 'Please, please, make this go away before I die. I don't want to die in a strange house with a boy I hardly know.'"

Melinda looked at her parents. "I haven't been the same since. The bad thoughts got worse, especially at night. That English teacher bitch made me feel like shit. She's always yelling at me. I didn't want you to know, because I knew you'd never forgive me for messing up my head."

"Did anything else happen to you while you were there?" Martin asked.

"You mean did Todd try and have sex with me? No, it wasn't like that."

Dr. Milroy spoke up, "Melinda and I are working on straightening out her thoughts. This is all a traumatic reaction in someone with bipolar tendencies. She has flashbacks, intrusive thoughts, and feelings of helplessness. Periodically her mind gets flooded with horrific images."

"You don't know how awful they are," Melinda cried. "They're bloody and they're always about you, Daddy, and Gregory. The idea of Gregory with his head split open makes me want to vomit. It's only been in the last two weeks that I've been able to read again," she said proudly. "The medicine makes me feel better."

"I'm sure talking helps, too," said Victoria.

Melinda said, "I like talking with Dr. Milroy."

"Good," Victoria said. "I have my own psychiatrist to talk with. He gives me medicine, too."

Dr. Milroy turned to Victoria, "She has your genes, which made it likely that, sooner or later, something would trigger a traumatic reaction, though not necessarily to this degree. It's interesting. Not only does bipolar disorder run in families, but often a medication that works for one family member works for another. Melinda's medication dampens her intrusive thoughts without making her a zombie. We can't have her up night after night worrying that if she goes to sleep she won't wake up."

"Now do you understand why I didn't want to go to sleep?" Melinda pleaded. "I wasn't being defiant; I was terrified. I kept myself up as long as I could, and when I did sleep, I had awful nightmares where I was paralyzed while spindly creatures that looked like tarantulas huddled together like they were going to swarm all over me."

"In addition to medication, we're working on techniques for Melinda to feel more in control of her mind," Dr. Milroy said.

"I'm getting better at stopping bad thoughts. And I'm starting to be able to write again, too. I was afraid my mind would never work again."

"Having Melinda tell her story over and over doesn't necessarily help," Dr. Milroy said, "but it's good you know where she's coming from."

Victoria said, "It all makes sense now. Thanks for telling me, honey."

"I believe that with time, therapy, and medicine, Melinda will recover," Dr. Milroy said.

"Completely?" Victoria said.

"That depends on what you mean by 'completely.' No one can promise that Melinda will never think about what happened that day."

"Will she be on medication forever?"

"It's way too early to speculate about that. The first order of business is for Melinda to get well and to stay well. Then, we'll decide what's next."

Melinda said, "What about family therapy? I never want to see that awful woman again. I know you're very busy, Dr. Milroy, but . . . maybe you could . . . "

"Sure I will. How's this? We'll arrange some day passes and see how it goes when you're home. And on one of them, the three of you can come to my office for a session. I'll put you down for a week from Friday at 5:00 PM. Okay, everybody?"

"Can I use one of my passes to go to Children's Hospital? I want to see my brother," Melinda said.

"We'll talk about it," Dr. Milroy said, glancing at his watch. "Whoa! It's late. I've got to go now. Is everyone okay about that Friday time?"

Melinda said, "Please, I really need to see him."

"We'll talk about that first thing at our next session," Dr. Milroy said.

"I promise nothing bad will happen. I promise," she pressed.

Victoria perked up, eager to observe how Dr. Milroy handled Melinda's insistence.

"Speaking of promising," Dr. Milroy said artfully. "I promise you and I will talk the whole thing out. Then we'll see."

"What is there to see?" Melinda contended.

"There's a lot about that night we haven't discussed," Dr. Milroy said. "Understand, Melinda. I'm not saying no. But we need to be sure that visiting Gregory won't cause a setback. Remember, I want you to go home as soon as you can."

"You're not sure I'm ready?"

"No. Not one hundred percent."

"How will you be able to tell?"

Dr. Milroy laughed impishly. "We'll know when you can tolerate not knowing whether or not you can visit Gregory without getting upset about it."

"Oh. Okay, I get it," Melinda conceded.

"Good," said Dr. Milroy, who ushered the family toward the door. "I think we've accomplished a lot tonight."

As they walked down the hall, Dr. Milroy said to Victoria, "It's obvious that you and Melinda are better with each other. You and Dr. Speller seem to be doing well, too. Please tell him I said hello."

52

December 21, 2004

For Jonas, the week before Christmas seemed endless. The first day of winter dawned raw with swirling gusts and single-digit wind chills that turned Manhattan's cross streets into wind tunnels. No one dared sit on Central Park's stone benches lest they adhere to them like ice cubes clinging to moist fingertips. Even the rats deserted the subway for the steam pipes and abandoned tunnels of Manhattan's subterranean world.

On the shortest day, the sun never really rose; instead it glowed dimly like a refrigerator light bulb, meandering across the sky barely above Central Park's treetops.

From the nonstop beeping of his telephone, Jonas concluded that his was not the only mood that was plunging. Whenever he thought about the holidays, his mind drifted back to Thanksgiving and how caught up he had become in Victoria's family. Guiltily, Jonas tried to reassure himself he cared as much about Gil and Gracie as he did about the Braun children. He could hardly wait for the family excursion to Puerto Rico the day after Christmas.

Hoping to break his mood, Jonas bundled up and walked south on Madison Avenue. When an arctic blast nearly toppled him, he ducked into Starbucks, which was teeming with gray-skirted girls in matching cardigans: Dalton School uniforms. A baby-faced strawberry blonde sat pigeon-toed, absorbed in her laptop. Jonas reckoned she was about fourteen, two years older than Gracie.

"This is so cool," she said to the friend on her left, a curly-haired round-faced girl who gazed out the window dreamily.

"Huh," her friend responded. "I can't see the screen."

The blonde girl adjusted her laptop. "Can you see it now?"

"Do you think they're coming?"

"Who?"

"Justin and his friend, the lacrosse player; I think his name is Dewitt."

"I don't know. Why?"

"Justin thinks you're hot."

The blonde girl's cheeks turned pink. "What? Who told you that?"

"Justin told Rhiannon Schlieder, who's friends with Shannon Parks, who told her sister—you know, that goofy-looking girl from Trinity Day who wears derbies and blood-red lipstick—that he thought you looked like Britney Spears."

"Britney Spears? That ditz. Is she for real?"

The round-faced girl didn't answer. She set her drink on the corner of an open book between the two of them. When the round-faced girl adjusted the laptop, she propelled her Frappuccino all over her friend's skirt and computer.

Instead of going ape as Jonas expected, the blonde girl laughed and grabbed a fistful of napkins, which she plastered to her clothes like paper towels.

"I always hated this skirt," she said.

"I'm sorry," her friend said unconvincingly. "Here, let me." She turned the laptop upside down, and a thin, steady stream of liquid poured out, reminding Jonas that Gregory Braun was still in a coma, hooked to an IV.

Two boys who looked like Abercrombie models walked in. One said something to the curly-haired girl, who wriggled around enough to make room for him to sit between her and her friend.

The barista called, "Skinny half-caff no-foam latte."

"That's mine, thanks," said Jonas, taking a last look at the two girls. Admiring the good-natured one, he thought he'd love to have a daughter like that. Or would he, given the challenges of parenting a teenaged daughter? Thanksgiving had made him painfully aware of how much he wanted to leave children of his own flesh and blood behind when he died.

Back at his office, Jonas had twenty minutes to kill before the weekly differential therapeutics seminar he conducted. He propped his feet next to a portable electric heater designed to look like a steam radiator. It reminded him of the scalding radiator at his grandmother's house on holidays where he used to play "I Spy" with his favorite cousins—blood relatives, too.

Jonas's reverie ended when his cell phone rang.

"Hello?" he said.

"It's me," Eddie said. "I just heard from the concierge at Dorado Beach. They're upgrading us to beach side."

"Well done," said Jonas, picturing five days in the South Atlantic sun. His beach reading included several medical record reviews and a biography of Richard Wagner. "Have you been outside today? It's freezing."

"Not really. I spent the morning taking the deposition of a guy from Greenwich who's suing an all-Jewish country club for not letting him in. He says they blackballed him after they found out his wife wasn't Jewish."

"Should you be telling me this?"

"Of course! You're my psychiatrist, Jonas," Eddie wisecracked. "Whatever I tell you is privileged."

"Do you care one way or the other?"

"Honestly? It's total bullshit. But it's an oral contract case. Something different."

"Anything else about the trip?"

Eddie hesitated. "Are Jennie and the kids excited?"

"Gracie would just as soon stay home with her friends. Gil's Gil. He goes with the flow." Jonas walked to his window. "Do you know anything about adoption law?"

"Huh? Why?"

"Gracie is interested in her biological parents. Jennie told me that adoption came up in Gracie's ethics class. The teacher said she had given up twin boys for adoption when she was seventeen and still wonders what became of them. Do you think Gil's and Gracie's parents think about them?"

"You said you didn't know anything about them."

"But they knew all about us. Both birth mothers thought long and hard. The adoption agency wanted a scrapbook detailing everything about our lives. Jennie and I lived on edge for months, not knowing if we'd be chosen. It was like being pregnant forever. There were home visits, neuropsychological testing, drug screening, credit checks, and criminal background reports. We even had to give access to our health records. It was worse than applying to med school, more like a psychological colonoscopy."

"You need a vacation."

"Sometimes, I wonder if Gil feels he's really my son."

"You *really* need a vacation," Eddie said.

"I hate winter. How about opening an office in San Juan?"

"Good idea. And we can advertise in the subway: '*Abogados* for slips and falls, asbestosis, and medical malpractice.'"

"If you do, I'll never testify for you again."

"Not to worry, Jo. Anything going on the rest of the week?"

"Jennie and I are going to *The Barber of Seville* at the City Opera tomorrow night. One of the residents' wives is singing Rosina. I wish I felt more enthusiastic."

"That's not like you."

"You're right. But I am looking forward to being warm. Can't you picture us jogging on the beach at sunrise?"

"Sounds like a plan."

"Great. See you Friday night."

"Remember, we're bringing the wine . . . " Eddie said.

Jonas knew there was more. "Yes . . . ?"

"And make sure to get somebody to be on call for you."

"So, that's the real reason you called," Jonas said. "To utz me about breaking up Thanksgiving dinner. You know, you're some character, Eddie. It's like Ahab and the whale with you. What do you have against *her*? What did she ever do to you?"

"Nothing. It's not that; it's . . . never mind."

"Never mind? Congratulations, Eddie, you're making progress. You're learning to keep your mouth shut."

"What happened with her kids?"

"They're alive. Barely," said Jonas sipping his lukewarm latte. He hadn't spoken to anyone except Stan about the ordeal before and after the bridge. Jonas's thoughts returned to his children. He made a mental note to spend time that evening helping Gil with homework, and to find out what Gracie really thought about the vacation.

"Thanks for the trouble you've gone through to set up this vacation. Jennie even asked me how to shoot dice."

"That's funny. Margo asked the same thing!"

"Well after what happened last month at Foxwoods . . . " Jonas's voice trailed off at the memory of Eddie's uppity attitude at the dice table when a very sexy woman sidled up to Jonas during a hot roll.

"I told Margo how you bet for all of us," said Eddie. "But I didn't tell her about the woman who shot the dice."

"Why not?"

"I didn't want her to tell Jennie."

"To tell Jennie what? Why shouldn't she tell Jennie?"

"I didn't want her to get the wrong impression."

"The wrong impression. Who?" Jonas asked indignantly. "Margo? Jennie?"

"Both of them."

The buzzer to Jonas's office went off. It was 3:00 PM exactly. "That's ridiculous, Eddie. I told Jennie everything the next morning."

"Including the hot blonde who shot the dice?"

"Why wouldn't I? I tell Jennie everything," Jonas added. "You know, I think you're laboring under some very mistaken assumptions, Eddie. I have a class. I gotta go."

"What if I stop by on my way home? Maybe we can grab a bite."

"Sorry, but not tonight," Jonas said, thinking about Gil and Gracie. "There's something important I have to take care of."

53

When Jonas arrived home, the aroma of Jennie's beef Stroganoff was wafting through the hallway. He found her in the kitchen over the stove with a spatula, sautéing mushrooms in a big skillet. Jonas snuggled up behind her and, after pecking her lightly at her hairline, he massaged her neck and shoulders.

"Mmm. That feels good." Jennie let her head flop around. She wiggled her shoulders until Jonas's thumbs kneaded a certain spot. "There. Right there."

Jonas squeezed Jennie's trapezius muscles rhythmically. "Where is everybody?" he said, hoping that Gil and Gracie were eating at home.

"Gil's studying. Gracie is at Jillian's preparing for a chemistry test. She should be home any minute."

"Have they said much about the trip?" Jennie remained silent. "I guess not," he said. "I heard from Eddie today. He said you and Margo are learning to shoot craps."

"You don't think you guys are going to have all the fun?"

"I hope everybody has a good time, kids included. Don't you think it's odd Gil and Gracie haven't said anything about it?"

Jennie turned off the gas and rapped the spatula sharply against the skillet. She opened her mouth, then grimaced as if she had bitten her tongue.

"What is it?"

"Jonas, all Gil wants is for you to be proud of him. He's your son. He needs that."

Jonas exhaled deeply. "He's so different from me, Jen. Nothing seems to move him. When I was his age, I was passionate about everything: girls, music, science. You know how emotional I am—how an aria can move me to tears. I get the sense that Gil feels I'm an emotional wimp."

"Just because he handles emotions differently from you doesn't mean he doesn't have them. He's more cerebral. He's passionate about his music, but he doesn't show it like you do. He feels you feel there's something missing in him, that you don't like being with him."

"What can I say? Sometimes I barely feel he's mine. I wish I didn't feel this way."

"And Gracie? Do you feel that way about her, too?"

Jonas flinched. "Are you talking about her ethics class?"

"It's way more than that. Gracie is a different animal," Jennie said. "Her life is becoming more and more about friends. Do you know why?"

"I assumed that was her strength. I encouraged her to do what she's good at. She's ten times more socially gifted than I ever was."

"That's not the point. I think the real reason she's searching for her birth family is because she wants a sister. I told you I hate the group she's involved with. Heaven help us if she picks one of them for a soul mate. Try and talk with her and find out where she's at. She's a lot smarter than you give her credit for. She's the one who could sit for hours and discuss chemistry and biology with you."

"I don't want to pressure her. You know that, Jen."

"What's important to you isn't necessarily important to them. We all know that music makes your heart sing, but expecting them to love Beethoven and Brahms doesn't cut it. Gracie thinks you think she's stupid. That's why she chooses the friends she does. *They* like her. At least I think they do. When's the last time you studied math or science with her?"

Jonas couldn't remember. "It's been a long time. I didn't want to stand over her like a taskmaster."

"She knows what a wonderful teacher you are—of *other* people's children, Jonas. I understand that you give all day at the office, but charity begins at home."

"I've given them the best of me: my enthusiasm and my encouragement."

"What if that's not what they need?"

This was not the evening Jonas had had in mind. "What's your point?" he said churlishly.

Jennie flung the spatula into the sink, splattering brown droplets on the countertop and backsplash. "Can the attitude and start listening, Dr. Wonderful!" she shot back at him. "Gil's incredibly closemouthed about his emotional life. His parents weren't from around here. You're the neurobiologist. Does it surprise you that people from different gene pools handle their emotions differently?"

"He's so stoic. Whenever I ask what he's thinking, he acts likes I'm prying. It's like trying to crack a bank vault."

"Then try another combination. I think you're so used to being admired by your students and your patients that you've lost sight of what your *own* children need from their father."

"I'm afraid they'll tell me I'm not their father. That would kill me."

"That's part of the package, dear. They didn't ask to be adopted by us."

"I think about that all the time," Jonas said.

Jennie's eyes blazed away. "They're not like patients you can refer out if you don't hit it off with them."

"Hold it right there, Jennie. I don't deserve that," he reacted self-righteously. "I have blind spots, I admit it, and you're right to point them out. But that's how marriage works, isn't it? You see things I don't, and I see things you don't. We're supposed to be on the same team."

"As long as you understand what I'm saying."

"Believe me. You've made your point."

"Apparently not. We talked about this a month ago, and nothing's changed. I'm trying to be patient, Jonas. I know you're having a tough time, but do I have to club you over the head with this skillet to get through your thick skull?" Jennie stretched her neck and back, which Jonas knew had begun to spasm.

"Here, let me. Where does it hurt?"

Jennie winced as she clutched the back of her neck and pointed Jonas's hand to the sore spot. "Ouch, it really hurts."

"Let your neck hang loose, and I'll stretch it. Let go of the tension. Just let go, and let me stretch."

Jennie complied hesitantly.

"Don't fight me," he said. He pulled Jennie's head to the right, ever so gently. "Take a deep breath and let it out slowly. Relax into the stretch."

"That's better," Jennie said.

"Good. I forgive you completely!" he said.

Jennie looked like she couldn't decide whether to embrace him or wring his neck.

Before she could do either, Jonas said, "I know I have to wrap my head around this. What do you see in Gil and Gracie that I don't?"

The telephone rang. Jennie handed him a whisk and pointed him toward a saucepan. She said, "It's probably Gracie calling to say she's on the way." Jennie picked up the phone. "Hello, kitten," she said, cradling the handset between her neck and shoulder. She winced again and stretched as Jonas had instructed. "That's okay," she said. "Dad and I will wait. *Dépêche toi.*"

Jennie looked at Jonas. "She needs to be pushed academically. You can explain science better than anyone I know if you put your mind to it. School has her working on complicated chemistry and math, but she's so into being with the in crowd, I'm afraid she'll get distracted and stop trying altogether." Jennie peered down the hall toward Gil's room. "He'll do better when you stop doing what you want to do with him and do what he wants to do with you."

"Which is?"

"Gil's much more comfortable writing his ideas than speaking them. Something tells me there's a girl in drama class who has a crush on him. I don't think he knows how to handle it. Musically, he likes alternative rock and roll. It's ironic. He's into classics, like you are, only it's music from the last decade, not the last century. It'd be a lot better for your relationship if you took him to a rock concert instead of *Der Rosenkavalier*. If you want know what he likes that's German, ask him about Rammstein. It's heavy rock with guttural German lyrics."

"It'll take work," Jonas said.

"Since when do you shy away from a challenge? All you have to do is express interest in music. *His* music. Or is playing the bass line beneath your dignity? How's that for a metaphor? And one more thing. Be thankful Gil's metal is in his music, not his tongue."

54

Jonas tapped on his son's door.

"Who is it?" Gil called.

"It's Dad."

"Is supper ready yet?"

"In a few minutes. Can I talk with you about something?"

"About what?"

"About the vacation."

"What about it?"

"Can we talk face-to-face?"

"Wait." It took another minute until he said, "It's okay to come in."

Gil's room was as neat as a marine barracks, everything in its place. Gil was on his bed, leaning against a corduroy chair-pillow, with a Tom Stoppard play open on his lap. So handsome and rugged he could have been on the cover of *GQ*, he wore a pullover sweater that complemented his black hair.

"How's it going?" Jonas began.

"Fine. Hang on a second, Dad," Gil said, preoccupied by a text message that had just arrived. "This'll just take a minute."

Jonas waited, but after several minutes, he got up to leave, telling Gil, "It looks like you're busy. I'll come back later."

"Don't leave. I'm just saying good-bye." Gil put his phone aside. "What's up?"

"Do you have everything you need for the vacation?"

"I'm all set."

"You sure?"

"Yup."

Each utterance sounded to Jonas like Gil couldn't wait to be left alone. "We haven't had a chance to talk much lately. I was hoping we could talk about Puerto Rico. I want you to have a good time."

Gil looked at Jonas for the first time. He sat up. "There's a lot of reading for drama class. They're putting on a production this spring, and I'm thinking of trying out. Mom thinks it'll help me be more comfortable around people."

"People? Anyone in particular?"

Gil fidgeted and his face flushed.

Not the right time, Jonas told himself, so he dropped the subject for the moment. "What play are they doing?"

Gil seemed relieved. "Actually, it's two plays: Shakespeare's *Hamlet*, and Tom Stoppard's *Rosencrantz and Guildenstern Are Dead*, which is a takeoff on it."

"That's quite an undertaking. When are auditions?"

"Right after winter break. We get the vacation to prepare."

"I've heard about *Rosencrantz and Guildenstern Are Dead*, but I never saw it."

"It's very witty. Did you ever read *Hamlet*?"

"A long time ago."

"Do you remember who Rosencrantz and Guildenstern were?"

"I'm not sure. Hamlet's friends?"

"More like acquaintances. Hamlet's mother and stepfather use them as part of a plot to have Hamlet assassinated. Hamlet figures it out, and Rosencrantz and Guildenstern are executed instead. In the last scene, the English ambassador announces, 'Rosencrantz and Guildenstern are dead.'"

"What's the play about?"

"It's *Hamlet* told from a different perspective. The minor characters in *Hamlet* become the main characters in Stoppard's play."

"Which role you want to play?"

Gil swung his muscular legs over the side of his bed, stretching his arms behind his head the way Jonas often did. "It's a long shot, but either Rosencrantz or Guildenstern. To be honest, I'll take any part as long as I'm in it." Gil put a bookmark in the paperback. "I'm memorizing everyone's lines, so that I can recite the whole play by heart."

"Wow, that's something." Jonas himself knew every line in *Carmen*. He thought, *Maybe we're not so different.* "Good for you, Gil. Do you practice with anyone from class? You know you can always have friends here after school if you want to practice in a smaller group or one-on-one."

"Well there is this one person . . . " Gil squirmed and looked at his father like he needed help finishing the sentence.

"Hmm. Let me guess," Jonas said. "Someone who wants to play the heroine?"

Gil started to blush again. "How did you know?"

"Well, let's just say that back in the day before your mother stole my heart, I had my share of encounters with the fair sex. When I was around your age there was a flutist named Cheryl who wanted to play Mozart sonatas with me. We knew each other from orchestra."

"Was she any good?" Gil asked

Jonas laughed. "'Good' is a relative term, son. Cheryl was far and away the best instrumentalist in school. Her intonation and technique were impeccable. The sounds she made felt like they came from on high. In that sense she was better than good. Back then I was very proud of being concertmaster, so the fact that she looked up to me musically felt good; so as long as were practicing or performing we got along great."

"What did she look like?"

"She was pretty; she had blonde hair and blue eyes. I remember her sweaters because the colors always matched her eyes. But outside of the practice room it was like she had no use for me. It was the weirdest thing. She hung around with a different crowd and never once introduced me to any of her friends. So in that way she made me feel bad."

"Whenever we have to pair off in class," Gil said, "the same girl always picks me."

"Do you like working with her?"

"I enjoy it. It's fun for both of is. I can tell she likes it, too."

"That's good. So she likes being around you. At least in class."

"Are you sure?"

"You betcha. You can't pretend to have fun . . . unless she's a professional actress, which I'm assuming she's not."

Gil assented, smiling.

"Do you know her outside of drama class?"

"Not really. But she smiles when she sees me in the hallway."

"Then she most definitely likes you. Cheryl never smiled at me anywhere! Do you like it when she smiles at you?"

Gil's face relaxed into a glowing grin that couldn't be faked.

"Can I ask her name?"

"Brandy."

"That's a nice name. Do you smile back when you see her?"

"I'm not sure if I'm supposed to. She's a senior."

"Ah. An older woman. I like her already. She has good taste. Well if you want her to know your better, you can always ask in drama class if she wants to work one-on-one with you some time."

"I could do that."

"I bet she'll say yes."

"And then what'll I do?"

"Be yourself and go with it. If what happens between you and

Brandy makes you feel bad, then stop doing it. You'll know if it stops being fun. If you're not sure about how you're feeling, I'm always here to talk about it."

"Supper's ready," Jennie called from the kitchen.

"We'll be there in a minute," shouted Jonas, reconsidering his beach reading. "Brandy aside, Gil, how about this? I'll read the play before vacation. Then, we can practice together: You play whoever you want; I'll read the other parts."

Gil's face brightened. "That'd be great, Dad. Really great."

"I'll enjoy it, too. We'll have fun."

55

As the three of them sat down to dinner, Jonas's twelve-year-old daughter Grace burst through the door and flung her backpack to the ground. Peeking into the kitchen, she said curtly, "Hi Mom. Hi Dad," then disappeared into her room.

"Dinner's on, Gracie," Jennie said.

"I'll be there in a minute," Gracie yelled back. A minute turned into two, then three, then five. Jonas looked at Jennie, then Gil, then Jennie again. Jennie's mushroom sauce had begun to solidify.

"Shall we wait for her or not?" Jennie wondered aloud. Jennie looked at Jonas liked like she expected him to do something.

Jonas, who felt hungry enough to eat gruel, said, "Let's eat. She'll be along soon enough."

"Someone knock on her door and tell her we're waiting," Jennie said.

Gil said, "She probably ate already, but I'll tell her if you want, Mom."

"Your father will get her," Jennie said peevishly.

Jonas said, "Let Gil do it. She'll listen to him."

"Dad will take care of it," Jennie resolved stridently while looking at Jonas. Jennie rarely argued in front of the family, but she shot him the same confrontational look from earlier.

As he rose from the table, Jonas said in exasperation, "Get started with dinner while it's hot. This may take a while."

When the telephone rang, Jennie bristled. "Who's calling in the middle of dinner?"

Jonas saw that the telephone cradle was empty. "Where's the receiver?"

"How should I know? Look for yourself."

Gil looked at his mother with an expression that said, "What gives?"

Jonas said to Jennie, "I'd like to speak with you. Alone," he added when she had barely moved. Jonas headed into the den, Jennie trailing behind slowly. "What's going on with you?" he said.

"It's time for you to get involved with her, too. Everything can't just be left to me. It's not right."

"What's been left to you?"

"It wasn't this way in my family. We all had to pitch in."

"What? I thought your mother wanted you to be her clone."

"You're off saving the world and forging new frontiers in psychiatry and psychoanalysis. I'm the one who has to deal with her issues."

"Okay, Jen. Enough! I'm starving. I had a good talk with Gil. I want to do the same with Gracie, but I need to eat first and clear my head. There's no way I'm going in there hungry and tired. Nothing good will come of it."

"I suppose," Jennie said dubiously.

Gil was easy, Jonas thought. *Gracie will be harder . . . much harder.* Jonas saw the parallel between his and Victoria's children.

56

After wolfing down dinner, Jonas grabbed a mug of coffee and disappeared into his den. He gazed at the bridges spanning the East River. Due east, a jetliner descended steeply toward LaGuardia Airport, about to make the hairpin turn over Shea Stadium that always scared him to death when he shuttled to Boston or Washington to testify or give a lecture.

Jonas moved onto the couch, where words and sentences began forming. "Jennie is my wife. Stan is my father-in-law; sometimes I wonder if Gil and Gracie are even mine," he said as if he were with Dr. Frantz. "Ah. I see. This thing about Gil and Gracie is about belonging."

Jonas went to his bookshelf and picked out his copy of Moses Maimonides' *Guide for the Perplexed*. He hadn't touched it in nearly a quarter of a century. A familiar smell tickled his nose and called to mind the conversation he had with his father a month before he died.

"What do you want to do after medical school?" Jonas's father asked.

"I'm not sure. It really doesn't matter where I'm going, I just see myself driving a used Volkswagen Beetle."

Willy Speller said, "I hope you get where you want to go. That car may have to last longer than you think. When I got my first car, I had no idea I'd use it to drive my first child home from the hospital."

"You mean Eddie?"

"No, we were going to name him after the first man in our family who settled in America, Jacob Spielmann; Jake for short. But the baby died before the Brith. Crib death, they called it."

"You mean I had another brother? Eddie never told me."

"He doesn't know."

"'SIDS,' they call it now. Sudden Infant Death Syndrome. Some people think it runs in families. I'm sure to be asked about it when I have children."

"I didn't know you were considering it."

"I haven't gotten that far in my plans yet, Dad."

"You'll get there."

"Having children scares me. I don't know if I'll ever be ready," Jonas told his father.

"Don't worry. You'll make a great father when the time comes. I hope you'll be blessed to have children that give you as much pleasure as you and your brother have given me."

Jonas returned to the present and clapped his hands in glee. "I get it!"

"You get what?" Jennie said through the closed door.

"Later," Jonas replied.

For the first time, something made sense. Children giving their parents pleasure, like that was all there was to parenthood. Jonas cringed at his naïveté—at the times he had distanced himself from Gil and Gracie when they weren't such a pleasure. And the connection to Victoria's children. The crisis with her children forced him to realize how vulnerable all children are. That they may be gone at any moment—like Jacob, the brother he never knew. It was so much easier to focus on Melinda's and Gregory's vulnerability than to feel it about Gil and Grace.

His hesitation *was* about adoption, he realized, but not in the way he thought. The real fear was that if the birth parents reappeared to claim their offspring, Gil and Grace would desert him in a moment. He hadn't appreciated that they would *become* his over time, the way Victoria and Jonas had become parts of each other's lives by being involved with each other's conflicts. That's why he had had to be there for Victoria on Thanksgiving night; because he belonged. Being involved: such a simple phrase with such far-reaching consequences. Conflicts are important, Jonas acknowledged. *Just because Dr. Fowler sucked at dealing with them doesn't mean I can ignore my own. Biological and psychological parenthood are far from the same*, Jonas realized.

It was closing in on 10:00 PM. Jonas rose and left the room. Jennie was nestled comfortably on the living room couch.

"I'll explain later," he told her on the way to Gracie's room. Halfway down the hall he turned around. "You know, it's really late, Jen. What I have to say will keep until tomorrow. Besides, I want to sleep on it."

57

At 4:00 PM the next afternoon, a new patient entered Jonas's office. Stewart Collier was a middle-aged, well-put-together man in an expensive business suit; he worked for a Wall Street investment bank.

After introducing himself, Jonas said, "So, Mr. Collier. What are you hoping we can do here?"

"I need something for depression," Mr. Collier said as if he were ordering lunch. "My divorce has been dragging on longer than I ever expected. I've tried everything, but nothing works for more than a few months."

"Who's been prescribing?" Jonas asked.

"Different doctors over the past few years. They all blend together in my mind. I have a psychopharmacologist, but my internist said you were good with medications. I guess you could call this a second opinion."

Mr. Collier produced two typewritten pages. Jonas perused the impressive list of antidepressants, antipsychotics, and mood-stabilizers. "Did any of the medicines work better than others?"

"I liked Paxil the best."

"Why was that?"

"Because it took away the pain and the anxiety. And it worked fast."

"The pain?"

"I was really hurting after my wife served me with divorce papers. I never thought Sandra would go through with it."

"How long ago was that?"

"Two years."

"So the Paxil numbed your feelings?"

"The relief was so welcome—I didn't care much about anything. It kept me together enough so I could work."

"Psychic anesthesia we call it," Jonas said. "Why did you stop taking it?"

"Because I couldn't have sex. I was trying to reconcile with Sandra. They tried me on Wellbutrin and Effexor, but nothing worked like the Paxil."

"You work where?"

"Duane Capital. I manage their high-yield corporate bond fund."

"Lots of late nights?"

Mr. Collier nodded wearily.

"Traveling, too?"

"Sometimes. I told Sandra that we'd only have to put up with it for a few more years. Then, we'd have enough, so I could quit and spend more time at home."

"How much is enough?" Jonas asked.

Mr. Collier looked at the family pictures on Jonas's desk. "No one ever asked me that question before."

"No one?" Jonas wrote the word "enough" in the margin of his note pad.

"After she served the papers, I agreed to go into couples therapy. Sandra told the therapist she felt she was living in an emotional vacuum. By then, my primary doctor had me on Paxil, but the therapist said Paxil could blunt emotions and cause sexual side effects."

"That's true," Jonas said.

"So the couples therapist referred me to a psychopharmacologist she knew. He said I would do better on Wellbutrin. But the depression got worse, so he added Effexor. Every few months, he would try me on something different or add something else."

"How often do you see the psychopharmacologist?"

"Once a month in the beginning. Then, they stretched it out to two, then every three—sometimes even a different doctor."

"How long are your visits?"

"Ten minutes or so. The doctor would ask about my symptoms. Then they'd type into the laptop."

"Ten minutes! How did he know how you were feeling?"

"I filled out a symptom checklist before each session. The nurse put it in the chart. Then, the doctor would go over it with me and decide about my medicine. I was supposed to call the nurse if had any questions. They must have a lot of doctors in the practice. The waiting room was always packed."

"Can you remember the last time you felt well?" Jonas asked.

Mr. Collier sighed. "Nobody who does what I do for a living feels well. Get up in time to catch the five twenty-five AM from New Canaan. Be at your desk by 7:00 AM to catch up on Europe. Wolf down lunch. Work until eight, nine, sometimes ten o'clock, depending on what happens."

"So why do you do it?"

"We need the money. Our youngest boy has Down syndrome. Between Thomas's therapeutic school and our daughter's college tuition, it costs a fortune."

"Do you have therapy?"

"We went to a local person for marriage counseling. I needed someone who could see us on Saturdays. Sandra stopped after six months. She said it was pointless, that nothing had changed. Mrs. Blackwell said I should come alone, so I began seeing her once a week in the beginning, then once every other week. Now I call her whenever I want to. "

"So, what happens in therapy?"

"We talk about how I'm feeling. About work. About the children. I like talking with Mrs. Blackwell. She says she's preparing me for the next step. She thinks I'm stuck on Sandra and need to move on."

"What's happening in the marriage now?"

"I'm living in a one-bedroom in Stuyvesant town. Sandra's still in the house in New Canaan. I really don't want to be divorced."

"Do you have a sense of where Sandra is at emotionally?"

"We see each other. It's not exactly dating; I don't know what to call it."

"She's still looking for something from you," Jonas observed.

"I feel like she's toying with me. Every time I think there's hope, something happens. Once, I got a call from the divorce attorney. Another time, I said I'd like to meet her for dinner, but she balked like she had a date. I was down for weeks after that. "

"Is it possible that that's why you felt your medication stopped working? Because your hopes were crushed?"

Mr. Collier removed his suit jacket and uncrossed his legs. "I never looked at it that way. You're probably right. My depression got a lot worse when Sandra's lawyer called in a forensic accountant."

"They think you're hiding money?" Jonas said. Mr. Collier smiled nervously. "Are you?"

"What I say is confidential, isn't it?"

"As long as no one's life is in danger."

"I keep a couple hundred thousand in an offshore account. I thought I hid it well. But now I'm not so sure."

"So you're hoping to get back together, but at the same time you're deceiving her."

"I thought I was here to get medication," Mr. Collier said harshly.

Jonas wrote down the words "nasty streak." "I don't just prescribe medicines, Mr. Collier," he said. "I treat patients with psychiatric disorders. To do that I have to get to know someone. Does Mrs. Blackwell know about the money?"

"No one knows about the money."

"It's only a matter of time until the accountant tracks it down. I see it all the time."

"I think Sandra's having an affair. But then again, my thoughts are so screwed up I don't know what to believe. Thomas is twelve. Neither of us wants to uproot him. When I come home, he throws his arms around me like he's afraid I'll disappear. He misses me."

"Do you have thoughts about death, dying, or killing yourself?"

"I would never do that to the children."

"That's not what I asked."

Mr. Collier reached for a tissue. "A lot of nights, I wish I would go to sleep and never wake up. Then everyone would be happy."

"No. It would tear your son to pieces."

"Please. Just give me something to get me through," he cried. "Anything. I read about a new antidepressant with no sexual side effects. Maybe that'll get me and Sandra back on track. You're supposed to be good with medicines. Just tell me what I need."

Jonas took off his glasses and faced his patient eye to eye. "Mr. Collier, you need a lot more than a pill. Sure; there are other medicines we can try. No one should have to put up with intolerable side effects from their medication. But what you really need is a different attitude. Deception has a nasty way of inveigling itself into every aspect of a relationship."

Mr. Collier nodded. "She's probably just as suspicious about me and the money as I am about her cheating, although I give her everything she wants."

"If she says she's living in an emotional vacuum, then what she wants is not a thing. What with you and your son, the stakes are high. Are you serious about working it out with Sandra?"

"Yes."

"Then that means coming clean about the money. And confronting how your work-life affects your family. You have to put everything on the line. Monetarily and emotionally."

Jonas and Mr. Collier discussed his mixed feelings about Sandra, whom he pressed to have the second child even though she was in her forties—a known risk factor for Down syndrome. After Thomas was born he more-than-partly blamed her for Thomas's condition.

"We can work with the medicine, Mr. Collier," Jonas said, summing up. "But to really stop the bleeding you need to see the world through your family's eyes. Not that you have to agree with it. But you do have to see it. What they feel. What they need."

"Do you understand what it's like living with a child with Down syndrome? They're so full of love. It's more than love; it's adoration. It's so hard to live up to."

"It has to be that way for Sandra, too. I wouldn't be surprised if that's at the crux of her feelings. Working all hours is a good excuse for avoiding your feelings. If you get working on that in therapy, you and Sandra might be able to talk it out. I can work with you on you as long as you, me, and Mrs. Blackwell are on the same page."

When Mr. Collier left the office, Jonas reflected on the session and what was awaiting him at home that evening. He thought about Gil and Gracie. Every child has special needs, he realized. Including his.

58

When Jonas entered Gracie's room after dinner, she was lying on her stomach reading *Teen People*. Grace Speller had the lithe build of a jockey and the face of a budding country-music star. She had just begun wearing makeup. Gracie had covered her walls with large nature scenes, mounted and matted in color-coordinated tones.

She looked up at her father and said in a distant voice, "Oh. Hello there. Do you want something?"

Instead of responding immediately, Jonas stopped to look around his daughter's room. A picture he had never paid attention to caught his eye: a just-before-dusk rendering of an abandoned barn camouflaged by unmown grass and leaves. In the upper left, a patch of sky glowed faintly with an orange tint.

"Is this a photograph or a painting?" he said. "It looks like something I saw at MOMA."

"What does?"

"Here. This is awesome."

"It's my favorite," said Gracie, rolling onto her back.

"The color jumps out like it's alive. Where did you get it?"

"My chemistry teacher is also a photographer."

"This is better than any photograph I've ever seen. It looks like an impressionist painting. How he did do it?"

"He uses digital imaging."

"Is this the teacher we met on back-to-school night?"

Gracie nodded. "Mr. Flynn. He said that professional cameras have more memory. They can record images more clearly, because there are more pixels. It's the same principle as high-definition TV."

"I knew you were interested in art, but I didn't realize you had gone digital."

"There's a lot of other things you don't know about me, Dad," Gracie japed, her tone uncannily like Jennie's.

"Touché," Jonas rejoined in kind.

Gracie stood up and, flicking away several strands of hair from her face, went over to the wall. "Have a look." She carefully removed the picture and placed it under her desk lamp. "Mr. Flynn takes pictures like these with a high-resolution camera mounted on a tripod so it won't move. He programs the camera to take six pictures per second, one right after the other. Then, he uses a computer to superimpose the images. This is the finished product."

"You mean that this is really six different photos, one on top of the other?"

"That's right. That's why it looks so alive. I like Mr. Flynn; he's a good teacher."

"What makes him so good?"

She hesitated thoughtfully. "He cares about us," she said. "Why are you interested in my teachers all of a sudden?"

"I'm interested in what you like."

"Oh."

"What are you working on in chemistry?"

"The first part of the year was about atoms, and now we're covering molecules and the kinds of bonds that keep them together."

"Mom said you were studying at Jillian's yesterday afternoon."

Gracie frowned. "That was awful."

"Is that why you were in such a bad mood when you got home?"

Gracie examined Jonas's face intently. He hoped she would open up to him.

She said, "We started studying, but Jillian didn't understand even the basics about atoms and atomic weights. It was like I was supposed to be her tutor, but when I explained, she said I made her feel stupid. I wanted help figuring out the difference between ionic bonds and covalent bonds, and electron clouds and orbitals."

"Mr. Flynn expects you to understand all that?"

"Yes, but Jillian turned the whole thing against me. She said everyone hates me, because I treat them like idiots. That even though I act like a stuck-up Jewish-American princess, I look like a trailer-trash *shiksa*."

"She said that?"

"Yeah. What's a shiksa, Dad?"

Jonas remembered seventh grade, when a girl he had a crush on sneered at him like he was some pimply nerd. "It's not a nice word," he said.

"What does it mean?"

"'Shiksa' is a very derogatory term for a non-Jewish girl or woman; the implication being she steals a Jewish man's attention."

Gracie said, "They've been using me, haven't they? I thought they liked me, but they have been talking behind my back the whole time."

"I was just thinking that, too. I'm sorry."

"There's nothing to be sorry for. I'm the stupid one. Some of this has to do with my Bat Mitzvah party next month. I couldn't invite everyone, and this is how they're getting back at me. Besides, there's a boy Jillian likes who likes me more than her. That's probably where this shiksa business is coming from."

"That's very insightful."

Gracie sat down in front of her computer and opened a spreadsheet with a long list of friends and acquaintances down the left side. "I invented this," she said proudly. "I know there isn't room for everyone at my party, so this is how I'll decide who to invite." She pointed to the headings of the columns; each contained a personality characteristic like temperament, friendliness, or responsiveness. Every cell in the grid contained a number ranging from one to ten. "I rate people on different traits and how they make me feel. Then I program the computer to derive a composite score—some factors are weighted more than others—which I sort from highest to lowest. That's the column farthest to the right. I'll pick the people on the top of the list."

"Brilliant! What an idea. How did you come up with it?"

"Chemistry lab. We're constantly doing experiments and then tabulating results based on variables like temperature or the concentration of the reagents."

"Reagents? I didn't learn that word until college. Are you sure you're not a closet geek?"

"Is that supposed to be a compliment?"

"I meant it that way."

"Well, the popular girls don't hang out in chemistry lab after school, that's for sure. You know who Hermione Granger is, don't you?"

"Is she a friend of yours?"

Gracie groaned like a parent going over multiplication tables with a seventh grader. "You, of all people—I thought you knew everything."

The conversation was getting interesting. "I guess not," Jonas said. "Who is she?"

"Hermione Granger is the heroine in all the *Harry Potter* books. She's the smartest, hardest-working girl at Hogwarts, the school where the books take place. At first, people thought she was a showoff know-it-all, but now, everyone respects her."

"Really? That's pretty sophisticated stuff for children's books."

"Children's books my ass. By the time book three came out, I had to look up new vocabulary words every other page."

"What is it about these books?"

"There's a lot to them. Everybody can find someone to identify with, a teacher they've had or someone they knew years ago. Each book corresponds to another year at Hogwarts, so you see Harry and his friends growing up."

"And Hermione?" Jonas asked.

"The business at Jillian's has me thinking more and more about Hermione. I'm more like her than I thought."

"Is being popular that important? There must be smart boys and girls who want to be friends with you."

"You're right, Dad," she said. "There's a boy named Manny Friedman who sits in front of me in chemistry, and we usually wind up being lab partners. He's friends with a lot of the smart kids who're into computers and imaginary games. I know they like me. Manny lives in Brooklyn. It's an easy subway ride, if you and Mom would let me go."

"I'm sure we can work something out. Is there a good place to start with the *Harry Potter* books?"

"You mean you want to read them?"

"Sure. It'll give us something else to talk about."

Gracie brightened. "Okay. Honestly, book four is the best, but if you really want to get into it, start with book one. Otherwise, you'll feel lost."

More interesting beach reading, Jonas thought. "As far as chemistry goes, would you like me to help you with it? I loved chemistry when I was your age."

Jonas and Gracie spent a delightful hour bonding over how atoms bond. "You're a good teacher, Dad," Gracie said.

Jonas felt tickled. "You're a good student."

She opened a thick botany book. "There's a lot more I want to understand; like what plants are made of and what happens when animals eat plants."

Jonas patted Gracie's back playfully. "It'll take a while. I never studied much about plants. Animals, I can figure out. Plants, we'll have to learn together."

Gracie hugged Jonas tighter than he ever expected. She didn't let go for a long time.

59

When Victoria arrived at Children's Hospital the day before Christmas, she found a huddle of interns and residents outside Gregory's door. The skull replacement, several days earlier, had gone well, but she worried that something terrible had happened. Instead, Drs. Bell and Breckenridge emerged from his room with smiles on their faces.

"You've noticed how he's begun to move in the last few days? Today, he's responding to commands," Dr. Breckenridge said. "That's huge! We noted it on rounds this morning when I asked him to squeeze my hand, and he did. I asked him to squeeze twice, and he did that, too. Then, I asked him to squeeze both hands at once, as hard as he could. The fact that Gregory can understand and follow commands means a lot of his brain circuitry is good to go."

Victoria said, "I want to see him now."

"They're changing his clothes and rearranging the monitors. It won't be long," Dr. Breckenridge said.

"How worried were you that he wouldn't wake up?" Victoria asked.

"I could tell that Gregory's a fighter."

"He's such a special boy."

"Isn't the brain amazing? If all goes well, he'll be skateboarding in Love Park before you know it."

"Skateboarding? Are you crazy?" Victoria caught herself. "I'm sorry. I shouldn't have said that. It's just that—"

"Don't apologize. I like it when people treat me like a civilian instead of a doctor. Can I ask you something, Mrs. Braun? I know you're a prominent lawyer. People must be intimidated by you. Every time a guy I meet finds out I'm a brain surgeon, he's blown away. I have a tough time with it."

"You know, Dr. Breckenridge, until now, I never thought of you as anything other than Gregory's doctor."

"Neurosurgeons are people, too," she laughed. "Can you think of me as Anna?"

"I'll try."

"You should see the way you look at Gregory. The love, it's awesome. I want to capture that look in a sculpture I've been working on. Until I started neurosurgery training, I was always chiseling away at a block of marble." Anna gazed out the window at Center City's glimmering skyline. "There's one piece I never finished. I never knew why until now."

"Which is?

"The face. I couldn't get the expression right." Anna eyed Victoria up and down. "Now I know. It's the look of love on your face. That's what I wanted to capture. Would you mind if I sketched you? It won't take long, I promise."

Marble made Victoria think of cemeteries and gravestones. "I suppose so. You see death every day, don't you?"

Anna nodded.

"How do you deal with it?"

"I look for the humanity. We all have to be technically competent; that's a given. But neurosurgery is a lot more than that. The week we started training, Dr. Liddle told us a story from when he was a first-year resident. He was called to evaluate a man with an enormous blood clot in his brain that came from falling on the pavement while he was dead drunk. Since the man had no identification, he was admitted as a John Doe. His blood alcohol was high enough to kill any nondrinker, and his blood clotting was so poor from chronic liver disease that surgery was impossible. Instead of berating the man for drinking himself to death, Dr. Liddle wrote in the consult, 'Although I greatly regret it, I feel that any surgical intervention would only cause unnecessary suffering. Comfort measures to ease this man's final hours are the most appropriate and humane treatment we can offer.'

"Three months later, the man's family identified his body, which had lain unclaimed in the local coroner's office. Someone must have read his consultation report, because the deceased man's mother sent Dr. Liddle a handwritten letter, which he shows to all the new trainees. It meant the world to her that her son had not been neglected in his final hours like a bum off the street."

Anna said, "You see, it's not just about sawing and stapling. It's about the brain, the seat of humanity. Unfortunately, not every doctor is like Dr. Liddle. Some surgical residents handle death with black humor. They use terms like 'organ donor' and say, 'Bring in the combine,' when they're going to harvest organs from someone who's brain-dead. I hate when they talk that way."

"Why do they do it?"

"Because they're afraid of recognizing how fragile life is, that the person on the other side of their retractors could just as easily be their wife or best friend. I can't help getting attached; it's how I'm made. Gregory gives me hope. Everyone needs hope. We do so much better now than we did a generation ago."

Anna lowered her voice. "When we were ten, my best friend Becky and I did something so stupid that I still can't believe it. Becky and I decided to race our bicycles. Back then, no one wore helmets. We rode off down the sidewalk in opposite directions going as far away as we could still see each other, equidistant from a driveway in the middle, which we picked to be the finish line. We agreed that at a given signal we'd take off toward each other. The one who got to the driveway first would win.

"Near the end I could see that the race was really close. With a hundred yards to go we were tearing down the sidewalk on course for a head-on collision. Both of us reached the driveway at the same time; we tried to peel off before it was too late, but we barreled into each other at top speed.

"I landed on the street, elbows and knees first. I still have the scars. The wounds went down to the bones. It felt like somebody had peeled off my skin. Becky ricocheted off the hood of a parked car then slammed onto the road. 'Get up. Get up,' I yelled, but she was knocked out cold. I told myself she'd be all right but when she didn't get up right away it hit me that she might be really hurt.

"Becky was in a coma for over a week and wound up brain-damaged with a lisp and spasticity on her right side." Anna's face furrowed as if she were reliving the scene. "Back then, brain-injured kids were never the same."

"About the skateboarding . . . ?"

"Tell him to wear a helmet. You'll make sure of that, won't you?" Anna asked.

"Don't worry. I'll kill him if he doesn't."

Several doctors and nurses emerged from Gregory's room. It was time for Victoria to go in.

Anna said, "Remember, it'll be like emerging from a thick fog. Eventually the fog will lift, but not before Gregory drifts in and out of consciousness."

60

Victoria didn't leave Gregory's side for the next twenty-four hours. On Christmas Day, his eyelids fluttered, and his throat moved, as if he were trying to speak.

As soon as she heard what was happening, Anna rushed in.

Victoria's eyes filled with tears. "You understand, Anna, no words can ever express how grateful we are for what you did for Gregory, and for us. If he had died, I'd never have recovered. Never."

Anna said, "It's why I do what I do. I had a feeling about Gregory last night. They made me go home early yesterday, because I hadn't slept in two days. I fell asleep on my couch. When I woke up, the movie *Apollo 13* was on TV—the part at the end where everyone was waiting to see if the astronauts had survived reentry. It was a shared moment of hope. Right then, I saw Gregory's face. I saw you two embracing, and I saw Gregory running in his schoolyard. Someone put me here on Thanksgiving to do that operation. I was supposed to be here."

"What if he doesn't know me?"

"He will. You'll see."

Victoria touched her son's shoulder. "Gregory?"

Gregory opened his eyes. They twitched noticeably, then closed.

"Gregory? It's your mother."

His eyelids moved again. He tried to raise his head, and it inclined slightly toward Victoria.

"Mu—Mudda?"

"He knows it's me!"

"I knew he would. I knew he would," Anna said.

"Wha—? Wha—? Where . . . ?" he whispered, his head drooping back down.

"You want to know what happened and where you are. Here." Anna placed Victoria's hand in his. "Squeeze once for yes, twice for no." Gregory pressed his mother's fingers perceptibly.

Victoria said, "Do you remember what happened? Once for yes. Twice for no." Gregory squeezed twice.

"You had a terrible fall and hurt your head. The doctors had to do a big operation. Do you feel any pain?" Gregory squeezed yes, this time more forcefully.

Victoria shuddered at the thought of Gregory having his skull violated with a buzz saw and his scalp peeled back.

"A lot?"

No, he squeezed twice. His throat muscles contracted again. "Ith . . . ithuzz," Gregory whispered.

"Ithuzz? Oh, I understand. You mean it itches."

"Yeth," he whispered. Victoria laughed and cried.

Anna said, "That's an excellent response. The self-dissolving stiches cause itching. That means he has sensation as well as motor control," she enthused.

Victoria caressed Gregory's forehead gently. "That's enough for now," she said. She let him rest.

She called Martin immediately to tell him what happened, then dialed Jonas's cell phone, which rang through to voicemail. Next, she called Lorraine and Morris.

"I'll be right there," Lorraine said on the other end of the phone. "Give me a minute to put myself together."

Anna said, "I can go away feeling better," and she headed for the door.

"Are you doing something for the holiday?" Victoria added

"I'm going on a ski trip, my first vacation in two and a half years. I'm on duty today until I finish rounds. I'll celebrate on the plane this evening. This is the best Christmas present I could get."

Martin arrived in minutes and embraced Victoria with tears of relief in his eyes. For an instant she didn't recognize him.

Lorraine appeared moments later in a white sweat suit, her eyebrows looking as if they had been painted on with a Sharpie. "I got here as fast as I could," she panted. "I ran up five flights of stairs. I knew he would be okay. I knew he would be okay."

"Let's not get ahead of ourselves, Mother," Victoria said testily. "There's still a long way to go."

"He'll be fine. I just know it." Lorraine eyed Victoria. "My God, you look awful."

"Thanks, Mother. So do you."

"I'm sorry. I didn't mean it that way. You've been through so much with them. It must be overwhelming."

Victoria knew her mother meant what she said. She regretted her nasty rejoinder about Lorraine's appearance. "I'm sorry, too, Mother," said Victoria, astounded with the comfort she took from her mother's apology. "You have no idea what it's been like to see my Gregory lying here, tethered to all these machines."

"He's my Gregory, too, you know. My only grandson."

Victoria was transfixed by the monitors chirping. "Do you hear this, Mother? This is all I've known of my child for the last month until an hour ago when he talked to me. When he woke up he wanted to know what happened. Thankfully he doesn't remember any of the bad from Thanksgiving night."

"I'm happy for him about that. I've been thinking a lot about things while I've been next to you at Gregory's bedside. I woke up, myself, only I do remember the bad between you and me. What happened to us?"

Forty years of sadness and hurt swept through Victoria like a tsunami. She glared at her mother.

"I don't know, Mother. You didn't like me. I never knew why. You said such mean things, it made me sick." Victoria caressed Gregory's cheek tenderly. "This could have been me. I kept thinking about throwing myself off a building every day for a month. I was so sick, Mother. It's a miracle I'm alive. I wouldn't have survived if I hadn't gotten help."

"I never knew," Lorraine said.

"Of course you didn't know," Victoria said bitterly. "You, Daddy, my brother. None of you cared whether I lived or died."

"That's not true," Lorraine recoiled. "Victoria, please believe me. I cared."

"Then why were you so awful to me? What did I ever do that was so terrible? All I wanted was for you to like me."

"I was mad at you. I was jealous. I was a fool."

"Mad at me for what?"

"I knew they loved you more than me."

"Who?"

"Your grandmother. Your father. My mother couldn't wait to get away from me; she couldn't wait to get back to work."

"Grandma went to work to get away from Grandpa. She wanted her own life and her own money, which is how she came to send me to college. It had nothing to do with you. Not everything is about you, Mother. And what about Daddy?"

"He lit up when he saw you like he never did with me. Even before you were born, he massaged my stomach so lovingly when I was pregnant."

"Is that why you poisoned him against me?"

Lorraine moved closer. "I didn't mean to do that. Please believe me."

"You treated Daddy like crap. That's one of the reasons he drank. The more you nagged him, the bigger his martinis. He let you abuse him, and I hated him for that. Thank God he got sober and learned to stand up for himself. I like the man Daddy is today."

"Believe me, Victoria, not a day goes by that I don't regret how I treated your father. I understand why he left. I don't blame him. I can't bear the thought of losing you, too. What can I ever do to make it up to you, Victoria?"

"It doesn't have to end like that for us, Mother. Just tell me you're sorry. Tell me you like me. Show me that you care. That's what I want from you."

Gregory moved again, trying to whisper. Victoria took his good hand. She said, "Do this, Mother. Help Gregory. He'll need a lot of help and a lot of love. Be with him. Read to him. Listen when he talks and make him know you understand."

"I promise I won't disappoint you, Victoria. I promise."

Morris arrived, a trench coat draped over one arm, his other around Carolyn's waist. Carolyn, a dark-complected woman with soft features, stepped back, but Morris took her firmly by the hand and led her toward Gregory.

Victoria held her breath. Lorraine and Carolyn had never been together in the same room. Victoria knew that Lorraine had never recovered from being left by Morris. The more he gave in to her demands for alimony and the Abington house—anything to buy his freedom—the more it hurt.

Lorraine said, "Hello, Morris. You two are well, I hope."

"Yes. Thank you," Morris said.

"I guess you heard Gregory's waking up. Although there's a long way to go."

"For everyone," said Morris. He looked at his ex-wife compassionately. "For everyone."

Victoria said, "Look, Gregory." She gently turned his head. "Look at all the people who love you."

Victoria wondered why she wasn't happier. She thought, *My son is waking up. My father has a woman who loves him. My mother wants to make a fresh start. My husband wants to . . . My husband wants to . . .*

Everyone toasted Gregory's awakening with a bottle of sparkling cider Morris had brought. Victoria went through the motions, but the feelings of disconnect between her and Martin wouldn't go away, and left her with doubts about whether Gregory, like she and her husband, would ever fully recover.

61

"Good morning, ladies and gentlemen," droned a bass baritone voice. "Captain Sean McBride speaking from the flight deck."

"What's he doing, making an announcement now?" Jonas asked Gracie and Jennie. "We haven't even pushed back."

"Shush, I want to hear," Jennie said.

"A storm system has stalled over the Delmarva Peninsula. We're going to skirt the storm by heading farther east than usual before we turn south. That will add a good forty-five minutes, maybe an hour, to our flying time today." Jonas strained to understand the pilot's words. "The flight will be choppy for a while, but we'll do all we can to keep you comfortable. It'll be another fifteen minutes until we leave the gate, so I suggest that anyone who might want to use the restroom do so now. The 'fasten seatbelt' sign will be on for quite some time once we're airborne."

Jonas, a confirmed white-knuckled flyer, sat on the aisle, Jennie to his left, Gracie in the window seat. "Just what we need," he said to no one in particular. Gil, directly across the aisle, next to his Aunt Margo and Uncle Eddie, was absorbed in his book, *Rosencrantz and Guildenstern Are Dead*, which Jonas had read the previous evening. Jonas noticed Gil mouthing the words silently.

"Choppy for a while" turned out to be an understatement. For the next three hours, Jonas felt like he was strapped to a paint-can mixer. Every few minutes, he glanced out Gracie's window to reassure himself the wing's rivets weren't coming loose.

To distract himself, Jonas read *Review of the Chemistry of Plants and Animals*, a study guide he had downloaded from the Internet. In fifty-six pages, it reviewed what had taken Jonas four semesters of organic and biochemistry and a lifetime of immersion in neurobiology to imbibe. Each section felt like swallowing butter. As he tried to take it all in, he wondered, *How did I ever learn all this?*

Fortunately, the material was dense enough to keep him occupied through the worst flight he had ever endured. Finally, as he was starting the section on proteins, the jerking stopped. The Atlantic Ocean peeked through billowing clouds, and the left wing rose ever so slightly as the plane turned south. As soon as the seatbelt sign went off, a parade of ashen passengers lined the aisle waiting for the restrooms.

When the plane touched down in San Juan, the passengers applauded, except for Jonas, who felt so relieved that he wanted to offer a sacrifice on the nearest altar. Most of the travelers wandered around baggage claim in shell-shock. Jonas and Jennie saw Stan and Marta.

"There he is," said Jennie, catching sight of her father. "Don't you think Mom and Dad look well?"

Stan and Marta, now in their mid-seventies, still appeared hardy, although Stan had more pigmented spots on his ruddy forehead and Marta's arms and legs were considerably less beefy. Gracie and Gil gave their grandparents big hugs.

"Hi, sweetie," Stan said to Jennie.

"How long have you been here?" Jonas asked Stan.

"About an hour, give or take." Turning to Gracie and Gil, he said, "I can't believe how big you two are getting, especially you, young lady. I think you grew two inches in the last month. How are you, Jonas? How did everything turn out with your patient?"

"I'm glad you asked. It'll be good to talk with you about that. Maybe over drinks tonight or tomorrow."

"Tonight or tomorrow? I'm dying of thirst right now. Besides, there's something I want to discuss with you. As soon as we're settled in our room, I'm changing into my shorts, making myself a rum punch, and settling onto the nearest lounge chair. I hope you'll join me."

"Give me half an hour to burn off my adrenaline with a quick jog on the beach," Jonas said. "I just spent the last three hours worrying that the plane was falling apart. You probably had it worse between the flight and the waiting."

Stan said, "Please thank your brother for getting everyone rooms on the beach. Oh, there he is. I can't believe how long it's been since I've seen him." Stan greeted Eddie and Margo warmly, leaving Marta and Jonas standing by the baggage carousel.

Marta said, "I know that Stan wants to talk with you, Jonas, so I'll be sure to give you two time and space. And don't feel you have to apologize about what happened with you and Jennie the other night. That's between you and her."

"Dammit, she told you?" said Jonas, angry at Jennie and embarrassed that Marta knew about their spat. That Jennie had talked about it with her mother felt like a betrayal.

"Mothers and daughters talk about their children all the time; you must know that. You don't think what she said came as a surprise, do you?"

Jonas sighed. "I guess not. Well, the good news is that I'm working on ways to connect with Gracie and Gil."

"I knew you would. They're great kids. You're a lucky man. I'm sure you and Stan have a lot to catch up on. You know there's nothing you can't tell him, Jonas. Nothing."

Marta must have seen the look on Jonas's face, because she back-pedaled quickly. "I'm sorry. That didn't come out right. I didn't mean to imply anything. It's just that he loves you like a son. He only wants you to be happy."

"I don't look happy?"

"Everyone knows you've been on edge since Thanksgiving. For what it's worth, Jennie felt horrible about jumping on you about Gil and Gracie. She really didn't want to kick you when you were down, but there's never a good time—"

"It's okay. She was right, and I spoke with both kids."

The fifty-minute ride to the resort over bumpy roads felt like being back on the plane. Jonas's motion sickness continued for an hour. As he headed to the beach for his run, he caught a glimpse of Stan lolling on a chaise longue, tumbler in hand, looking like a man without a care in the world.

62

"C" an I get you one of these, Jonas?" Stan said, tipping his glass in Jonas's direction. "We have all the ingredients. Have a sip; I'll never finish it."

Jonas looked at Stan's glass, from which a pineapple chunk and a maraschino cherry protruded. "No thanks," he said, pulling over two deck chairs. "Eddie wants to have a drink before dinner. If I have one of those things now, I'll be asleep in five minutes."

After an awkward silence, both men began speaking at once. Jonas said, "After you, Alphonse."

Stan took a sip. "No use beating around the bush."

"Beating around the bush," said Jonas, squinting in the afternoon sun. "I wonder where that comes from."

"It's a hunting term. You rustle the bushes near where the birds nest, to flush them out, so the shooters can get at them."

"That doesn't sound like much fun for the prey."

"It's better than bushwhacking, spraying the bush with buckshot. At least the prey has a chance to get away."

"Maybe I should have one of those," said Jonas, pointing at Stan's glass. "That way, the prey won't feel it so much."

"Jesus, Jonas, relax. You look like I'm going to perform an autopsy on you."

"Well, can you blame me? I didn't exactly expect Marta to come out swinging."

Stan broke into a wide grin. "She's like that. All women are, don't you think? Do something that threatens their children, as they see it, and you might as well be facing a firing squad."

"So you've been on the receiving end yourself, Stan?" Jonas smiled. "You should have seen your daughter in action."

"She comes by it honestly, that's for sure. You weren't around to see Marta and Jennie go at it when Jennie was Gracie's age."

"Good Lord. That must have been something!" Jonas looked at Stan's cigar. "Pass me one of those things, so I can think better," he said. Both men laughed, but the truth dawned on Jonas; it was getting late in the game for Stan. Who else besides Marta could he confide in? Jonas borrowed one of Stan's favorite therapy lines and said, "I can tell there's more you want to say about that."

"Correction, my son. There's more I want to say about that *to you.*"

The late afternoon sun had turned the South Atlantic into a dappled orange reflecting pool, reminding Jonas of Fridays on Dr. Fowler's couch. If the guard were going to be changed, this was as beautiful a spot as any.

Stan took a big swig of his drink. "To understand Jennie, you have to understand Marta and me. How much has Jennie told you about us?"

"Not much. Just that the two of you were crazy about each other right from the beginning and moved heaven and earth to be together."

"That's the party line. Has she said anything else?"

Jonas said, "No."

"Which means Marta never told her."

"Never told her what?"

"Understand, Jonas," Stan said. "What I'm about to tell you goes no further; maybe Jennie, that's up to you. And Marta doesn't need to know I told you. Agreed?"

"Sure, Stan. Sure." This certainly wasn't the grilling Jonas had anticipated.

"When Marta and I met," Stan began, "neither of us were prepared for what happened. My father was a rabbi; Marta's father was a Eucharistic minister. No one would have picked us for each other. No one. But what we felt for each other was so strong, there were no words for it. We were young for our age, so naïve. It wasn't anything like the era in which you and Jennie came of age. Back then, young people couldn't live by themselves and experiment relationship-wise without seeming loose."

Jonas moved closer.

"You know, we met at the airport during a snowstorm. I was going to a wedding in Kentucky. Marta was going home, but that's not the whole story by a long shot." Stan took off his Panama hat to swat some fruit flies. "After finishing in Lexington, I met up with Marta in Louisville. Marta told her family she needed to return to Switzerland early to prepare for exams. She and I snuck off to the Brown Hotel in Louisville. I remember the place like it was yesterday. The lobby reeked of so much booze and cigarette smoke, it felt like a gin mill. Once we were alone, we couldn't keep our hands off each other. It felt like being possessed.

"Since both of our families were religious, we were sure they'd be furious, but neither of us was prepared to break with our families. They meant too much.

"After Louisville, we flew to New York, and I saw Marta off on her return to school in Switzerland. She didn't have enough money to come back to the States anytime soon, and I was in analytic training and barely supporting myself. So, we weren't sure when we'd see each other again.

"We wrote constantly. There was a trunk line her hospital maintained for international calls, so we managed to hear each other's voices, but only for a few minutes at a time. Then, I got a call at six o'clock in the morning one Saturday. She was hysterical."

Jonas knew exactly what had happened. "Oh, no," he whispered. "Not that." He maneuvered his chair to face Stan head on. He wished he'd taken Stan up on the drink offer.

"You have to understand, Jonas. To Marta, abortion meant murder, end of story."

Seeing beads of perspiration forming on Stan's forehead, Jonas offered him the napkin from under his drink.

"There we were," Stan continued. "Two kids; we barely knew each other. All alone in the world."

"Jesus, Stan. What did you do?"

"We decided we'd be better off away from home, where no one could bother us. That Monday morning, I called the director of my psychoanalytic institute to ask about suspending my training while I attended to important family business overseas. I told no one other than my training analyst.

"The plan was for me to go there and we'd get married discreetly in some nondenominational chapel. Married! Can you imagine that? We hardly knew each other. I begged and borrowed enough for the airfare. Marta found us an apartment next door to one of her friends. We had no plan. Except for the rent money Marta earned teaching at a girls' finishing school, we had no income. I had no working papers. We had nothing."

Stan continued, "Marta had two close friends: Jausienne Moriellion, a nurse at the university hospital—she lived with her parents in a chalet with an in-law suite; that's where we lived—and Anne DePaquier, a fellow medical student who was married and had young twins.

"Anne and Marta persuaded Professor Christian Mueller, the equivalent of the Dean of Students at Marta's medical school, to find me a part-time job as a lab assistant earning five Swiss francs an hour, which was a lot of money back then. Mueller introduced me to Professor Georges Van Claire, the chief of psychiatry at l'Hôpital de Cery and the head of the Lacanian psychoanalytic institute in Lausanne. I'll never forget Van Claire, so stocky and inscrutable. He looked more like a ski instructor than a psychiatry professor.

"Marta had terrible morning sickness, but she never missed a class. She spent her evenings with me studying; I spent the evenings emptying the plastic bowl we used to catch her vomit. Even though the fetus was only eight weeks old, she bonded with it as if it were one of her vital organs."

Stan's eyes drifted toward the wall of flowering bushes beyond which the waves were breaking against a craggy jetty.

"We barely slept," Stan continued. "Marta woke up night after night, breathless from panic attacks, but except for being there for her, there was nothing I could do. My parents called day after day, wondering what was going on. Eventually, I stopped answering the phone.

"Then one afternoon, my older sister Sharon showed up at the chalet. From the way I embraced her, she must have thought I was desperate.

"When she saw us together, Marta assumed my family sent her to get me to come home, but once Sharon saw Marta heading for the barf bowl, it took all of fifteen seconds to figure out what was going on. She immediately took Marta into her arms like a sister. Marta couldn't stop sobbing. I thought about calling Monsieur Van Claire that night, but Marta didn't want anyone knowing our business."

Stan's drink was disappearing rapidly.

"In the middle of the night, I heard panting and soft moans, and the toilet flushing. At first, I thought Marta was having another anxiety attack from all the emotional upheaval she'd been through."

"Did you realize what was happening?" Jonas said.

"Not at first," said Stan, covering his eyes like he wanted to blot out the memory. "Marta pointed at some red-stained mucus in the toilet bowl. Then, she started pacing. It went on that way for a while, me rubbing her back and neck like I always did, when all of a sudden, she doubled over and started howling like she'd been disemboweled. Sharon woke up, and when the two of us carried Marta back to bed, all I could see was bright red blood staining her nightgown."

Stan began rubbing his hands agitatedly. "I pounded on the Moriellions' door.

"'*Où est ta femme? Maintenant. Venez vite. Si vite que possible*,' I said to Monsieur Moriellion in the best French I could manage. Out came Madame Moriellion in her nightgown. I told her, '*Prenez votre voiture. Venez. Ma fiancée Marta est là-dedans. J'ai peur qu'elle mort.*'

"I'm sorry. I remember it in French. Did I lose you?"

"Absolutely not," Jonas said. "I'm right there inside the chalet with you. You told them you were afraid Marta was dying."

"The next ten minutes are a blur. Madame Moriellion, Sharon, and I dragged Marta into the cold night and laid her in the back of Monsieur Moriellion's pickup truck. He sped through the windy streets like a grand-prix driver. At every traffic signal the road split into two or three directions. It's amazing the things you remember. The street to the Salle Des Urgences was named Rue de Bugnon. '*Au secours. Au secours*,' Madame Moriellion yelled the moment we arrived."

Jonas had become so engrossed in Stan's story that he could barely breathe. With the late afternoon wind dying down, the only things moving were two egrets diving from the sky like a pair of fighter jets.

"Marta had bled out six pints. An arterial-venous malformation in her uterus had ruptured. She was in shock. They said she'd have died if we'd gotten there ten minutes later. The doctors operated immediately to see if they could save her from needing a hysterectomy, and that's how things stood when Marta came to. We were so relieved that she had survived that all we could do was hug each other.

"But when Marta saw us celebrating, she threw a fit. 'Where is our baby? What happened to our baby?' she wailed on and on. The doctors hadn't told her yet about the damaged uterus. She was thrashing around so much it took all four of us to keep her from disconnecting her IVs. I remember the glass bottles of blood—that's what they used in those days—swinging back and forth.

"Someone summoned Professor Van Claire, who dismissed us summarily. He didn't leave Marta's bedside for the next two hours. Then, he said he wanted to speak with me. Alone. By then, it was late morning, and I could see Evian and Mont Blanc in the distance. 'French or English?' Van Claire asked sternly. The look on his face told me everything. I was in for it. '*Anglais, s'il vous plaît*,' I said.

"'Do you understand what just happened, young man?' he asked gravely.

"I told him yes. He asked again. I told him yes. He asked a third time, irately. 'I love her,' I told him. 'I love her with all my heart.'"

"'You love her?' What do you know about love? You run off to some shabby hotel like a pair of rabbits and call that love? You didn't even use protection. What sort of man does that? Do you have any idea what kind of woman Marta Koetter is? What it meant to her to be pregnant? What it'll mean if she can't bear children? You—ready to run back to Mommy and Daddy and leave us to clean up your mess.' Monsieur Van Claire glared at me like I was scum."

Stan's shoulders shot back to attention. "I saw red. '*Assai!*' Enough, I told him. '*Pas un autre môt.*' Not another word. 'You know nothing about me. I'm the son of a rabbi. A man of faith. I would *never* run away from my responsibilities.'

"I wanted to grab the man by his neck and pin him against the wall, but he apologized for talking to me that way. It must have dawned on him that I might be as grief-stricken about the baby as Marta was.

"'Marta Koetter is a simple girl,' he said. 'She's devoted to family. She'll stay with you forever. It's in her nature. But she deserves better than someone who stays with her out of obligation.'

"I thought Monsieur Van Claire was finished. He opened the door as if to dismiss me; then turned back and said, 'So do you.'

"'*Je reste ici*,' I told him. '*Je m'appartiens avec elle.*' I'm staying here with her; where I belong.

"Monsieur Van Claire and I made peace. He saw how devoted I was to Marta and that I would never desert her. Later on, he recommended me to the Lausanne psychoanalytic institute and found me work at l'Hôpital de Cery. He became Jennie's godfather."

Stan collapsed into his chaise lounge. "Does any of this sound familiar?"

Jonas nodded. "Yes, but about Marta . . . ?"

"We were lucky. Her uterus healed enough for her to conceive Jennie, but Marta spent the entire pregnancy in bed. That was all we were prepared to risk. We thought about adopting but never pursued it. Not until a certain someone showed up in our foyer one Thanksgiving with two bottles of Swiss wine."

"It must have been devastating to Marta when Jennie couldn't have children," Jonas said.

"Not really. There had always been tension between Marta and Jennie. Marta is and always was a farm girl. That's what I loved about her, but Jennie wanted a gentrified sophisticate for a mother. That's the real reason she took up with that fool from Hollywood. It wasn't solely that Peter snowed her with the lifestyles of the rich and famous; Jennie bought into it because she thought she'd become the woman her mother never was. God knows exactly what happened—I have my suspicions—and I know Jennie landed hard, but it was the making of her."

"Ironic, isn't it?" Jonas said. "Life sends Marta two kids from the farm for grandchildren. You know, I always believed Gracie and Gil came from somewhere in the Midwest."

"You don't think that was an accident, do you?"

"What?" Jonas said.

"Marta turned the whole Koetter clan onto the fact that 'a couple she knew well and trusted'—that's how she phrased it—wanted to adopt. Koetter was one of the most respected names in southern Indiana; they put out the word to every diocese within fifty miles."

"Did Marta know the birth families?"

"No. And she didn't want to. That whole episode with Jennie's cancer scare and the adoptions gave Marta and Jennie a second chance to bond, which they did. That's all I wanted to tell you."

"That's all?" Jonas chuckled. "It's going to take a while to process this. I feel like I just discovered that Beethoven was a plagiarist. What about Jennie? Should I tell her?"

"I trust your judgment. Other than that, I don't have much to say."

Both men laughed. Jonas broke the silence. "I'm glad you told me."

"You're the first person I've ever told the full story. I'm glad you're here for me to tell it to," Stan said as if he had read his last will and testament.

"Let's hope it stays that way for a long time," Jonas said.

Off to their left, the sinking sun backlit the stratus clouds above like the corner of Gracie's photograph.

63

After dinner and an uneventful hour in the casino, Jonas and Jennie returned to their room. Jennie wore a flowing negligee that made her feel plush and satiny. She initiated the lovemaking that night, which Jonas knew was her attempt at reconciliation. He tried hard to accept her apology, but the sting of feeling betrayed lingered, like the ache after a muscle spasm that heals in its own time; he knew his anger at Jennie would fade away soon. Jonas turned face up promptly after they finished and said, "That was nice. Good night, Jen. I love you," after which Jennie burrowed close to his chest and fell asleep quickly.

Jonas slipped out of bed and threw on some clothes; he headed out the sliding doors toward the ocean. With the palm trees swaying, the full moon cast eerily bright shadows, the evening breeze echoing the sounds of the surf. Jonas sank onto a wooden bench, his mind swirling. Stan's story reminded him of his own vigil after Gregory's surgery. He thought about Jennie's breast cancer and infertility, and Marta's miscarriage—how women face death to bring life into the world.

Moments later, he heard footsteps, and caught a whiff of cigar smoke mingling with the scent of the tropical blossoms. Jonas said, "Stan? What are you doing up so late?"

"It's me," said Eddie, emerging from the bushes.

"Since when do you smoke those things?" Jonas said.

"Stan gave it to me. Mind it I sit down?"

"It's a free country."

Eddie sat down as far from Jonas as he could get. "Am I disturbing you?" Eddie said.

Neither man spoke for a moment. Then Jonas said, "Yes, to be honest, but don't take it the wrong way. It's been a long day. I just wanted to unwind."

"Peaceful, isn't it? Not like holidays in the city." Eddie turned to face Jonas. "Whatever happened Thanksgiving night is still affecting you. Everyone's noticed."

"Evidently it's open season on my psyche," Jonas said.

"You told me you tell Jennie everything. Just exactly how much does Jennie know about *her*?"

"So, we're back to that again?"

"That's how Dad wanted it."

"What!"

"You heard me."

"What does our father have to do with this?"

"The year you went to college, he made me swear I would always look out for you. Maybe he had a premonition he would die young."

"This is looking out for me? Harping on me because of something you don't understand?"

"You've had this thing for her forever. Admit it."

"So, we're back to cross-examination. Leave it at work, Eddie. I'm on vacation."

"So, Jennie doesn't know?"

"Know what?"

"That you love someone else."

"Did it ever occur to you that someone could love more than one person? And that there's more than one kind of love?"

"What's that? Psycho mumbo jumbo for cheating?"

"Cheating?" Jonas reacted vehemently. "How many times in the last twenty years have I had to endure your accusations? It took me all this time to figure it out; you're jealous, because I have something in my life that you don't. Do you really believe I would skulk off from my family to attend to a mistress? Are you out of your mind? What kind of person do you think I am?"

"Explain it to me, then."

"Why should I?"

"Because I've always been there for you. Because I stuck up for you every time Pete doubted you. Because I helped you get started in the city. Because I've done a million things for you over the years. You owe me an explanation."

"Back off, Eddie. I'm warning you for the last time."

"You owe me an explanation," Eddie insisted.

White heat surged up Jonas's spine. "I'll explain myself to you after you explain to me why you fucked some twenty-year-old babe three days before you got married."

"What?"

"Don't bother to deny it. I know all about it. How many others have there been since then, Eddie? One? Ten? A hundred?"

Eddie stared at the ground for a long time. "It happened only once," he said.

"I don't believe you. I saw her in the neighborhood more than that."

"How did you know?"

"You left the used condom in the kitchen trash can. It was disgusting. How do you think I felt, finding that right before your wedding?"

Eddie hunched forward.

Jonas said, "She passed by me on her way out just as I came in with coffee and *The Morning Sun*. You never knew I was there."

"We did it only once, Jonas. I swear. She lived around the corner. I went jogging, and there was this beautiful girl with auburn hair and a figure to die for. She smiled each time I circled the neighborhood. But I barely remember her face."

"I do," Jonas said. "Drop-dead gorgeous. She looked like a movie star and carried herself like a debutante."

"Her name was Jane. From Weymouth. She had a British accent. I remember her outdoorsy smell; I'd never been that close to someone so beautiful.

"She said she was in Baltimore temporarily, nannying for a friend of the family. I was so naïve. Jonas, you could have knocked me over with a sledgehammer. I couldn't believe she was hitting on me."

"Why not?"

"Because I was just another average-looking guy about to marry some nice Jewish girl I'd been dating forever. I was nothing special; I played by the rules."

"Rules. Whose rules?"

"Whose rules?" Eddie grunted plaintively. "You think anybody sat me down and told me?"

"What happened that night?" Jonas asked.

"She said she had the evening off. Her accent made her seem older. She wore a dark brown skirt with buttons down the side. She was thirsty, so we went to No Fish Today on Howard Street. She ordered ginger ale. I told her I was getting married soon, but instead of being put off, she seemed curious. She talked about her parents. Her father was a doctor, or a diplomat, I'm not sure. She asked where I lived, so I showed her my room."

For the first time in his life, Jonas felt his brother was speaking to him as an equal.

"Something came over me, Jonas," Eddie continued. "For an instant, I was a different person. No one expected anything from me. Time stopped. I'm sure I was trembling, because it took forever to undo all those buttons. She looked so beautiful when she was naked." Eddie looked off into the night. "She was disappointed by the sex, I could tell. I think I hurt her. I never got the chance to make it right. In the morning, she thanked me for the evening, very properly, as if she were thanking a parlor maid for having poured a lukewarm cup of tea. I tried to walk her home, but she wanted to go alone. She must have passed you on the way out."

Jonas said, "I wondered what she was doing there. I went to the kitchen, because I needed a paper towel. When I opened the trashcan my first reaction was astonishment. I thought, 'How did this get here?' Then I remembered that you never went to sleep without emptying your bathroom wastebasket. 'How can he be doing this?' I asked myself. 'He's getting married in three days!'"

"Did she say anything?" Eddie said.

"No, but she looked at me as if there was a family resemblance. So, was it worth it?"

Eddie seemed to smile and cry at the same time. "Yes and no. Mostly no. I felt awful about having disappointed her. And about being unfaithful to Margo." Eddie scooped some sand with his right shoe and flipped it over. "I was scared shitless about getting married, and I had no one to talk about it with."

"You never thought of saying something to me? Your own flesh and blood?"

"I was the older brother. I didn't want to disappoint you."

"It's too bad you didn't know me better. There's still time."

"Time for what?"

"To get to know me better. You might be pleasantly surprised. Your Jane was a beautiful young woman. I would have wanted to know her myself. She wasn't sleazy at all."

"No. She was a gentlewoman. I was the one who felt that way."

"So, that's what you've been projecting onto me all these years; that I'm a sleazebag, because I have a thing for a woman I've known half my life—a lot longer than you knew Jane."

"Well . . . what about when Jennie finds out about this 'thing' of yours?"

"She knows all about her. How many times do I have to tell you that I don't keep secrets from Jennie? I hadn't heard from the woman in twenty years, until the week before Thanksgiving. You'd be one lucky man to have someone like her in your life," Jonas said. That simple statement crystallized coherently what he had been feeling.

"She must be something. You've never slept with her?" Eddie said.

"For the last time, no."

"You admit you love her?"

"That's right. I do."

"What about her? Does she love you?"

"She's married to a man who adores her. She'd fall apart without him. I could never do anything that would threaten her stability or their marriage."

"How do you live your life married to one woman while you love someone else?"

"Don't you understand? I love them in different ways."

"You don't want to sleep with her?"

"No, I don't."

"So, what do you get out of it?"

"She needs me; at least for the time being. I matter to her. Knowing that makes life better."

"What is she, some friend from high school?"

"It's more than that."

"What is it, then? I want to understand."

"We grew up together. It's as simple as that."

"I didn't think therapy was supposed to work that way."

"Neither did I."

"I don't understand."

"I don't know if you can. You see, twenty-five years ago, psychoanalysts believed therapy was a one-way street. Analysts were expected to be blank screens onto which their patients played out their conflicts. It looked pretty on paper, but the result was a stilted pseudo-relationship. A natural connection goes both ways, but back then, analysis was an exercise in mutual deprivation. Analysts cared more about their patients' conflicts and free associations than they cared about their patients' lives. I knew that wasn't right, so I searched for another way to look at therapy. She was one of the people who helped me find my way. We nourished each other. Do you see?"

Eddie said, "It's like a dance."

Jonas smiled. "You must have read my mind. I was just thinking that. Therapy is music, spontaneous and intuitive. Sometimes it feels like improvisational jazz. The music I make with Jennie is like the waltz in Tchaikovsky's *Serenade for Strings*, lilting and melodious. Even though I'm still mad at her right now, I wouldn't give that up for anything. The music I make with *her* is different, more like Stravinsky's *Rite of Spring*. She's fiercer and more unpredictable, but that doesn't mean I want to live my life with that. I've met her husband; he's devoted to her. And they trust me."

"I'm sorry I was so hard on you all these years."

"It's over and forgotten."

"That's easy for you to say, Jonas. It doesn't mean that *I* forgot my night with Jane."

"Oh," said Jonas, moved close to tears by his brother's revelation. The breeze stopped and the night went silent.

Eddie ground the remains of his cigar into the sand. He said, "Why didn't you say something before?"

"Dad told me the same thing he told you. The summer before he died, he asked me to look out for you. I didn't want to hurt you, or Margo."

"Are you going to say anything to her?"

"I'll take it to the grave. I always knew it was because you were scared about your future. Isn't everyone?"

"You were that insightful even before you went to shrink school?"

"It's the way my mind works. It's too bad I didn't have that same natural talent for music as I did for figuring out how people worked."

"You would have gone for a life in music?"

"Probably. But that would have meant a whole different life: no Jennie, no Gil and Gracie." A wave of sadness and nostalgia came over Jonas. "Suppose you had met Jane earlier when you were unattached. Have you ever thought you're living the wrong life? Someone else's life?"

"There's no way of going back, is there?" Eddie said.

"No, there isn't. I dream about it sometimes. Four days from now, some man will mount the podium in Vienna and conduct the New Year's Eve concert. At that same moment, I'll be sitting on this beach; or maybe having a drink with my in-laws; or rehearsing Gil's play. I've dreamt about conducting that New Year's Eve concert since I was ten years old. I can smell the flowers decorating the proscenium. I'm holding the conductor's baton. I can feel my hands quiver during the opening tremolo of the *The Blue Danube Waltz*, which is always the second encore."

Eddie meandered toward the waterline, where the moonlight turned the breaking waves into foamy swirls. Jonas followed, but not too closely. Eddie went a good ways out before he turned around.

"I envy you, Jonas," Eddie said, "the fire, the life within. I live my life in black and white. You live yours in high-definition color. I wish I felt emotions like you do."

"It's not all sunshine and roses, Eddie. Believe me. My world can smell very dark and musty. Nobody gets through life unscathed by regrets. Nobody."

"Do you know how much it hurts? How sad it makes me feel?"

"You said you want to feel your emotions. Welcome to the world of the living. It's not all it's cracked up to be, is it?"

"I'd rather deal with it."

"Good for you," Jonas said.

"I want the next part of my life to be different," Eddie said.

"Are you and Margo all right?"

"Who knows, Jonas? Who knows? I'm a cliché: a middle-aged attorney with an overpriced co-op I can barely give away, much less sell. The kids'll be gone before I know it, and unless I reinvent myself I can see Margo taking up journalism and running off with one of her writing professors. I need something more. I need passion."

"Of course you do, Eddie. We all do. It's what I mean about *her*."

"We married young, not like you and Jennie. It was straight down the rails for me. College, law school, kids, partnership, Speller and Bodenheim."

"You did well, Eddie. I'm proud of you. You'll figure this out. Maybe I can help."

"Really?"

"Don't act so surprised. No one knows you better than me—except for Margo, and even she doesn't know you like I do. I know how much there is to you. Pete gets the limelight, but you were the person who taught him how to talk the other side's expert witnesses into supporting your argument while getting them to expound *their* beliefs. It's just this side of devious. That's more than talent, Eddie. It's a gift. You get people to admit things after half an hour that would take me two vials of truth serum. You've turned interrogation into an art form. Don't you want to share that with the world?"

"Sure, I'll put it in my autobiography."

Jonas grabbed sprig of dried seaweed and pointed it toward Eddie. "If you don't, who will?"

"Seriously, Jonas. Who wants to know that half a lifetime ago, some wet-behind-the-ears lawyer made love with a beautiful young woman who's lost to the pages of history? Who wants to know that I got married the following Sunday and every so often I wonder about that woman? What happened to the rest of her life? Did she become a mother? Did she die young? Did she change the world? Does she even remember that night?"

Jonas thought about the afternoon he and Victoria met, and what would have happened had their paths not crossed. "I bet she does."

"Does it even matter?"

"Of course it matters," Jonas said. "Everyone has a story to tell, just like everyone needs someone to tell it to. You never know whose life your story touches; that's why every person's story is precious. It's the only way I can reconcile the minutiae of every day with the vastness of the universe without feeling that life is meaningless. I don't know what's on the other side of my last breath any better than you do, but this I know for sure: We create our own stories one memory at a time. Whether you choose to type it up and show it to the world is your business."

A blank piece of music paper formed in Jonas's mind. In an instant, staves and notes sprang to life across it. "Your story can be a building, a symphony, a painting. Or Gil's play, or Gracie's photographs. Or it can be a book about legal strategy. Think of the stories you have to tell."

"There's a lot," Eddie said.

"You bet, brother. It's the best we can do in the battle against mortality. You. Me. We're all warrior poets. Damn if I'm going down without a fight. Neither should you."

"What about you, Jonas? Besides your family, what will you leave behind?"

"My students for one thing; someone needs to teach the next generation. It's an honor. Then, there're the cases I testify at. Every time we win, someone gets hit hard in the pocketbook. Do it enough and people will think twice before messing with someone's mind. That's my contribution to destigmatizing mental illness. I'm doing a case of legal malpractice where a colleague was wrongfully sued in connection with one of his patient's death. If I have my say I'll bankrupt the law firm that sued him. Call it my contribution to tort reform.

"And my theories and approaches to therapy with teenagers. What's happening with Gracie and Gil makes it clear there's still plenty more I need to learn. Gracie got me reading *Harry Potter*, which I want to mention in my chapter on adolescent development."

"And your music? How many symphonies have you composed?"

"I'm writing one right here, right now. This is our symphony. Yours and mine. We all need more than one *her* in our lives, people who make our dormant seeds germinate. Margo can't tend your whole garden; just like Jennie can't tend all of mine."

"I met *her* once, at the baseball game. I never forgot the way she looked at you. Or the way you looked at her. I remember her name, Jonas, just like I remembered Jane. Her name was Victoria."

Jonas remembered the scene as if it had just happened. "It still is."

"Thanks, Jonas."

"For what?"

"It still hurts, but having you takes the sting out of it."

64

Victoria's initial euphoria about Gregory's survival gave way to a steadily mounting dread that his basic character might not have survived intact. His body's functions were recovering more every day, but when she considered the possibility that the banter that they shared might be compromised or forever gone, Victoria felt paralyzed. Without her talks with Jonas to keep her grounded, her mood plunged violently in the days before New Year's.

With Anna Breckenridge gone until January, the hospital just wasn't the same. Not that the fill-in doctor, Dr. Percy Walker, a descendant of the whiskey-maker, wasn't well qualified and sympathetic, but he didn't have the same investment in Gregory, or in her, that Anna did. He always seemed tentative, as if he was afraid to get families' hopes too high.

Victoria's in-laws were unexpectedly supportive. Charles, who had bonded strongly with Melinda, visited frequently. Martin's sisters sent Gregory multi-colored helium balloons with a get-well message, and they were friendlier to Victoria than they had ever been. They even canceled their Caribbean cruise, to be nearby. But nothing could counter

Victoria's increasing disconnect from Martin. Victoria found little comfort in her husband, with whom she discussed the mundane—who would do what, and when—as if he were a newly hired employee.

By New Year's Eve morning, the temperature inside 1912 Rittenhouse Square South was as cold as it was outside. Victoria awoke exhausted from dreams reminding her of childhood, angry that no one had offered her help when she was Melinda's age. Stiff and sore, she felt as if she had run a marathon in cold rain. She wrapped herself in a lamb's-wool throw and, brooding silently, sipped her morning tea. She stared blankly out the window onto Rittenhouse Square, trying to stop the sickening fantasies moving through her mind: picturing herself dead and gone while an imbecilic Gregory lay strapped to a urine-soaked, stool-ridden bed in a nursing home.

Martin entered the room quietly. He came up behind Victoria and laid his hand on her shoulder tenderly.

Victoria withdrew with a jerk. "Don't do that. You know I hate to be surprised."

Since the nightmare with Melinda and Gregory, flecks of gray hair had begun to frame Martin's brow and temples. "Jesus, Vic. Every time I touch you, you act like I'm a child molester. How long is this going to go on?"

"I don't know," she whispered.

"What is it that you don't know?" Martin said.

"I don't know; I just told you. I don't even know who I am anymore. All this running around between CHOP and Pennsylvania Hospital has me exhausted. Now, I'm supposed to do it again," she said, referring to the day pass that would release Melinda that afternoon for a test run. "I want the day off. You get her."

Martin said, "We agreed to do this together. It's supposed to be a special day. Dr. Milroy said that since this is Melinda's first time seeing Gregory, both of us should be there. Now that Gregory's better—"

"I don't call wearing a bib and slobbering over himself while he eats applesauce getting better. He looks like a drooling infant."

"What is the matter with you, Vic? Look at the progress he's made in the last week. Since this whole thing began, you've been treating me like a stranger. What did I do?"

"This whole goddamn thing never should have happened. You know as well as I do that something should have been done about Melinda months ago."

"You mean that *I* should have done something? And what is it you think *I* should have done?"

"You don't know?"

"No, I don't."

"How can you not know? What kind of father are you? You're supposed to take care of things like this."

"What in God's name do you mean?"

"You spent the summer buried in spreadsheets getting your mock-jury business off the ground, while Melinda hung out with that grungy kid. Aren't fathers supposed to protect their daughters?"

Martin rolled his eyes. "Excuse me for auctioning my shotgun collection. Or was I supposed to stalk her with a fish knife between my teeth and gut the first boy who came near her?"

"Your glib hyperboles won't work, Martin. I'm not some starstruck judge in Ashtabula, Ohio, presiding over slips and falls. I saw the look on your face when Melinda talked about that Todd character."

"What look?"

"The look of a man realizing for the first time that his darling daughter might have other interests in the male sex besides sitting on her father's knee playing pat-a-cake."

"You know as well as I do that we had no idea of what was going on. We were both happy she had a group to hang out with."

"It never occurred to you she might get involved with someone older?"

"Of course boys would be interested in her, but from what she said in therapy, it's not like this Todd fellow was just out to put her on his trophy shelf."

"You don't know that, Martin. And about what she smoked; she sees you with your glass of wine every night. Where do you think she got the idea to try marijuana? You enable her."

"Enable her? What?" Martin slammed his fist against the couch. "Just because you don't like it, doesn't mean everyone who enjoys a glass of wine with dinner is an alcoholic. Like your father."

"That's not fair."

"But it *is* fair for you to asperse my parenting? It *is* fair for you to imply I'm a drunk? Wake up and smell the bathroom vents, Victoria. Whether you like it or not, kids experiment with dope all the time. Just because you hated marijuana doesn't mean everyone is like you. For all we know, she inherited the same sensitivity to marijuana you have. Her temperament's a hell of a lot more like yours than mine. You both have the same mood disorder, yet you've never heard me say a word about that, have you?"

Victoria stared out the window in silence.

"Of course not," he said. "And why is that? Because I'm not built that way. I would never, ever, come down on you for being in therapy. If there's any blame, it belongs to both of us. You heard Melinda. She said she was afraid to call home, because she thought we'd yell at her."

"She was speaking to me, not you. She meant *I* would yell at her. How come the burden always falls on me?"

"Look, Victoria. You're making much too much out of what that Blount woman said."

"That's another thing, Martin. You stood by and let that woman rip me to shreds without one single word. How am I supposed to feel about that?"

"I apologized to you. But I'll say it again. I'm sorry. I should have said something sooner."

"So why didn't you? Why was it me that had to take all her shit? Why didn't you protect me?"

"I should have; you're right about that, Victoria. I don't know what I was thinking. But you're not the only one who's worried sick about Gregory and Melinda. I didn't know what to do in those sessions. It's not an excuse, but like I said, I'm truly sorry. I never said I had no role in this, but how many teenage girls discuss their first crush with their fathers? Did you?"

"She should have told you about it, at least after the fact. If you'd had a better relationship with her, you would have known something was wrong and been able to get her to talk about it."

"'Get her to talk about it'? You're out of your mind!" Martin shouted. "Since when has any parent been able to get their fourteen-year-old to do anything? That's ridiculous."

Out of your mind and *ridiculous* resonated with every accusation Victoria had heard as a child. She raised her hand to slap him. It took every ounce of self-control to fight the urge.

Martin had finally had enough. "You'd better use your other hand if you're going to hit me, or do you want to shatter your wrist again?" Martin taunted.

"Ridiculous. Ridiculous? Don't you dare try and turn this around on me."

"Christ almighty. Is there any use talking to you? What makes you think she should have talked with me any more than you? How much of your personal life did you share with your parents?"

"My father was weak. He let my mother run roughshod over him and me just like you stood by while that Blount witch cornered me into the ropes. Like you let Melinda dump on me. It's like it always was. My father, now you. There's no man I can count on to protect me. No one."

"Are you finished yet?" Martin said unrepentantly.

"Damn you! Damn all of you," Victoria exploded in a rage that overshadowed all the good Martin brought to their marriage. "You're not a man. You're just like him."

You're just like him. You're just like him. As she said the words, Victoria began to tremble, and the room started spinning. Reeling, she staggered to the couch.

Martin looked as though she'd ripped out his heart.

And then Victoria felt the tingling she had experienced as a teenager. It spread through her body like the panic attacks she had suffered since

Thanksgiving. When it centered deep in her pelvis it resonated with the lust she felt as a teenager. For the moment the man in front of her wasn't Martin. Instead, he became her father's friend Mr. Brendel, a weak man who squandered his power and good looks through drunkenness and debauchery.

Something was very wrong with her, Victoria realized. Very wrong. For sure, Martin may have had faults, but weakness was not one of them. He had always been kind to her. How could she turn on him so viciously?

Martin said, "I'm going to Pennsylvania Hospital at noon to collect Melinda. I'll take her wherever she wants to go for lunch. Then, Melinda and I are going to see Gregory. As for you, do as you like. I'm leaving."

Martin's tone made Victoria's blood run cold. Feeling more terror than rage, she cried, "Martin, please. I didn't mean it. I—"

"We'll see about that later. This changes everything. I'm going to see *my* son and *my* daughter."

"Martin, please. I'm sorry. I didn't mean that. I shouldn't have . . . "

"You don't need to apologize, Victoria. Now, I know how you feel. All these years, I thought you loved me."

"No, Martin. It's not that. Please. You don't understand."

"What's there to understand?"

Victoria tried to think of something, but all she could do was beg, "Don't go, Martin. Please."

"Melinda's going to ask where you are," Martin remarked coldly. "What do you want me to tell her?"

Victoria looked at her fingers, wondering whose they were. "I don't know. Tell her whatever you want," she whispered.

"Get ahold of yourself, Victoria," Martin said icily. "I will not tolerate your upsetting my daughter."

Martin turned and left, leaving Victoria with an overwhelming sense of déjà vu and a pulse rate of 150. She stared at the gazebo in the square in a trance, knowing that her outburst at Martin had little to do with him.

65

It took Victoria an hour to stand up and get going. On the way upstairs to dress, she passed the chair in which she sat during phone sessions with Jonas. She longed to hear his voice and make sense of what was happening.

She made it her business to be at CHOP before Martin and Melinda arrived there. At two o'clock, she settled into her chair next to Gregory, who had been able to sit up off and on for several days. Pie-eyed and somnolent, he acknowledged his mother with a weak smile.

A bleached blonde, plump-but-not-frumpy woman, whose name tag read 'Janice Raines, RPT,' entered the room and announced it was time for Gregory's first session of physical therapy. "We need to do a thorough evaluation and come up with a plan. Today's goal is to see if Gregory can support himself."

Still consumed with the ugly scene between Martin and herself, Victoria barely heard the woman. "Are you sure he's ready?" she managed.

Janice said, "We have to start somewhere. Even if he can't support his weight on his own, it'll be good for his heart to reacclimate to pumping harder. Remember, except for the few hours he's been sitting, Gregory's been lying flat for a long time; his heart hasn't had to work against gravity the way it normally does. Don't worry, Mrs. Braun. There'll be several of us to make sure he doesn't fall."

"I'd like to come with you," Victoria said.

"That's fine. Here, let's get him into the wheelchair."

Victoria scrawled a message on a get-well-card envelope, which she taped to Gregory's bed: *Martin. We're in the Physical Therapy suite on the third floor. Join us. PLEASE.*

CHOP's physical and occupational therapy departments were very different from the drab surroundings in which Victoria had felt quarantined at Gregory's bedside. Children of all ages and colors, some in wheelchairs, most in slings and casts, cavorted busily under the watchful eyes of a legion of therapists encouraging their charges like the Dallas Cowboy Cheerleaders. *Thank God he'll see colors*, Victoria told herself, thinking of all the birthday pizza parties they had attended when Gregory was four, five, and six.

An athletic man with a crew cut met the threesome at the sign-in station. After introducing himself as Mark, he spent half an hour testing Gregory's muscle strength, then turned Gregory over to a pear-shaped speech therapist.

His right side was considerably weaker than his left. Because he had trouble with his tongue, Gregory had problems forming sibilants, as well as Ls and Rs. The pronounced lisp and lack of mental acuity intensified Victoria's worries.

Mark retrieved Gregory from the speech therapist and wheeled him over to a set of parallel bars. "Okay, let's see what we've got to work with."

"Hold on a second. Let's do this first," said a familiar voice from behind. Dr. Jonathan Bell, still in his scrubs, placed a blood-pressure cuff around Gregory's arm. "Oh," said Dr. Bell, noticing Victoria. "I'm glad you're here."

"I didn't expect to see anyone from the team. How did you know where we were?"

"We keep track of everything. You don't think we'd miss a moment like this, do you?"

Victoria had never looked so closely at Dr. Bell's boyish face. His dark brown eyes seemed older than the rest of him.

"Percy's in the OR with Dr. Liddle. I volunteered to come to PT to make sure they were taking good care of our young skateboarder." Dr. Bell gave the stubble on Gregory's head a playful tousle.

"That's very considerate."

"Thanks, but Dr. Breckenridge would be one angry neurosurgeon if she came back from vacation and found Gregory with his head cracked open after fainting in PT, and rightly so. For your information, she's not as demure as you might think. Let me tell you, you don't want to make that woman mad."

"I never pictured her that way."

"Gregory's recovery will look like watching a baby grow, only speeded up like in a time-lapse movie. You don't see it as much as we do, because you're with him every moment, but the change the past week is phenomenal. Once Gregory can feed himself and get around, we'll send him to a rehabilitation unit for the next phase. Keep this in mind: Don't be spooked if he's very concrete at first, the way young children are."

"Concrete?"

"Concrete as in literal. If you asked him about an operating system, it wouldn't surprise me if, instead of computers, he talked about the saw we used on his skull. Abstract thinking comes later in development or, in other words, his recovery.

"How long are we talking about?"

"I can't say for sure, but even Dr. Liddle is amazed at Gregory's progress this week. I don't know if anyone told you, Mrs. Braun, but even though Gregory ruptured an artery when his head hit the ground, he was actually lucky because the way he landed concentrated the damage to one area, as opposed to shearing the ascending and descending nerve-cell pathways, the brain's version of a spinal cord transection."

"You could have sent one of the pediatric residents to check on Gregory, couldn't you?"

"We don't operate that way, Mrs. Braun. We take care of our own." Dr. Bell checked Gregory's blood pressure, and said, "That's one hundred over seventy-five. Not bad. Okay, let's see what happens."

Two women grasped Gregory under his arms, while another stabilized his wheelchair and steadied him from behind. They hoisted him up slowly, stopping every few degrees to give him time to acclimate.

Halfway to vertical, Dr. Bell halted the crew and took the second reading. "Ninety-five over seventy. Let's go nice and slow."

Mark said, "That's it, Gregory. You're doing great. Now try and get your arms over the bars. That's it. Just like this. Here, we'll help you." The women draped Gregory's arms across the metal beams.

Dr. Bell took the third measurement. "One-ten over eighty. That's some ticker you've got there, young fella. Gregory must have been in fine shape to begin with."

Not quite as limp as spaghetti, more like a garden hose, Gregory's arms sagged and his knees buckled, but even before the group could brace him, Gregory locked his knees. As if awakening from a deep sleep, he said, "Who aw awl deeze peepawl?"

Everyone laughed except Victoria.

"Let me introduce myself. I'm Dr. Jonathan Bell from the neurosurgery department, and these are the physical and speech therapists who are going to help you regain your strength. I thought this might happen. I bet everyone five bucks that when we got Gregory's heart pumping, he would wake up like Rip Van Winkle."

"I hate that thory," Gregory said. He looked around the room until he caught his mother's eye. "Witthen to me, I thound wike an idiot."

"That's what this woman is for," Dr. Bell said, nodding at the speech therapist. "Her name is Jolanda, but we all call her Jolly. She's the best in the business. She'll have you doing tongue twisters inside of a week."

"Ith obviuth I cud ooth thum help with that," Gregory said.

Victoria was overjoyed that Gregory still had his sense of humor. She hugged him so tightly that she had to be restrained, tears smudging the mascara and eyeliner she had applied carefully to look her best for Martin.

Gregory scanned the rest of the crowd. "Wheaw ith Mawtun? I wanna thee Mawtun."

Thank God he still thinks of his father the same way. "He'll be here soon, Gregory," she said.

Mark said, "That's plenty for today. Great job, Gregory. I'm sure you and Jolly are going to be best of pals. Thanks for coming," he said to Dr. Bell, who gave Gregory's good hand a parting high five.

When the elevator stopped to return Victoria and Gregory to his hospital room, who should be there but Martin and Melinda. Melinda, who hadn't seen Gregory in over a month, turned pale when she saw her brother in a wheelchair and with most of his hair shaved off.

"Oh my God! I can't believe I did this to you, Gregory!" she said.

"Hewwo Mewinda," Gregory said. "Whea haf you been? I miffed you."

"It's a long story. I think about you all the time. You don't remember what happened, do you?

Pointing at his head, Gregory said, "Oh thith? Mutha thaid I fell down the theps. I don't wemembah a thing. The doctahs had to opawate on my bwain. Ith a good thing they found thomething in thewe. I hope you'we feewing better. You hawen't been yowthef for a wong time."

"Oh Gregory, I love you," Melinda cried. "Thank God you're getting better."

When everyone had settled into Gregory's room, Victoria tried to seize the moment. "Martin, he's back; Gregory's back. I heard it in physical therapy. It just happened again when he joked about his brain. Isn't that good news, Martin?"

"It is," Martin said to Gregory as if Victoria weren't in the room. She went to hug Martin, but he moved away and stared past her.

"Welcome back, Gregory," he said tearfully, extending a hand to caress Gregory's cheek. "Welcome back."

66

Saturday, February 5, 2005

"I'd like a word with you," Dr. Frantz told Jonas at the early February meeting of the American Academy of Psychoanalysis. "We need help with something."

Jonas had just conducted a seminar on the pros and cons of the therapist's self-disclosure in psychotherapy. He felt pleased that his former analyst wanted his opinion. "Who is we?" he asked.

"Me, Sid Pulver, and Phil Escoll. Remember them from the Institute?"

"Of course." The men came over and shook hands warmly.

Jonas had seen Dr. Frantz occasionally over the years, but not since Frantz's wife, the cellist, had died. The cheekbones of his once-stout face protruded like a scaffold, and he had lost a good twenty pounds since his wife succumbed to pancreatic cancer.

Dr. Frantz said, "Here's the situation, Jonas. Phil Fowler has been deteriorating. We've heard that he gets his patients confused, and his mind wanders so much that he forgets his point. Either he stops practicing and gets treatment, or the Institute will suspend, possibly revoke, his privileges. He doesn't seem depressed; he's convinced we want to steal his ideas."

"Sounds manic to me," Jonas said. "It could be neurological, you know. Was he ill? He didn't fall or have a mini-stroke, did he? People Fowler's age don't just suddenly become manic."

"Now that you mention it, he complained of dizziness after a tennis match a few months ago," Dr. Escoll said.

Dr. Pulver said, "He thinks he's completing Freud's *Project for a Scientific Psychology*. His notes are pure gibberish, scribbled in the margins of science journals and on the backs of envelopes. Between his crumpled clothes and the key ring full of flash drives attached to his belt loop, he looks like a janitor. According to his wife, one time when he couldn't find a file he was working on, he hurled his laptop against a wall and accused her of conspiring with us. Maybe you can get through to him."

"Me? We haven't spoken in more than twenty years. Why would he listen to me?"

"Because he respects you," said Dr. Frantz.

"Respects me? After what happened when I dumped him and went to you?"

Dr. Frantz said, "A lot happened to Phil after that. The bottom line is that you were the one who got him to stop and think about what he was doing. You must have really sobered him up, because he became a lot less doctrinaire. At first, we didn't know if it was because we had a policeman at his shoulder or if he had a true change of heart, but over time, he convinced us he'd learned to keep an open mind. People change. You have to respect him for that. Will you try to help out?"

Jonas had hoped to discuss his feelings about Victoria with Dr. Frantz, but his former analyst looked too frail to be up to it. Reluctantly Jonas agreed to meet with Fowler, but his major motivation in going to Philadelphia was to talk things over with Stan.

* * *

Two days later, southbound on the Jersey Turnpike, a string of jetliners on final approach to Newark Airport caught Jonas's eye; they looked like fireflies. One after another, they descended. As soon as one plane passed, another followed in a line extending to the horizon. Appearing to head toward them were planes taking off from LaGuardia Airport. For an instant Jonas wondered how the air-traffic controllers could put them on a crash course. Then, he realized that his collision fantasy reverberated with long-forgotten airplane dreams from his final days on Dr. Fowler's couch.

Jonas drove directly to Marta and Stan's.

"How about a cigar?" Stan asked when Jonas said he needed to talk something through.

"Sure, it'll help us analyze better." Both men smiled as they shared the same flame to light up.

"So what's up, Jo?" Stan asked.

"I don't even know if I should be talking about this with you, Stan."

"Talk to me, Jonas. There's nothing you could say that would surprise me."

"It's about Victoria. You remember I was talking about her in Puerto Rico?"

"Sure."

"Well, it got worse. A lot worse. Now, I'm not sure what to do. She stopped therapy a few weeks ago; disappeared just like that. In all the time I've known her, she's never done that. It's just not her."

"Did you say anything or do anything unusual?"

"I don't think so. When I got back from Puerto Rico, she told me how she lit into her husband Martin. I drew the parallel between the way she treated him and the way her mother treated her father. She seemed to accept the interpretation at the time, but now that I think about it, my timing might have been off. Maybe she wasn't ready to hear it."

"She could have easily dissociated her emotional reactions."

"Goddammit, I should have thought of that before I opened my mouth. Come to think of it, that's when things began to change. Can't you just picture her? Seething on the inside while yessing me to my face. The last few times we talked, she sounded like she was in another world."

"In person?"

"No, she made several appointments to meet me in New York, but she called at the last minute to cancel, saying something had come up and the best she could manage were phone sessions. She sounded burnt out and disconnected."

Both men puffed away thoughtfully. "It's resistance," Stan said.

"I was thinking that, too. What do you think it's about?"

"Let's put our heads together. What would you tell a supervisee?"

"That's a very good question, Stan. Most likely I'd tell him it's a transference resistance. Feelings about therapy Victoria doesn't want to talk over with me."

"Let's not forget feelings about you."

"That's right. Do you think she's retaliating against me for abandoning her over Christmas?"

"Yes, maybe, but it can't be that simple. If it was that and that alone you would have worked it through by now."

Jonas said, "I got a call from her pharmacy a few weeks ago to renew one of her medications. I told them to give her a week's worth and have her call for an appointment. I still haven't heard from her. You don't think she stopped her meds, do you?"

"Could well be. Have you heard from her husband?"

"I was just getting to that. Martin called the other day. Other than the night her kids nearly died, he's never contacted me. When she came back into therapy, Victoria made it clear she didn't want me communicating with her husband; I knew she was holding back, but I didn't want to break confidentiality. But with things the way they are now, I felt I could use the man's viewpoint, so I told him I'd listen, even though I couldn't reveal anything about Victoria's therapy. I can't be stumbling around in the dark. That was right, don't you think, Stan?"

"Absolutely. Everyone agrees you can't treat bipolar disorder without feedback about how the patient is doing outside therapy. What did Martin say?"

"He sounded frightened. He says the better Gregory and Melinda are doing, the more Victoria's falling apart. She's always on the phone when he wants to talk with her, and she waves him away whenever he tries to communicate about the most commonplace issues. He said she's up all night working on briefs and teaching herself computer programs she's never even taken out of the box before. That high-profile case she was working on is starting up again. Martin's in D.C. for the next few days, but he wants to meet with me in person after he gets home. My gut tells me not to."

"I agree. Follow your instinct. This could cause a permanent rupture; she could easily get paranoid that you and Martin are colluding. Maybe she'll meet with you while you're in Philadelphia."

"You mean a home visit?"

"Doctors have made house calls before."

"That's not a bad idea," Jonas said.

"Then again, she might get the wrong idea. Especially with Martin away."

"You don't think she's having an affair?"

"I doubt it. I think this has more to do with her feelings for you. Don't be alone with her outside an office. You can use mine if she agrees to meet. But watch out, Jonas. If she's manic and off her meds, she could easily misinterpret your motives."

67

lipping into his clinical mode, Jonas went to Dr. Fowler's office, now at Eighth and Spruce Streets, a short walk from Stan's house. The man who buzzed Jonas in was wild-eyed and unkempt.

"How are you, Dr. Speller? You look exactly the same as when we—" Dr. Fowler's greeting melted into befuddlement. "Would you like to lie down?"

The offer about the couch seemed inappropriate. "No thanks," Jonas said. "It seems like such a long time since we've talked."

"Come now," Dr. Fowler said. "It's only been a long weekend."

Jonas stared in disbelief.

"Metaphorically speaking. Hahaha. Hahaha," Fowler tittered. "You didn't think I was serious, did you, my boy? Remember that weekend?" Dr. Fowler winked. "Did you enjoy the concert?"

"What concert?"

"The one where they played *Invitation to the Dance*. You didn't think I forgot, did you?" The chaos in Dr. Fowler's office was palpable. Every inch was consumed with scrawled notes and pages torn from electrical engineering journals. On the desk was a dog-eared Volume I of *The Standard Edition of the Works of Sigmund Freud*, open to *Project for a Scientific Psychology*, a work of historical interest only.

"Speaking of which," Dr. Fowler said, "can't you feel the energy field between us? I see micro-volts radiating from your head like the earth's magnetic field. Kandel deserved his Nobel Prize, but he didn't put his observations together with Freud's and Galvani's, like I have. We're constantly recharging each other's batteries, funneling energy into neural networks that underpin the transference-countertransference paradigm during the middle to late phases of analysis." Dr. Fowler grabbed Volume I. "It's all here!" He pointed at a sketch he had drawn in the margin of page 188.

Dr. Fowler's demeanor changed abruptly. "I never thanked you for stopping treatment with me. I've thought about it many times, Dr. Speller. You were right about the oedipal struggle I enacted with you. When I finally accepted that you knew more than me, I felt myself opening up to a new understanding of the psyche."

Such lucidity surprised Jonas. He said, "I had such mixed feelings about what happened in analysis with you. I felt like you wanted me to hate you. Was that your intention?"

"It took a long time to recognize that your idealization of me made me uncomfortable. That was my issue, not yours. I interpreted it as a boundary violation; that you didn't just want to be *like* me, that you wanted to *be* me."

"What's so terrible about that? I can't be the first analysand who felt that way. Why did you have to be so nasty?"

"Honestly, I was full of myself for making training analyst so young. Not that that makes it right. My own training analyst had been a tyrant; he wouldn't tolerate the smallest departure from orthodox practice and ideology. Sad to say, I internalized his intolerance and analyzed like him. I shouldn't have. It took your blowing the whistle to awaken me to the fact that one size didn't fit all, that each analysand had his own needs. I wished I had figured that out earlier, like you did."

"I can't believe you couldn't see that your attitude colored the analytic situation. You completely dismissed the relational component of psychoanalysis. And every time I said something about that, you dealt with it like I was a rebellious child. That wasn't right."

"You're right. It wasn't right. You were ahead of the curve, and it threatened me. I analyzed how I was taught. It was the best I knew at the time. You were trying to enlighten me. I was too full of myself to listen."

Jonas noticed a blue vase of tulips. "It was her, I mean your wife, who made sure you had fresh flowers, wasn't it?"

Dr. Fowler's smile turned vacant. "My wife. You mean Iris? We were discussing something else. That's right, open-mindedness and giving people what they need. You would agree that some people need tough love, wouldn't you?"

"Sure. I treated a woman whose husband was a flaming rageaholic. The wife's earlier analyst was a protégé of the husband's therapist, who was afraid of becoming the object of the man's tirades. By the time the woman got to me, she believed her husband's rages were normal. I was too late. The fallout royally screwed up the couple's daughters, one of whom killed herself when her fiancé dumped her after a vile outburst."

Dr. Fowler nodded, then began scratching furiously behind his shoulder. "Goddamn laundry, they make my shirts stiffer just so they'll itch, and since I called them on it, they've made them even stiffer. They're doing it on purpose to torment me. I know it."

"How can you be sure?"

"The smell. I hate the smell. How would you like it if someone tried to poison you with cleaning solvent?"

"You haven't been ill in the last few months, have you?"

"What are you getting at? Did those thieving magpies from the Institute put you up to this?"

"Let's get something straight. There is no conspiracy. I see where your theory is going; they don't. You picked up that when Freud wrote the *Project* he didn't understand that the brain worked both chemically and electrically."

"It could be the pills they gave me."

"Pills? What pills?"

"My eyes bothered me one day after tennis. Iris got me into the Will's Eye Institute. At first, they thought I might have a brain tumor, but they diagnosed pseudo tumor ceribri."

"You look weary. Are you sleeping okay?"

"Sleeping? What with all this work to do on the *Project*? I'm so close." Dr. Fowler pointed at three formulae-laden sheets of legal-sized paper taped together like a foolscap. "I want this so badly. After you terminated with me, the Institute never really trusted me again, which is what I want this paper to fix."

"To do that you need a clear mind, a rested mind. What about the pills?"

"That day after tennis my eyes became so blurry I could hardly see a thing. The ophthalmologist said the optic nerves were inflamed, and he prescribed high doses of steroids for three days, after which I was supposed to taper off. But I didn't get any better, so I doubled the dose, figuring I'd get quicker results."

"You what? Where did you get the extra pills?"

"I called in a prescription for myself."

"I can't believe you did that. It's very dangerous."

"I only did it for a week."

"One whole week? That's enough to throw you into a—"

"Into a what?"

"Mania or hypomania—you know, an altered state of mind. In the old days, they used to call mania brain fever."

"Is that what you think happened?"

"I think it's still happening. You need to calm down."

"I am exhausted," Dr. Fowler said. "I try to sleep, but the equations flit through my mind like an electric billboard. You don't think I'm crazy, do you? That's what *they* think about me."

"Crazy is not in my lexicon. Overworked? Yes. Exhausted? Yes. Affected by high doses of steroid pills? Most definitely."

"What about my theory? I can't afford to lose it. You promise you won't steal my ideas?"

"Of course not. You helped me through the worst time of my life that first year after my father died. You were there for me. Do you trust Stan Amernick? Or if you prefer a woman, his wife, Marta, is excellent, too. Either one will take good care of you. I promise."

"I'm so exhausted," Fowler repeated. "Oh. I just told you that, didn't I?"

"I'll talk to them as soon as I leave here."

"Thank you, my boy, thank you. I didn't have it in me back then to tell you that I admired you. I'm sorry if I caused you grief."

"It all worked out, Dr. Fowler. I learned to trust my unconscious mind. Everything turned out for the best."

68

Tuesday, February 15, 2005

Victoria felt exhilarated. The windowless, magazine-strewn cubicle outside Jonas's office felt like a cage. She had been counting the days until the February 15 double session, yearning for a furlough from the sterility of her relationship with Martin.

When Jonas had heard about her fight with Martin, he pointed out how Victoria's treatment of Martin paralleled Lorraine's attitude toward Morris. Victoria was so agitated and depressed, she couldn't process his comment fully at the time. When it sank in after a few weeks of family sessions, Victoria began fuming—who the hell was Jonas to compare her to Lorraine?—which rekindled smoldering resentment of every man she had ever counted on. *The hell with Jonas*, Victoria told herself, determined that she could do her own therapy. Besides, if Jonas could take a vacation from her, she could take a vacation from therapy. She became so maniacally furious with him that she couldn't think of one good thing Jonas had ever done for her. The more heated she felt toward Jonas, the more dissociated and disconnected she felt from Martin. Dr. Milroy became the "good doctor" in Victoria's mind; his work with Melinda seemed nothing short of miraculous. It astounded

Victoria how quickly Melinda came to see her as a confidante, chatting with her busily as if they had always been best friends.

Instead of asking Jonas to renew her medication, Victoria asked Dr. Milroy to take over prescribing. When he deferred, Victoria interpreted the refusal as a sign that she didn't need medicine anymore, so she stopped taking it toward the end of January. Within only a few days, the bad thoughts returned; however, she was convinced that Jonas would ream her out royally for consulting Dr. Milroy, so she was afraid to call.

There matters stood until Victoria heard the warmth in Jonas's voice message. Clearly, he wanted to see her, which rekindled another flame within her that hadn't burned so brightly in twenty years. She stayed up the entire night before their appointment, trying on different blouses and sexy lingerie. With Martin away on business and the children well situated with family, she called the swankiest hotels in New York City, dreaming about having wild anonymous sex with men overcome by her sexual allure. Even though she hadn't slept in forty-eight hours, a sense of total well-being intoxicated her. Victoria's raw sexual appetite screamed for relief. *If only I got a good screwing*, she thought, *all my angst would disappear*.

For the appointment, Victoria wore her usual business suit over a creamy silk blouse with a plunging neckline. She added a gray-and-white Wedgwood cameo pendant suspended from a black ribbon choker to draw Jonas's eyes toward her décolletage. Her round diamond earrings sparkled, as did the hint of glitter on her face. She left her jacket open to reveal the sheer bra she had chosen.

Somewhere between Trenton and Newark on the train to New York City, she took off her wedding ring. The anticipation of being alone with Jonas, whom she hadn't seen in over a month, had her feeling like a teenager planning a secret rendezvous the night her parents left town. The idea of being alone with Jonas created a pleasant tingle throughout her body. As the train neared Penn Station, Victoria exchanged her black boots for a pair of sexy heels.

At 4:31 PM, Jonas's office door opened, and several people came out, everyone in a good mood. One of the men reminded Victoria of the young Jonas minus the big hair. Another had the build of Bucky Bleyer, her first lover. At that moment, Victoria felt more like twenty-three than forty-three. The intense mood swing of the past forty-eight hours felt so welcome it didn't occur to her that anything was amiss.

Jonas seemed unable to take his eyes off her; he looked her up and down like never before. "Whoa," he said. "You didn't come from court just now, did you?"

Jonas looked very manly that day, in a muted gray sweater-vest over an off-white collarless pullover. His tailored pants drew Victoria's eye to his muscular buttocks and thighs. Until that moment, she hadn't consciously registered how handsome Jonas had become.

Victoria said, "No, I came from the office. Martin's away again until Thursday. Charles and Danielle are with the children. Melinda loves being with her grandfather, and you should see how she hovers over Gregory; I've never seen her so devoted to someone other than herself."

"That's good," said Jonas, continuing to eye Victoria up and down.

"I'm in the city by myself," she said.

"What's Martin doing?"

Victoria tossed her head back, letting her hair fly freely. "He's in D.C., preparing a mock jury trial in a huge case—millions upon millions at stake. Fourteen teenagers and a pregnant woman died when a man who worked at D.C. Bank & Trust jumped off the Calvert Street Bridge onto a tour bus. The deep pocket is the bank, which had just fired the man who committed suicide. There's a five-year paper trail of complaints against the nasty bastard—his specialty was harassing older employees into quitting—that D.C. Bank & Trust sent to manage the branch. There's even an internal e-mail from upper management congratulating him on the fine job he had done 'clearing out the dead wood so quickly and efficiently.'"

Jonas hadn't taken his eyes off Victoria. "Are you sure you're not making too much of it?"

"This is huge. Huge," she said feverishly. "I'll show that Denise Mather—the attorney on the case I just finished dealing with—a thing or two about media presence."

"I'm surprised Martin left Philadelphia," Jonas said.

"He has no idea that I'm in the city. I like it that way."

The room seemed secluded; Jonas's couch looked more like a divan in a brothel than anything therapeutic. She imagined bolting the door. "It's just as well. I wanted Martin gone. He and I might as well get it over with. It's not so much that I *want* to be divorced; it's that I can't see staying married to him. The only thing we talk about outside of family therapy is work. It wouldn't surprise me if he's screwing one of the women attorneys he's working with in D.C." She pictured Martin pinioning his panting mistress and humping her with abandon.

"Hopefully, he'll start talking about something other than work and the children once he gets laid. But it's only a matter of time, and the suspense of not knowing when he's going to ditch me is hell. I can't remember liking him, let alone loving him."

"Oh." Jonas blushed. He didn't stop looking at her. When his eyes settled on her torso, occasionally drifting lower, Victoria felt even sexier. The idea that he found her alluring intensified her tingling and the ache. She wondered if he was undressing her mentally.

Jonas said, "I've never seen you looking this way. Are you going somewhere after here?"

"That depends."

"Depends on what?"

Victoria had never conjured explicit sexual fantasies about Jonas until that very moment. She pictured herself dressed in the skimpy negligee she'd packed for the trip, drinking expensive champagne with him in the sleek room she had booked for the night at The Carlyle, one of New York's classiest hotels.

"On how the session goes," she said.

"Oh." Jonas crossed then uncrossed his legs uncomfortably. "How are Melinda and Gregory?"

"Please, not today. I want a break from them."

"You don't want to fill me in on what's happening?"

"Not really," she sighed impatiently, when what was really happening was her longing for Jonas to lead her to the couch and strip her.

Slipping into dissociation, Victoria said, "You get thirty seconds for the bullet points, and that's all. Gregory's coming along. It's getting easier to accept what Dr. Liddle and Dr. Breckenridge say about his progress without my mind taking off in horrible directions. Melinda's group therapy with Dr. Milroy has catapulted her forward socially. It's all in here." She handed Jonas three singled-spaced pages she had brought with her to the session. "Melinda left this on the kitchen counter. It's an essay she wrote comparing her brother to Harry Potter. She's taking Gregory to Barnes and Noble the night the sixth *Harry Potter* is released, so they can be the first to get it. And the Barlow case settled, I'm thrilled to say. You can't imagine what a load it is to have that off my mind.

"That's enough of that." Victoria's voice trailed off.

She recalled the last session in Philadelphia, when Jonas told her he liked her. She stretched her arms behind her back, her chest protruding even further. "I sure feel better than when I went to bed the other night. It must have been my dreams."

"Your dreams?"

"I think I was dreaming about you. Only this time we weren't in a bakery!" Victoria looked Jonas up and down. The Carlyle fantasy sharpened. She pictured Jonas with his shirt off. "All I remember about those dreams is that I woke up feeling warm."

"I remember that bakery dream," Jonas said. "That was a long time ago. You've changed a lot."

"Really? How?"

"You're all grown up! And you seem so much better than the last time I saw you."

"I hope that means what I think it does."

"What's that?"

She tilted her head slightly. Her throat felt dry. "That you like what you see." She removed her jacket and placed it on the couch. The fantasy became more graphic. She hoped Jonas would want to ravage her as much as she wanted him. She imagined being enfolded by him while she maneuvered herself on top of him.

Victoria moved to the part of the couch closest to Jonas and leaned toward him, reaching for his hand. "I want to get caught up with you," she said. "Let's talk about us," she said lasciviously.

69

*T*alk about us, talk about us, Jonas thought. One look at
Victoria's face, and he knew he'd never seen her that way. His
temples and scalp felt prickly and his insides quivered like
when he was a hormone-crazed adolescent. Victoria had always been
attractive, but this felt different. This felt animal.

*She's wild today, scary wild. Stay with it; stay with the feelings. You
can do this. Just let your thoughts and feelings go*, Jonas told himself.

He could smell Victoria's perfume. An aura radiated from her hair's
reddish highlights, like heat waves over asphalt on a scalding day. With
his genitals about to explode, Jonas struggled to reflect on what he was
feeling.

*Give in to the moment. Enjoy the feeling. Let the fantasy come to
mind. Don't fight it. Just let it be.*

Jonas pictured stripping Victoria, derriere and legs first, bending her
over the couch, coming at her from behind, grabbing her wildly swaying
hair, penetrating her as deeply as he could over and over. The fantasy
made him weak in his knees.

He started to speak but stopped and inhaled deeply. The sensation made him think of flying.

Floating. Soaring. Flying. Breaking free. Something unexpected came to mind: the scene between the two girls in Starbucks months earlier, with the pretty girl in pewter earrings whom he imagined as his daughter. Images of Victoria and pretty girl merged in Jonas's mind. They became one and the same.

Daughter? Is this what Gracie will look like in thirty years? Jonas thought, imagining his daughter all grown up. *Gracie. The child who threw her arms around my neck.* Jonas wondered how the pretty girl's father would react to seeing the boy with the dark brown hair creeping closer to his daughter. Jonas became that boy. He pictured himself making out passionately with the girl, dry humping her until he came.

Jonas scanned the office ceiling. One of the overhead lights had burned out. *Stay with the feelings of Victoria and me.* Still, he went back and forth between Victoria and the pretty girl.

I'm old enough to be her father. Old enough to be her father? Whose father are we talking about? The girl from Starbucks? Gracie's? Victoria's?

A bolt of insight hit like an electric shock.

It's about how Victoria sees me unconsciously: the handsome, strong father she longed for as a child. With her, I'm the man I always wanted my father to be: worldly and potent. What a pair we are! A matched set. No wonder our chemistry is so strong. The forbiddenness has to do with her being my patient, my first analytic daughter. Incestuous feelings for my daughter! Victoria's repressed sexual feelings for Morris. How trite. How—true.

Then a second shock: *There's something more going on. Victoria's trying to live something out. Or relive something. What is it? Maybe she'll talk about it.*

The elapsed time since anyone had spoken was less than a minute.

Jonas composed himself enough to talk. "What are you thinking?" he inquired gently.

"I'm in room 802 at the Carlyle." Victoria grasped Jonas's hand and pulled him toward her. "If we walk fast, we can be there in fifteen minutes," she said brazenly.

"What?"

Victoria maneuvered herself even closer to him. She stared at the bulge between his legs and reached for his zipper.

Jonas withdrew instinctively. "Don't do that!"

"Let's not pretend anymore, Jonas," Victoria panted, grabbing for his belt. We're both grown-ups. I want you so badly, I can taste it."

Jonas scrambled to his feet and started to back up, but his desk stopped him. "Victoria, I said, 'Don't.' I mean it."

"Don't what?" exclaimed Victoria. She grabbed a sharp letter opener from his desk and menaced his bulging trousers. "What's that? A banana?"

"I'm your doctor, Victoria. My job is to understand your needs, not give in to them. Your job is to put your fantasies into words, not action."

She glared at Jonas. "I know what I want right now."

She began unbuttoning her blouse.

"Wants and needs are not the same, Victoria. You're a beautiful woman. I am attracted to you. I don't deny it. If we knew each other in another context, it might be different, but that's not how it is. As for your thoughts and feelings, our job is to *talk* them out, not to *act* them out. Anything that touches you today will be through words, not actions."

Victoria dropped the letter opener and stared at it in dismay. She turned to Jonas. "So you are the dashing professor Lorraine warned me about. Are you enjoying playing with me?"

"This is not a game. Something important is happening here. It's about how you see me and what it means."

"What about that?" said Victoria, pointing at the tumescence between his thighs. "What does that mean?"

"It means I'm turned on."

"By me?"

Jonas laughed. "Is there someone else here I should know about?"

"I want you to want me."

"I do."

"So why not—?" Victoria halted.

"Because I don't give in to every impulse. And neither should you. Like when you tore into Martin."

"You sure know how to spoil a mood. This is so degrading." Victoria wrapped her jacket around her. "You, the handsome psychoanalyst whose patients fall madly in love with him. Me, throwing my hotel key at you like some pathetic groupie after a Springsteen concert."

"It's not like that."

"Then what is it like?"

"I'm your doctor."

Victoria dug her fingernails into her knees. "Now what am I going to do? I'm confused. I need you to make sense of this. Please don't say you won't see me anymore."

"Who said anything about that?"

"What a mess I am. What am I supposed to do now?"

"Do? We do what we always do. We're going to talk about what happened."

"That's it?" Victoria shuddered.

Jonas felt split in two. The sex fantasies about Victoria and the pretty girl felt so real that he could hardly wait to get home and go at it with Jennie like a twenty-year-old. Meantime, the rest of his mind had switched into analytic mode. "There's a lot to discuss."

"Like what?"

"Your Carlyle fantasy, to begin with."

"You expect me to talk about that?"

Jonas adjusted his clothes. "It would be good for your therapy," he said wistfully.

"We've been here before," Victoria said. "Haven't we?"

"I was just thinking that," Jonas said. "That last day in Philadelphia when you told me to do my job."

Victoria wiped her face with her sleeve. "This is it, isn't it, Jonas? Our day of reckoning. It had to come."

"This is the way it has to be, Victoria."

They stared at each other intently for a shared moment, looking deeply into the other's soul. Jonas waited.

"It was such a nice fantasy," Victoria said. "Just us. You and me and a bottle of Veuve Clicquot. Like the rest of the world didn't matter."

"Veuve Clicquot? You don't drink."

"You're right. I don't." Victoria's right hand traced circles on the table to her side. "I just thought of something. When I was little, my father's friend, Mr. Brendel, took us out to celebrate when one of his horses won a race at Saratoga, and he ordered champagne in a green bottle with an orange label. That's how I remember the name.

"Daddy wore a dark blazer and a pink shirt with a brilliant white collar and a white tie clasped with a pearl tie bar. He looked so handsome. My mother got mad at him."

"What did it have to do with you?" Jonas asked.

"I was little. Only five or six. Daddy picked me up in front of the whole restaurant while he toasted Mr. Brendel. Everyone made such a big fuss about how pretty I was. I tingled with excitement. Bing Crosby, the movie star, was there. He said what a pretty girl I was and that if Daddy wanted me to be in pictures he should let him know. His breath smelled like disinfectant. Later on, someone said Crosby wasted his money on racehorses that never won."

"So your mother got jealous."

"She was always jealous. That's why she hated me. I've told you that before."

"About the jealous feeling?"

"It intensified the tingling."

"I'm not surprised. What about your father?"

"What else is there to tell?"

"How you felt about his handsomeness. What it felt like for him to treat you as though you were more special than your mother. How tingling with excitement connects to your fantasies and feelings about handsome men. I'm glad you think I'm handsome, but so is Martin."

Victoria laughed bawdily. "I never told you this before, Jonas. When

I saw you with Jennie at the pizza joint that time, I felt like I was burning up. I almost jumped into bed with Bucky that night. So, guess who bought me the lingerie I wore the first time I got laid?"

"Your father?"

"He didn't know what he was getting me, but he knew I had a date that night and he told me to get something special."

"He knew, but he didn't want to know."

Victoria readjusted her blouse and reached for her jacket. "I'm not sure I like where this is going," she said.

"It's heading straight from room 802 at The Carlyle to the master bedroom at 1912 Rittenhouse Square South." This was Jonas's chance to connect Victoria's desire for him with her forbidden feelings about Morris and Martin. Gregory was a part of this, too: Gregory, whose boyish charms Victoria clung to lest she realize that the objects of his adoration would soon be females much younger than she, and that the feeling between Gregory's and his admirers' legs would be very different than adoration. It was one of those pivotal moments in therapy, like the pregnant pause before a symphony's finale.

Victoria gazed across the room at her Robert Frost poem. "It's complicated. Isn't it?"

"It usually is."

"You changed my life, Jonas," Victoria said. "I wouldn't be me if it weren't for you."

"You changed my life, Victoria," Jonas echoed. "I wouldn't be me if it weren't for you."

"We could have been so good with each other. Don't you think?"

"We already are."

"I bet you're as good on the couch as you are behind it."

"It's time you had that in your life, not just in your fantasies."

"I used to feel that way when I was young. Remember that person? I miss her. Can you help me get her back?"

"You've got it in you already. You felt it not ten minutes ago. You need to allow yourself to feel it with your husband."

"I like the sound of that!" Victoria said.

"He will, too. I promise."

"And just how is this erotic explosion going to take place?"

"Give me a second to think it through." Jonas smiled. "Here. I'm going to muse out loud. First, I'll send you and Martin to the best damn relationship counselor I've ever met: Eileen Bremen. She's head of the Marriage and Family Center in Philadelphia. After you and Martin work on your communication she'll send you off to a marriage encounter weekend." Jonas laughed out loud. "By the time you and Martin are finished there you'll be panting for each other like wildebeests. You'll be the hottest dark-haired woman Martin's ever met. You won't be able to keep your hands off of each other."

"You're the best friend I've ever had," Victoria said.

"Maybe so," Jonas said. "But to get the job done right, you'll need more than a friend."

Victoria walked over to the picture window. The scene reminded Jonas of the final day of her therapy in Philadelphia.

She said, "Why does someone like me need a 'you' in my life?"

"It's in our nature. We weren't made to go through life alone. Nobody's life is real unless we share it with someone who matters."

"Are you lonely with Jennie?"

"Not at all. She knows me like no one else. I'm grateful to have her and our children. Same for my father-in-law and my brother. And you. I'm a lucky man. I love a lot of people."

Victoria broke into a broad smile. "I love you, Jonas. I always have."

"I love you, too, Victoria, from the moment we met. I didn't have words for it back then. But here we are now, and there's a lot of unfinished business."

"What do we do now?"

"Take a few moments to catch our breath. After that, we need to get your meds straightened out. I know you stopped taking them; the pharmacy called."

"You know," Victoria said, "everyone says that medication for bipolar disorder either makes you gain weight or lose your mental sharpness. Or you lose your sex drive. I don't want any of that."

"Of course you don't," Jonas replied.

"Are you sure that won't happen?"

"Years ago we had fewer medications to choose from. Now we have excellent mood-stabilizers that don't make people gain weight or lose their mental edge. About the sex drive. . . ."

"Yes?"

Jonas laughed. "You don't think I expect you to take something that would get in the way of what we're working on, do you?"

Victoria blushed.

"Do you?" Jonas teased.

"No. I know you wouldn't."

"Good. Let's go to work on the Martin issue. You take him for granted. I said it before, but my timing was off."

"I knew you were right. I just wasn't ready to admit it."

"You accused Martin of being like your father."

"Why do you think I said that?"

"Because of conflicted feelings about sex."

"Why is this coming up now?"

"For one thing, your children are getting older," Jonas said. It's hard for parents to deal with their kids coming of age sexually. Bipolar or not, Melinda's probably got a lot of your sexual drive in her."

"Oh, God. I remember those years," Victoria said.

"And don't forget Gregory. Give it a few years and the girls will be fighting to get their hands on your son."

"Parenthood. I suppose you have to deal with it, too, Jonas. Don't you?"

Jonas smiled. "Oh yeah. Meanwhile, don't forget: Martin loves you very much."

"How can you be sure?"

"Masculine intuition. If he didn't love you deeply, he wouldn't have been so hurt. But you have issues with his handsomeness."

"You're right, Jonas. You're right. Me of all people. Who would have thought it?" Victoria looked troubled.

"We're not going to run out of things to talk about anytime soon, if that's worrying you." Jonas looked at his watch. "I'll meet you back here in a few minutes. Let's get going on it today, while The Carlyle fantasy is still fresh."

Jonas ushered Victoria into the hallway and pointed her toward the restroom around the corner. As she disappeared, he remembered the ferryboat metaphor she had used to describe life's journey. Minutes later he heard sounds in the distance that reminded him of his last day on Dr. Fowler's couch.

Bawm bibawm bum bah, dah diddle dada, dah diddle dada, Bawm bibawm bum bah, dah diddle dah daaah.

Faint at first, the sounds fell into waltz time. Could it be *Invitation to the Dance*? Jonas smiled as he heard Victoria's footsteps approaching, picturing her and Martin's steamy romance.

The lights dimmed three times and soft chimes announced intermission was over; it was time for act two. Though his and Victoria's dance would continue, the ballet would end in a Schone-Braun *pas de deux*.

About the Author

Jeffrey Deitz grew up in Baltimore, Maryland, where he was a prize-winning instrumentalist at the Peabody Conservatory of Music. Between undergraduate and postgraduate years at Philadelphia's University of Pennsylvania, Jeffrey graduated from Baltimore's University of Maryland Medical School, where he received an award for academic excellence. He spent the last half of his senior year conducting neuroscience research at The Johns Hopkins Medical School.

After psychiatry and psychoanalytic training in Philadelphia, Deitz and his wife moved to Connecticut, where he entered private practice, contributed widely to the professional psychotherapy literature, and conducted a series of seminars about the theory and practice of psychotherapy. He also participated in the psychotherapy research group at the Albert Einstein College of Medicine and taught psychopathology at a New York psychoanalytic training institute.

In 2007, Deitz turned his attention to wider audiences when he began publishing in the *New York Times*, *Huffington Post*, and other media outlets on topics including sports psychology, sleep deprivation, and the power of psychotherapy. He also contributed regularly to *The Rail*, the *New York Times* blog about horse racing, one of his lifelong interests.

In addition to his writing and psychotherapy practice, Deitz is

Assistant Professor of Psychiatry at the Frank Netter School of Medicine of Quinnipiac University, where he lectures second year medical students on diverse topics.

Deitz and his wife JoAnn live in Norwalk, Connecticut. They have two grown sons who live in Brooklyn. *Intensive Therapy: A Novel* is his first book.

Acknowledgments

No one writes a first novel without a village; or in my case, a town. I am very grateful for the many people who helped take *Intensive Therapy: A Novel* from inception to publication.

Writing coach and mentor William Greenleaf grounded me in the fundamentals of story telling. Every time I discuss the book, I realize how well he taught me my ABCs. Editor Beth Haddas's deft critique led me reconceptualize and restructure the original manuscript. Teacher and friend William Zinsser, a sharp-witted literary economist, taught me to spend my adjectives and adverbs wisely. I felt Bill's presence at the keyboard as the story was distilled into the finished product.

No one could have championed the story better than my editor at Greenleaf Book Group, Brandy Savarese, who believed in the project from the beginning. She relentlessly shepherded the manuscript through rehearsal after rehearsal—line by line, oftentimes word by word—until it was performance-ready.

Greenleaf Book Group designer Neil Gonzalez worked tirelessly on the book's cover and interior layout; indeed, the entire Greenleaf organization has been a pleasure to work with.

I would also like to thank editors Tom Connelly, Melissa Hoppert, Tara Parker Pope, and Patty Laduca at the *New York Times* for giving me the opportunity to publish; same for Lloyd Sedler of the *Huffington Post*.

I deeply am indebted to Dr. Philip B. (Jay) Storm, Chairman of the Division of Pediatric Neurosurgery at Children's Hospital of Philadelphia (CHOP). Under Jay's preceptorship, Dr. Anna Breckenridge came to life and I learned of the miracles CHOP performs every day to save the lives and futures of children suffering from traumatic brain injury.

I also want to acknowledge Dr. James Krinsley, Director of the Stamford Hospital Intensive Care Unit, for his insight, and Bill Lipton, Marjorie Marlowe, and Amy Weiss for their careful reading and comments about the manuscript.

Thanks go to former mentors and supervisors, Drs. Perry Ottenberg, George Roark, and Stanley Olinick. There will always be a special place in my heart for my training analyst, Philip J. Escoll, MD. I am also grateful to be part of the Training and Research Institute of Self Psychology (TRISP) in New York City, where it has been a privilege to teach and study.

Finally, I want to thank my patients, whose everyday courage in the face of adversity testifies to the indomitability of the human spirit and the potential for human growth throughout every stage of life. It is a privilege to share their journeys.